PRAISE FOR NANCY CANE
KEEPER OF THE RINGS

"A dark, dangerous hero and imaginative adventures make *Keeper Of The Rings* an entertaining read."
—Phoebe Conn, Bestselling Author Of
Ring Of Fire

"Prepare yourself for exotic locales, evil doers galore, and two splendid romances! Ms. Cane's done it again!"
—*The Paperback Forum*

"For fans of futuristics, Nancy Cane is the name to watch. Her books capture the imagination with their originality!"
—*The Literary Times*

"The spellbinding action gets more terrifying and enthralling as the uniquely different plot thickens. The conclusion is stunning. Kudos to Ms. Cane!"
—*Rendezvous*

Futuristic Romance

SWEET SURRENDER

Taurin let Leena fuss over him in their cabin. She brought him a drink and a cool cloth for his forehead. He didn't feel the need to lie down but was too glad for her ministrations to refuse. He'd never had a woman care for him before.

"Leena," he murmured.

"Yes?"

She was standing on the edge of her bunk in order to be head level with him. Tentatively he reached out a hand to cup the back of her head. Her hair felt like spun silk, and suddenly his resolve dissipated. He'd been able to push away from her at Hathers Beach, knowing it wasn't right for him to steal kisses from her no matter what their legal relationship was. But now he drew her toward him until his mouth hovered inches above hers.

The words escaped his lips before he could stop them. "I want you."

NANCY CANE

Keeper of the Rings

LOVE SPELL NEW YORK CITY

LOVE SPELL®

February 1996

Published by

Dorchester Publishing Co., Inc.
276 Fifth Avenue
New York, NY 10001

Printed in the United States of America.

This book is dedicated to:

Alicia Condon, Editorial Director at Leisure/Love Spell, for giving me the opportunity to achieve my dreams.

Lydia Paglio, my first editor, for helping me shape those dreams into a better reality.

Rob Cohen, literary agent, for believing in me and having faith that I'd make that first sale.

With special thanks to:

Donna Creekmore, for her keyboarding skills.

Gary Shpritz, for his creative input.

Chapter One

"If we don't start soon, I'm going to faint!" With trembling fingers, Leena adjusted her flowing royal-blue robe. It was the first time she was privileged to wear the sacramental vestment, and she wasn't accustomed to its length. Glancing down, she grimaced at the sight of her satin slippers barely peeking out from beneath the hem. "Dear deity, what if I trip over this thing when we're called up to the dais?"

Karole, her friend during the past six weeks of training, patted her shoulder. "You'll do fine. You always appear so well poised."

Leena's blue eyes widened. "But today we're getting inducted into the Caucus! My father is in the congregation, and so are Malcolm and his family." Her face blanched. "Bendyk isn't here yet. What could have happened to him?"

Karole, a raven-haired beauty, gave her an indulgent smile. "Your brother might have arrived by now. You wouldn't see him if he entered the Inner Sanctum." She swept her arm in a broad gesture encompassing the room they were in. Other young men and women, initiates like themselves, stood about, fidgeting nervously like school graduates. "No one else is allowed in the Robing Salon except for us and the Synod."

"Of course." By being formally inducted into the Caucus, Leena and her newfound friends would become official participants in the aide corps that served the fourteen-member ruling body of priests called the Synod. At its head was Dikran, the Arch Nome, whose signal they were awaiting now. The annual Renewal service was about to begin, and at its completion Leena and the others would take their places in the religious hierarchy.

As she placed her headdress over her crown of blond hair, Leena's pulse raced with excitement. Ever since she was a child, she'd wanted to learn more about the Apostles who had established the religion called Sabal on her world. Her father, a high-ranking Candor, first inspired her interest in archaeology by his study of ancient religious texts. Growing up beside a crumbling ruin had sparked her imagination as she thought about what life must have been like in days of old. Where had the Apostles originated? They'd established the magnificent reign of Lothar, their god, and then vanished. Why did they leave after so many years? Where had they gone?

Craving knowledge of her forebears, Leena realized the Synod held the key to wisdom. The ecclesiastical leaders were privy to secrets known to no one else. Joining the Caucus was the swiftest route to enlightenment as far as she was concerned.

A solemn bearded figure marched into the room. Planting himself firmly in the center, he peered around at the young initiates. He raised his hand and then waited until everyone fell silent. "It is time," Zeroun intoned.

"Holy waters," Leena whispered to Karole. "I can't believe we've made it this far. May Lothar guide us!"

"You're supposed to be near the front," Karole reminded her. "Get in line."

Leena wiped her sweaty palms against her flowing robe.

Not even her graduation from the archaeological college had made her this nervous. Was it because Malcolm was in the congregation? Her wealthy neighbor had been after her hand in marriage for several years now. Lately Leena had been inclined to accept him, mainly for the security he could offer her. She felt a modicum of affection toward him, having known him ever since she was a child, but something within her made her hesitate. He was here now, waiting inside the congregation for her to make an appearance. Also present was her father, and even though their relationship was strained at times, she still hoped to make him proud.

Lining up behind the others, she tilted her chin resolutely in the air and marched forward with Zeroun in the lead. Leena had been in the cathedral-like Inner Sanctum many times during the six weeks of her training period, and they had even had rehearsals for this event, but that hadn't prepared her for the sea of faces that greeted her when she entered the cavernous hall. A front row of seats was reserved for the twenty young people who were to enter the Caucus. As she filed in, Leena noticed the members of the Synod taking their places on the dais. Sitting on a center thronelike chair was Arch Nome Dikran, wearing his gold robe with the dignity that befit his eighty years. A towering headdress covered his head, and it was much more resplendent than the simple ones Leena and her friends wore. She didn't care for such an elaborate style of dress, although since her father held a high position, she was accustomed to attending fancy dinners and parties. As she sat on a plushly upholstered seat, smoothing her robe about her legs, Leena wished for the comfort of the breeches and short-sleeved shirts she wore on her archaeological digs. There was no pretense when you were systematically examining a site for ancient treasures. You did your work, and everyone pulled his own weight on the site, regardless of gender or age. She knew Malcolm didn't approve of her career. He would expect any wife of his to stay home and manage the household of his large estate. Leena had plenty of experience in managing her father's property, which she had done since her mother's death, five years ago in the terrible accident that had given her brother his true calling.

Good Lord! Where was Bendyk? She craned her neck, searching the crowd for her brother's handsome face, but she couldn't spot his blond head anywhere. Nor was her father or Malcolm visible, even though she knew they were in the congregation. It was simply too crowded, or else her mind was in such a state of nervous agitation that everything appeared to her as a blur. Focusing her attention forward, Leena scanned the dignitaries on the dais. Sirvat, the most prominent woman on the Synod, looked stiffly proper in her white robe tied with the gold sash of office. Magar sat beside her, his eyes twinkling beneath a crop of white hair. Karayan, a family friend, caught Leena's eye and smiled. Flushing, she looked down at her blue robe, eagerly anticipating the moment when she would be given the gold cord identifying her as an ordained servant of Lothar.

Impatiently she shifted her position, watching as Dikran rose from his throne and approached the podium. His shuffling gait proclaimed his age, but his dark eyes were sharp as they pierced the crowd like two orbs of glowing embers. The service began with a hymn praising Lothar for his beneficence.

"We come here today," began Dikran, in a voice that projected to the rear of the audience even without a microphone, "before the face of our deity, the miraculous Lothar. Together in worship, we sanctify our existence and praise Lothar, ruler of Xan. Who is like unto you, O Holy One, majestic and awesome in splendor? Who can compare to your generosity? Let us extoll your name! Let the name Lothar be hallowed unto the world for the creation he willed. Let his name be glorified and exalted although he is beyond praise, because he is so mighty and powerful."

The congregation raised their voices in a hymn, and Leena's song joined them. The familiar melody brought her the same calm serenity that it had throughout her life at similar services. Renewal was a time to recall one's past deeds, one's joys and triumphs, tragedies and sorrows, and to look ahead to the new year with reborn hope.

"May this new year bring us peace, joy, and exaltation," exclaimed Dikran, raising his hands toward the pyramid-shaped vaulted ceiling. "May you bless us, O Lothar, with plentiful rains so our crops may grow bountiful and our fields be fertile. May our rivers flow and our lakes remain unblemished. We count on you, O Holy One, to maintain our land and to provide us with your special blessing that keeps us from ill health. May our redemptive labors make us happy and our struggle for purity not fail. Let us strive for the good we can do by toiling at our work to the best of our ability. Blessed is the vision of holiness that exalts us from on high."

Leena joined in a series of responsive readings. Her heart opened to Lothar and his generosity to her people. Truly they were all blessed to have such a wonderful god looking out for them. He provided them with fertile soil with which to grow adequate foodstuffs. Xan was a rich, bountiful world. The lakes and rivers teemed with fish. The land blossomed with fruit, and the air was pure and clear. What more could anyone want?

Zeroun got up and exchanged places with Dikran. Minister of Religion, Zeroun's presence was powerful, the hunch of his shoulders indicative of his forcefulness. "Praised be Lothar who unifies all creation," he said, his eyes piercing the congregation as though he would read their souls. "May the Holy One fill our minds with knowledge and our hearts with wisdom, and praise those who labor to bring harmony to our world. The new year should be a fruitful one for us. Be gracious, O Lothar, and treat us generously. Be our teacher and guide," he shouted, raising his hands toward the heavens.

A choir began singing, and melodious music filled the clerestory. Leena felt her heart soar with faithfulness and love for Lothar. *Please help me to clear my father's name*, she prayed. *I know the answers are here in your Holy Tem-*

15

ple. I vow that I will find them before the next Renewal. The communion of those around her filled her with comfort and peace as she followed the words of the service.

"Let us bend in humility before Lothar," said Zeroun, bowing low so that his headdress tipped in front of him. "Let us give praise unto the one who established our land."

"May the Holy One be gracious and bring us peace," everyone in the congregation intoned in unison.

"As the new year begins, so is hope reborn in us," said Zeroun. "Lothar has been resting after the toil of the harvest, but now is the time for Renewal. We must blow the sacred horn to awaken our god from his rest so the life cycle may begin anew. Behold the vessel for summoning Lothar."

Karayan, Minister of Justice, and Eznik, Minister of Labor, rose and approached a set of immense carved wooden doors at the rear of the Grand Altar. Uttering their own incantations, they reached out to draw the doors apart in front of the awed congregation. Leena held her breath. The sound of the horn was more than a symbol for ushering in the new year. It summoned Lothar, and when he awoke he reset the climatic cycles of Xan for another year. Without his beneficence, her world would revert to the wild, untamed fury of the past. No one ever wanted that to happen; it would mean the end to civilization as they knew it. Renewal was the pinnacle of all the seasonal holidays.

"Show us the horn," shouted Dikran, standing as he faced the rear.

Karayan and Eznik drew the doors apart, and a collective gasp went up from the congregation. Emptiness yawned from within the richly lit interior.

"Dear deity," Leena whispered. Where was the sacred horn? She saw the stunned look on Dikran's face and the shocked expressions on Karayan's and Eznik's countenances. The other members of the Synod looked horror-stricken. Dikran gave a quick glance at Zeroun before indicating that the doors were to be closed. Stepping forward to the podium, he raised his hand to signal the choir. A trumpet was always played after the horn to reflect the holy voice. Now the trumpet player began a haunting melody that reverberated through Leena's soul. When it was over the congregation remained mute. Dikran, his expression stony, spoke into the microphone.

"Our opening of the holy chamber this year was symbolic. The sacred horn, after so many years of continuous use, has required a cleansing in sacramental water. We have blown the trumpet in its stead. It is Lothar's will that this be done. Hear us, Holy One, and awaken from your rest." He raised his hands toward the congregation. "Bless our people and grant them freedom from sickness and sorrow. Let us love our neighbor as ourselves, walk humbly with our god, and convert our thoughts into faith and our words into good deeds. Here and now, as everywhere and at all times, teach us to serve you, O Lothar. And so we say Mahala."

With the final pronouncement, he lowered his head and uttered a blessing. "And now," he continued, beaming pontifically, "it gives me great pleasure to call upon our new initiates. These young people are dedicating their lives to serving the members of our Synod. By their faith, they serve Lothar. By their service to the Synod, they aid you, the people. Treat them with the respect due their station. Hereafter they are to be accommodated with the same consideration as those they are appointed to serve. You may step upon the dais," he ordered the trainees.

Leena shook in anticipation of this moment. Holy waters, it's time, she said to herself.

Squaring her shoulders, she gracefully made her way up to the elevated platform and stood facing the congregation in a line with her fellow initiates. One by one they were called before Zeroun, who gave them a lit candle and the gold sash that would signify their new station. Holding their candles, the initiates repeated the words they had been rehearsing diligently.

"We pledge ourselves to serve the members of the Synod in good faith, with loyalty, dedication and compassion, and in so doing we pledge ourselves to you, O blessed Lothar. Praised be the power that brings us peace and prosperity. Praised be Lothar, who sanctifies us all. Mahala.''

They blew out their candles, signifying the end of the Renewal ceremony. As was the custom, the congregation remained in place while Dikran, the members of the Synod, and the new Caucus left the sanctuary to head for the reception hall. A huge feast had been prepared, for Renewal was a joyous occasion. Lothar was awakening. He would provide for them for another whole year: a year free from ill health, a year blessed with bountiful fruit and produce of the land. Leena's heart soared with joy as she followed her robed companions through the nave toward an archway at the rear.

Someone planted a hand on her shoulder in the reception hall. Whirling her around, he planted a kiss firmly on her lips.

''Malcolm!'' she exclaimed.

''I am very proud of you,'' he told her, flashing a grin that showed his white, even teeth.

Leena scanned his handsome features. His brown eyes reflected warmth and something more when he looked at her.

''Thank you,'' she murmured, pleased by the sincerity of his remark. ''Have you seen Father?''

''He's over by the refreshment table. Can I get you a drink?''

''Yes, I'd like that.'' She looked around for Karole, wanting to introduce her friend to Malcolm, but it was difficult to locate her in the crowd. People stood about in clusters, drink in hand, chatting and laughing in good cheer. Friends and relatives had come from miles away for this special occasion. Most people attended religious services in their hometowns or at the regional worship centers, but guests of the elite were invited to participate in the service at the Holy Temple, and such invitations were highly coveted.

Frowning, Leena wondered where Dikran had gone. She wanted to put in a good word with the Arch Nome for her father. But Dikran was nowhere in sight, and neither, she noticed, were the top members of the Synod. Where had they gone? Dikran should be here to give his blessing to the bread so they could eat. But it was Jirair, Minister of Agriculture, who offered the prayer. A moment of doubt overwhelmed her as she recalled the stunned looks on Dikran's and the others' faces when the doors were opened and the horn was gone. Had it really been intentional that the horn not be here for Renewal, or was this a surprise to the Synod that Dikran had hastily covered up? They were certainly experts at cover-ups, as she well knew.

Malcolm interrupted her thoughts by offering her a cup of fruit punch. "Thanks," she said, a preoccupied frown on her face.

"What's the matter?" Malcolm asked, concerned.

She lowered her voice. "The sacred horn . . . do you really think it's being cleaned? This seems an odd time to be doing a chore like that. We need the horn to be blown for Lothar to reset the cycles!"

Malcolm raised an eyebrow. "Are you calling Dikran a liar?"

Leena paled, for it *was* Dikran's veracity that she was questioning. "No," she responded, afraid of incurring retribution should anyone overhear them. "Look, here comes Father!"

Cranby strode over and embraced Leena in a huge bear hug. He was a large man, and in his crimson robe of office he seemed even more imposing.

"Congratulations," he murmured in her ear.

"Thank you, Father."

Standing back, she gazed at her father with love and affection. His blond hair, receding from his high forehead, was sprinkled with gray. Blue eyes similar to her own had been dulled by years of grief over the loss of his wife. Clearly a pressing matter weighed heavily on his mind now as he regarded her with an anxious expression.

"Have you heard from your brother?" he asked pointedly.

Her brow creased in concern. "I tried to contact him before the ceremony, but communications to Amat were out. I can't imagine what might have happened, and he should have arrived late this morning. I hoped he might come in and sit with you."

Malcolm raised his hand. "I'll go make inquiries," he said. "Amat is located at Seacrest Bay, is it not?" At Leena's nod, he hastened away.

"He's a fine young man," Cranby said, eyeing her carefully.

Leena lowered her lashes. "I'm still not sure about him, Father."

His look grew stern. "You've achieved a great deal for a woman of twenty-five years, daughter. Now it is time to think about your future."

"I've just been admitted into the Caucus. My immediate future is here." Her heart sank, knowing where the conversation was leading, but she tried to head him off regardless.

"Do you hope to be promoted to Docent, as do many of your peers?" Cranby asked. "I hadn't known you to be so religiously inclined."

Leena compressed her lips. Her father didn't know the true reason for her wanting to join the Caucus, and it was best that he remain in ignorance or he would warn her against her chosen course of action. She didn't mean to stir up trouble; she merely wanted to uncover the truth about the origins of her religion in order to put to rest the doubts in her heart.

She wasn't the only one who questioned the faith. The Truthsayers were protesting rule by the Synod. They demanded reforms, claiming Lothar was a false god created by the priests. The spate of recent weather disasters gave solidity to their words and shook the very credibility of the religion. The Synod proclaimed that Lothar was angry at the people and was punishing them for their doubts, but Leena knew Lothar was a god of mercy and compassion. There had to be some other reason for the disruption of the climate on Xan, something only the Synod knew about—and that was another item of information she hoped to discover while she was here.

"Mark my words," said Cranby, "not another Beltane will pass with Malcolm and you unpledged. I shall speak to his father myself. It is still within my authority to troth you a husband, miss, and so I shall. You dilly-dally too long, and such indecisiveness is unbecoming in a lady. You'll lose the young man if he isn't snared now."

"But I'm not ready yet—"

"Nonsense; you'll never be ready at your pace. The matter is settled."

Leena bit back a retort as the Minister of Justice bore down upon them.

"Cranby, my old friend." Karayan slapped a hand on Cranby's shoulder, then vigorously shook both his hands, as was the custom. "How good to see you again, and what a thrill to celebrate your lovely daughter's success." His pale gray eyes swung to Leena, expressing approval.

"I'm looking forward to serving the Synod," she told him, smiling warmly. Karayan had always been a supporter of her father, even during his censure.

Karayan gave a slight bow. "You honor your family by your service." He tilted his head at Cranby. "Your son Bendyk is earning a name for himself as a missionary," he said, a note of admiration in his voice. "We have word that requests are pouring in from the villages for his counsel. If he keeps going at this pace, I see him being appointed soon as a Docent. Where is the young man?" he asked, glancing around. "I thought he was supposed to join us today."

"He never got in. I called Amat but couldn't get through," Leena said worriedly, adjusting her headdress, which had begun to tilt. The heavy piece was beginning to give her a headache, and she wondered when she would be able to change into more comfortable clothes. Probably not until this reception is over, she thought resignedly. It was then that she caught sight of the stunned look on Karayan's face.

"You said Bendyk is in Amat? Why, we've just received notice that there's been a terrible disaster at Seacrest Bay."

Leena's face paled, and Cranby cried out, "What? What did you say?"

"A tsunami struck last night. There have been casualties, and a rescue effort is underway. I'm uncertain of the details."

"Dear Lord," Leena said. "Bendyk was supposed to leave last night. I wonder if he made it out."

Karayan laid a hand on her arm. "The Synod has called for an emergency meeting. You are to come with me. Perhaps we'll learn more information."

Of course, Leena thought, giving her father a brief kiss and hurrying after Karayan. The Synod must be convening to discuss the tragedy. Muttering a quick prayer that her brother had either left before the disaster or had miraculously survived, she followed Karayan through the mazelike corridors of the Palisades complex.

Anxious to be on his way to the Palisades for Leena's induction into the Caucus, Bendyk hoped the town council meeting in Amat wouldn't take long. Wellis, the village priest, had requested his presence. Now, as he sat across from the older man in the living area of his oceanside bungalow, he fingered the medallion at his chest and fumed with impatience. It was the day before Renewal and he'd hoped to leave earlier, but dusk was already approaching and it didn't seem his departure would occur anytime soon.

"I fail to understand your meaning when you say the people are straying from the Faith," Bendyk said. "The turnout at the service this morning was phenomenal."

"That's because the villeins are putting on a pretense of piety for your benefit," said Wellis. "They're afraid you'll report to the Docent about their indiscretions otherwise."

Pursing his lips, Wellis felt he knew his flock better than

any representative from the central authority, such as Bendyk Worthington-Jax. He'd sent for help realizing the situation could get out of control. After all, on whose head would the wrath of Lothar fall if he failed? His, of course! But the golden-haired missionary, despite his zeal, had found nothing amiss. It wasn't Bendyk's fault, considering how fearful the villeins were about retribution. The blasphemous talk circulating throughout the town was bound to bring dire repercussions. Wellis had hoped Bendyk would inspire a renewal of faith and, indeed, the service he'd conducted this morning had been exemplary. Perhaps his visit had done some good after all.

Facing the black-robed priest across a table laden with fresh fruit and nuts, Bendyk cocked a blond eyebrow. "Don't forget it is tithing time. The tax collector is here even in the midst of Renewal celebrations. That's enough to cause heightened tensions."

A tired smile creased Wellis's craggy features. "Not in this case. We've been fortunate to have the same agent each year. She counts in our favor and exacts a toll of ten percent on less than the amount actually produced."

Bendyk's eyes darkened to a shade of indigo. "What say you? This agent does not report an accurate count? Why . . . why that is criminal!"

Wellis leaned back in his chair, relishing the warm salty breeze that blew in from the open windows. His bungalow, a short distance from the ocean, stood on stilts like the rest of the houses by shoreside. Further inland, other dwellings rose along a gentle slope that footed the Jerrise mountain range. Life there was simple, with people living off the bounty of the sea and their industries of ropemaking and small boat construction. They didn't have enough revenue to be the focus of an investigation, so he didn't see any harm in telling Bendyk of the favoritism showed them by the tax agent.

"It appeases people," Wellis said. "There is grumbling

enough that the laws don't take into account the needs of individual districts.''

Bendyk scraped a hand through his short wavy hair. ''That's not true! The Docents are responsible for making adjustments. If they rule unfairly, you can appeal to the Candor.''

''The Candors are concerned mainly with their own wealth. Things have gotten out of hand.''

Agitated, Bendyk jumped up. ''My father is a Candor. He's always judged his people fairly and considered their needs.''

''Cranby is an exception.'' Wellis regarded him wisely. ''Do you deny that dissatisfaction with the Synod's power structure is growing? Aren't your services widely in demand in an attempt by local priests, such as myself, to stem this tide of disloyalty?''

''It is the work of the Truthsayers!'' cried Bendyk, struggling to control his rage. ''They seek to undermine the Faith and establish anarchy in its place.''

Footsteps sloshed outside, and the elderly priest held up a hand to silence his guest. ''Hush; here comes the village council. I have summoned them to harken to your advice. Go easy, young man. Your fiery tongue serves you well in sermons but not in debate.''

At his signal, Bendyk hastened to open the door. Five older persons, the village leaders, shuffled in. To his surprise, a young woman accompanied them. Possessing a willowy frame, she moved with the gracefulness of a forest *lyier*. Bendyk's surprised gaze swept from her pretty face to the short-cropped black hair that dipped inward toward her chin. The thrust of her jaw hinted at a stubborn streak, and her unorthodox style of dress confirmed it. Shocked, Bendyk peered at the skintight breeches she wore and the dark green sweater with its revealing neckline.

''I hope I meet with your approval,'' she said in a sarcastic tone as he continued his blatant stare.

Startled, Bendyk's gaze flew up to meet hers. Flashing

amber eyes, like two torchlights in the dark, glared at him fiercely.

"I'm Bendyk Worthington-Jax, representative of the Saballic Order of Missioners," he replied, giving a slight bow.

The woman came up to him and stretched out a hand. "And I'm Swill Braddock," she said boldly.

He caught her hand in a firm handshake. Her palm was small, fitting into his larger hand like a ball into a catcher's mitt. He liked the weight and warmth of her. "Swill?" he asked, giving her a questioning glance.

"You got a problem with that?" she retorted, her brows furrowing angrily.

Clearly this woman was one who took any remark as a challenge. Bendyk was amused. He'd never met anyone as bold and brazen as she before.

"What is your function?" he inquired. "Surely you're not on the town council." She didn't fit in with the other robed members with their dignified miens and conservative dress.

"I'm the tax agent," she said. "I'm here for the tithing count."

"So you're the one! I hear your counts are favorable to the villeins."

She cocked an eyebrow. "Perhaps."

His eyes fired righteously. "Dishonesty is a sin."

"It all depends on who's in the know," she said. Smiling sweetly, she brushed past him and joined the others, who were already seated around Wellis's oval table.

"Come, Bendyk, sit down," said Wellis.

"Why are your feet all wet?" he asked, approaching the table. He'd noticed the trail of moisture they left from the door to the table.

"The tide is washing in," spoke one white-haired gentleman. "It's higher than normal tonight."

"Aye," said another. "It is most peculiar. I can't remember it coming up this far in recent years."

"Never mind," said Wellis. "Our visitor here"—he gestured toward Bendyk—"has to leave for the Palisades soon,

25

so let us begin our discussion. We asked for Brother Bendyk to serve our village because of the rumblings of discontent that have been more pronounced of late. During his sojourn here he says he has noticed no such problem, but I assured him that is because the villeins are afraid of retribution should they loosen their tongues in his presence.''

''Indeed,'' spoke an older woman, leaning forward, ''ever since the hurricane that devastated the Rockmount Islands and the tornado on the Ruas Plains before that, people have been questioning Lothar's actions. Why would our Lord bring such retribution on his people? He's always been gracious and merciful. Why does he deal us such catastrophic blows?''

''It is because of this Truthsayer movement,'' Bendyk said, hunching forward in his seat. ''Those who would protest rule by the Synod would leave nothing but chaos in its place. Our laws were put here for a reason, and we must abide by them to please Lothar. Health care, education, and housing are provided for everyone. I don't understand what the Truthsayers want instead.''

''They want freedom to control their own destiny,'' spoke Swill in a low tone.

All eyes swiveled in her direction, and Bendyk became aware of the seductive pull of her presence. She sat across the table from him, but every nerve in his body stood at attention when she directed her gaze at him. Those eyes, round as dew drops, could draw a man into their depths without any effort, and Bendyk found himself eager for her next word.

''People resent the fact that they have no choice over where they can live. If we want to move from one village to another, we must submit an application. Populations are strictly regulated. It's not fair, and people are tired of having an impersonal central authority making these decisions for them.''

''There is a reason for every law,'' Bendyk countered. ''A town's population is limited so it doesn't overgrow the needs of its citizens. The cities of old were rife with problems: poverty, crime, lack of sanitation. Lothar placed limits on a town's population for that very reason. In smaller villages people are loyal to each other. They care about what is happening to their neighbors. In large cities no one takes any concern for what's going on next door. I believe the ruling is a wise one. These Truthsayers are just trying to stir up trouble any way they can.''

His eyes narrowed suspiciously. ''And what do you know of their beliefs anyway? What right do you have to report a false count on the tithe? I should turn you in for your dishonesty.''

''Be my guest,'' she sneered. ''The people I serve are happy because I let them keep more of their produce. If you worked a farm, wouldn't you prefer to earn the profits on what you grew yourself? Why give it to a central authority that doesn't even care what happens here?''

''You speak blasphemy,'' Bendyk snapped, slamming his fist on the table. A strange banging echo caught his attention, only it wasn't an echo. It was a rhythmic thump-thump that sounded from somewhere below the house.

''What's that?'' one of the elder councilwomen said nervously.

Wellis's face darkened. ''It can only be the empty oil drums banging together beneath the foundation. That means the water has risen to nearly the level of the steps outside. I fear this is an ill omen. Let us look outside to see what is happening.''

Bendyk hastened to the outer porch, not wishing to get too close to the woman named Swill. What an unusual name! But then, it went along with her strange manner of dress, cropped hair, and abrupt manner. He didn't know what to make of her. Clearly she was a rebellious sort, yet he found her oddly attractive, and that discomfited him. He was aware when she came outside; he could almost feel her hot breath wafting on his neck. He didn't glance in her direction, merely kept his gaze turned out to sea, and what he saw alarmed him.

It was dusk, and the lights from town lit up the heavens with an orange glow. Out to sea, he could still discern the outline where the horizon met the darkened sky, but it was the water by the shore that disturbed him. The color was unusual, a dark swirling green. As he watched, he noticed the water was receding. The beach widened, and the sea bed gradually became exposed. Several beachgoers who'd been observing the sunset rushed out delightedly to pick up stranded fish flopping on the sand. Others, shouting a warning, turned and fled toward higher ground.

"What in the world?" Bendyk said.

Behind him, he heard Wellis suck in a breath. "Dear Lord," the priest exclaimed. "A big sea is coming. We must flee!"

Swill gave a cry of alarm. "Do we have time to reach our riders?"

"We can try," Wellis said.

Four feet of water sloshed about their legs as they rushed toward their vehicles, only to find them jammed together by the latest wave. With cries of dismay, the group turned to run across the yard of the nearest house, charging inland as fast as they could go in the rising water.

As he ran, Bendyk was aware of a strange calm pervading the region. His ears picked up a new sound—a dull rumble, like that of a distant train. It came from the encroaching darkness and turned into a thundering roar. Glancing over his shoulder, he saw an incoming wall of water that seemed to grow in height as it moved toward the village center.

Seconds later, the wave washed into town with crushing force. Brilliant blue-white sparks marked the impact of the wave as it shorted out electrical circuits and loud crashes accompanied the destruction of buildings. A brief greenish arc flashed through the sky, signifying the fact that the wave had reached the power plant at the south end of the bay. The lights went out abruptly, plunging the area into near total darkness. But it wasn't so dark that Bendyk couldn't make out the terrifying wall of water surging in his direction.

Praying he'd make it to high ground before catastrophe struck, he moved his legs as fast as they could go, charging onward.

Chapter Two

Loud booms announced the sound of walls being crushed and buildings being demolished as the wave progressed. Bendyk heard Swill's scream as the tower of water descended upon them. He was lifted by the wave and swept inland. As he was submerged, his pants' cuff caught on a piece of debris and his body was battered to and fro. Dazedly, he found himself on the surface, floundering amid fallen beams, pieces of broken furniture, and heavy appliances.

A wood plank floated past, and he heaved himself onto it as a terrible sucking noise indicated the fact that the water was returning to its home. All around were the cries of people fighting the current among the swirling debris. Some people rode on the tops of their houses; others clung to treetops. Some people swam, but everyone was screaming in fright. A body swept past, and Bendyk's heart thudded in sudden recognition. Letting go of the plank, he swam with the current, grabbing Swill by the shoulder and flipping her over so that her face was out of the water. It was difficult to support her while they were both being swept along, but he managed to keep both their heads up. She had a gash on the side of her face, but she was breathing, and that was all that counted. As the water ebbed back to the shore, one of his feet touched firm ground. Bracing his legs, he prevented them both from being pulled out to sea. Nearby, one of the other town leaders became wedged with an arm trapped between a tree and a rock. Of the other council members, he saw none. Along the edge of the shore were piled, collapsed cottages, lumber, tree branches, and smashed vehicles. After the sea subsided people lucky enough to have survived on land began to stir and call out. Frantic parents began searching for their children. Children wept for their missing parents. Husbands and wives sought absent spouses, and the first rescue efforts began. Not one residence remained standing, and the center of town yawned as an empty, dark hollow. In the ocean, heads bobbed in the heaving water as those swept out to sea struggled for survival.

Walking to a grassy knoll, Bendyk put Swill on the ground and examined her head wound. As he touched her skin, her eyelids fluttered open and she gave a soft moan.

"Don't move," he told her, annoyed with himself for noticing how her sodden clothes clung to her body. He knelt at her side, ignoring the discomfort of his own wet shirt and trousers. "You've been injured. How bad does your head hurt?"

She stared at him, her amber eyes wide with fright and confusion. "I feel dizzy. What happened to the others?"

"The tsunami demolished everything, and I saw only one member of the council. I don't know if anyone else who was in that meeting survived. I don't understand it," he said, shaking his head. "This region hasn't had waves like this in hundreds of years. It must be a sign of Lothar's wrath," he concluded. "Wellis admitted to me that the people were harboring doubts. This must be Lothar's retribution."

Sighing, he surveyed the sorry scene about him as people cried for missing relatives and their destroyed homes. "Per-

31

he villeins will confess their sins and give themselves
e Lord as a result of this tragedy.''

will brushed away his hand and sat up, her limbs trembling. ''Is that all you can think about? Your stupid religion?
People here need help. Where are the healers? We need
lights. No one can see anything.''

It was a terrifying darkness, as frantic wailings, like
sounds from hell, rent the air. Bendyk became aware of a
cool breeze raising the hairs on his arms.

''You'll get chilled in those wet clothes,'' he told her.
''We need to find shelter.''

''We need to help these people,'' she stated, but when she
tried to rise to her feet she stumbled dizzily and would have
fallen if it hadn't been for his steady arm around her waist.
''I can manage by myself, thank you,'' she snapped.

''I think not,'' he said, leaving his hand in place. She
didn't protest as he drew her closer. Rather, she seemed to
lean more heavily against him.

''I wonder if even one structure is left standing,'' she said,
her voice more subdued, as though she'd reckoned with her
weakness and accepted it.

Bendyk considered how long it would take for word to
reach the outside world about what had happened here. For
now, there was no means by which to communicate with
Leena, and she'd be worried when she learned of the tsunami. His departure was unavoidably delayed; he was needed
here. The survivors might wish to express their gratitude to
Lothar, and he wanted to be the one to lead them in worship.

Holding on to Swill's slim waist, he hoped he could convince her to join them.

When Leena entered the meeting chamber of the Synod
she noticed at once that Kolb and Voshkie were engaged in
a heated argument.

''We need to assemble an emergency response team,''
Kolb was insisting. As Minister of Health, the lean, thin-
faced gentleman was responsible for the worldwide network

of trained healers. While Lothar's lozenge, which everyone swallowed each year at the festival of Mistic, would prevent disease, injuries still required the care of skilled personnel.

"The expense would not justify such an alarming action," said Voshkie. In charge of commerce, she was constantly railing against the people's demands for a broader choice of consumer goods. In the short time she'd been here, Leena had assessed the attitudes of most members of the Synod, and Voshkie's dislike of materialism was well known. The black-haired woman led an austere life, setting an example for those who wished to emulate her. In contrast, Sirvat, who was in charge of the Treasury, and the other prominent woman on the Synod, dressed attractively from what Leena had seen when they were derobed. Sirvat had thin red hair that she liked to wear coiffed beneath veils and hats. Her manner of dress was stylish, but her reedlike figure did not accentuate her womanliness. Her unsmiling mouth and the permanent frown on her face bespoke her frustration as a spinster of fifty-two years.

Sirvat's green eyes, pale as a frozen sea, flickered briefly in Leena's direction. Seats were arranged around a central table in concentric circles. The members of the Synod had the first tier of seats, directly against the table. Behind them were the aide corps. Leena found a seat next to Karole and sat down as unobtrusively as possible.

"I trust you are discussing the tsunami at Amat," said Karayan, settling his robes as he took his chair. "Missionary Bendyk was last known to be at that location. Has anyone heard from him or had news of survivors?"

"Communications have not yet been established," said Lendork, Minister of Communications. "In any event, that's not what we're gathered here for."

"Ah, yes," Karayan agreed, a sudden light of knowledge in his eyes. "We have a much more pressing matter that needs our attention."

With those words, all eyes turned to Dikran, who sat silently at the head of the table. Nodding for the door to be shut, Dikran spent a few moments in silence, peering at each one of them, including the members of the Caucus.

"We have a grave matter before us," Dikran intoned. Despite his age, his voice retained its forcefulness, and when he spoke it sounded as if he was giving a sermon. "The sacred horn is missing," he pronounced, to the shocked gasps of the members of the Caucus. From the looks exchanged by the Synod, it appeared this knowledge was already known to them. "I only said it had been taken out for cleansing to avoid panic," said Dikran, "but sooner or later questions will be raised. We must find the horn as soon as possible."

"But what happened to it? Where is it?" demanded Zeroun, his dark brows drawn together. "This whole matter is an abomination."

Dikran raised a hand for silence. "No one has access to the sacred closet," he said, referring to the small chamber in which the horn was kept. "Except for us. That can mean only one thing as far as I'm concerned." He paused, eyeing each one of the fourteen-member Synod. "One of *you* has stolen the horn."

Gasps of outrage were heard throughout the room. Leena glanced with fright at Karole. By all that was holy! One of the ministers had taken the horn? But why? For what purpose? All of her doubts came rushing back to her, and she stared at Dikran, her mouth hanging open, waiting to hear what he would say next.

"This is absurd," Karayan said quietly. "You are accusing one of us of being a thief."

Dikran nodded solemnly. "I see no alternative. Only the fourteen of you plus myself have access to the Inner Sanctum. The horn must be returned."

"Dear deity," Leena whispered to Karole. "What will happen if it's not found? Truly, the trumpet is insufficient to awaken Lothar. He needs the special frequency of the sacred horn. If he is not awakened, our climatic cycles will not be reset. Rains will not come during the winter. And what of the lozenge? Lothar provides it for us every year at Mistic. If we do not partake of his bounty, sickness could devastate the land.''

"We have three months," said Dikran. "We are now in the final cycle of the year, following the harvest. Lothar times his renewal to begin in Fearn, our winter season. If we do not find the horn within this three-month period, other disasters of greater magnitude than you can imagine will afflict our world. It must be found. Unless, of course, one of you wishes to return it immediately. If you do not wish your identity to be known, you may place it in the sacred closet when no one is about. No further questions will be asked. But if the horn is not returned by this time tomorrow, we must convene and begin an investigation. And I assure you," he told his underlings, "every piece of information that was ever known about you will be uncovered."

Silence descended upon the room. Leena's mind reeled with the possibilities. No horn to awaken Lothar? No resetting of the weather cycles to keep her world's climate on a steady course? No lozenge to prevent sickness and ill health? Surely great disaster would befall them.

The gathering was dispersed with instructions that they reconvene in the same place at the same time the following day if the horn had not been returned by then. The members of the Caucus were directed to assume their duties immediately. To Leena's disappointment, she had been assigned to Zeroun, Minister of Religion. She had hoped she would be with Karayan, since he was her father's friend, but the artifacts she had been studying were the property of the religious order of Sabal. She followed Zeroun to his offices in another section of the Palisades. Each department had its own suite. Most of the clerical functions were assumed by civilians. By being assigned to the religious hierarchy, Leena had become a personal aide to Zeroun. With the privileges accorded to her status, she could attend private meetings with him, sit in on the Synod councils, and carry out his direct orders.

Marching into his office, Zeroun sat behind his desk and

indicated that she was to take the seat opposite. His close-set ebony eyes pierced her like an avenging angel. Dark, thick-slashed eyebrows converged into a frown as he stared at her sternly and reviewed her duties. His thin compressed lips and hawklike nose completed the image of a man who would let nothing stand in the way of his goals. Even the puffs of black hair rising up behind his ears and flanking his receding hairline proclaimed his aggressiveness. Disciplining his body as well as his soul, Zeroun maintained an athletic figure, which was an accomplishment for a man of sixty-four years.

Leena trembled in her seat as she listened to him. Zeroun was vehement in his faith, and he allowed for no dissension. Those who spoke against Lothar were even known to have disappeared, if not being outright banished to the pagan Black Lands. It didn't make her feel any better knowing that Zeroun had played a role in her father's censure.

Had it been just over five years since Father's misinterpretion of the ancient scrolls? He'd been severely disciplined for his indiscretion. Rather than face banishment, as would have been the punishment for one of his station, he'd been given the option of renouncing his words and submitting to a year of penance. Leena knew he had Karayan to thank for interceding in his behalf. Father never talked much about the incident, having been greatly disturbed by it, but she could see how it had changed his life. One of the reasons why she'd joined the Caucus was to find a way to clear his name. Although he maintained his position of Candor, he was diffident in the presence of his superiors, and it hurt her to see him behave in such a humble manner.

Her father's background wasn't the only reason she didn't care to work with Zeroun. About six months earlier she'd found a unique item on one of her digs at an ancient temple. The ring—it could almost be called a small bracelet—was constructed of the same creamy, translucent material as the sacred horn. Unlike any other substance on Xan, it inspired her to seek more information about the origins of her religion. She'd been astounded when the Department of Religion confiscated the piece, ordering her to keep the discovery confidential. When she received an invitation to join the Caucus a month later Leena realized she was being bribed in return for her silence. She wanted to ask Zeroun what had been done with the valuable relic but was afraid to mention it for fear of being disciplined and summarily dismissed.

Since her own background was less than exemplary, she scurried to obey his commands, consoling herself with the thought that she would soon learn the secrets of the Synod.

It was a relief to retire to the dormitorylike quarters she shared with the other female initiates at the end of the day. They ate their evening meal in the dining commons and then were free for the rest of the evening. Everyone was eager to discuss recent events, and so the time passed quickly. Leena's father came by and gave her the good news that Bendyk had contacted him. He was safe and would be arriving within the next forty-eight hours, having made plans to take the first transport out. In the meantime, he was busy helping with rescue efforts in the village. Leena tried to discuss the matter of the missing horn with her father, feeling she could confide in him if no one else, but Father didn't seem to want to hear her news.

"You have an important position now, daughter, but don't abuse it. Keep your ears open and your mouth closed." He gave her an indulgent pat on the shoulder. "If you follow the rules, your efforts will be rewarded."

Karayan was more sympathetic, listening to her fears and worries and reflecting them with his own. "Indeed, this is a grave matter," he told her when they encountered each other in the corridor the next morning. His handsome, solid features brought her a measure of comfort as he gazed at her with an open, friendly expression. "Dikran checked this morning, and the horn still is not in its proper place," he informed her. "I'm going to recommend that you be put in charge of the investigation."

"Me!" Leena gaped at him, openmouthed. "Why me?"

He laid a hand on her arm and smiled. "You're the only one among us who has knowledge of these ancient artifacts. With your dedication and energy, you're the perfect choice to lead an investigation. The new members of the Caucus can aid you."

Leena stared at him. A stickler for propriety, Karayan always presented a well-groomed appearance, from his carefully styled brown hair to his manicured fingernails to his personally tailored frock coats and trousers. As Minister of Justice, he supervised the higher court system, led by the Candors, with the same enthusiasm that he exhibited for his favorite hobby of art collecting. Leena was impressed by his air of quiet confidence. She had visited his estate and knew that he kept his affairs in the same meticulous order with which he presented his appearance. At fifty-eight years old, Karayan was one of the youngest members of the Synod, and also one of the most energetic. Leena glanced down, and her eye caught the large gold pinkie ring on his left finger.

"I shall do my best to follow any instructions I am given," she murmured, aware of her father's admonition.

Dear deity, Leena thought as Karayan left to perform a task. How can I be put in charge of finding the horn? Dikran and the others won't agree. I have no status here, no power; I'm just a simple aide. Why would they choose me? Actually, as Minister of Justice, Karayan should be in charge of the investigation.

But when the Synod and the members of the Caucus met later, Dikran didn't agree with that notion. "The thief is one of us," the old man said, his voice trembling with distress as he glared at each one of the robed members of the Synod. "Therefore whoever leads the investigation must check into our backgrounds."

"Exactly," Karayan agreed, rising. "This requires a two-pronged effort. We need someone here at the Palisades to investigate each one of us, but we also need someone to search for the missing horn if it has left the grounds. There is one among us whose life work has been studying the relics of our past. It is my recommendation that Leena Worthing-ton-Jax be placed in charge of this investigation.''

All eyes turned in her direction, and Leena felt like sinking through the floor. Why me? she thought again. I wouldn't even know where to begin.

''May I make another suggestion?'' Karayan asked. ''Her brother Bendyk is due here in the next few days. He's a missionary with an exemplary track record. We need an objective person to check into our own backgrounds while Leena pursues the missing horn. Why not select Bendyk to work with her?''

Zeroun shot to his feet. ''I object! May I remind you of Cranby's censure? His son might harbor resentment against the Synod, as may his daughter.'' His dark gaze swung to Leena.

Leena rose proudly, squaring her shoulders. ''I beg to differ with your opinion. My brother Bendyk was fully in agreement with the Synod's sentence regarding our father. As for myself, I yield to your superior wisdom and hope to show you my loyalty through my service in the Caucus.'' She bowed her head, hoping her display of humility would persuade them in her favor. Although she didn't wish for the burden of the responsibility of finding the horn, she felt excited by the prospect of conducting an investigation. Such a pursuit of justice would serve her own purposes well.

A heated discussion ensued, during which Zeroun's protests were overruled. Leena and Bendyk were empowered with the full authority of the Synod in order to conduct their investigation. A letter would be given to each one of them, authorizing them to seek whatever help or counsel they'd need.

Leena felt a glow of satisfaction as she left the chamber, but her spirit was dampened later that day. Passing by a partially open door in one of the many corridors winding through the Palisades complex, she heard her name mentioned. Without hesitation, she flattened herself against the wall to eavesdrop.

"How can you let her take charge of such an important matter?" Zeroun demanded. "She's a danger to our faith. You know we invited Leena to be a member of the Caucus in order to keep a closer eye on her."

"She has the background to verify the horn's authenticity," replied a muffled male voice. "As an expert on the carvings left by the Apostles, she's familiar with the symbols etched onto the horn's surface. No one else has the same level of knowledge or experience."

"I suppose you're right. The Truthsayers may try to prevent her from recovering the horn. They're trying to destroy the credibility of our religion. It would further their goals if the holy relic was never found."

"Perhaps they stole it in the first place."

"I wouldn't even be surprised if Leena is one of them. She asks too many questions. Let's keep a sharp watch on her!"

A rustling noise indicated that the speakers were about to leave the room, so Leena hastily slipped inside the next open doorway, waiting until she heard their footsteps pass. Trembling at what she'd overheard, she considered the repercussions. Zeroun didn't trust her, yet she came under his authority as a member of the Caucus. Not anymore, she told herself. He was subject to her investigation the same as the others. His words about the Truthsayers gave her pause. Maybe they *were* involved in the theft. They were claiming that Lothar was a false god whom the priests created to serve their own purposes. If the horn wasn't blown, Lothar wouldn't awaken from his rest, and disaster would ensue. Chaos would only benefit the Truthsayers. Her heart was heavy as she envisioned a society disrupted by anarchy. The world must never be allowed to come to that. She had to find the horn. But the awesome responsibility made her shudder.

"Bendyk, come quickly," she whispered to herself. She needed her brother's help to start the investigation; who else could she confide in?

Bendyk finally arrived two days later. Sister and brother embraced while Cranby looked on and Karayan beamed at all three of them. Leena and Bendyk retired to a private corner of the dining commons and exchanged their news.

"Many people were lost in the tsunami," Bendyk said, his face haggard, dark shadows under his eyes. "I did what I could to help," he said, shrugging, "but there was still much to be done. At least communications have been restored."

Bendyk was shocked when told of his new assignment. "The sacred horn is missing?" he cried.

"Hush! Lower your voice," Leena whispered when she realized that others in the dining commons weren't aware of the news.

"What do you mean I've got to check into the background of the Synod?" he asked. "Why me?"

Leena gave a small laugh. "That's what I've been asking myself," she said. "But you're not attached to the Synod. You can pursue this with an objective mind."

"I'll need help," he told her, his forehead furrowed. "Their individual records will have to be examined, background checks made, financial records inspected. I can't go about this alone." His eyes brightened. "When I was in Amat I encountered the local tax agent, a woman named Swill Braddock. She's supposed to be a whiz at finances. Perhaps I could convince her to be my assistant."

He didn't tell his sister that he'd like nothing better than an excuse to see Swill again. A lump rose in his throat as he recalled how they'd worked side by side to help the villagers. Swill Braddock was a strong, assertive woman who hadn't encouraged him in the least. If anything, she had tried to dampen his interest in her. They'd gone their separate ways thereafter, much to Bendyk's dismay, but he knew how to contact her. He wondered if she'd agree to help him on her own, or if he'd have to use his newly given authority to order her to do so. He hoped she would be agreeable. It

41

would bode well if their business relationship began on the right note.

Mentioning his plan to Leena, he was pleased to receive her approval.

"Where do we start?" Leena said.

She didn't have long to wonder; a strategy session was called with the Synod.

"You'll need protection," Magar said. As Minister of State, the seventy-year-old silver-haired gentleman supervised relations among the different districts. His twinkly blue eyes and warm smile engaged her trust as he regarded her. Entertaining visiting dignitaries was part of his job, and his preference for fine wines and good dining was evident in his portly figure and rolling gait. A casual dresser, Magar favored comfort over formality; quite the contrast to Karayan, who always dressed in an exemplary manner.

"The Truthsayers may try to stop you from recovering the horn," he went on. "Or your search could take you into dangerous territory, where our representatives are not available to render aid. I know someone who can offer you assistance, if he'll agree to accompany you."

Leena was aware of no one on her world who could come to her defense if need be. Her people were a peaceful race. Few had experience in fighting or aggression, though it seemed as though the Truthsayers were heading in that direction. If Magar was correct, she might have need of such assistance.

"Who is this person?" she inquired, although the possibility made her shiver with dread.

"His name is Taurin Rey Niris," Magar replied. "He has the experience you seek."

"What do you mean? Where is this man located?" Karayan demanded, casting a protective glance in her direction.

"I will give Leena the necessary information later," Magar said. "Leena, have you thought about where to begin your investigation?"

Leena understood that he didn't want the others inquiring

too deeply into the background of this man named Taurin and wondered why. Who was the fellow? Where did he come from? Where would she have to go to ask for his assistance?

Sirvat spoke up. "If the horn has been stolen, it's very likely it passed through the hands of Grotus."

Leena's eyes lit up. Grotus was a renowned dealer in stolen artifacts. It was suspected that he controlled a worldwide network of smugglers, but nothing had ever been proven, so he'd never been prosecuted. It was true that if someone had stolen the horn for money, it would very likely have gone to Grotus. It seemed as good a place as any for her to start her investigation.

"Very well," she agreed. "I will seek out the help of this Taurin Rey Niris, and we shall travel together to Grotus." She'd heard that Grotus lived on a fortified island. She had no idea how she would get herself admitted to see him, let alone why he would share information with her. But she could worry about that later. First, she'd better see if Taurin Rey Niris was willing to help her. It would be better if she didn't have to go about her escapades alone.

But as she and her brother were saying their good-byes— he was on his way to seek the help of Swill and Leena was off to find Taurin—her brother regarded her solemnly.

"I don't like this notion of your traveling with a strange man," he said, stroking his jaw.

"I don't even know if he'll agree to help me," Leena replied. "If not, I'll send a message to you and we'll figure out another route to take. You'll have to let me know if this tax agent will work with you. It would be useful for you to have someone who knows about financial records."

Bendyk nodded. "It's possible one of the Synod members needs money and that's why the horn was stolen, although I find that idea doubtful."

"Don't you think Father might have some helpful suggestions?" Even if he tried to brush her off again, she'd make him listen. After so many years in the service of Sabal, her father might possess knowledge of priestly secrets of which she and Bendyk were unaware.

"I don't think we should tell him what we're doing," Bendyk said, the corners of his mouth turning down. "Let's keep this between ourselves. But promise me, Sister," he added, his blue eyes flashing, "you'll call me as soon as you make contact with this man."

"Of course. I'll let you know what happens."

"If he agrees to your proposal, you must not travel with him."

She widened her eyes. "Whatever do you mean?"

"Traveling alone with a strange man, Sister? Have you no notion of the harm that would befall your reputation?"

Leena almost laughed. "We have no such strictures in our society, Brother. Why would you think such a thing?"

"This is not Beltane, when coupling is encouraged and trial marriages take place. If you are allowed such freedom, your future plans may be jeopardized."

"Oh," she said, catching his meaning. "You mean Malcolm? He need know nothing about this."

"And what if he finds out?" Bendyk inquired. "Do you think he would take it lightly that you were traveling about with an unattached male?"

"If he hears about me, he'll understand. At any rate, he's not supposed to know anything about this mission."

Bendyk glowered at her. "Let's hope your suitor doesn't learn about it from someone else. Call me the minute you and Rey Niris reach an agreement!"

"*If* we reach an agreement," Leena corrected.

Her brother's expression turned sly. "I shall see to it that you behave with propriety. Leave the matter to me."

He turned away, leaving Leena filled with misgivings. Just what did Bendyk have up his sleeve?

Chapter Three

Leena drove her sleek red rider along a rural road flanked by rolling green fields and wooded hillsides. Osbrets swooped and soared over a broad stretch of brown stubble, the remains of a recent grain harvest. Their graceful bodies were starkly white against the muted earth tones. The Blenheim region was one of the most fertile in Celia, the province that housed the Palisades in its central hub, and this area supplied a bounty of fresh produce, milk, and cheeses savored around the globe. Magar's estate was close by, his family being one of the largest landholders in the area. Leena hadn't realized Taurin resided in the same locale and was surprised that Magar hadn't mentioned it.

Glancing at the paper with his written directions on the seat beside her, she noted that the turn-off to Taurin's place should be coming up ahead. Sure enough, it was just around the next bend. She followed an oak-lined private road that ended in a circular driveway. Stopping her rider with a squeal of brakes, she shifted gears and turned off the ignition. An attractive, tidy house faced her, and beyond it were cultivated fields. Was Taurin a farmer, and if so, what did he raise? Her curiosity climbed a notch as she examined his home.

A trimmed yard spread out in front like a brown-tinged carpet, the grass obviously too dry. Bordering the foundation of the house was a rounded evergreen hedge. A short flight of steps led up to a wraparound porch on which sat a couple of cushioned lounge chairs, a small table, and various potted plants. The one-story dwelling was painted pastel blue, with white shutters edged in a scallop design, giving an impression of neatness and simplicity that appealed to Leena the way a home-cooked meal would appeal to a weary traveler.

The quiet, still exterior of the house greeted her as she emerged from her vehicle. Unseasonably warm autumn air struck her skin like a blast from a furnace. Glad that her gown was made from a lightweight silk material, she strode the few steps up to the portico. No one responded to her loud knocking. Disappointed, Leena realized that the driveway held no other vehicles besides her own, and she hadn't noticed a garage. Taurin must have gone out.

Taking an appreciative sniff of the rich, earthy scent coming from the freshly plowed fields off to the side, she was startled at the sweet fragrance that drifted into her nostrils. Following her nose, she moved around to the rear of the house to stare at row after row of brilliantly colored flowers.

Flowers? The man grew flowers? Picturing Taurin as a rural farmhand, she couldn't conceive of him as being able to protect her from danger. Laughter bubbled into her throat at the absurd notion. Moving closer, she noticed that the soil was parched and the blooms wilted. The weather had been unusually hot and dry lately, and apparently the climatic disorder was taking its toll on local farmers. Was this a result of Lothar's wrath at his people's unfaithfulness, as the Arch Nome proclaimed, or could it be taken as another sign that something was deeply wrong on her world?

Squinting in the bright sunlight, Leena decided to return to the house before her shoes became encrusted with dirt. The shade of the porch beckoned to her as she climbed the steps, approaching a back door.

A glimpse in a window showed her that the small gold circlet covering her head had become tilted. She straightened it along with the attached blue veil that matched her elegant gown. She wore her hair loose, preferring a freer style in defiance of propriety, which demanded that unwed females comb their hair into a modest upsweep.

Beyond her reflection, Leena's eyes fell on a pile of books visible through the window. Oddly enough, they were archaeological texts. Disregarding her innate caution, she pressed her nose against the pane in order to get a closer view. The books were spread on a kitchen table. Her gaze swept to a broad tile counter, on which rested several woven baskets holding yellow onions, polished red spommes, potatoes, and green stiglers. They were arranged in rows like the flower beds outside. Not a dirty dish was in sight. Was Taurin so tidy, or did he have a housekeeper? Even his kitchen utensils were hung with an eye to precision. Then again, what made her think he lived alone? She'd gotten that impression from Magar, but maybe it was wrong. And if not, what kind of man would live in isolation, raising flowers and studying archaeology texts?

She strolled to another window to search for more clues as to the man's puzzling nature. She spied a living area, a cozy room with a stone fireplace and couches you could sink into and—what were those?—drawings? Yes, it appeared as though Taurin was working on something. An easel stood in a corner.

So now she had a flower farmer with aspirations of becoming an artist. But wait—weren't those figures in his sketch a bit familiar? She stepped to the side, and her ankle banged against a solid object. A loud crash made her jump, and she glanced down in dismay. She hadn't seen the flowerpot. Stooping to gather the broken pieces from among the spilled dirt, she heaped them in a pile and then straightened, flushing with guilt. Lord, now Taurin would know someone had been snooping around!

Brushing off her hands, she trudged toward her rider, deciding she'd return later. In the meantime she was thirsty and could use something to eat. On her way through the town, she'd noticed a pub. It would be a good place to get a snack while seeking information.

The dimly lit interior of the pub was a welcome respite from the unusual heat of the late-afternoon sun. Leena stood just inside the doorway in order to give her eyes time to adjust. After a few moments she let her gaze wander. Straight ahead was a polished mahogany bar with gleaming brass trim. Glasses hung on racks overhead, and behind the bar were various bottles and kegs in different sizes. The tantalizing smell of food drifted into her nostrils, and she noticed a small dining room off to the right. It being near the supper hour, a few of the tables were occupied already. There was a fancily dressed young couple at one, visitors like herself. A family with three noisy children occupied another table. Roughly dressed farmhands used a number of seats, drinking brew and chatting vociferously. Deciding she liked the atmosphere, Leena strode to the bar to place her order.

"I'll have a glass of claret, and I'd like to see a menu, please," she said.

The bartender, a large burly fellow with a shock of red hair, complied. As he handed her the menu, Leena smiled sweetly at him.

"I'm looking for a man named Taurin Rey Niris," she said in a low tone. "Would you know where I can find him? He isn't at home."

The bartender looked over her elegantly styled gown and his eyes widened as he realized the significance of the gold circlet on her head. He leaned forward in a conspiratorial manner.

"Rey Niris sits in a booth yonder," he whispered, nodding toward a dark corner at the rear of the pub. "Be cautious of the man you seek, madam. He's a strange 'un."

"What do you mean?" Leena hissed back.

The man's face closed, and he withdrew to pour her a glass of red wine. ''Just heed my words,'' he cautioned.

Leena took her glass of wine and the menu and sauntered toward the rear of the pub. She could barely make out who was sitting in the far corner. With his back to a wall, the man facing forward was barely visible in the gloom. No wonder, she thought nervously as she approached.

The man was swathed totally in black, including a covering wrapped around his head. The cloth shaded his eyes so she couldn't read his expression, but she sensed an air of tension about him. His broad shoulders were hunched forward, as though he were ready to spring up at a moment's notice. She could imagine his eyes darting toward the entrance, searching for the first hint of a threat. But what threat could there possibly be in this peaceful village?

If he turned out to be Rey Niris, how could she convince him to assist her? He appeared formidable in his isolation. Nearing his table, she muttered a quick prayer to Lothar for guidance.

Taurin had noticed her the moment she stepped through the door. Backlit from the sunlight streaming in the entrance, the woman appeared a vision of loveliness. A mass of golden hair floated about her head and shoulders like waves of spun silk, framing a face with features as fine as porcelain. He couldn't see the color of her eyes; only that they were large and round as saucers as she peered about the room. Her body, slender and curvaceous, was encased in an exquisitely styled gown that was cinched at the waist and flared out in a skirt that drifted about her ankles with each graceful movement.

What was a woman of her obvious wealth doing here? he wondered, watching as she exchanged words with the proprietor. Holding a glass of red wine, she approached in his direction, and he realized she wore the gold circlet and blue veil that signified a member of the Caucus. Her eyes matched the royal blue hue of her gown, and he could only stare in awe as she neared.

"Good and welfare, brother," the woman said, issuing the standard greeting when she'd stopped before his table. "I'm looking for a man named Taurin Rey Niris. Might you be the one I seek?"

Her voice, sweet and musical, rang in his ears like a spirit calling him to worship. She inspired idolatry, he thought, gazing into her eyes. Mentally shaking himself, he focused his thoughts on reality. Was he forgetting his reasons for being here, and the enforced isolation he must maintain?

"What is it you want?" he asked bluntly.

"I have a proposition to make."

"Who are you?"

"My name is Leena Worthington-Jax."

"You're in the religious order."

"So I am. Look, are you Rey Niris or not?"

At his curt nod, she placed her glass on the table and took a seat.

Taurin shrank further back into the shadows so she couldn't see his face. "I have no interest in anything you have to offer."

"Please listen to me. I need your help, but this is something we should discuss in private." Her hands trembling, she took a sip of her wine.

His gaze lingered on her slender, tapered fingers. He couldn't possibly imagine what she wanted or who had encouraged her to approach him, but she obviously posed a threat to his solitude. Except for occasional excursions into town, he'd succeeded in keeping a low profile. Why, then, was she here to disrupt his status quo?

"There's a room upstairs," he conceded, curiosity overwhelming his better judgment. "I'll ask the owner if we can use it for a few minutes."

"Very well." Leena felt a wave of relief that at least he was willing to listen. Following him toward the bar with her glass of wine in hand, she was gratified when the owner agreed. Taurin stood aside so she could precede him up the staircase. Brushing against his arm, a shiver racked her body.

The man radiated such a menacing aura, and she could barely make out his face under the covering that swathed his head. The broad set of his shoulders and the width of his chest were punctuated by the strange garb that he wore.

Upstairs they entered a private dining room that reeked of stale liquor. Taurin had ordered a drink brought up from the bartender, and they waited in tense silence until it was served. This room was brighter than the downstairs section, and she caught a startling glimpse of his steely gray eyes and the shock of black hair that curled onto his forehead. A forbidden thrill warmed her blood, but she pushed it aside to focus on her mission. His aquiline nose and firm jaw proclaimed him a man of character. Hopefully his sense of honor would prevail and he'd agreed to help her.

"What I'm about to tell you," she said, "must not leave this room. You will not reveal a word of it to anyone. Swear it upon your sacred honor."

Taurin quirked an eyebrow. "Go ahead."

"You swear you will tell no one what I am about to reveal?"

He inclined his head in acknowledgment.

"Someone has stolen the sacred horn, and it has not been blown at this year's Renewal ceremony. We are facing total disaster if it is not recovered by the month of Fearn. I have been assigned the task of retrieving the horn, and I need your help to do it."

"Absolutely not!" he snapped.

"Magar told me to ask for your assistance," Leena persisted.

"Magar!" Taurin's eyebrows shot up.

"There might be danger involved in my quest," she explained. "The Truthsayers could be involved in this plot, and they might try to stop me from succeeding. I need your protection. Magar said you're the only one who can help me."

"What else did he tell you about me?" Taurin growled.

"Very little," Leena admitted.

Taurin stood abruptly. "I cannot do it. I will not be involved in the affairs of your kind.''

"They're your affairs too! Don't you realize that all of us will be affected if the horn isn't blown? Catastrophe will result, with everyone suffering the consequences.''

"I don't care. You'll have to find someone else to help you.''

She opened her mouth to make an angry retort, but just then a loud commotion erupted from downstairs. Raised male voices resounded over a couple of crashing thuds. Without so much as a backward glance in her direction, Taurin thundered down the stairs into the dining area, where the workers, Leena saw, following on his heels, were engaged in a brawl. Shouting and cursing, their fists were flying. The other clientele had fled. Leena gasped as Taurin threw himself into the fray. A series of well-placed kicks and punches subdued the opponents within a few moments' time. Stunned, they lay sprawled about the room, staring at him in fear and wonder.

"Fighting is not to be tolerated,'' he told them. "You will make reparations to the owner of this establishment. Is that understood?''

The men nodded their agreement, their expressions making it clear that they feared reprisal should they refuse. Hunching his fists at his side, Taurin hovered over one cowering miscreant, as though wishing the fellow would lash out at him so he could react in violence once again. A shudder racked his body as he straightened. Without another word, he stalked toward the door and was gone.

"Wait!'' Leena cried, rushing outside. They hadn't finished their discussion. But when she emerged into the sunlight, he wasn't anywhere in sight. She glanced at the riders parked along the curb. One was just pulling out, and as she tried to identify the driver it roared away.

"Kripes!'' she cursed. That had to be Taurin! Now a trip back to his farm had become a necessity. Angrily raking her fingers through her hair, she strode off toward her rider, hoping he'd go directly home.

The violence she'd seen unleashed in the pub disturbed

her greatly. It was truly a sign that the people were straying from the Faith. Hardly anyone ever fought on Xan, even in a drunken brawl such as the one she'd just witnessed. It wasn't their way of life, and it defied Lothar's teachings. Change was in the wind, and she feared it didn't bode well for her world.

Taurin had jumped into the fight without so much as a second thought. That demonstration of his skills proved that he could serve as her protector. The man was no gentle flower farmer. Dressed in black, with tension emanating from every pore, he appeared more as a representative from the legendary Demon's Lair than a gentle farmhand. His choice of occupations and hobbies continued to intrigue her. The differing sides of his personality didn't mesh, and she wondered at his origins. His farm occupied a corner of Magar's huge estate. Was he a tenant farmer, offering part of his produce to Magar as a rental payment? Or was he a freeholder, owning the land himself? She couldn't conceive of their relationship and resolved to question Magar about it at the first opportunity.

Looking at her timekeeper, Leena noticed that it was six o'clock. She'd missed having a snack at the pub, and now her stomach grumbled with hunger. Stopping at a local market, she bought a loaf of crusty bread, a hunk of cheese, and a couple of bottles of cider. After putting her purchases into the back seat of her rider she slid into the driver's seat and turned on the ignition. A warning light glowed red on the dashboard, but Leena ignored it, as she had on her way into the village. She'd take care of it tomorrow; today her business was too pressing.

Approaching the front of Taurin's house, she noticed that the windows were open, letting in a breeze that cooled the air. The sun had begun its descent, and it would soon be dark. Not wishing to drive at night, Leena decided to plead her case quickly and leave. If the man agreed to help her, she'd return tomorrow morning to further their discussion.

Gathering up her bundle of groceries, she marched toward

his front door and knocked loudly. The door swung wide at her summons.

"What do *you* want?" Taurin snapped, scowling at her. "I thought I made it clear that I was unable to help you."

Leena stared at him in response. He'd removed the cloth swathed about his crown and a riot of black curls covered his head. Angry slate gray eyes slammed into hers with a fierceness that took her breath away.

"I brought some food," she said. "May I come in?"

She used her sweetest, most beguiling tone of voice, but it didn't budge the man. He stared at her unmovingly.

"Go away," he said, about to shut the door in her face.

Leena wedged her foot inside. "We haven't finished our discussion."

"Indeed we have." The hunch of his shoulders told her he would resort to force to remove her if necessary.

"I told you Magar sent me," she said hastily, hoping the name of his neighbor or landlord, whichever it was, would move him.

Taurin hesitated, and Leena snatched at another opening. "I see you have an interest in archaeology," she said, nodding toward the easel in the far corner. "I'm an archaeologist. It was because of my background and experience that I was the one assigned to find the missing horn."

"An archaeologist?" he queried, staring at her with renewed interest. "Perhaps we should continue our conversation." His voice had softened ever so slightly, but Leena perceived the change and felt relieved that he might consider her offer.

He stood stiffly aside, allowing her to enter. Her breath came short as she passed by him. He presented such a dark, menacing aura that she trembled in his presence. But her mission was too important for her to be awed by him. She needed his help, and she was determined to get it any way she could.

Stalking straight into his kitchen, she put down her package on the counter and began unpacking the contents. "I brought a loaf of bread, cheese, and cider,'' she said. ''Would you like some, or have you already eaten?''

''No,'' he said quietly from behind. ''I haven't had the chance yet. Your repast is welcome.''

''You could get me some plates and a knife. I'll cut this cheese into wedges.''

He complied, watching her silently as she busied herself with nervous fingers. The man totally unsettled her. It was his kitchen, she reminded herself. She was the intruder, and he undoubtedly resented her presence. Whirling around, her gown swishing at her ankles, she smiled bravely and offered him a plate of bread and cheese. Without uttering a word of thanks, he took it from her, helped himself to a mug of cider, and sat down at the polished wooden kitchen table. She took the seat opposite him and looked at him openly. His irises were a dark shade of smoky gray, but something greenish flickered inside them whenever a shadow crossed his face. Fascinated by the dancing lights in his eyes, she didn't realize she was staring until he glanced away.

Taurin was aware of her interest, and it deeply disconcerted him. He had never been so profoundly affected by a woman before. A relationship with a female of her stature was strictly forbidden—not that he could afford to get involved. And even if he *did* fancy a relationship with her, she belonged to a higher social status and was a member of the religious order. As if the social strictures weren't enough to discourage him, her loose hairstyle proclaimed that she mated, even though she didn't wear the ring of bonding.

''Does your mate know that you have come on this errand?'' he blurted out, and was instantly horrified at his words.

Leena cleared her throat. ''I have no mate,'' she announced. ''My brother Bendyk knows I am here. So do the members of the Synod who sent me.'' Realization dawned as she noted his gaze lingering on her defiant waves of hair. ''You are wondering why I wear my hair loose? I prefer the style.''

So she chose to defy convention; what an unusual female! Stuffing a piece of bread into his mouth, he sought distraction from her charms. The bread was crunchy on the outside, but the inside melted as he ate, leaving a rich taste in his mouth. "Tell me about the missing horn," he said.

Leena couldn't keep her gaze from being drawn to his finely chiseled mouth as he chewed. Belatedly she realized that she was alone in a house with a strange man whose violent nature had recently been demonstrated blatantly to her. *Magar wouldn't have sent me here if he didn't trust the fellow*, she told herself calmly, but she still felt uncomfortable in his presence, especially with that brooding look on his face.

"The horn could only have been taken by someone with access to the Inner Sanctum," she told him. "That means it had to be one of the fourteen members of the Synod. My brother Bendyk has been assigned the task of looking into their backgrounds to determine whether any shows a financial strain that could indicate a motive. It was suggested that you and I contact Grotus, a dealer in stolen artifacts, to see if the horn has passed through his hands. And if he has it, we'll offer a ransom. I am prepared to give you," she said, leveling her gaze on him, "a substantial sum for assisting me."

Taurin took a large draught from his mug of cider. "I have not agreed to help you," he reminded her. But he couldn't conceive of this fragile female meeting with Grotus herself. He had heard of the man, and though they'd had no personal contact, Taurin knew Grotus wasn't the kind of person Leena should encounter alone—if she was even able to procure an audience with him. "I have my farmlands to tend," he told her, denying the flame of desire that flared unbidden from his core. The wistful look in her sapphire eyes tugged at a soft spot in his heart that he didn't want to acknowledge.

"Your crop isn't doing well," she told him, hoping to appeal to the farmer within him. "If the horn is not blown, how will your fields prosper? This drought will worsen, and your blooms will die. Nothing can grow in this unusual hot spell. Do you not wish to see Lothar awaken from his rest?''

''Lothar be damned,'' he said, knowing very well that her god was not responsible for the climatic cycles—at least not in a direct sense. He didn't understand what was happening on this world, but it wasn't his job to find out either. He simply wanted to live in peace, undisturbed and unmolested. He had been through too much horror to seek violence now. This was his haven, and he had no desire to leave it.

''I'll take my chances like everyone else,'' he told her, glancing at her from under his thick brows.

Leena's hand curled tightly around the handle of her mug as she tried to suppress her rising anger. ''Don't you care that people are going to get sick and die if Lothar's lozenge isn't made available in the month of Mistic? People are facing sickness and hunger, not to mention the weather disasters that cause havoc around the world. My brother Bendyk was just in the village of Amat on Seacrest Bay. It was hit by a tsunami. Scores of people died, and many others were injured or lost their homes. Do you want to see this continue to happen? You're being given a chance to help. This is not something I can do alone,'' she said, hating the way her voice began to quiver. Moisture flooded her eyes as a desperate edge entered her voice. ''I need help, Taurin. I trust that Magar sent me to the right place.''

Taurin didn't answer, considering the reason why Magar had sent her to him. Magar knew very well who he was and where he had come from. Indeed, he was the only person in this region who could protect her from trouble. But by involving him, Magar put them both at risk of exposure. Damn! What was he to do? The woman appeared as though she was about to burst into tears at any moment. Shoving his chair back, Taurin got up abruptly and paced the kitchen, dashing a hand through his unruly dark hair. So she was an archaeologist, was she? Maybe she could help him interpret the secrets he'd kept hidden from everyone all these years.

Leena watched him pacing and was afraid he'd refuse her

again. She felt as though she'd insulted him by offering money. Didn't he understand that his own livelihood was threatened?

"I'm sure I can get the Synod to send someone to tend your farm, if that's what worries you," she said.

Taurin wouldn't want to see all the work he'd put into the place gone to waste. He'd toiled long and hard to make this piece of land he called his own prosper, and the flowers he grew were important to a significant person in his life. He didn't want to disappoint that person by not being able to make his monthly shipments.

"Let me show you something," he said to her, before disappearing through the doorway into the living area. He returned a moment later, holding the sketch she'd spotted on the easel. She recognized the symbols instantly as being the same inscriptions that appeared with frequency at crumbling ancient ruins around the globe.

"Where did you get that from?" she asked him suspiciously.

"I've made a study of these symbols," he said. "Since you're an archaeologist, perhaps you can interpret them for me."

Leena rose, her skirt swaying about her legs. "I am afraid I've been unable to decipher them. I suspect it is some message left to us by the ancient Apostles, but I cannot imagine what it means. My life's work has involved studying the ruins. I'd like to learn where the Apostles originated and why they left. There are many more things I need to learn as well," she murmured, thinking about her father's misinterpretation of the scrolls. Was he so far off the mark that his censure was justified, or had he been too close to the truth?

"Will you help me or not?" she demanded.

"All right," Taurin muttered, "but I'd like someone to work the fields in my stead."

"I'll make the arrangements. I need to return to the Palisades to pack. How long of a journey is it to Grotus? Do you know anything about him?"

"Not much."

"I'll ask Sirvat for details. She's the one who suggested his name to me. Sirvat is in charge of the Treasury," Leena explained. "Anyway, I'd better leave now. I'd like to get back before it's too dark."

Accompanying her outside, Taurin watched as she got into her rider. He didn't make a move to open the door for her or render assistance. He stood on his porch, as still and silent as a statue, his expression stony. Leena wondered how far they would have to travel to reach this Grotus person, and hoped it wouldn't be a long trip. Certainly her brother Bendyk's concern was justified. How could she go on such a journey with someone who was so disinterested in her welfare? Reflecting upon her goals, she determined that it was worth any peril if she could recover the horn.

Fumbling nervously with the key, she turned the ignition, but nothing happened. The engine didn't turn over, nor did the headlights come on. Oh, no! she thought, pounding the steering wheel in frustration. The recharger must be dead, and all the stations would be closed. She couldn't have it fixed until tomorrow. Now what? Biting her lower lip, she supposed she could call Bendyk to see if he could come pick her up, but it would be an hour-and-a-half-drive for him in the dark. She hadn't noticed any hostelry nearby either.

Taurin approached and peered through the open window. "Having a problem?" he drawled.

"My charge is drained." Leena felt foolish. She'd never ignored a warning indicator before, and now look what had happened! Once emptied, the circuit chamber needed hours to renew.

"The nearest station is closed. You'll have to wait until morning to request assistance." Taurin stared implacably at her, as though unwilling to burden himself with her difficulty.

With an annoyed frown, Leena stepped away from the rider. "I'll call my brother. He'll come and get me."

But when she messaged him Bendyk wasn't at the Palisades, presumably having departed to seek the help of the Swill woman. Inside Taurin's house, Leena turned to view her host with trepidation.

Bendyk remembered Swill saying she'd be going home from Amat to spend her earned leave time with her family. The town of Kameron-by-the-Knoll was located in one of the most desolate, uncomfortable settings in which he'd ever set foot. Having arrived by special air transport, he'd hired a vehicle to take him to her address, which had been supplied by Sirvat. As a tax agent, Swill was an employee of the Treasury Department.

The town was at the heart of a dustbowl, where dried weeds tumbled through the streets on every breath of hot wind. Digging for scaly grubs was the main industry, the rental agent had told him. A food delicacy in certain parts of the world, the grubs commanded a high price, but the cost of living in such a place discouraged all but the most solitary souls from pursuing the trade.

Swill's parents owned a squat tan house in a sparse development that ran up a hillside. The sun blazed overhead, and cactuses and hardy weeds provided the only greenery in sight. Hopefully he wouldn't have to stay long, Bendyk thought, ringing the doorbell on the front stoop. The pilot had orders to wait for him at the airfield.

Shuffling footsteps approached from inside the house, and then the door was thrust open. "Yo! Who be you, young 'un?"

"Good and welfare, brother." Bendyk took a step backward. The smell of spirits was strong, and from the bloodshot eyes of the stout man facing him, Bendyk would say he'd been drinking. The man's plaid shirt hung loose over a pair of baggy pants, and his work shoes were encrusted with dirt. He reeked of liquor and sweat, and Bendyk had to force himself to smile politely.

"I'm Bendyk Worthington-Jax, servant in the Sabalic order of Missioners," he said, fingering the medallion dangling at his chest. Because he worked among the people, he could wear clothes of his choosing. The medallion signified his station.

"So?" Clearly unimpressed, the fellow scratched his balding head.

"I'd like to see Swill if she's at home."

"Swill? You're here to see my daughter?" The man's face broadened into a grin, exposing yellowed teeth.

Krimas, Bendyk cursed under his breath. This was Swill's father? No wonder she had such a tough attitude.

"Come in," Braddock said, grabbing both Bendyk's hands and shaking them. Bendyk entered the house directly into a living area decorated with faded second-hand furnishings. "Swill!" her father yelled. "See who's here!"

Swill appeared in the hallway and stood stock-still at the sight of Bendyk. His gaze swept over the rust-colored top that barely bound her breasts and the white shorts that halted midthigh. Inadvertently, his eyes slid down her shapely legs.

Another woman with a worn, tired face and wearing a soiled apron entered the room, diverting his attention. But it was apparent that Braddock had noticed the appreciative look in his eye.

"Gemma, this young man is here for Swill," he told his wife, thumbing at Bendyk.

"Swill, why didn't you tell us?" her mother said, rushing forward to shake Bendyk's hands in greeting. "Oh, I'm so glad she's found someone!"

Bendyk flushed in embarrassment. "I'm not . . . I mean, I need her to come with me." He dropped his arms at his side.

"Of course," Gemma gushed. "You'll have to tell us all about how you two met. Royce?" She addressed her husband. "Now you don't have to worry no more about Swill finding a man. She's gone and gotten herself a beau."

Royce Braddock gave a loud belch. "About time it is too. Let's go mix up some drinks to celebrate while the lovebirds greet each other."

"Pa," Swill said, "I think Bendyk may be here on business."

"Nonsense; he's got eyes for you, girl. You've got a good thing here." Braddock winked. "Give him a proper greeting now." And he staggered after his wife into another room, leaving them alone.

"Well?" Swill queried, facing him with her hands on her hips. "Are you here to arrest me?"

"Arrest you?" Bendyk stared in astonishment. "Whatever for?"

"For misrepresenting the tithing count. That *is* why you're here, isn't it? You reported me to your superiors and they sent you to bring me in?"

Bendyk saw the flicker of fear in her eyes that was quickly hidden by a mask of defiance. "I am here to bring you back with me to the Palisades, but only because I need help with a special project."

Doubt crossed her expression. "A project? You need *my* help?"

"That is correct." Stepping forward, he took her hands in his. The contact sent delicious tingles up his arms. "I cannot tell you the details now, but your interviewing skills and financial expertise are what made me consult you. I need to conduct an investigation and have little experience in that type of endeavor."

She moved back, withdrawing her hands as a wary look came into her eyes. "What's in it for me?"

"An increase in pay and the knowledge that you're doing the people a service. That is important to you, isn't it?" he asked.

Her chin tilted upward. "Everyone needs a break. I do what I can to help."

"So I've noticed." He couldn't help his sarcastic tone, knowing that she didn't play by the rules. Unlike her, he chose to live with restrictions, believing that discipline strengthened the spirit. He wondered at the state of her soul that she mocked their laws.

"This isn't about anything religious, is it? Because if it is—"

"I can't give you the details now. You'll have to trust me."

"Trust you?" she scoffed. "With that fanatic gleam in your eye? I'd just as soon throw myself into a kougar pit."

"Dammit, just agree, will you?" he snapped, losing patience.

Her lips compressed. "I don't like to be told what to do. I've had enough from my Pa in that regard. Sorry; find yourself another assistant."

Bendyk regretted his outburst of temper. He was constantly striving to control his emotions and had prayed for tolerance many times. But her irreverence annoyed him beyond reason.

"Very well; then I shall have to assert my authority. If you don't cooperate, I'll inform Sirvat of your conspiracy with the villagers about the tithing count. You'll all be punished."

"Bastard!" Her eyes glittered dangerously. "I'll make you regret this."

He grinned broadly. "And I'll look forward to your retribution." He heard her howl of frustration as he turned toward the door, intending to wait outside for her to join him. What was it about this woman that so intrigued him? By all that was holy, she irritated him, but she also stirred his blood. The woman is dangerous, he warned himself. Look to your soul or she'll steal it as she did from Lothar's tribute.

He exited the house, resolving to offer a special prayer to ask for forgiveness. His thoughts of Swill were far from pious, and that was a weakness he considered a sin.

Taurin saw the look of dismay on Leena's face as she switched off the messager. Drat; he couldn't help feeling sorry for her, a weak emotion he despised, but she appeared so ethereal in her long gown and with her golden blond hair streaming down her back. If only her eyes weren't so large and such a unique shade of azure, he wouldn't feel so threatened. But her presence was a danger because he was so aware of her.

She wears a circlet, he reminded himself. That means she's pledged to serve Lothar.

"What does your brother do?" he asked, wondering if her sibling was also a member of the Caucus.

"Bendyk is a missionary. He's very dedicated to the principles of our religion. He must have left to seek help from that woman he met in Amat."

"Too bad. Now you're stranded here." He stepped forward until their bodies nearly touched. Her scent pervaded his nostrils, tempting him to do something wicked.

No! he thought in panic. There was no telling what might happen if he lost control.

"I can drive you home," he gritted out. "Leave your rider key with me and I'll take your vehicle to the station in the morning."

Leena agreed, an unhappy expression on her face, as though she realized there was no alternative. After retrieving her cloak from her rider and handing him the keys she followed him to his vehicle. Taurin held the passenger door open for her, watching intently as she gracefully slid inside.

Marching around to the driver's side, he forced away the unwanted surge of desire that held him in its powerful grip and pulled a dark cloth from his pocket to swathe about his head. He couldn't risk the woman seeing his eyes as dusk deepened into night. Shadows and darkness were his enemies; he had to guard his vision from others when light dimmed.

Gripping the steering column, he set off, rushing along the winding country roads to make the trip as brief as possible. The black-painted rider had a low-slung design that made it hug the road like a tightrope walker on a wire. Beside him, Leena clutched her seat, pressing her lips together tightly.

"Can't you please slow down?" she pleaded, giving him a sideways glance.

Taurin noted her pallor. Without commenting, he eased back on the accelerator.

"I'll get a ride out here tomorrow morning," she said. "It's best if we don't delay our journey. Will that give you enough time to get ready?"

He nodded, displeased at the idea of visiting Grotus. He had a feeling Captain Sterckle might have sold his bibliotomes to the unscrupulous artifacts dealer. Sterckle could even have told Grotus about him. Was the danger involved worth the possible rewards? He sought only two things in life: peace for his troubled soul and knowledge of his origins. The first he'd already achieved, but Leena could help him obtain the second.

The fact that she herself unknowingly presented a danger to him didn't go unnoticed. Her delicate beauty and single status offered a temptation too strong to resist, but Taurin realized she was off limits. Normally her station forbade her from associating with people like himself. As far as she knew, he was merely a farmer. She must never find out about his other persona. Magar had sworn him to secrecy in exchange for giving him the small plot of land he called his own. He was obligated, upon his honor and for his safety, to remain silent. But that wouldn't prevent him from learning what the symbols carved into Xan's ancient ruins meant. If Leena didn't know, perhaps they could find out together. The strange inscriptions were linked to his history, and by deciphering them he might discover his destiny.

The time had come for him to emerge from his secure cocoon. Magar was sending him on this errand, which meant the situation was critical. The personal danger to himself was minimal compared to what threatened Xan. And yet, as he sped his vehicle along the rural roads, he had the feeling they'd merely touched the tip of an iceberg. An even greater threat loomed—one that none of them could fathom in its immensity. The signs were there: the missing horn, the Truthsayer movement, the weather changes. Xan was plunging inexorably toward disaster. Would he and Leena be able to stop the forces of evil from overwhelming her world?

Where he came from they'd already won. Taurin swore he wouldn't let the same thing happen here.

Chapter Four

Bendyk and Swill arrived back at the Palisades late that night. In the morning they held a strategy council with Leena, who took an instant liking to Swill, noting the rebellious gleam in the girl's eye. Leena smiled warmly and grasped both her hands in welcome.

"I'm so glad you've agreed to help my brother," she said. Bendyk had told her that Swill was twenty-one, four years younger than herself, and two years younger than her baby brother.

Awed by the magnificence of the Palisades, Swill was glad she'd changed into a wraparound skirt and a sweater for her appearance in the religious center. She sized up Bendyk's sister and wondered how the two could seem so different. Leena wore her long blond hair loose in defiance of the custom, and her blue eyes sparkled with warmth and friendliness. She didn't possess any of the righteous airs that her brother radiated.

"I didn't agree to anything," Swill confessed. "Your brother blackmailed me into coming here."

Leena cast a startled glance at Bendyk, whose eyes glowed with amusement. "Oh?" Leena said, raising an eyebrow. "Would you care to elaborate?"

He shook his head. "It's a private matter between Swill and me. We'll do fine together," he asserted confidently.

Swill muttered an expletive, then apologized to Leena. "Sorry. I forget I am in a holy place."

Leena suppressed a grin as she studied the fine contours of the girl's face and the upward tilt of her chin, which indicated strength of character. Her blunt haircut and unadorned clothes showed that comfort and practicality were more important to her than the mores of society. Clearly Swill must offend her brother's sense of propriety!

Her gaze swung to Bendyk, whose eyes hadn't lifted from Swill from the moment they'd all stepped into the room. Leena wondered at his interest. What had occurred between the two of them to make Swill have such antipathy toward him? Bendyk appeared entertained by the girl's attitude. She thought about the fact that her father had been wishing that both of them would settle down. Bendyk was young yet; he had time to seek a mate. But Leena had often wondered how he would find a woman who appealed to his sense of moral righteousness. She'd always thought the daughter of a Candor, someone like herself, would attract him, but it appeared instead that this rebellious young woman might have captured his attention.

Leena grinned broadly until her brother snapped, "What do you find so funny?"

"Nothing," she shrugged. "Let's discuss how we're going to keep in communication with each other. I've asked Sirvat to join us so she could give me further instructions about locating Grotus, and Karayan said he would stop in also. Have you partaken of your morning meal yet?"

"Aye," Bendyk said. "We had breakfast delivered to our apartments earlier this morning. I'm not sure where we should begin our investigation either."

"It's too bad we can't ask Father to advise us."

"Tell me about this Taurin fellow."

Leena's expression grew thoughtful. "He's very strange. . . ."

Before she could say another word Karayan marched into the room, greeting each one of them, including Swill, to whom Bendyk introduced him. "Good and welfare, children," Karayan told them, beaming at them all. "Have I interrupted your discussion?"

"Leena was just telling us about this Taurin person," said Bendyk, addressing his father's friend.

"The man agreed to help me," Leena told them, "but he wishes for someone to tend his farm while we are gone."

"His farm?" Karayan asked. "Where does he reside?"

"He raises flowers down at Lexington Page," she said, indicating the nearby town.

"Isn't that where Magar has his estate?"

"Yes, it is. If you recall, Magar is the one who suggested I approach Taurin."

"Indeed." Karayan's brows furrowed. "What else did you find out about this fellow?"

"He lives by himself," Leena said. "He has an interest in archaeology. I saw some sketches of the carvings I've been studying, but I'm not really sure of the reason for his pursuit of the subject. My mention of being an archaeologist seemed to sway him in favor of accepting my proposal."

"Did he say where he came from?" Karayan asked.

"No. He told me nothing about his background. The man is a skilled fighter. He broke up a brawl in the town pub. I feel he is the right choice for a protector, but it will be difficult traveling with him. He has a taciturn nature and reveals little about himself."

Karayan's face took on a troubled look. "I don't know if I am pleased by your words or not. Your safety is our prime concern. How do we know we can trust this man?"

"Magar recommended him," she reminded him. "The Minister of State would not have sent me to someone untrustworthy."

"What is your destination?" Bendyk cut in.

"Sirvat still needs to give me that information," Leena answered. "I believe I hear footsteps outside. Maybe that's her coming now. Swill, could you please open the door?"

Sirvat, her thin red hair coiffed in an upsweep atop her head, walked in amid a swish of white robes. "Karayan," she snapped, "what are you doing here?"

"I was just looking after these young people's welfare," he stated amiably, flicking a speck of imaginary dust from his tailored frock coat. Aside from religious ceremonies, he preferred his own style of dress to ecclesiastical garb. In contrast, Sirvat liked to flaunt the embellishments of her station.

"Our conversation must be private," Sirvat said, giving him a meaningful glance.

"In that case I was just leaving." Karayan gave her a mocking bow, then turned toward Leena and Bendyk. "Message me if you need any assistance, children. I am always available to help you."

"Good and welfare," Bendyk cried as Karayan stalked out.

"This is your brother?" Sirvat asked.

Leena hastened to introduce him and Swill, realizing Sirvat hadn't had the chance to meet them before.

"Where are you going to start your investigation?" she queried Bendyk.

"Perhaps we should look into the Treasury funds," he said mildly, watching for her reaction.

Sirvat stiffened. "My department can undergo any kind of scrutiny. You'll find our recordkeeping is exemplary," she responded. Her eyes narrowed at Swill. "Haven't I seen you somewhere before?"

A smile quirked the corners of Swill's mouth. "I work for your department, your honor. I'm one of the tax agents."

"Ah, I thought you looked familiar."

Leena cut into their conversation, hoping to get the information she required. "Taurin Rey Niris has agreed to accompany me on my journey," she said. "What can you tell me about Grotus? Where can I find him, and what makes you think he might have the horn?"

"I have no idea if he has the horn," Sirvat confessed, "but I believe he's the best person to ask. If anyone stole it for money, it would have crossed through Grotus's hands by now. And if not, perhaps his agents possess useful information. You can always suggest a trade," she said, a sly look coming over her face.

"What do you mean?" Leena asked.

"If Grotus has not heard that the horn is missing, you'll have valuable information to offer him. In return, there are things he might know that you could find of interest."

"Such as?"

Sirvat shrugged. "That'll be for you to find out."

Leena peered at her suspiciously. Sirvat appeared to know more than she was willing to tell. It would be interesting to see what Bendyk's investigation uncovered. "Where do I have to go?" she asked, curiosity taking hold.

Sirvat reached into a pocket in her voluminous robe and drew out a piece of parchment. "Come." She strode to a table and unfolded the document, which turned out to be a world map. "We can provide air transport for you to Port Donner, located here." Sirvat pointed to a spot on a coastline in a subtropical region halfway around the world. "From there you'll have to find a means to cross the Tortis Sea to the Black Lands."

Leena gasped. Those who defied the Faith were banished to the Black Lands, and since they didn't worship Lothar, the region lacked his protection. She had never dreamed that her quest would take her into such a wilderness.

"There is a commerce between Port Donner and Garu, the southernmost village in the Black Lands," Sirvat went on. "Transport should be available between those two points. You may have greater difficulty traversing the land mass. The Black Lands, as you can see, is one of the largest islands on Xan. With an area of over three hundred thousand square miles, its terrain varies from rugged, snow-capped mountains in the central portion to hot and humid coastal lowlands. Many rivers and streams flow down the mountain slopes and cross the lowlands. The largest river, called the Kile, has a broad swampy delta. Steep mountain ridges, grassy plateaus, and deep forested valleys cover much of the interior.''

Leena swallowed hard. Missionaries had gone into the area to convert the native tribes, as well as to counsel the dissidents, but their reception had been hostile. Indeed, some of them had never been heard from again.

''It is said Grotus resides on an island in this archipelago.'' Sirvat indicated a series of dots in the Pavian Ocean, located off the northern coast of the Black Lands. ''No one knows his exact location. You'll have to find some means to reach his island, assuming you're able to pinpoint it. Grotus must have his own secret method of transportation because his movements are untraceable. Be cautious when you make inquiries: Anyone attempting to search for Grotus's hideaway has vanished.''

''Vanished!'' Bendyk exclaimed. ''What do you mean?''

''He guards his privacy as a *langmuir* does its den. It is impossible to get close to him. As you know, there has been an ongoing theft of artifacts from holy sites around the world. We suspect the smugglers are linked in a worldwide network reporting to Grotus, but no one has been able to determine their methodology. Unscrupulous collectors would pay anything to get their hands on these valuable objects, which is why I am sending you to Grotus to search for the horn,'' she added. ''It is a dangerous journey. Even if you managed to reach his island, he might have you killed.'' Her cool jade eyes focused on Leena. ''Take your circlet along to convince Grotus of your identity, but keep it hidden during your voyage. If the Truthsayers get wind of your mission, they're apt to try to stop you. It would be best if you travel incognito.''

''But how would the Truthsayers know what she's doing?'' Bendyk said. ''Only the members of the Synod and the Caucus, along with Swill and I, know of her assignment."

"One of us stole the horn, remember?" Sirvat said, her eyes flashing. "I don't trust anyone in this place."

Brother and sister exchanged glances. Leena was fast learning that she had no one to turn to except her own brother. How sad indeed that her world's leaders couldn't even be trusted. For that matter, how did Sirvat know so much about Grotus? Her detailed descriptions were odd unless she'd had the smuggler investigated by her Treasury department.

"After you've seen Grotus," Sirvat told her, brushing a wisp of red hair off her stern face, "message me immediately. I will do what I can to aid you in your return journey. Dikran said he wishes for you to report back to the Palisades when you have accomplished this task."

"But what if we fail to obtain news of the horn?" Leena asked. "Grotus may know nothing about the theft."

"That is true, but once he learns it is on the market he may pursue the matter himself. You can keep an eye on each other."

"What an exciting prospect," Leena murmured sarcastically.

Brother and sister spent a few moments alone before Leena's departure, talking about Sirvat's strange manner.

"I like Swill," Leena said, changing the subject. "She seems to have a sensible head on her shoulders. I'm sure she will give you good advice."

Bendyk grimaced. "If she talks to me," he said. "In your presence she is polite, but when we're alone she barely speaks."

"Do you insult her with your religious dictates, Brother?"

He stiffened. "I merely comment on the moral standards applicable to our society."

Leena snorted. "No wonder she resents you. Go easy, and you may find her more likable."

Bendyk put a hand on her shoulder. His eyes, as deep a

blue as her own, held a serious expression. "I am worried about you, Sister. Your journey is dangerous, and you travel with a stranger. I do not like the tone of this mission. It is I who should be going on that pursuit. I am used to traveling and meeting with all types of people."

"But only I can identify the horn," Leena said. "What if someone produced a counterfeit and tried to ransom it back to the Synod? The horn is inscribed with the same carvings I have been studying. It is an amazing piece," she told him. "There is nothing else like it on our . . ." Halting abruptly, Leena bit her tongue. She had almost said there was nothing else like it on this world. What had she been thinking, to nearly blurt out such a thing to her brother? It was the same type of observation, made about the ring she'd found in the ruins on her last dig, that had gotten her into such deep trouble with Zeroun. No one was allowed to question the teachings of Lothar, or to speculate about where the Apostles had originated. To even conceive that they might have come from another world was to doubt their divinity. She'd tried to interpret the inscription on the ring's thin band. It was the same sequence of symbols she'd noted on the walls of ancient ruins and on the horn, but now she didn't have any more success than in the past. Taurin's sketch displayed the same markings, she reminded herself sharply, vowing to learn more about him at the earliest opportunity.

"What type of clothes should I take on my trip?" she wondered aloud.

"You're liable to run into savages in that untamed land."

"Perhaps I should take my archaeological garb."

Bendyk stared at her in horror. "How dare you think of such a thing? Wearing breeches goes against your womanly nature. It is unnatural, Sister. You'll take your gowns, lest this Taurin fellow thinks you're a loose woman."

He's probably right, Leena thought, but still she would pack a couple of her outfits into her valise just in case. And perhaps some of her tools as well.

And so it was that several hours later she was packed and

ready to depart. Dikran, the Arch Nome, summoned her for a final audience.

"I wish you to report directly to me upon your return," the old man said, shaking a finger in her direction.

"Yes, your eminence." Leena was dismayed by the distressed look on Dikran's face. He was terribly shaken by recent events, she realized, and now even he could trust no one among his senior counselors. She pitied him because age had claimed his strength, and he no longer had the power to command his people with the rigid authority that was required. Zeroun would do well in his stead, she admitted, but she feared that under Zeroun's dominance, oppression would rule the land. There was no easy solution, except for her to find the horn and bring the situation to rights. The dissension and uprisings were for people like her brother to eradicate. Her job remained within the archaeological realm, and for the first time a sense of excitement filled her veins. This would be the ultimate adventure, and the recovery of the horn, her greatest find. She must succeed!

Bidding farewell to Dikran, she hastened through a series of elegantly appointed chambers to the exit. Bendyk was waiting for her in a rider outside, her luggage already secured in his trunk.

"I'm looking forward to meeting your escort," he said, squinting in the sunlight. "If he doesn't measure up, I will not allow you to go with him."

"Nonsense," Leena scoffed. "Who else is going to protect me? I've witnessed with my own eyes his prowess as a fighter. The violence of his nature does not please me. Nevertheless, he has been chosen to be part of this mission. Where is Swill?"

"She has already begun to audit the records of the Treasury. I will meet with her late this afternoon. Since you have agreed, I used our authority to enlist the aid of the Caucus in running background checks on each member of the Synod. I will be supervising those efforts myself."

"Be cautious," she warned him. "One among them is a

thief who would not want his perfidy to be discovered. There could be danger for you at the Palisades, even though it is not as evident as the road I follow.''

"Understood," he acknowledged. A frown creased his forehead. "It disturbs me that I won't be able to contact you."

She laid a hand on his arm. "I promise I'll message you at the earliest opportunity."

The drive took an hour and a half, and Leena enjoyed the breeze that blew in from the open rider windows. Bendyk's vehicle was a sedate, forest-green sedan. Like Voshkie, Minister of Commerce, Bendyk didn't believe in conspicuous consumption. Modesty was his byword, and he looked with disapproval at the two huge suitcases she'd brought along.

"You told me to pack my gowns," she told him.

"Yes, but you've brought enough for months of travel."

Leena shrugged. "Who knows how long we'll be gone?" she joked. But inwardly she quivered at his words. For all she knew, they could be true, and she dreaded spending so much time in Taurin's taciturn company.

Taurin obviously was expecting her. As soon as their vehicle pulled into the driveway, he flung open his front door.

"You must be Bendyk," he told her blond-haired brother, shaking both his hands in greeting. Addressing Leena, he said, "I took your rider in for servicing this morning and got a lift home. Perhaps your brother can retrieve it when the work is done, since you and I will be gone."

"I'll take care of it," Bendyk agreed as Taurin handed him the receipt from the station. He stared at the tall, darkly handsome man. Taurin's muscular build was barely concealed beneath a belted black longshirt and a pair of hip-hugging trousers.

Leena was pleased to find his head uncovered by the cloth he favored. Recalling that he'd only worn it in the tavern and the darkened interior of his rider, she wondered at its purpose. Unencumbered, his striking features captured her attention.

"I am going on this journey because your sister and I hope to learn the answers to similar questions," Taurin told Bendyk, a steely expression in his gray eyes. "I know little about your god or this missing horn but will do my part to help you find the holy object."

Bendyk pounced on his words. "What do you mean, you know little of *our* god? Do you not worship Lothar?" Disapproval rang in his tone.

A half-smile twisted Taurin's countenance. "I have my own beliefs, or lack of them," he stated. "What I feel is irrelevant to our mission."

Bendyk's hair glinted gold in the sunlight. "Indeed, your beliefs have relevance. I will not allow you to travel with my sister in sin."

Leena glanced at him in shock while Taurin quirked an eyebrow at Bendyk. In truth, Taurin was amused by the difference between brother and sister. Surely Leena looked angelic, with her blond hair streaming over her shoulders and the ruby-red gown accentuating every curve on her body, but her attitude seemed impious compared to her brother's serious intensity. He kept his gaze off Leena, aware of the way his heart thudded in her presence. She looked too lovely by far, and it unsettled him. He would do his best to keep as great a distance between them as possible, but her brother's next words shattered that resolve.

"I will see you both wed 'ere I go," he said.

"What!" Leena shrieked.

"Normally a trial marriage may only take place during Beltane," Bendyk said. "But exceptions can be made, and I have the authority to make such a decision. I repeat, Sister, you will not travel with this man in sin. I will marry you, and when you complete your mission the vows can be annulled. They need be in name only, but it will legalize your companionship."

Taurin's face darkened with fury, and the menace looming from him was like a huge thundercloud blotting out the sun. "This is absurd," he snapped. "Let's get on with our business. We must leave immediately."

"We have a flight to catch in forty-five minutes," she reminded her brother. "We cannot waste time."

Bendyk's hand clasped her arm. "I insist on this, Leena, or I shall tell Father what you're about."

"So what? It would only spoil my chances of marrying Malcolm."

Taurin's ears perked up. "Malcolm? Who is that?"

"A man to whom she will be wed come next Auden," Bendyk said. "Malcolm may understand the circumstances once your role in recovering the horn is explained, but he would never forgive you if he learned you traveled with a stranger under immoral conditions."

Leena's heart twisted with indecision. At the moment she didn't care what Malcolm thought about her, but she had been considering accepting his proposal. She'd messaged him and Father to let them know she'd be away on ecclesiastical business without going into any details. Malcolm had wanted to see her to discuss a date for a formal betrothal, but she'd put him off. Facing him upon her return would be easier if she didn't have to rationalize her situation. She and Taurin had no idea what arrangements they would have to make in traveling together. It would be convenient if she could say he was her husband, although the notion was extremely distasteful.

Slowly she raised her eyes. The dark expression she saw on Taurin's face brought a shiver to her spine. "It would bring me a measure of comfort," she told him quietly. "It need mean nothing. My brother is empowered to conduct the ceremony. We shall be wed in name only, and you will have no further obligations when our task is finished." Meeting his gaze, she swallowed hard, afraid he would reject her offer, but the man stared at her with an odd light in his peculiar gray eyes.

"All right," he said slowly. "I agree. But like all good wives you must obey my commands thereafter."

"A fair agreement," Bendyk said, a beatific smile on his

face. He hated his part in this deception, but he wouldn't want it said that he let his sister travel with a strange man in an improper fashion. This was the best solution, as he saw it. "Where do you come from?" he asked Taurin, hoping to learn more about the man who was about to become his sister's temporary mate.

Taurin's eyes skittered away. "I'm from Iman," he stated.

Bendyk nodded. He knew of the remote region, even though he'd never traveled there himself. That would explain the man's abrupt manner, Bendyk thought.

The marriage ceremony was performed with haste in Taurin's living room. When it was over Bendyk glanced around with interest. Sketches were everywhere, ink drawings of inscriptions that he assumed were copies of the symbols from ancient ruins, as Leena had stated. The man did appear to have an interest in archaeology; various books on the subject were placed around the room. The house was kept in a meticulous fashion, and he approved of the man's cleanliness and tidy habits.

Taurin had only one valise. Bendyk put it, with Leena's luggage, in the trunk of his vehicle. He would drive them to the airfield and then return to the Palisades to pursue his own investigation. Leena sat in front beside him, as though afraid to be near Taurin, who climbed into the back seat without a word. At the last minute Taurin had decided that he didn't need anyone to tend his farm in his absence, and Bendyk realized he didn't want anyone snooping around his place. I'll have to come back, he decided, and make inquiries as to his relationship with Magar. Taurin's piece of property seemed to occupy a corner of Magar's estate, but it wasn't fenced off, which normally would be the case if Taurin owned his own land. Maybe he'd find out when he checked into Magar's background. But he could also send a few inquiries to Iman, which was where Taurin said he originated. He'd like to know more about this man whom Leena could now call husband. He glanced at his sister, noting her impassive expression. He was worried for her safety, although he felt Taurin would protect her and keep her from harm. He prayed to Lothar for the success of their mission, and he was still praying when Leena and Taurin's flight took off from the airfield thirty minutes later.

Leena sagged back in her seat, tired from the emotional strain she'd undergone that day. The unexpected marriage ceremony was the crowning blow, especially after Bendyk had said he would enter the marriage in the ecclesiastical books to make it legal. Such was acceptable for trial marriages, and annulments were common after the handfast ended. Beltane only lasted for a month, although some trial marriages were known to have continued for years at a time. Leena hoped their farce wouldn't go on for long.

Taurin sat stiffly in a seat beside her. There were only the two of them in the aircraft, it having been commissioned for their use. The crew was up front, behind a cockpit door. A self-service refreshment center was available if they required nourishment, and magazines and books were provided in a rack to the rear. Leena couldn't concentrate to read; she was too nervous in Taurin's presence, afraid of what lay ahead.

Taurin sensed her fear and wondered how he had gotten himself into such a predicament. How had he let himself become responsible for this fragile female? She was dedicated to the service of Lothar, and he, an unholy soul, was put in charge of her. Demon's blood! He had never been so surprised as when her brother had made his proposal. Too stunned to argue, he had merely let the trial marriage take place. Of course, it would be annulled as soon as they returned. He'd have to keep his secrets from her in the meantime. She'd be repulsed if she learned who and what he was.

Raking a hand through his hair, he shifted in his seat. The flight was supposed to take approximately eleven hours, with a refueling stop along the way. Without a moving picture to entertain them, it would be a long journey indeed.

"Tell me more about the missing horn," he said, forcing a note of encouragement into his voice. It was necessary for them to work together effectively if they were to succeed, and Taurin knew he'd have to put aside his personal feelings until their task was complete.

Deep in the bowels of the Palisades, a revered member of the Synod was also discussing the horn, using a scrambled messager system so no one else could detect the subversive communication.

"They are heading for Port Donner," the Synod member told the person who'd answered the line. "Leena and Rey Niris seek an audience with Grotus. They must not return. Do you understand?"

A chuckle sounded at the other end of the line. "Of course. It is best if the horn is not recovered."

"Never mind the horn. Leena knows too much already. You'll know where to pick up their trail now. Be sure that they're intercepted."

"Your will shall be done, your honor. Hail to the cause!"

The Synod leader terminated the communication, smiling grimly. The orders would be carried out, and the threat from Leena would be eliminated. The leader would keep an eye on her brother, and if he posed a problem, the young man would be disposed of as well. The plans had already been set into motion, and no one would be allowed to interfere.

Glory will be mine! Soon all of Xan will bow before me. Lothar's time is nearly over, and my reign is about to begin!

Leena glanced at Taurin with relief. She couldn't have stood another moment of this silence. The man totally unnerved her, and she trembled at the thought of remaining at his side in the days and nights to come.

"You already know the horn's function," she told him. "It is needed to awaken Lothar. I had a chance to examine the horn once. It is made of a strange material—a creamy, almost translucent color. Have you ever been to the Holy Temple during Renewal?" she asked him.

"No," Taurin replied, frowning. He was intrigued by the

description of the horn. It sounded similar to the entwined rings he wore as a band around his right arm, hidden under his clothes where no one could see it. When separated the three rings were a baby's toy. They had been left with him when he was abandoned by his parents, and the gang leader who'd found him had let him keep them. Spinning the rings had been one of his favorite pastimes as a child on Yllon. The musical notes had delighted him, and there had been few joys on that violent world. It wasn't until he was older that he'd learned how they fitted together into a wide bracelet. Viewed as a single band, the symbols carved into the material became evident. Taurin realized those symbols were significant when he saw them engraved into books hidden in the repository on Yllon. Those same carvings had shown up on Xan, and it was one of the reasons why he'd settled here. He hoped to learn more about his heritage and how the two worlds, total opposites in nature, were linked.

"What do you know of the symbols carved into the horn?" he asked, expressing mild interest.

"They represent a repetitive sequence," Leena said. "I haven't been able to decipher what it means. There are many things I don't understand about our past and would like to learn about. The horn is made of a substance unknown anywhere else on Xan. And so is the ring I found on my last excavation."

As soon as the words left her mouth, she realized she'd made a mistake. Hopefully he wouldn't catch her on it. But Taurin was sharp.

"What ring?" he asked, glowering at her.

Leena bit her lower lip. "I'm not supposed to talk about it," she muttered.

"If we're going to be working together, you have to tell me everything you know," he said glibly, aware of the secrets he was keeping from her.

Leena sighed. It probably would be best if he knew her background. "I uncovered a strange circular object at my last dig," she said. "It was made of the same pearly substance as the horn, which I recognized at once. I reported it to my superior, who in turn told Zeroun. He impounded it, saying it was important for the security of the land that we keep this find under wraps. It was after that incident that I received the invitation to join the Caucus. I realized he didn't want me to report my find to anyone else, and I wondered why. What was the significance of the object? Where had it originated? Where had the Apostles come from? They must have brought these materials with them. Why did they establish the rule of Lothar and then leave?'' She shook her head in confusion. "I wish I had the answers. I feel they would help us deal with the weather disasters that are plaguing us now. I don't believe they're due to Lothar's wrath. Something isn't right.''

She debated informing him about her father's deviation from the Faith but decided it wouldn't be in her best interest to do so at this time.

"How did you become interested in archaeology?'' he asked her, watching as she repositioned herself. Her slender hands were folded one on top of the other in her lap, and he tried to quell the surge of desire that rose within him. Demon's blood! How was he going to tolerate being in such close contact with her for the weeks ahead?

Leena explained how fascinated she'd always been with Xan's past history. Living near a ruin, she was able to explore the site in her childhood, and her father's teachings had encouraged her curious mind.

"I love the excitement of digging for secrets of the past,'' she told him, her eyes sparkling. "But what gives you an interest in the ruins, Taurin? Why do you have sketches of those symbols all about your house?''

His expression darkened. "I'm merely interested,'' he lied, knowing that she would see through his falsehood but hoping she wouldn't pry. "Here comes one of the crew,'' he said suddenly.

Leena glanced up sharply. She didn't see anyone coming from the cockpit, but a moment later the door opened and out came the co-pilot to offer them refreshments and see to their comfort. How did Taurin know the man was coming? She accepted a fruit drink and a snack and waited until the crew member returned to his duty before turning back to Taurin.

"What made you decide to raise flowers for a living?" she asked.

Taurin munched on a handful of nuts. "I owed someone," he said, and she wondered if he meant Magar, who'd provided him with a plot of land. His next words refuted her idea. His face took on a wistful expression as he explained. "I was befriended by a baker once. He did me a great service, and I wished to repay it. I remembered that the candied flowers he used on his sweetbreads were extremely expensive, so I decided to raise edible flowers myself. I send him a shipment every month, and the others I sell on the free market. It's quite a lucrative business. There aren't that many other flower farmers who grow edible blooms."

"I would think not," Leena agreed. "And do you pay Magar with produce as well?"

"Magar?" Taurin arched his dark eyebrows.

"I noticed that your property abuts his estate," Leena stated, smiling sweetly. "I was wondering if you rented from him."

"No," Taurin said bluntly. "I own my piece of land."

Leena fell silent, realizing that he didn't wish to talk about his relationship with Magar. Still, it puzzled her. There was something going on between the two, but this wasn't the appropriate time to make further inquiries. Besides, Bendyk was working at the other end. He might find out more about Magar and his relationship with Taurin.

"You have no woman," she blurted out.

Taurin nearly choked on one of the nuts. "Does that disturb you?" he asked, wishing he couldn't smell the tantalizing scent of her perfume.

"It must be a lonely life, tending your farm alone, living in a small town."

"It's what I've dreamed about," Taurin answered. "Peace and harmony. That's what I've sought my whole life, and I'd found it. Until now."

Leena dozed off, puzzling over his words but too fatigued to think clearly. Taurin sat rigidly in his seat as her head drifted onto his shoulder. Honeyed tresses trailed across his chest, their fragrance as sweet as the blossoms in his garden. With trembling fingers, he touched a lock, relishing the silken feel of her hair as it rippled through his fingers. She breathed softly, her breasts rising and falling with each respiration. His eyes drifted down the length of her gown. She was perfection, he admitted, not only in body but in spirit. She was devoted to her god and loyal to her people. Intelligent as well as beautiful, she'd make a fabulous mate for a man. If only he could hope for a union with someone like her! But it was an impossibility. She was too good for him, too pure, never mind their difference in station in life. She would be horrified if she learned his true background.

He'd spoken of peace, but now that peace was threatened. The harmony throughout Xan was on shaky ground. Dark forces were marching across the land, and Taurin feared their evil. He'd grown up with it and had cast it away, and now it was creeping inexorably in his direction again, drawing him into the darkness.

Chapter Five

Leena's senses sharpened as she came awake. With sudden clarity of thought, she realized her head was leaning on Taurin's shoulder. It was a remarkably comfortable position, but a too familiar one. Despite her being able to call him husband, she wished to avoid personal contact between them. His slightest touch had the power to unnerve her, and she regarded that as an improper response on her part.

Clearing her throat, she straightened up. "I'm so sorry," she murmured.

She smoothed down her dress, and that motion seemed to discomfort Taurin, who'd been sitting with a rigid posture. Abruptly he got up and strode toward the rear of the aircraft, where the restrooms were located. Leena ran a hand over her face. The man was so dark and imposing, and yet she experienced such a forbidden stimulation in his presence. He'd only left her for a few moments, and already she felt bereft of his company. It was with relief that she watched him return and settle into his seat.

Edging herself away from him, she smiled shyly. "Will we be landing soon?"

Taurin averted his eyes so he wouldn't have to gaze upon her rumpled hair and the sleep-laden heaviness of her eyes. "We have an hour left before the layover."

They devoured a light meal before landing, spent a couple of hours on the ground while the plane refueled, and then resumed the flight. The rest of the trip passed easily as Leena told him what she knew of each Synod member. They finally arrived at Port Donner on the afternoon following their departure.

Outside, Taurin gathered their luggage and surveyed the scene. The small airfield was not frequented often, and theirs was the only plane in sight. According to what the pilot had told him, outcasts from society were brought here and then taken across the Tortis Sea to the Black Lands, where they spent the rest of their lives in exile. No one else ventured far from here except for some merchant ships, which made regular runs to Garu for trade and mail.

"I'll find us a ship," Taurin told Leena after a driver transported them to the wharf. "Perhaps we can sail around the eastern tip of the Black Lands to the archipelago."

Leena nodded, excited by the idea. It would be much better if they didn't have to cross the width of the Black Lands. Her eager gaze scanned the bustling waterfront scene: masts and spars from sailing vessels reached toward the sky like outstretched fingers; mountains of goods were piled high on the dock; a surging crowd of sailors, tradesmen, and fishing crews toiled laboriously, oblivious to the heat and humidity that caused perspiration to trickle down her face. She longed for a cooling ocean breeze, but dark clouds lumbered overhead and a heavy stillness filled the air, which stank of fish. Distant rumbles of thunder sounded, and she feared it would rain before they found transport.

"Wait here with our luggage while I make inquiries," Taurin ordered.

Marching off, he strode along the pier, stopping at each ship until he found a captain willing to accept passengers.

Captain Riez picked at his rotting teeth while contemplating Taurin's request.

"The facilities ain't much," Riez told him, "but you can jine us if you're able to pay."

"How much?" Taurin asked wryly.

"Fifty chekels each, and I only got one cabin."

"What do you mean, *one* cabin? We require two staterooms."

"I thought you said you was married."

"Well . . . er . . . yes, but the lady requires extra space for her dressing room."

"One cabin; take it or leave it." Riez spat into the water.

"We'll take it," Taurin said hastily. "Is there someone who can help us with our luggage?"

The captain gave a short, raucous laugh. "Sorry, brother. We ain't sailin' for another two days. You'll have to put up in town if you want to ship out with us."

"Two days!" Taurin exclaimed. "You didn't say that before."

"You're not going to find anyone else to take you. I'll need a cash deposit."

Taurin saw the avarice glinting in the captain's jaundiced eye. "Very well." He pulled a ten-chekel note from the wad in his pocket. "Here," he said, handing it over. "Is there anything else I should know?"

"Our grub ain't the best, so if you want to bring any of your own chow aboard, you'll want to visit the village market 'ere you board."

"Thanks for the advice." Tilting his head in acknowledgment, Taurin turned on his heel and left.

Leena had been amusing herself by watching the frenzy of activity on the wharf. Bins labeled with the popular Chocola Company's logo were being off-loaded from several vessels by huge cranes. Bags of mail, crates of canned foods, medical supplies, bales of fabric, machinery, and other goods were being loaded onto container ships by brawny workmen.

As some of them caught sight of her standing by in her finery, they gave her lecherous stares that made her pray for Taurin's quick return.

She saw the dark scowl on his face as he approached. By all that was holy, now what was wrong?

"I booked us a passage, but the ship doesn't sail for two days. We'll have to find accommodations in town until then," he told her, his expression grim.

Leena's brows arched. "Where do you expect to find a hostelry here?" The town was nothing more than a cluster of taverns, warehouses, and small businesses catering to the marine trade.

"We'll ask in one of the taverns," Taurin suggested. "I'll take my case and this one of yours. Can you manage the other?"

"Of course." She'd carried heavier loads on her archae-ological expeditions. Glancing with dismay at her pristine gown and low-heeled pumps, she yearned for her work clothes. Giving a resigned sigh, she lifted her valise and ac-companied Taurin across the cracked and uneven pavement, careful to watch her footing. He halted in front a tavern, its open doorway allowing the raucus din from inside to pene-trate the street. The scent of liquor wafted to her nostrils, mingling with the stench of garbage from a bin at the corner, and she wrinkled her nose in distaste.

"What are you doing?" she asked, curious when Taurin pulled from his pocket the familiar black cloth that matched his trousers.

"It may be dark inside," he said enigmatically. "You wait out here until I assess the situation." He swathed the cloth around his head so that his eyes were shadowed.

Leena squinted in the bright afternoon sunlight that was rapidly becoming obliterated by the clouds. Soon it would rain, she realized, feeling a salty breeze gust into port.

"Why do you cover your head like that?" she asked, un-able to read his expression under the hooded cloth.

"I choose this garb for my . . . security. It is necessary

when the light is dim enough to cast shadows or when it's dark."

"But why?" she persisted, wondering what possible effect the darkness might have upon him.

Ignoring her question, he strode into the tavern, and it wasn't long before Leena heard a commotion ensue from within. A few moments later he sauntered outside, his clothes rumpled and disorderly. "You may enter," he said, his tone gruff. "I've rented us a room upstairs."

"In *there?*" Leena cried, horrified. The place appeared to be a den of impropriety, and she dreaded entering the foul-smelling interior. He must have noticed her hesitation because his voice softened with his next words.

"I will see to your safety," he said reassuringly. "Pretend you are my dutiful wife and follow me directly to our room."

Our room? Leena thought to herself, swallowing hard as she obeyed him, picking up her bag and trailing after him with her head bowed. Were they to share a room here and a cabin on the ship as well? In truth, they were man and wife, but in name only. Surely Taurin didn't expect her to perform her wifely duties, did he? Her brother had made it quite clear that this marriage would be annulled after their mission was over. Of course, Taurin couldn't be thinking in that vein. He must have rented the only accommodation available, or else he was simply seeing to her safety.

And for that I'd be very grateful, she told herself, entering the smoky, dimly lit interior that reeked of liquor. Men in rough garb stared at her as she passed by, her head down. She'd never felt more glad for Taurin's presence than at this moment. His shoulders seemed broader than she remembered, his body taller. Dressed as he was, all in black, he appeared as menacing as a demon. A loud clap of thunder sounded from outside, as though Nature were in agreement with her. Surely none of these men would dare offend Taurin when his very being emanated a dangerous aura.

Feeling less than brave herself, she followed him up a flight of stone steps and into a cramped, musty bedchamber.

Dear deity, were they to spend the night in here together? Her gaze swept the wide bed with its tattered coverlet and alighted on a dented bureau and a small table with a set of chairs. Off to the side was a door to what she assumed must be a lavatory. ´

"Where are the lights?" she asked. Electrical appliances were noticeably lacking.

"I don't think this area has electricity," Taurin remarked, lining up their suitcases in a corner. "We'll have to use that oil lamp on the table and the candles on the bureau. Those will suffice."

"No electricity!" Leena was horrified. Their situation was rapidly deteriorating, and she dreaded what lay ahead. "Where are we going to sleep?"

"That bed looks comfortable enough to me."

"But, you can't expect me to . . . you and I can't . . ." Leena sputtered, unable to complete her sentence.

"If you would rather sleep in the chair tonight, madam, be my guest, but I for one intend to get a good night's rest. I've ordered a meal to be served in our room. Thereafter, I intend to scout around the town to learn what I can of our destination. We may need more supplies."

"What about the ship that is supposed to take us there?" Leena strolled inside the room. "Did you ask about sailing around the tip of the island in order to reach Grotus's place?"

"Unfortunately, I couldn't find a ship's master willing to charter a boat, nor does anyone else go to a port other than Garu on the Black Lands. I was lucky enough to find us the cabin space I did."

Leena hadn't been impressed by the condition of most of the ships in port, so she did not venture to inquire as to a description of their vessel. "How long will it take to cross the Tortis Sea?"

Taurin shrugged. "Could be three or four days, depending on the weather."

"That long?" Leena stared at him. She'd thought it would be an easy crossing.

"Look, you either take the breaks or you go back to your sanctuary at the Palisades and let me handle this."

Leena drew herself upright. "I've been in worse places on digs," she retorted. "Perhaps I should change out of this gown and into my work clothes. That might convince you that I don't need your protection."

"Oh, no?" Although she couldn't see his shadowed face, she could imagine him quirking his eyebrow. "Would you care to venture downstairs by yourself and see what happens?"

Leena shuddered. "I didn't ask to be put in this position. You're being unfair."

"Am I?" He sauntered closer, and she could almost feel the powerful warmth from his body as he neared. "Do you expect your faith in Lothar to get you through the days ahead?"

"Of course I do. Don't you?"

"I believe in myself, Leena Worthington-Jax. No one else will look out for me. I would advise you not to rely on any supernatural entity to come to your assistance."

"How dare you mock Lothar!" Leena cried, clenching her fists at her side. "He is watching over us to see to our safety."

"You are wrong," Taurin said quietly. "It is I who sees to our safety." *Although who is going to keep you safe from me is anyone's guess.* Taurin watched as she moistened her lips, and his heart thudded in his chest. Cosmos, he would be hard pressed to keep his distance from her this night.

Turning away abruptly, he stared out the window as the first splattering of rain hit the panes. As the room darkened, he hastened to light an oil lamp. A soft glow filled the room, casting shadows into far corners.

"Why don't you sit down?" he grouched. "You're hovering about like a nervous mother hen."

Leena felt so infuriated by his presence that she wanted to

scream. How could she endure a night with this man? He didn't even trust her enough to uncover his head before her. Seething inwardly, she did as he suggested, testing the edge of the bed against her weight. The mattress sagged.

"What do you believe in, Taurin?" she asked. "Are you a heretic?"

"I told you," he said, "I believe in myself." He sank into one of the chairs while the fury of the storm raged outside. Flashes of lightning and cracks of thunder rent the air. But inside their room, away from the storm, a momentary sense of security pervaded the atmosphere. He wished he could pull the cloth from his head and gaze directly at her, but it wouldn't be advisable in the dimness of the room.

"The place where I grew up," he said, "was a violent society."

"I thought you came from Iman."

Taurin didn't comment. "You had to scrabble for survival," he mumbled half to himself. "It was a brutal existence. You learned to trust no one, to rely on no one but yourself. Life is in the here and now, and it is what you make of it."

"What a cynical attitude! I pity you, Taurin. Without the Faith, your life holds no meaning. No wonder you live by yourself."

"This is the life I choose!" He rose abruptly. "Now, if you'll excuse me, I'll check on the delivery of our meal." He stalked out, closing the door none too gently behind himself.

Leena sat on the bed, her hands folded, contemplating their conversation. Taurin didn't believe in Lothar, but could he possibly be aligned with the Truthsayers? He hadn't said anything about going against the Synod or their structure of government. He appeared to want to live his own life in peace, regardless of his or anyone else's beliefs. She should be able to trust him as long as he did his job of protecting her. And that was why he'd come along, wasn't it? Still, it troubled her that he didn't believe in the Faith.

How can anyone not bend their knee before Lothar, who provided them with such blessings as a fruitful land and a temperate climate? And what about Lothar's lozenge? Did Taurin partake of it, even though he didn't acknowledge the source?

Troubled, she went over to her luggage to see if her tools were intact. They might have need of them; who knew what dangers faced them at the Black Lands? This trip was folly, she thought. How would they ever cross that wild territory? Would they be able to locate Grotus's island even if they made it to the other side? How would they get there, and would Grotus agree to see them? There were so many problems they had to face. Lothar, she prayed, please help us! Please let us succeed in our mission.

Taurin returned shortly thereafter, followed by the proprietor, who set them a decent table and delivered their meal. After he left Taurin and Leena sat facing each other. Taurin's head was still covered with the cloth, but she could see his stormy gray eyes.

"We must pray," she chided as he reached for a piece of bread.

"I'm hungry!" Taurin growled, tearing a piece off the crusty loaf.

"Please," she implored. "We must thank Lothar for his bounty."

He couldn't resist the pleading look in her eyes. Again, he was reminded of her similarity to his image of an angel—not that he believed in them. Golden blond hair floated about her shoulders like strands of gossamer silk. The color of her gown accentuated the startling blue of her eyes. Taurin's gaze traveled along her arched brows, down along the bridge of her nose, and lingered on her slightly parted pink lips. A sudden urge to take her in his arms and kiss her nearly overwhelmed him with its intensity. Hastily, he stuffed the bread into his mouth to suppress his unwanted desire.

Tears sprang into her eyes at his blasphemy. "You have insulted Lothar! Now we shall be punished."

"Don't be absurd. You'd better eat or the food will get cold."

Leena closed her eyes and prayed for their absolution. "Please forgive him!" she begged Lothar. "He has strayed from the faith that I know is in his heart. He must believe in you because he raises your beautiful creations for a living," she said, meaning his flowers. Surely he acknowledged the importance of the elements. "It is you who provides the sun and the warmth, and the moisture for us, O Lothar. We thank you for your bread and sustenance and your generosity in the past. Please stay with us on this journey, and forgive this man for his digression." I have to help him see the light, Leena told herself.

Dear deity, now she sounded just like Bendyk. She didn't want to turn into a moral activist like him. Opening her eyes slowly, she was dismayed to see Taurin chomping away, obviously enjoying the meal without any regard for her feelings.

You'd better eat or there won't be anything left, Leena told herself. Eating silently, she avoided looking Taurin directly in the eye. Upon completion of the meal, her hand inadvertently brushed his when they were straightening the table. A delightful tingling sensation assailed her fingertips, and she snatched her hand away.

"I'm heading out to scout the premises," Taurin said gruffly. "Don't leave this room!"

The storm had ended, but Leena still heard a faint pattering of rain on the roof. She had no desire to go anywhere and longed to make herself comfortable in the soft bed.

"Be careful!" she warned him, thinking that the characters around here would just as soon beat and rob you as let you pay your own way.

"No one will come near me unless I approach them." Taurin's tone of voice was so menacing that Leena shuddered. Yet after he had left she couldn't make herself feel glad about his absence. She busied herself rearranging the items in her suitcases until fatigue overwhelmed her. She took off her gown and spent a few moments washing up before donning one of her simple nightdresses. It was made of a thin maille fabric and came to just below her knee. The short-sleeve top was comfortable and allowed her ease of movement in her sleep. She crawled into bed, neither caring that the mattress was too soft and lumpy nor that the sheets appeared somewhat soiled. It was a haven for the night, and she sank into blissful repose with barely another thought.

Hours later, Taurin entered the room. The oil level in the lamp was low, and he could scarcely make out the shapely form lying in the bed. Quietly, he stripped off his clothes down to his briefs and slid between the sheets. His bones were chilled, but his throat still burned from the liquor he'd drunk downstairs.

He'd gotten valuable information tonight, but all that he had learned fled from his mind as the warmth from Leena's body penetrated his senses. His loins responded with an answering heat of their own. He tensed, experiencing a throbbing need for release. Tossing and turning, he tried to find a comfortable position, but Leena's soft breathing and tantalizing scent continued to tempt him. In a frenzy of desire, he finally leapt out of the bed and paced the room until his muscles relaxed to the point where he could settle down. But as he approached the bed, his gaze fell on her bared shoulder, which peeked out from under the blanket that she'd thrown back, and his eyes slid along the edge of the thin shift that she wore. Demon's blood, he'd never sleep tonight!

And so it was that when Leena awoke the next morning, her gaze lit upon Taurin sleeping in the chair. Poor dear, she thought. He looks so different in repose. His face was relaxed and his manly jaw was covered by an early morning stubble. Dark eyelashes fanned his cheeks like black bristles arranged in a half moon shape. His hair, tousled from his restless movements, was tossed across his forehead. Besides removing his head cloth, he'd removed his clothes and now lounged in a short, snug pair of briefs.

Leena stared at his strong body, mesmerized by the sight

of his virility. The man fascinated her, and she longed to touch him, to explore his hard muscles and rugged angles. Chastising herself, she decided she'd better stop gawking and get dressed. But as soon as she stepped from the bed, his eyes popped open and he straightened up, instantly alert.

Leena halted, blushing beet red as she stood in front of him in her thin ivory-colored shift. "I was just going to get d-dressed," she stuttered.

Taurin gave her a slow, lazy smile. "By all means, go ahead." His hooded gaze made her body tremble.

"Do you have to look at me so ... so ... ?" Leena faltered, unable to finish her sentence. The blaze of desire she saw in Taurin's eyes shook her to the core. He is aware of me as a woman, she thought in alarm. By all that is holy, what do I do now?

Taurin continued to watch her, an unfathomable gleam in his smoky eyes. Acutely embarrassed, Leena hastily pulled the first gown she could reach out of her valise and rushed into the lavatory.

I can't go on like this, she thought. How can I continue to share a room with this man when every glance, every movement he makes causes me to tremble like a foolish schoolgirl?

That would be all right if they could observe the proprieties, but it was impossible to do so under their current circumstances. *I will just have to make the best of it,* she decided, pulling the bright yellow gown over her head. She brushed out her hair until fine waves cascaded over her shoulders like a curtain of topaz gemstones. Her eyes sparkled as she gazed into the mirror. It suddenly seemed important to present herself in a most feminine way, unlike with Malcolm, whom she always wanted to shock by wearing her breeches. Leena had no desire to earn Taurin's disapproval. Indeed, she thrilled to that heated look in his eyes when he gazed at her. Giving herself a final admonition to behave with decorum, Leena reentered their sleeping chamber.

"By Lothar, what are you doing?" she cried. Taurin was

performing sit-ups on the floor.

"I am exercising. It should be obvious," he told her, continuing his exertion. Leena stared at his massive chest and bulging muscles, which rippled with each movement. A sheen of sweat covered his body, and she moistened her lips, her mouth having suddenly gone dry.

"You can't do that here!" she told him.

"Why not, wife? I always exercise in the morning. You had better get used to it."

"But . . . but we have to say our morning prayer."

"You say the prayer; I'm working out."

Too shocked to make a retort, Leena turned toward the eastern side of the building, facing the rising sun. She prayed to Lothar for a peaceful day, ending her worship with a silent meditation. When she was finished she spared a glance at Taurin, who was now running in place, his bare feet thudding on the floor. Thanks be to Lothar, he had put on a pair of black trousers.

"Do you not partake of any of the ritual prayers?" she asked him, her brows furrowing at the notion that she was now wed to a heathen.

"I told you, I don't pray to anyone."

"But how can you not believe in our god? You've seen what he does for us by providing us with the lozenge that prevents sickness and by moderating our climate. How can you not offer him thanks for his graciousness?"

He stopped his efforts, his face taking on a thunderous expression. "Look, you have your beliefs and I have mine. Don't intrude on my life."

Leena stiffened her spine. "I beg your pardon. Have you forgotten that we are wed?"

"In name only, and as soon as this journey is ended, I intend to have our vows annulled."

Turning away from her, he stalked to his suitcase, from which he grabbed a clean shirt, and then marched into the lavatory, slamming the door behind himself. Leena sank miserably onto the edge of the bed. How were they ever going to get along when their personal philosophies were so different? She'd never thought about what it meant to respect someone else's right to his own beliefs, because nearly everyone she knew worshiped Lothar. It had always been that way throughout recorded history, at least as she'd been taught. Without Lothar's rules of order, chaos would reign. Her god's commandments held their society together. The Truthsayers proposed to establish a separate government, but she didn't see how they could separate governing of the land from Lothar's laws.

These are matters Bendyk deals with every day, she realized. *I commend him for his work. Truly, I'd rather be spending my time at an excavation site.* At least one dealt with concrete topics in the field of archaeology.

When Taurin came out of the rest room she asked him if he'd learned anything interesting during his tour last night.

He nodded, drops of water glistening on his damp hair. "We'll need a guide to cross the Black Lands. The best route is through one of the valleys. We'll have to see who's available when we get to Garu." The other things he'd learned he would keep to himself for now. They'd find out more when they got to the Black Lands. If his suspicions were confirmed, he'd have her pass the information along to her brother. In the meantime, they had a day to kill before their ship left on the morrow. He'd obtained a few extra supplies, and early the next morning they could visit the market to shop for groceries. But for now they were free.

"Did you bring nothing but those gowns?" he inquired.

Leena gave him a startled look. "I brought along the outfits I wear on my archaeological digs: breeches and loose-fitting, short-sleeve tops."

"We have a free day today, so I thought we could spend it at Hathers Beach. It's south of here, and within easy walking distance."

He'd had rare opportunities to spend time at the shore. Such a frivolous activity was unheard of on his world, and here he'd been too busy establishing his farm to engage in leisure pursuits. Sitting on the beach, gazing out to sea, seemed to him the ultimate relaxation. He'd looked forward to sharing the experience with Leena, but after their conversation this morning he had his doubts it would be so pleasurable. If she kept expounding on her faith like her brother, he'd be tempted to clamp a hand over her mouth and toss her into the waves. He'd just have to steer the conversation in another direction.

"We'll buy something at the marine shop," he said. "You'd be too hot in your gown or in breeches." Studying her fair, unblemished skin, he added, "We'll have to get you a hat to shade your face from the rays."

Leena didn't know what to make of his suggestion. Spend a whole day at the beach with Taurin? The idea titillated her in a wicked sort of way, but she couldn't refuse. Wondering if she were making a serious mistake, she followed him out of the room.

Chapter Six

On the beach, Taurin watched Leena as she tested the water. She wore a short tan tunic, which they'd found in the marine shop. He'd suggested she buy a couple of extras for their journey; tunics were less cumbersome than her long gowns and would make traveling easier. He stared at her long, shapely legs as she faced the water, soaking her feet in the sun-kissed surf.

Removing his shirt, he enjoyed the warmth from the sun's rays penetrating his skin, but it was nothing to what he felt as he watched Leena. Every movement she made bespoke grace and good breeding. His loins stirred, and he yearned to take her into his arms, lower her onto the soft sand, and taste the outline of her body with his lips.

No doubt she's thinking of her god, he thought ruefully. Xan was a beautiful world, and those who lived here were truly blessed. Perhaps there was a Creator who had designed the perfections of life. Certainly the flowers he grew indicated a higher intelligence at work. The brilliant colors, concentric circles of the petals, and uniqueness of the different varieties couldn't have developed from random evolution, could they? Is that what he believed in—that all things came to be from the fortunes of Nature? Or was there something more?

He'd seen that Lothar gave comfort to those who believed in him. He couldn't explain where the lozenges came from, except that they materialized in a sacred receptacle in each regional worship center during Mistic. The people attributed this miracle to Lothar. Nor did he know who controlled the weather satellites stationed in orbit around the planet, which he'd seen during his approach. Was it the hand of god or the hand of man at work? One thing was for sure: only Dikran and the members of his Synod knew the answers.

Leena knelt down and splashed water on her face. Taurin observed her, wishing he could believe as she did. It would make life easier to feel you were not alone. His journey through life thus far had been a hard one. He'd earned his peace and harmony, thanks to his own personal resources. But who knows? Maybe someone was guiding his destiny. Unfortunately, Leena couldn't be part of it after their assignment was complete.

His yearning for something he couldn't have saddened him, and to shake off the mood, he decided to go for a swim. Exercise would get his mind off his dark thoughts. After stripping off his pants he strode toward the water in his swim trunks. A moment later, he plunged into the ocean, his strong strokes taking him past Leena toward deeper waters. It felt good to plow through the waves, the vigorous exertion energizing him.

As he emerged onto the shore, Leena was sitting on the blanket he'd obtained, a wide-brimmed hat shading her face. As he toweled himself off, her admiring eyes drank their fill of him. Slowly her gaze roamed from his hairy chest downward to where his wet shorts clung to his hips. As though her mouth had suddenly gone dry, she grabbed for one of the water bottles they'd brought along and gulped down several swallows.

Taurin plunked himself down beside her. "Your arms are getting burned. Shall I apply lotion?" He couldn't help wanting to touch her and used the first excuse he could find.

"I can manage," Leena said, reaching for the tube.

Taurin snatched it up first. "Let me do it," he insisted, squeezing a line of white creamy liquid onto his fingertips.

His touch on her hot skin sent spirals of delight along her nerve endings. Leena closed her eyes as his smooth hands trailed up and down her arm, rubbing in the lotion. Even when she was sure the sunscreen must be fully applied, he continued to caress her skin. Both his hands moved to her shoulders as he gave her a light massage.

"You're too tense," he murmured, his low voice seducing her into a curious languor.

His fingers kneaded deep into her muscles, and her body relaxed into a pliant state, like putty being molded. His practiced fingers knew just where to apply pressure or lighten the touch. A small cry of pleasure escaped her lips when he tickled the back of her neck. Never had she imagined that a man's hands could feel so wonderful!

She opened her eyes and half turned so she could gaze into his face. The desire that blazed in his eyes made her breath come short. Her mouth parted, and before she knew what was happening she was being swept into his arms, his mouth descending upon hers with crushing force. Her mind reeled with the incredible sensations he created within her with his sensual movements. His kiss had a desperate edge to it as he slanted his mouth over hers again and again. Then he was pushing her back on the blanket, covering her body with his, his kisses becoming more urgent.

Taurin moaned her name, and her heart thudded faster. The weight of his body pressed her down, and the mere strength of him rendered her senseless with wanting. She snaked her arms around him until her hands splayed on his bare back. By the Faith, she could feel his muscles rippling beneath her fingers. Leena had never craved a man's touch before, but suddenly she longed for him to move his hands across her body, touching her in all the places that burned with fire.

Taurin's mouth moved with the desperation of a man consumed with thirst. When his tongue plunged inside her mouth she jerked beneath him, startled by the unexpected action. After she grew accustomed to his exploration she hesitantly reached out with her own tongue to meet his. A swirl of sensations drove her to a frenzy she didn't understand.

Suddenly she felt a release, and when she realized his weight had lifted from her body she opened her eyes, knowing her disappointment would be evident.

"Forgive me. I never meant for this to happen," he murmured, hovering above her, his eyes dark with remorse.

Leena swallowed. "Please don't offer apologies. I allowed it to happen."

"Well, it won't happen again." Taurin stood abruptly, brushing the sand off his body. "I wouldn't want your brother's disapproval to greet us upon our return to the Palisades."

Leena could imagine Bendyk's reaction. "Of course," she replied, flushing with embarrassment at her wanton behavior. With his riot of ebony hair, piercing slate-gray gaze, and powerful physique, Taurin presented an overpowering masculinity that she found difficult to resist. *Truly our journey is fraught with danger,* she thought, *my own interest in this man being the most serious!*

Taurin carefully kept his distance from her as he helped pack up their belongings. Nor did he touch her again as they went into town to catch a quick meal at a café hidden away on a side street. Only when they were back in their room did he address the subject that caused such tension between them.

"I cannot sleep next to you," he confessed, "or I shall be sorely tempted to turn to you. I shall stay in the chair again tonight."

Leena quivered at his words. He desired her, and yet there were too many gulfs between them to allow them to give in to passion, even if she were willing to do so. Sadly, she nodded her agreement, then changed the topic of conversation. Again that night he went out, leaving her alone, and she fell into a troubled sleep.

The next morning, when she awoke, the smell of liquor lingered in the room. He must have gone drinking, she realized, dismayed. Did I cause him to do that? It didn't seem likely, though, when he faced her with a stony expression that morning.

"I hired a porter. Our cases will be brought to the dock. I've ordered breakfast to be ready downstairs."

"I must perform morning prayers," she said. "Would you care to join me today?" Her tone was hopeful, even though she knew he would refuse.

"No," he said abruptly. "I'll meet you downstairs." Without a backward glance he stomped out.

It was with a sense of trepidation that Leena followed Taurin to the market for provisions and then to the ship he'd hired to take them to the Black Lands. The wharf was bustling with workers, and the scene was similar to the one that had met their eyes the day they had arrived. Leena's mouth gaped when she saw the ship, which was named *The Predator.* A two-masted sailing ship, her hull was painted black and her bulwarks white. The two masts were square-rigged, and the bowsprit stood out like an *elgar*'s antler. The rigging rose high above, and Leena saw that the sails were secured while the ship was moored to the dock. A man with a shuffling gait came out to greet them as they stepped onto the deck. His unshaven face held a permanent scowl, his dark eyes a hostile glare.

"I am Captain Riez," he introduced himself to Leena. "Welcome aboard. Haddok will show you to yer quarters." He gestured to a thin fellow with a gray beard and tattered clothes, who had been hunched over the deck, pounding some kind of material between the planks. At his master's command Haddock hastened to join them.

"Show our passengers to their cabin." Riez smiled

broadly, revealing his crooked yellow teeth. "I hope you find the place comfortable."

The crewman indicated an entryway that appeared to lead below. Wrinkling her nose in distaste, Leena followed him, with Taurin bringing up the rear. They entered a narrow, dark passageway with a low ceiling. A door stood on each side, with another door at the far end. Haddok opened the door on the left, indicating a space so small that Leena thought her closet at home must be bigger. A stench of rot permeated the air, and she drew back, affronted.

"We are not going to be confined in *there!*" she cried.

"If you don't like it, you can leave, madam, but it's my understandin' there ain't no other ship to take you where you want to go."

"Never mind." Taurin brushed past her. "This will do."

Leena forced herself to step into the cabin. A couple of bunk beds rested against one wall. On the opposite side was a sink, and a small partition concealed the toilet. A built-in chest on the bulkhead wall was the only other item of furniture.

"This is *it?* Are there no other cabins available?" She stalked outside and yanked on the door opposite. It was locked, and so was the one farther down the passage.

Captain Riez showed up, his face darkening. "If you wish to jine us on this voyage, you will follow orders."

"We are guests," Taurin said quietly, "not crew members."

Something in his voice must have warned the captain, because he gave Taurin an oily smile. "Of course, Brother. And we hopes you and the lady will enjoy yourselves. Chow is at five o'clock this evening. To reach the galley, go back down the passageway and up the steps to the waist of the ship. On the other side is a companionway that'll take you there."

At the evening repast, Leena and Taurin met the other crew members, as well as two passengers, who had joined them at the last minute. Puzzled, Taurin turned to Captain Riez, who sat at the head of a warped wooden table, his hand on a mug of ale.

"I thought you had only one cabin available," he stated.

Captain Riez smiled avariciously. "Your fellow passengers were in desperate straits. They're clergy—how could I refuse them?"

Taurin examined the couple, a man and a woman wearing medallions professing their membership in the Order of Missioners. The medallions bore the antlerlike design representing the branches of life that Lothar sustained. A few of the crew members, a scurvy lot to be sure, wore pendants made of different materials, also bearing Lothar's branch of life, which showed they followed the Faith. The couple were introduced as Brother Aron and Sister Bertrice. Brother Aron led them in the evening prayers.

He was swarthy-skinned and dark-haired, with high cheekbones, while the woman beside him had platinum-colored hair, hazel eyes, and a long nose that gave her face a waspish expression. No pair had ever seemed more incongruous, Leena thought, wondering how they came to be aboard. From the richness of their garments she assumed they'd paid Captain Riez well for their berths.

"What takes you to the Black Lands?" Leena asked them.

"We are going to try to contact some of the native tribes," Sister Bertrice answered amiably. "There remain many unconverted heathens on the island."

"Is it not dangerous for missionaries to go there? Those in exile would bear a grudge against the Ministry of Religion."

"Lothar will be guiding us," said Brother Aron, slurping up a spoonful of the brownish glop that the cook aboard called stew.

Leena ate very little, thinking of the cheese and bread she and Taurin had stashed in their cabin. She'd partake of those items later. They were much more appealing than this repast. She kept her gaze averted from the crew; they were an uncouth lot—unshaven and ill-dressed. There was a newcomer aboard, who had replaced a sailor who'd injured his leg in an accident just before the ship was due to sail. He appeared a bit more lively than the others, wearing clean clothes and having neatly combed hair.

While he devoured his meal, Taurin surreptitiously studied the crew. He would have hoped that while they were aboard *The Predator* he could relax his guard, but he could see that wouldn't be a wise course. Any one of the crew members could be a Truthsayer or a paid spy for the Synod member who'd stolen the horn. The safest path was to trust no one.

"I've heard tell that the best way across the Black Lands is through the central valley," he said to the captain. "We need to reach the northern coast. Have you any advice on how to get there, or who we can hire as a guide?"

"Don't go into the central highlands," Captain Riez said, chewing on a soggy breadstick. "There's tribes in those mountains who've never yet seen an outsider. You go in there and you'll never come out."

"What about the lowland areas?" Leena asked, remembering Sirvat's instructions. "Is it possible to go around the island on the outskirts?"

Riez shook his head. "Too swampy. You're crazy to cross through, but the valley following the river is your best bet."

Taurin leaned back in his chair, a casual look on his face. "I also heard that the Chocola Company has an interest on the island." His steely gaze met Captain Riez's rheumy eyes, which skittered away at the contact.

"That so?" he muttered.

"I saw a lot of crates at the wharf," Taurin went on. "From what I learned, beans are grown at plantations on the island and crated across the Tortis Sea by ship. From there they must go to a processing center. There are very few flights out of Port Donner. Where do those crates go?"

"They travel by rail, if you must know. And, yes, the Chocola Company does own plantations in the Black Lands.

But it won't do you any good to stick your nose into that business.''

His tone of voice held a warning that Taurin didn't miss. Chocola plantations in the Black Lands? Who was working there? The exiled dissenters? Who oversaw the operation and made sure it ran smoothly? And how could the Chocola Company have gotten permission from the Ministry of Religion to use the land for this purpose? Or did it come under the Ministry of the Interior? He wasn't sure, but this could bear looking into. If the information proved useful, Leena could pass it along to her brother. Somebody was fattening his pockets with the proceeds, and the trail could lead all the way to the Synod.

Later he voiced his opinion to Leena as they were strolling on deck, and she agreed that they should learn all they could. Night had fallen, and there were myriads of stars gleaming overhead. Their topic of conversation forgotten, Leena gazed upward in enraptured delight. Never had she seen so many stars in the sky. Even though her hometown wasn't big enough to produce much of a glow, nevertheless the effect dampened the view of the nighttime sky. Now, at sea, she gazed with awe at the twinkling dots of light overhead.

''Have you ever wondered what those stars are like?'' she asked Taurin. His head was swathed once again in the cloth, so she couldn't read his expression, but she saw that he, too, was staring at the darkened sky. ''Do other worlds circle them, and do they harbor life? Has Lothar's presence visited them, or is ours the only planet blessed by his bounty?''

''Would you be shocked if you learned that there was life on other planets?'' Taurin asked.

Leena sensed a feeling of tension behind his words. ''I don't think so.'' She frowned at him, wishing she could read his expression. ''That ring that I found in the ruins, and the horn, are constructed of the same type of material. It's like nothing I've ever seen on Xan. Either the Apostles were able to construct items using a process unknown to us, or else they brought this material from somewhere else. Perhaps up there.'' She rolled her eyes toward the heavens. ''They came out of nowhere, established the order of Sabal, and then left. Where did they go? Back to where they'd come from? Perhaps even now they are watching over us from somewhere else. I hope not, because they probably wouldn't like what they see. People are losing the Faith, and it bodes ill for our future.''

She rested a hand on the rail. Just then, Taurin's head jerked up. With a cry of alarm he grabbed her by the shoulders and pushed her to the deck, throwing his heavy body atop hers. Something crashed by with a deafening roar and splashed into the sea.

''What was that?'' Leena gasped, when he rose off her and helped her to stand.

Taurin scanned the rigging on the foremast. It was too dark to make out details—at least for Leena's eyes—but he picked out the figure making a hasty descent along the ratlines.

''Stay here,'' he said, charging after the shadowy figure. But the person made it below before Taurin could reach him, and he couldn't figure out who it had been. Somebody had tried to knock them overboard, which meant they had been betrayed. Now he would surely have to watch their backs. Hearing a soft footfall behind him, he whirled around, tensing his muscles, but it was only Leena.

''Did you catch him?'' she asked, her eyes wide with fright.

''No, I didn't. Let's return to our cabin.''

''Who do you think it was?'' she said when they were back in the confines of their quarters.

Having nowhere to sit or pace, Taurin climbed up on the top bunk and stretched himself out. Leena sat below him on the lower bunk, her head ducked.

''I'd say the best bet is the new crew member.'' Taurin's voice, low and rumbling, came from above. Leena reacted to the richness of his tone. Alone in the cabin with him, she was vitally aware of every breath he took, every movement he made. His presence made it difficult for her to formulate her thoughts, but for the sake of their mission she made the effort.

"Didn't Captain Riez say the regular crewman had had an accident before sailing? It was awfully convenient that this man was available."

"I'll ask him a few questions tomorrow," Taurin determined. "It's likely he'll make another attempt. If I'm not with you, I want you to stay in this cabin with the door locked. Understood?"

Leena was about to sputter a protest, but she acknowledged that his request was reasonable. "As you wish."

A long silence ensued during which neither one of them spoke. Leena could tell Taurin was awake by the restless movements he made and the erratic sound of his breathing. She wondered if he was worried about the success of their mission. It seemed as though there were so many obstacles yet ahead, and she was grateful she wouldn't have to face them alone.

Taurin lay on his back, his arms folded and hands under his head as he gazed at the low ceiling. Every fiber of his being was aware of Leena's lovely shape lying on the bunk below. The scent of her perfume tantalized him, and he heard the rustle of her gown as she changed positions. Demon's blood! How he'd like to roll off his bunk and sweep her into his arms. Her image danced before his eyes, tormenting him. When they'd entered the cabin the light from the flickering oil lamp had cast her in an ethereal glow, and he'd felt as though she were his personal angel, come to soothe his soul from its torment. But the sweet torture she brought him was even worse; he craved to touch her, to smooth his hands over her exquisite body, to run his fingers through her golden waves of hair. But he could never have what he wanted.

Shifting to his side, he squeezed his eyes shut, hoping to erase her image from his mind. *You can't have her.* Those words haunted him until he finally fell into an exhausted sleep.

The next morning, when they were walking on deck, Leena noticed that the crew seemed edgy. Her stomach, queasy ever since they'd set sail, rebelled as increasingly tumultuous waves rocked the vessel. Wondering if a storm was brewing, she decided to ask Captain Riez while Taurin questioned the new crew member.

Ignoring Taurin's orders for her to remain in their cabin, she located the captain, who was downing a quick meal in the galley. She breezed in through the open hatchway, her billowy yellow gown floating about her ankles.

"Good and welfare, Captain. I was just on deck and noticed the crew going about their duties in a grim silence. The sea is rough this morning, and the sky has a peculiar yellowish tinge. Is anything amiss?"

The captain, unshaven and wearing clothes that hadn't seen soap in a fortnight, grimaced at her.

"We're entering Fool's Quadrant. The passage isn't always safe."

"Not safe?" Leena's voice cracked. "What do you mean?"

"The water can thicken."

"I don't understand. How can water thicken?"

"It has something to do with the growth of microbes." Riez scratched his ample belly. "The sea turns to the consistency of glue. Eventually the water liquifies again, but it ain't good to be stuck here in the meantime."

"Why not?" Leena asked, fearful of the answer.

Stuffing a forkful of mashed tubers into his mouth, he gave a furtive glance at the cook, who stood by listening to their exchange. "The flying lungefish, Sister. They'll swarm a man." His voice lowered. "I've never seen one, but I've heard tell they have suckers on their tentacles. The things secrete an enzyme that can dissolve a man's flesh."

"We wouldn't be here if we wasn't steered off course last night," the cook blurted out.

Startled, Leena glanced in his direction. The portly fellow wore a stained apron that sported several hairs from his graying head.

"I means what I says, lady. That new crew member, Sprawls, he was on duty last night. He didn't know his charts too well, did he?"

The captain nodded grimly. "Now it's too late to circle around Fool's Quadrant. We have to go through it. I just hope we make it without any trouble."

Leena hastened away, eager to find Taurin. He'd be interested to learn this news. She wondered if he had found that fellow Sprawls and was even now questioning the man. But neither could be found.

Troubled, she strode across the deck, a strong breeze whipping her long hair about her head. Salt spray stung her face, and she had to grip the railing to steady herself. As the planked flooring rose and dipped beneath her feet with the movement of the ship over the high swells, her attention was drawn upward by shouts and curses. Appalled, she saw Taurin's lithe body climbing among the sails.

Taurin was chasing the new crew member, who had fled as soon as he saw him coming. Apparently the man hoped to lose Taurin by climbing into the rigging, but Taurin had no regard for his own safety. He'd started after Sprawls immediately. He wasn't able to shimmy up the mast like the crewman, so he chose to climb the shroud, using the ratlines as a ladder. The main mast towered above the deck, supporting four levels of sails, and the crewman had already reached the topsail. Taurin reached up, grasped the lowest deadeye, and hauled himself atop the rail. He stretched as far as he could into one of the middle shrouds, grabbing a ratline to ease his climb. He needed to pull with his arms as well as boost himself up with his legs. Line by line he proceeded.

Glancing down, he saw the deck of the ship grow smaller and smaller. Leena's bright yellow dress stood in contrast to the rolling green sea. He felt as though he were climbing into the clouds. He neared the crewman, who was resting at the trestle tree just below the top gallant spar. Every muscle in Taurin's body ached from the exertion, and his heart pounded in his chest, but he didn't stop for even a momentary respite. He kept on going upward, ratline by ratline, cursing as his hands grew slippery and his senses reeled. Pausing with the rigging inches from his face, he let his breathing slow.

"You come any closer and I'll throw you off," said Sprawls, one arm wrapped around the mast.

"You tried to knock us overboard, didn't you?" Taurin shouted. A sudden wind blew up and whipped his hair into his face.

"Aye, that I did. And I'll see to it that you and your lady don't reach the Black Lands. I've got me orders," he hollered.

"Orders from whom?"

Taurin lurched upward, hand over hand, vowing to get closer still. As he reached the height of the crewman, he noticed the gleam of metal in the man's grasp just as he thrust his arm out. He kicked with his foot, slicing the knife from the assassin's hand. The weapon arched downward and away. With a growl of rage, the crewman launched himself in Taurin's direction. The two men grappled wildly as the lines flapped around them.

"Who sent you?" Taurin yelled, his hands tightening on the man's throat.

"That's no concern of yours." The man's words came out as a choking gasp.

"I think it is."

Taurin squeezed harder, and the man's face turned a dark shade of red. The crewman loosened Taurin's grasp with a vicious kick.

"Once I get rid of you I'll take care of the lady. Neither one of you is supposed to leave this ship alive."

The uppercut to his jaw caught Taurin unawares, and he reeled from the force of the blow. His grip on the line was the only thing that saved him from slipping off and falling to the waves below. Sprawls jumped on his advantage, pummeling Taurin about the head and face. With a roar of rage, Taurin lashed out, striking his adversary with a glancing blow in the rib cage. Fury filled his veins, and he felt a maniacal urge to throttle the fellow until he was dead. Before he could give in to his bloodlust, the ship dipped. With a howling scream, the crewman lost his grip. Flung off the rigging, he fell to his death in the depths below.

Clutching the mast, Taurin swayed in place, his muscles trembling, his hands on fire. Sweat dripped into his eyes, blinding him. He waited while the wind cooled his fury; then he contemplated the hazardous journey down.

Chapter Seven

As the ship rocked against the strengthening waves, Taurin clung to the rigging while making his descent. The horizon kept tilting and dizziness assailed him, but he forced himself to place one foot below the other. Sails filled and smacked about him, at times nearly smothering his breath. He heard Leena screaming his name as he reached the mainyard and climbed down the final few feet to the wooden deck. His legs were so rubbery that he tumbled to his knees once he felt a solid surface beneath him.

"Taurin!" Leena shrieked, rushing over to him. "Are you all right? I've never been so scared in my life!"

Taurin glanced at her, wonder in his eyes. "You care about what happens to me?"

"Of course I do." She helped him to his feet. "Can you stand steady?"

"Yes, I'm all right now." He shook out his aching arms. "I haven't practiced rope-climbing in a while," he said ruefully.

She told him about the exchange in the galley. "Did

116

Sprawls admit to trying to push us overboard last night?''

"Aye, so he did. He said his orders were to keep us from reaching the Black Lands.''

Leena grimaced. "It seems we were betrayed. Only the Synod and Caucus members knew we were going on this mission.''

"We'll have to be doubly cautious. Either the traitor sent his own assassin after us, or he's tipped off the Truthsayers about our purpose and Sprawls was one of them.''

"We're safe for now." She gave him an assessing glance. "Let's go below. You're exhausted from your exertions.''

Taurin let her fuss over him in their cabin. She brought him a drink and a cool cloth for his forehead. He didn't feel the need to lie down but was too glad for her ministrations to refuse. He'd never had a woman care for him before. Having been raised by one of the dominant gangs on Yllon, he'd had no real parents. Baker Mylock and his wife were the only ones who'd ever shown him kindness.

Leena smoothed his cheek with her hand, and Taurin let a deep sigh escape his lips. Her touch was like an angel's kiss. His body burned, and it wasn't from the heat or the energy he'd expended. He burned with desire for the beautiful woman nurturing him. Tenderly his gaze scanned her face. Her expression, full of concern for his welfare, moved him deeply. Looking into her eyes, he thought he had never seen anything so pure in his entire life.

"Leena," he murmured.

"Yes?"

She was standing on the edge of her bunk in order to be head level with him. Tentatively he reached out a hand to cup the back of her head. Her hair felt like spun silk, and suddenly his resolve dissipated. He'd been able to push away from her at Hathers Beach, knowing it wasn't right for him to steal kisses from her no matter what their legal relationship was. But now he drew her toward him until his mouth hovered inches above hers.

The words escaped his lips before he could stop them. "I want you."

Leena's eyes widened, as though doubting she'd heard him correctly. Her body trembled, but instead of pulling away as he expected her to do, she parted her lips and tilted her face upward. "Kiss me, Taurin. I want to be close to you."

With a cry of exultation, Taurin smashed his mouth onto hers.

His kiss was deep and passionate, and Leena thought she'd never experienced anything more heavenly than the press of his mouth on hers. She'd been so afraid for him on deck that now she had to be close to him, just to reassure herself of his safety. Standing on tiptoe so that she could meet him more fully, she thought that kissing him was more rapturous than anything she'd ever imagined. Malcolm's feathery touches were mere polite formalities in comparison. In contrast, when Taurin kissed her she felt consumed by a hunger too wild for words, and she never wanted him to stop.

His arm wrapped around her shoulder in a protective embrace. Closing her eyes, she gave in to the ecstasy of the moment, relishing the feel of his mouth on hers as his lips moved frantically, expressing his need. He desired her! The wonder of it took her breath away. But it shouldn't be his arms around her; it should be Malcolm's. Guilt ate at her consciousness, giving her pause, so that when his hands roamed toward her breasts she jerked away, stricken with remorse.

"No!"

Taurin's eyes darkened to a slate-gray shade. "Why not?" He heaved himself into a sitting position and then jumped down so he stood facing her directly. "I want to touch you, Leena. Kissing you isn't enough. I want to have all of you."

"I'm not yours," she whispered, her heart thudding wildly in her chest. By the Faith, how handsome he looked, with his dark swirl of hair curling onto his forehead and his piercing gaze. "Our marriage is in name only," she reminded him sadly, wishing it were otherwise. But too many obstacles precluded their staying together, even if she or Taurin desired it. Not that she was considering such a possibility! Malcolm was waiting for her, and although he wouldn't necessarily expect her to be a virgin, he might rescind his offer if he learned the circumstances of her journey and suspected that she and Taurin had coupled.

"It would dishonor us were we to consummate our union without an emotional commitment," she said, feeling an explanation was necessary.

A cloud came over Taurin's face. "Of course," he sneered. "Your brother wouldn't approve, would he?" With those words, he spun around and stormed out of the cabin.

"Taurin!" Leena cried. But he was already gone, and she felt it best to let him go. She should never have let him kiss her again; it was her fault for responding in such a shameless fashion. But she couldn't help it if her limbs weakened and her body fired with tension whenever he was near. The only solution was for her to maintain a safe distance from him. Once their mission was over she'd resume her station in life, and that didn't include socializing with people like Taurin.

A short while later, she noticed that the ship's motion had quieted. She went out on deck to see what was the cause and found Taurin, along with some other crew members, staring out to sea.

"What is it? What's going on?" she asked.

When she caught sight of the sea Leena gasped. The consistency of gelatin, it had taken on a strange amber hue and entrapped the ship in its viscosity.

"We're stuck," Taurin said, giving her a disdainful glance.

Captain Riez, who was worriedly conferring with his men, called out to her. "Ye'd better go below, miss. You don't want to be caught here if the flying lungefish attack."

Before she could heed his words, a giant sucking noise erupted off the port bow. Leena shrieked as the sky filled with scores of fluttering wings. Dozens of flying bodies hurled themselves at the crew member standing on the forecastle deck, engulfing him so completely that he couldn't be seen. His screams could be heard, however: blood-curdling shrieks that were quickly silenced. When the swarm flew away a murky puddle remained on the deck, all that was left of him. The creatures soared into the sky and then veered downward in a spiraling turn, heading back toward the ship.

"Take cover!" Taurin yelled, pushing her toward the companionway.

She screamed as they charged past, crowding another crew member, who howled in terror. The captain shouted orders as the crew frantically scurried to obey them. Stepping backward in an effort to flee, Leena didn't notice the open hatchway located in the center of the ship's waist. Suddenly she felt herself toppling into empty space. Screaming, she was barely aware of the total blackness engulfing her before cracking her skull on a solid surface. White-hot pain exploded in her head and then all went dark.

Taurin's breath caught in his throat as he saw her disappear. "Leena!" he howled, rushing forward, his offer to help the crew forgotten. Climbing down the ladder into the cargo hold, he fumbled in the darkness until he felt her soft form, limp on the floor. His heart hammered in panic as he felt for her pulse. A weak, erratic beat brought him a measure of relief, but she needed treatment.

After a moment his eyes adjusted to the dark, and he could see as clearly as though it were daytime. With a grim smile, he noted that if she could see him now, she'd be frightened by the glowing luminescence of his eyes. It was the reason why he swathed his head in cloth—so no one could see that he wore the demon's sign. A gash on the side of Leena's head showed him what had rendered her unconscious. Carefully, he scooped her up into his arms and climbed up the ladder onto the waist of the ship. The siege from the flying creatures continued as he hustled into the passenger quarters and entered their cabin. Gently, he placed her on her bunk. As he was doing so, her eyelids fluttered open, and she moaned with pain. Taurin took the same cloth that she had used on his forehead and moistened it with cool water. He tenderly cleansed her wound.

"Don't move," he cautioned. "It's my turn to take care of you."

His touch sent shivers through her body. She reminded herself of her vow not to let him get close to her again, although it wasn't necessary. He seemed to be doing his best not to look at her face and was tending her wounds in an impersonal manner. But then his hand wandered to stroke her cheek.

"I'm sorry," he murmured, and this time his eyes did meet hers. She saw contrition in them, and remorse.

"It was my fault," she said, embarrassed. "I shouldn't have let you . . . I mean, I could have stopped . . ."

Taurin put a finger to her lips. "Hush. It's not necessary to explain. We both enjoyed it, but it shouldn't have happened. Let's leave it at that." Seeing the hurt look in her eyes, Taurin cursed inwardly. He had never wanted to possess a woman as much as he wanted her, but it was an impossibility. Why waste his time with someone he couldn't have? Even if she agreed, she was too good for him, and the life she was meant to lead was far different than his.

Pretending to freshen the cloth, he walked to the sink so she wouldn't see the longing in his eyes. Honest intimacy with a woman was something he could never have. It would frighten her if she knew his true nature. Some of it showed already, but she didn't know the whole of it. She'd be repulsed if she knew the rest.

Squeezing out the rag, Taurin returned to her side, ministering to her wounds until their throbbing eased. Screams and cries came from above, and Leena shuddered.

"What if those creatures get all of them?" she asked, her frightened gaze capturing his attention. "We'll be left alone."

Taurin couldn't think of anyone else he'd rather be stranded with, but he didn't believe that would happen. "The water should be liquefying soon; then we can get underway again. If you'll be all right here by yourself, I'll go out and take a look.''

Leena grabbed for his hand. ''Stay here,'' she implored. ''I . . . I don't want to be left alone.'' In truth, she feared for his safety should he leave the confines of the cabin, but she would never admit that to him.

Taurin saw the look of concern etched on her face and smiled briefly. ''Wait here for me.''

With that lingering promise, he left. Leena closed her eyes and allowed her body to relax. Fear and the blow to her head had left her energy drained. She must have fallen asleep briefly, because when she came to her senses the ship was rocking, telling her that they were moving again. The danger was past. Thanks be to Lothar!

Leena tried to sit up, but her head swam dizzily. Taurin walked in at that moment and cried out in alarm.

''You've been injured. You must rest!''

Leena gingerly lowered herself onto the mattress, touched by his concern. By all that was holy, how she wanted him, even with the ache in her head! She glanced away, not wanting him to see the yearning on her face. It was disconcerting having him so near, and yet it was herself she feared more than him. She had never known herself to be a weak woman, but around Taurin her willpower seemed to evaporate.

With a heavy grunt he heaved himself onto his bunk and lay down. Leena listened to his movements for a long while, wondering if she could bear for them to be parted once this mission was over. First things first, she told herself. Tomorrow they should reach the Black Lands, and then they'd see where their assignment took them. The attack from the flying creatures might seem mild compared to the dangers ahead.

The approach to the Black Lands was a delight from Leena's viewpoint. At first a shadowy shape on the horizon, the island grew larger as *The Predator* sailed toward land. Soon verdant green slopes and mountainous rises became visible.

She leaned against the rail, a breeze tossing her hair about her head as Captain Riez maneuvered the ship into a wide harbor.

The wharf area was a morass of squalor, but the forested mountains rising behind it promised a land of lush beauty. As the ship approached the dock, a frenzy of activity energized the wharf. Vendors, traders, and stevedores prepared for the new arrival. After the mooring lines were secured Captain Riez assigned a porter to assist the passengers with their luggage. As soon as they were safely on the pier, they were left to fend for themselves.

"Excuse me," said Brother Aron, the richness of his cloak making him the object of envious stares. "I understand that you're going into the interior. Perhaps we can share a guide." The missionaries stood beside Leena and Taurin, bewildered looks on their faces as they observed the bustle going on about them.

"What is your destination?" Taurin's hand shaded his face. The tropical sun blazed overhead, momentarily blinding him.

"It is our intention to contact the native tribes and teach them the ways of Lothar. I have a map of sorts that we can follow." He withdrew a document from a pocket in his long-skirted garment, showing it to Taurin.

Leena addressed Sister Bertrice. "Aren't you afraid to approach the primitive tribes?" she asked. "Some of them might never have seen an outsider before."

Sister Bertrice smiled benignly. "Lothar will protect us."

Taurin and Brother Aron hurried off, apparently on their errand to find a guide. Leena watched in astonishment as workers on the dock began distributing the ship's stores. Bags of mail, containers of food, first-aid supplies, and medicines, as well as sundry goods, were packed onto trucks belching foul-smelling fumes. Vehicles carrying loads of packed crates bearing the Chocola Company's name rumbled onto the wharf. None of the smaller vehicles appeared to be motorized. The only private conveyances were simple carriages or carts drawn by *enixes*—strong, proud beasts known for their easy domesticity. An operator drove out a large crane and began hoisting the Chocola crates into the cargo hold of *The Predator*.

"I understand the motorized equipment is guarded vigorously," said Sister Bertrice, nodding at the crane. "Those in exile might build boats, you know."

"The waters are patrolled. Even if some of the inhabitants did make it off the island, they'd be intercepted." Leena knew that those who were sent here rarely received a reprieve; it was their fate to live out the rest of their lives on this large island, their only company being their fellow dissidents or the natives in the interior.

"Do most of the . . ." She almost said *prisoners,* but guarded her tongue. "Do most of the people who come here reside in the lowlands?"

"In the lowlands and at the foot of the mountains." Sister Bertrice patted the bun at the nape of her neck to make sure her hair was still bound in its proper place. Her hairstyle gave her face a severe look, and her eyes, as she studied Leena, held no hint of friendliness.

Leena had no time to ponder Sister Bertrice's puzzling demeanor; Taurin and Brother Aron had returned, accompanied by a white-haired gentleman whose pompous swagger was undercut by his faded, worn clothes. If a person exiled here did not receive packages from home, she thought, they were dependent on charity. What a sad existence! For the first time she wondered at the harsh sentence prescribed by the religious order for those who disagreed with their tenets. Lothar's grace and compassion were absent from this place. Although the island was lush with greenery and boasted a pleasant climate, its watery boundaries were the same as prison walls for the people entrapped here. Modern technology was lacking, no doubt because the people could convert sophisticated items of machinery to their own use. It was a harsh existence, she acknowledged, staring at the ramshackle wooden buildings that lined the wharf.

Realizing the fate that might have been her father's had he been exiled here, she felt a rush of gratitude toward Karayan for speaking in his behalf. A year of penance, no matter how unpleasant, was much preferable to a lifetime in this lonely place. Renewing her vow to see her father totally exonerated, she studied the new arrival.

"Ives will be our guide," said Taurin, introducing the man. "He says our best route is to follow the lowlands to the east and then cut across the island through the main river valley."

"It'll take days without any motorized transport!" Leena exclaimed.

Taurin pursed his lips, clearly displeased with the prospect. "We have no choice," he snapped. "Ives will take us to a place where we can stay for the night. We'll get an early start tomorrow morning so we can cover a longer distance."

Ives helped them load their luggage onto his cart, a large conveyance drawn by four spirited *enixes,* who snorted and pranced as they waited for their passengers to board. A wooden bench seat lined the inside perimeter. Leena and Taurin took seats together; Sister Bertrice and Brother Aron sat opposite them. Ives climbed onto a raised platform in front, gripped the reins, and uttered a cry that spurred the beasts forward. They galloped through the town, raising a dusty cloud in their wake, and were shortly following a trail alongside a marsh that stank of sulfur and rotting vegetation.

Leena held on to the seat with one hand and her hat with the other. She was glad Taurin had insisted she put on one of the shorter tunics he had bought for her in Port Donner. It was forest green, with a sleeveless top and a scooped neckline.

The cart jostled and rose beneath them as they rushed along the bumpy trail. A salt-laden breeze cooled Leena's face as they progressed. After about an hour of driving they stopped to share a drink from a jug of water provided by their guide and to eat a snack of fresh *karanas,* a soft yellowish fruit that peeled easily and satisfyingly filled the stomach. The cart lurched onward as they resumed their journey, turning inland toward the foothills. Scrub brush grew in profusion along the hillsides, but there weren't many tall trees in this area. Leena felt the ride was rockier than the cruise on the ship. If she'd thought being on land would be easier, she'd been incredibly wrong. The contents of her stomach heaved as the cart bounced beneath her.

"What are we going to do once we reach the other side of the island?" she shouted at Taurin, her voice carried by the wind.

His black hair was being blown wildly about his face, but she caught the instant warmth of his eyes as he responded to her question, an enigmatic smile on his face. "I have a plan." As though recognizing her need for reassurance, he held out his hand.

Leena slid her way along the bench and gratefully sank against his solid chest as he wrapped his arm around her. Brother Aron's gaze fell to her exposed legs, making her feel uncomfortable. Sister Bertrice gave her a disapproving frown. To avoid looking at them she closed her eyes, letting her body melt into Taurin's contours. She forced herself to focus her thoughts on their goals rather than on the jostling ride and the unpleasant couple sitting across from them.

After what seemed like an interminably long period of time, when dusk was falling and Leena despaired of ever reaching shelter for the night, they turned down a path heading west onto higher ground. The trees were taller, shading the road. When they broke into a clearing she gasped with surprise. Cultivated rows of plants met her gaze, and in the center of the fields was a two-story mansion built from brick and stone.

"What is this?" Taurin exclaimed, straightening up. "A plantation house?"

His farmer's eye looked with interest at the plants as they passed. The stalks looked strong and healthy, and the large oval leaves were bright green and tapered. Clusters of brown beans hung from the different offshoots. The ripened plants must stand about three feet in height, Taurin figured. Into his mind's eye came the image of the crates on the dock. Of course; this must be one of the Chocola Company plantations he'd been told about. Again he wondered how property rights had been granted in the Black Lands when this was prohibited territory.

They drove up to the front of the manor house. A bright glow from within welcomed them as the door was flung open and a well-dressed gentleman stepped outside.

"Ah, Ives." The dark-haired young man spoke. "You have brought guests for the night?"

Ives introduced them and nodded in a nervous manner. "I hope you don't mind our unexpected visit, Master. But you always said to show outsiders to your place."

"Indeed I did, Ives. Indeed I did." He thrust his hand into his pocket and then threw a few coins to the old man. "You can take your meal in the common house. I'll take care of our guests."

He ushered the missionaries, Leena, and Taurin inside. Snapping orders to several servants who hovered about, the young man led them into a furnished library.

"My name is Alber," he said, offering them a drink of wine.

"What's going on here?" Taurin demanded, after accepting a crystal glass filled with a rich burgundy. "I thought commerce was prohibited in the Black Lands."

"This operation is a closely guarded secret." Alber gave a conspiratorial grin that reminded Leena of the face of a cat about to devour a dead mouse. "I trust you will not reveal my company's presence on this island to anyone else."

"But who authorized it?" Leena put in.

The missionaries could care less, she noted. They were circling around the room, perusing the texts lining the bookshelves. She accepted a glass of wine gratefully. Her throat was parched, and the tart liquid eased her thirst. Briefly her eyes flickered about, alighting on several statuettes and other objets d'art. None were of exceptional value, but Alber at least had an eye for aesthetics.

"It's of little concern to you who gave authorization for this facility. The Chocola Company is a major producer on Xan, and certain allowances have been made to encourage productivity. After all, the processing of the beans creates jobs, and we all want our people to have satisfactory tasks to keep them occupied. Chocola is a product enjoyed by everyone. Why not use the richness of this island for such a productive purpose?"

"But where do you get the workers?" Leena asked.

As she saw the smirk on Alber's face, her eyes widened in understanding. "You employ those who are exiled here."

"I wouldn't say *employ* is the correct term. I offer a trade: They provide me with their services and I give them food and shelter. It's an amiable exchange."

"Slave labor," Taurin muttered.

He and Leena exchanged glances, both of them having the same thought. She would instruct Bendyk to look into this matter. Only someone at a high level could have skirted the regulations regarding usage of the Black Lands. The authorization had to come from one of the ministers. Someone's pockets were being lined on this place, Leena thought with disgust. She didn't know who to believe, who to trust. Taurin, she thought; I can trust Taurin. He and Bendyk and Swill; they're the only ones.

"Do you have a line to the mainland?" she asked, hoping to contact her brother.

"I am afraid direct communications are forbidden. We conduct business via the mail boats that ply these waters more regularly than the ship on which you sailed. The system works, madam. I pray you will not betray us."

Leena didn't like the warning note in his voice and neither did Taurin. His body tensed as he gave the man a dark scowl that would have made a lesser man quiver in his shoes.

"Let us discuss the continuation of our journey," Taurin said gruffly, realizing that if this man wanted to detain them, he had only to give the word to his servants.

"We haven't considered the payment for your accommodations," Alber stated, smiling amiably, as though the warning tone in his voice had been nothing but a figment of their imaginations.

"Ives said nothing about us having to pay you."

"You travel in luxury, Brother. Surely you can share some of your bounty with those of us who are less fortunate."

Taurin glanced around, a sardonic look on his face. "Your place doesn't appear to be lacking in the accoutrements of comfort."

"No, but you forget I have to maintain a work force. That costs money. Any extra contribution I can obtain aids the cause. Thus I take in visitors when they arrive."

"How many visitors do you get?" Leena asked curiously. She'd had no idea that people could come and go from this island. How were the dissenters kept in line?

"Representatives from my company come through here on occasion, and sometimes other guests pass through." Alber didn't elaborate, but Leena was liking the man less and less.

"How much did you have in mind?" Taurin demanded.

"Oh, I'd say a hundred chekels for each of you should do. And twenty-five more each for your meals. That's a total of five hundred chekels."

Sister Bertrice, who'd been listening off to the side, snorted with derision. "We don't carry that kind of money, Brother."

"I'm sure your friends would be willing to share their wealth," Alber said, keeping his eyes fixed on Taurin.

"What if I refuse?"

"We have other accommodations available in the common house. You can join the rabble there."

The man's meaning was clear. If Taurin didn't pay, they'd be imprisoned with the rest of the work force. In that case, their chances of leaving the island were almost nil.

"Very well," Taurin consented, not wishing to cause trouble. He'd be on his guard through the night, lest his purse be taken from him by force.

So it was that after a generous repast the four guests were assigned comfortable suites on the second floor.

The evening passed without incident, and early the next day after morning prayers—Alber apparently followed the teachings of Lothar—and a simple meal, the travelers started off on their journey once again. To their pleasant surprise, Ives was standing between two riders that Alber had supplied for their continuing journey. They were open-air vehicles with a transparent shield in front to provide protection from the wind and huge tires to allow passage through difficult terrain. Square-shaped, the riders had seating for four and an additional space in the back for luggage or equipment.

Ives and the missionaries took the lead in one vehicle, Leena and Taurin following in the second rider.

"Have a safe journey," Alber called to them, standing on his front stoop.

The missionaries raised their hands in farewell, but Taurin didn't give the man the courtesy. He didn't like Alber's tone, nor the secretive look in his eye. It might have helped had they been able to communicate with Leena's brother, but under the circumstances he felt isolated. Whereas before such a feeling had brought him a measure of comfort, at the moment it only served to heighten his sense of unease. Being cut off from civilization had suddenly lost its appeal, and Taurin wondered what dire consequences might result.

Chapter Eight

Bendyk and Swill were making slow progress. Swill had nearly completed her examination of the Treasury records but was dissatisfied with one of her findings. Each month, exactly on the thirty-fifth day, collections were entered into the Receipts account in varied monetary amounts. Sirvat claimed these were miscellaneous categories for income that didn't fit into any of the other classifications.

Feeling she was being misled, Swill had demanded a more detailed explanation and was told to consult Magar; his department was responsible for the revenue.

Meanwhile, Bendyk was looking into Sirvat's personal background by interviewing her acquaintances. He found out that she lived a rather frugal life and kept a quiet residence in one of the larger towns where her family resided. Her penchant for traveling had taken her to some of the more exotic locales on Xan. Apparently she traveled alone but "met friends," as one of her neighbors said.

Bendyk wanted to tell Swill what he'd discovered and was waiting for her in their shared office one afternoon when

Karayan and Zeroun stormed in.

"How is your research progressing?" Zeroun asked, his tone as sleek as oil.

Bendyk stared at the man's dark-complected face. "Well enough, thank you. Did you come to see me for a particular reason?"

"Don't get your hackles up, my boy," said Karayan, casually examining one of his manicured fingernails. As usual, he wore an impeccably tailored frock coat and a pair of matching trousers. "You know, you really should learn to control your temper. It isn't suitable in a missionary and a disciple of Lothar to be so turbulent."

Bendyk stifled a retort, knowing he was right. He'd always had to struggle to keep his volatile emotions in check. Praying for serenity hadn't helped him thus far. He feared it was a state he would never attain, and he envied Leena's sense of inner peace. Where in tarnation was Swill? She was late for their conference.

"Did you learn anything more about Rey Niris?" Karayan inquired.

Bendyk answered him with a smile. Now he knew why they had come to see him. "Perhaps." Leaning on his elbows, he steepled his hands on his desk.

"His residence is located in the same town as Magar's estate, is it not?" Zeroun demanded.

"Aye, and so what if it is?" He wanted to look into the matter himself but hadn't had the time. After he was finished investigating Sirvat he'd start with Magar.

Karayan and Zeroun had other ideas. "Did you see his home when you took Leena to him?" Karayan asked. "What was the fellow like? Was he eager to go on this quest?"

Bendyk rose. "I believe my sister and I are the ones in charge of this investigation, gentlemen."

"Yes, but we are concerned for Leena's safety," Karayan said. "Zeroun and I are going to take a look around Rey Niris's place. If you want to come, you're welcome."

"How did you get the location?" Bendyk narrowed his

gaze suspiciously. He didn't think Magar would share that information so readily.

"We have our sources."

Pretending to adjust his shirt, Bendyk considered his options. Better to go along with them than have them snoop around on their own. "When are you leaving?"

"Right now," said Karayan. "Will you join us?"

"Very well."

Hastily, Bendyk scribbled a note for Swill, explaining the circumstances of his departure. Fingering the medallion hanging over his tan longshirt, he followed the ministers outside.

The drive into the countryside seemed to take little time as he sat in the rear passenger seat, lost in his own thoughts. Before he knew it they were turning down the private drive that led to Taurin's tidy house. Zeroun's white robe, cinched at the waist with his gold sash, fluttered in the breeze as they emerged from the rider. The weather had cooled, but rain had not yet come, and Taurin's fields lay fallow. After walking about the grounds the trio climbed onto the porch that wrapped around the exterior.

"You know," Karayan mused, a thoughtful gleam in his eyes, "I believe this piece of land is considered part of Magar's property. He showed me the boundaries once, and I could have sworn this plot was included." He looked over the fields that eventually ended in a forest, beyond which, Bendyk had learned, was Magar's family residence, a large mansion by most people's reckonings.

Zeroun peered into a window. "I'd be interested to learn where Magar met this Rey Niris gent." His gaze fell on something in the interior that made him cry out. "What is that? Karayan, come here!"

The two men huddled together, staring through the windowpane.

"An archaeological text," Karayan muttered. "And those drawings."

"Magar said the man fights like a warrior," Zeroun

mused. "Where do you suppose he comes from? No one around here possesses such skills."

"Magar is concealing his knowledge of this man," Karayan concluded. Turning his gaze to Bendyk, he fixed the young man with an intense glare. "You'll have to learn what Rey Niris's purpose is here. Magar would be the best source of information."

"I'll question Magar when I'm ready," replied Bendyk.

"It can't be soon enough. If you won't interrogate him, then I will."

Bendyk raised a blond eyebrow. "I'll handle this," he said quietly, hoping to leave no doubt in their minds that he'd assert his authority if necessary.

During the return drive to the Palisades, his brow furrowed in thought. Zeroun sat stiffly in the front, morosely silent. Karayan drove faster over the winding roads than Bendyk would have liked, but he said nothing, immersed in his speculation. He wondered if he should pursue his investigation of Sirvat or interrupt it to question Magar. He'd like some answers from the man. Feeling uncomfortable with the lack of information they had on Rey Niris, he didn't deem it wise to acknowledge the bonding ceremony he'd performed between Leena and Taurin, though he'd registered the event in the village ledger.

Returning to his office, he found Swill reviewing her notes. She glanced up from her desk as he entered, a guarded expression clouding her face.

"I need to discuss my findings with you," she said.

The hour was growing late; she must have been waiting for him. Bendyk was weary from the unexpected trip but also wanted to compare notes with Swill.

"Sorry I'm late. Zeroun and Karayan set off to snoop around Rey Niris's place, and I thought it best if I accompanied them. How about joining me for dinner?"

Swill had never yet accepted an invitation from him, though he tried every day. But this time she seemed to have a change of heart. Maybe she noticed the lines of fatigue etching his face or the concern showing in his eyes, because her expression softened. When her face relaxed she became attractive, and Bendyk felt himself drawn to her like a moth to a flame. Theirs was supposed to be a business relationship, and yet he found himself curious about her personal life. His interest was acceptable: Missionaries were not expected to remain celibate. Indeed, mating was encouraged within the religious order—not that he had any intentions in that regard!

"Do you propose to eat in the dining commons?" she inquired.

Bendyk's eyebrows shot up in astonishment. She was actually considering his offer? "Er . . . no. I thought we might try a new café that's opened up in town. The chef specializes in roast game. It's a quiet place, and we can talk there undisturbed."

"Fine," she agreed.

All thoughts of work fled from Bendyk's mind when they were seated in the restaurant at a small table with a white cloth and a votive candle in a cobalt blue glass holder. The decor was provincial and cozy, with a fire lit in a stone fireplace to ward off the chill of the evening.

Taking a sip from his glass of white wine, Bendyk let his eyes feast on Swill. She wasn't taken to wearing feminine frills; her style of dress was simple, almost rebellious. But Bendyk was getting used to her ways and now found her viewpoint to be refreshing. She wore a burgundy blouse with a low scoop neckline and a long black skirt. Around her neck hung a string of beads. An inexpensive piece of jewelry, it provided a splash of color that complemented her healthy tanned complexion. In the muted candlelight her amber eyes glowed like polished topaz gemstones.

"Let's talk about you," he suggested. "It's a far more interesting topic than the Treasury records or Sirvat's background."

"Me?" Swill was startled. She didn't like to talk about herself and had hoped to continue their work discussion in more comfortable surroundings. But the atmosphere was intimate—moreso than she'd expected—and it discomfited her. Bendyk was a handsome man when his righteous airs didn't pucker his face and tighten his jaw. The way he was looking at her now made her limbs go slack, and a warm feeling settled into her stomach. A shock of blond hair fell across his forehead, contrasting with the deep blue of his eyes. He'd removed his cloak and sat facing her in a fawn-colored longshirt that did nothing to hide the wide set of his shoulders and his broad chest. She wondered what he did to stay in shape; so many of the priests she had known had grown flabby from years of indulgence. But Bendyk was young. He had his career ahead of him, and it struck her that he might be aiming for a position in the very Synod that they were investigating.

She'd resented the way he'd recruited her to this task, but after beginning work she had realized its importance. Bendyk and his sister had a weighty responsibility on their shoulders. She admired the way he bravely forged ahead, assuming the leadership role as though he were born to it.

"I'd rather learn more about you," she told him, hiding her shyness by taking a hasty swig of wine.

He smiled, an even, white flash of his teeth. "You don't like talking about yourself, do you? I've seen where you live. You've accomplished a lot with your life so far. Why did you take the job you did? Was it for the travel, or do you just like to help the villeins along on your tithing counts?"

Her eyes flashed indignantly; then she realized he was merely curious. "I like to help people who don't have the same advantages as others. But I also needed to change my environment. You met my parents. The atmosphere at home is stifling. This seemed like a golden opportunity to get away."

"But is this job what you're going to do forever?"

Her eyes narrowed and she glanced away, her long lashes like crescent moons against her cheeks. Bendyk noticed her hesitation.

"Well?" he urged, aware that she was reluctant to answer.

What dreams did she harbor? What hopes had she for a future life? Surely she didn't want to maintain this position. Suddenly her eyes met his, and moisture tipped her lashes.

"I want a family like I never had." Her voice was tremulous. She'd never confessed her dream to anyone before, but when Bendyk acted normal it was easy to talk to him. She was pleased by his interest; few men were attracted to her unorthodox style of dress and abrupt manner. So she shared her dream with Bendyk, hoping he wouldn't laugh at her. "I'd like a small house in a quiet neighborhood with several children running about and a man who makes enough of a living to support us. That's all I've ever hoped for. It's not very modern, is it?"

Bendyk was touched by her sad, wistful expression, the more so because she'd shared part of herself with him. He'd never expected someone with as abrasive a personality as she had to confess to wanting to be a housemate. This was a side of her that was totally unexpected, and Bendyk found himself warming to her even more.

"Is that so?" he said, his eyes radiating admiration. "Perchance we share the same ideals."

"What do you mean?" A flutter of hope swelled within her breast. "I would have thought you'd want to advance up the ladder of the clergy, perhaps to become a Docent or even a Candor like your father. Or maybe you have your eye on the Synod."

Bendyk cocked an eyebrow. "I always thought that was the route I'd take, at least after I entered the calling. Before that . . ." He let his words trail off, and his face closed in painful memory.

Swill reached her hand across the table, closing her palm over his. Bendyk gazed at her, taking strength from the warmth of her skin. He made tiny circular movements in the palm of her hand with his fingers.

"Before the accident I wasn't sure what I wanted to do with my life," he told her. "I was spoiled, having always gotten what I wanted. A particular ambition hadn't come to me then. If I hadn't been so rushed, I might not have driven that night, but . . .'' His voice faltered, and he couldn't go on. How could he tell her about the night that had changed his life, the night that Mama had died and he would have embraced death himself, if it hadn't been for Lothar's intervention. He'd pledged himself to Lothar for saving him, and now was following the vocation that allowed him to assuage his guilt. He downed the rest of his wine, awash in memories he'd rather forget . . . that horrible night, the snow falling outside, the drive on the dark, winding road, the steep hill and the icy surface. If only he'd let his mother drive instead. . . . A shudder racked his body, and he squeezed his eyes shut, blocking out the haunting images.

''Bendyk?'' Swill's voice roused him from his reverie.

''I don't want to talk about it.''

''I'd like to listen whenever you're ready.'' She changed the subject, aware that she'd stumbled onto a painful topic. The realization that she wanted to help him struck her with the full force of irony. Here Bendyk was, a missionary whose purpose in life was to help others. Yet she sensed that he had a need deep within himself for solace. Swill had never thought of herself as the nurturing type. She'd struggled too hard to meet her own goals to think often of others, except for the villeins she aided. She'd never allowed herself to become personally involved, fearing that any emotional entanglement could leave her too vulnerable. She'd had enough pain throughout her childhood, and she'd wanted to spare herself any further anguish.

But looking into Bendyk's world-weary face she felt a sudden urge to comfort him. It was a new feeling for her, almost like a new bud that had grown upon a bush and was about to burst into blossom. Did he have this effect on anyone else? she wondered, or is it only me? He truly did have the power to inspire and to change one's outlook. And such, she sensed, was only found in men destined for greatness.

* * *

"I hope Bendyk is being successful in his efforts," Leena told Taurin as they bounced along the trail, heading inland. "Hopefully we'll be able to confer with him once we finish this part of our mission. How do you propose we reach Grotus's island?" she asked again, worry nagging at her.

"I know a way. Trust me. I've brought along some of the supplies we'll need, and we can salvage the rest."

The lead vehicle turned west toward higher ground, the route punctuated by tall, leafy trees and a profusion of wildflowers whose perfumed scent weighed heavily in the air. Splashes of pink, orange, and orchid-colored blossoms lined the paved roadway. Taurin's eyes took them in appreciatively. He'd bet there were some exotic specimens here that would flourish in his gardens. Too bad he didn't have time to look around.

Leena settled back in her seat, enjoying the caress of the warm breeze on her skin. The rider jolted and bounced over the rocky road. A canopy of tree branches provided shade, and the air cooled slightly. After a while they stopped and had a drink from the cooler in the back of the missionaries' rider and a snack from the provisions Alber had supplied. Taurin wondered why the plantation owner had been so accommodating when he hadn't wanted them to reveal the Chocola Company's involvement in the Black Lands. Did he actually trust them not to speak of what they knew, or was there some other way Alber planned to silence them? He was surprised the man hadn't offered them a bribe, but that could have been expensive for all four of them. Taurin decided to be on the alert just in case.

His suspicions proved wise when, two days later, he and Leena and the missionaries found themselves abandoned on the trail. They were high up in the mountains, and their guide, having stopped the journey to take a break, suddenly vanished. The road didn't appear well-traveled, and Taurin deduced that their route had been chosen for nefarious purposes. He said as much to his companions.

"Native tribes are supposed to reside in the interior," he

warned them. "I'm not so sure we should have gone in this direction."

"I did think we were heading too far west," Leena commented, wrinkling her brow. Shivering in the cool mountain air, she folded her arms around herself, glad she'd donned the work shirt and breeches she'd brought along.

"Which road should we follow?" Sister Bertrice asked, pointing out the fork in the road ahead.

One branch led down the mountainside toward what Leena imagined was the valley they'd been advised to follow. The left-hand trail veered upward in slanting, dangerous curves. At least they'd filled up with fuel recently, so that wasn't a worry. But if they took the wrong trail, they'd risk running dry and would have to proceed on foot. With dismay, she glanced at her two suitcases, resting in the rear of their vehicle, realizing how ludicrous it was to have brought so much luggage. One of the suitcases held a backpack with her archaeological supplies. She could stuff a few outfits in there and just use that if necessary.

"We'll take the road heading down," Taurin decided, indicating that the others should board their vehicle. "If the river's there, we'll know we're on the right track."

"I'll send a prayer to Lothar that he may guide us," Brother Aron shouted.

Taurin rolled his eyes. "Do as you wish. Maybe it'll help."

Slowly they started down the decline, a thick wood on either side obstructing the view. The hill rounded out into a flat run. They were halfway along when the woods seemed to move straight into their path. Coming to a screeching halt directly behind the lead vehicle, Taurin and Leena gasped in astonishment, while the missionaries in the forward vehicle turned and waved their hands frantically.

Facing them were scores of natives, their brown bodies plastered with a covering of leaves. Their headdresses contained several antlerlike twigs along with colorful feathers. Streaks of paint adorned their cheeks and foreheads. The warriors glowered at the unexpected visitors—or *were* they unexpected?

"He knew we'd go down this road," Taurin mumbled. "Ives knew these people were here and would stop us. He led us into a trap."

Leena's eyes rounded in fear. "He's obviously following Alber's orders. Do you think many visitors to Alber's plantation disappear this way?" Looking at the warriors surrounding them, primitive spears pointing in their direction, she shuddered.

A fierce-looking warrior stepped forward and nudged Taurin with his spear, indicating that he should get out of the vehicle. He did what he was told, realizing it was useless to resist when they were so outnumbered. He motioned for the others to copy his action. Talking amongst themselves, a group of natives began ransacking their supplies, while Taurin and the others were herded away at spearpoint.

Her heart hammering in fear, Leena stumbled over the dry roots and rocks underfoot as they were forced to march through the woods. The scent of rich, earthy humus mingled with the aroma of evergreens, but she was too frightened to care about her surroundings. Could these natives speak Xanese, the standard language? And if not, how would they communicate? Their dialect was incomprehensible to her.

"Can you understand them?" she whispered to Taurin, who strode beside her. Whenever they had to cross a particularly difficult stretch of territory he held her elbow to assist her. She was grateful for the comfort of his presence and wondered if they'd have any chance for escape.

"I have no idea what they're saying," Taurin replied, his face grim.

They seemed to walk for hours. By the time they reached the encampment dusk was falling, and Leena was nearly sobbing with exhaustion. She felt ill from hunger and thirst, though they'd been given drinks of water along the way, and her muscles ached from exertion. Feeling like a zombie, she obeyed without question when they were directed to enter a small round hut built of mud bricks with a thatched roof. There was one slitted window for ventilation, but it was high up and didn't provide much light when the door was shut and sealed. Enclosed by darkness, despair overwhelmed her, and she sank to the ground, covering her face with her hands.

Taurin took out his cloth and quickly swathed it about his head so his eyes would be screened. His hearing picked up a conversation outside the thick walls of the hut, but he didn't understand the language and couldn't make out what was said. They're probably deciding what to do with us, he thought ruefully. The situation didn't look good. If necessary, he'd use the blaster secreted on his person. Magar had forbidden him to bring any objects of violence when he'd offered Taurin sanctuary, but being used to fending for himself, Taurin had slipped in the weapon unnoticed. He'd kept it locked in a cabinet in his house, but this mission had necessitated its removal. As Leena's protector, he deemed it his job to give them every advantage, and Taurin admitted that it gave him a measure of reassurance to feel the weapon strapped under his pants' leg against his calf.

The air outside had grown quite chilly by the time they'd reached the encampment, but the inside of the hut seemed warm. Peering around, Taurin noticed a grating in a far corner from which steam arose.

"Look at that," he said to the others. "Where do you suppose these people found a source of heat?"

Leena raised her head. "There could be a hot spring nearby that they tap via a series of conduits to their huts. It would mean they're more intelligent than we thought."

"We'll have to see what happens next before formulating a plan for escape." Taurin strode to Leena's side and lowered himself to a spot beside her. A covering of hay provided soft cushioning over the cold dirt floor.

Brother Aron stood firmly in the center of the hut, peering at them. It was difficult to read his expression in the gloom. "We must pray for deliverance," he said, folding his hands in front of his robe.

"You do what you want," Taurin muttered, putting an arm around Leena's shoulder and drawing her close. If they were to stay here for the night, he needed the comfort of her body. Apparently she appreciated his gesture; she snuggled closer, giving a soft sigh of pleasure. His arm tightened around her involuntarily. He'd get them out of this, one way or another.

The first rays of sunlight piercing the room brought Taurin to full wakefulness. The air was cool and crisp, and he realized the steam had been turned off for the night. Leena was still asleep, leaning against his shoulder. Her golden tresses streamed over her bosom. Her sweet, womanly scent and the quiet sounds of her breathing made him wish they were alone, but the missionary couple snoozed across from them in the tiny hut.

Gently he roused her, unable to keep his lips from brushing hers in a tender good morning kiss. She smiled up at him, her eyes dewy. Glancing at the missionaries to make sure they were still asleep, he pressed his mouth to hers with greater urgency. She responded eagerly, moving her body so that she molded into his body's angles. He held her closer, his need escalating, the desperation of their situation driving him to seek the oldest comfort known to mankind.

His mouth slanted over hers again and again as he sought solace in her sweetness. When her hands roamed his broad back he moaned with pleasure before thrusting his tongue into her mouth. She took it greedily, playing with him, her own need evident in the tautness of her nipples against his chest that he could feel through the fabric of her blouse. By the stars, he'd like to take her right here and now, regardless of who was watching!

A loud throat clearing told him that someone else was awake. Releasing her reluctantly, he glanced across the hut's interior, his eyes meeting Sister Bertrice's disapproving frown.

Footsteps approached from outside, and the door was flung

open. A bright stream of sunlight poured inside the hut. Brother Aron awoke noisily, muttering a prayer. A native woman who was too afraid to look into their faces brought them a simple meal of gruel and water.

As they ate, Leena surreptitiously studied Taurin. He'd removed the cloth from his head and looked magnificently handsome with his thick ebony hair and clear gray eyes. She'd awakened once during the night and had glanced up at him. She thought she'd seen a faint glow coming from the front of his face, but because his head was swathed in the cloth she couldn't be sure. This morning, when he woke her with a kiss, there was enough light in the hut for her to see him clearly. Her mouth still burned from his kiss, and the pleasure of it brought a hot flush to her face. She'd been disappointed when he drew away, but they couldn't very well continue with Sister Bertrice looking on.

Flinching from the brightness, she followed the others outside as they were led to an outhouse. Then they were prodded, again at spearpoint, to follow a troop of native tribesmen clothed in furs and shell necklaces, their faces streaked with paint. Huts similar to theirs dotted the hillside. She noted that they'd come quite a distance the day before. The elevation made her breath come short, and her exhalations were steamy from the cold. They were led along a wooded trail into a shady grotto bordered by crumbling stone pillars and other structures familiar to Leena.

"By the grace of Lothar!" she exclaimed. "It's a ruin." Her eyes glanced excitedly at Taurin, who strode beside her, a look of nonchalance on his face.

Her heart thumping wildly from the discovery, Leena's fear evaporated in her excitement. She wished they could explore, but they were driven in front of a flat, rectangular stone, which had the ominous appearance of an altar. Forced to kneel in front of it, she gazed in dread at the ornately feathered tribesman who stood facing them. The tribal leader's features were fierce, his movements menacing as he raised his staff above their heads and muttered incantations

144

in a strange language. Circling tribespeople chanted and swayed rhythmically, their voices rising into a shrill crescendo. A stone pillar stood behind the altar. Behind it, Leena caught sight of a lazy stream, and her ears picked up the sound of gurgling water intermingled with a strange sucking noise. When the rising sun reached the top of the column a ray pierced forth with sparkling radiance, and she noticed what hadn't been visible before—a round, faceted crystal embedded inside the stone column. In the direct light of a sunbeam the crystal began to glow, and the sound of the stream changed from a happy bubbling to a hissing boil.

"Holy waters!" she exclaimed, startled.

"The crystal appears to provide some kind of energy," Taurin remarked.

Brother Aron, who stood slightly off to the side, pointed. "The water is divided. Part of it siphons off below."

"I'll bet this is the source of their heating system," Leena said, glancing at Taurin. His expression was harsh in the dappled light penetrating the grotto, the angles of his face gaunt. Dark stubble covered his jaw, and circles shadowed his eyes. Having had the presence of mind only to notice his sensual attractiveness after he'd kissed her awake, she hadn't realized how tired and worried he was.

The tribal leader muttered at them angrily, and a thrust of spears indicated that they were to remain silent. Pointing at Sister Bertrice, he shouted instructions to several of his followers. They advanced upon her and, ignoring her screams, seized her by the arms and dragged her to the altar, where they forced her onto her back. The tribal leader withdrew a long curved dagger from his belt and held it above the shrieking missionary while the tribesmen restrained her.

"Dear deity! They're going to sacrifice her!" Leena cried.

"Not if I can help it." Taurin realized the time had come to play his hand. In another instant he would have retrieved his weapon, but a cloud drifted across the sun, thrusting the grotto into near darkness. Purposefully, he gazed at the tribal leader, whose eyes widened as the true nature of Taurin's vision was revealed to him. The dagger dropped from his hand onto the stone ledge at the floor of the altar. With a shriek of terror he turned on his heels and fled. The tribesmen, following his example, dropped their spears and wheeled away, as though pursued by demons of the underworld.

The cloud broke, and as the sun brightened the sky, Leena stared at Taurin in puzzlement. "What happened?"

Sister Bertrice sat up and rubbed her arms, a dazed look on her face. Leena hastened forward to assist her off the sacrificial altar.

"Something frightened them away," Taurin said mildly.

"They were looking at you."

He shrugged, unwilling to offer an explanation. "We don't have time to analyze their rationale. I suggest we get away from here."

"Correction!" called Brother Aron, who'd been standing behind the rest of them. "Sister Bertrice and I will escape. You and your lady will be viewed as unfortunate sacrifices to the native tribes. You shouldn't have wandered so high into the mountains."

Taurin spun around to find Brother Aron pointing a blaster at his chest. "Where did you get that?" he said, his voice dangerously quiet.

"Never mind. If you believe in a god, I suggest you pray to him now. And you, madam"—he nodded toward Leena—"may request Lothar to receive you."

"Receive me! What do you mean?" Stunned, Leena watched Sister Bertrice take a stance by Brother Aron's side, an evil sneer on her face. Surely the two didn't mean to kill them and leave them here? "Why are you doing this?" she cried.

Brother Aron smirked. "I have friends in high places who don't want you to succeed on your quest. My instructions were to intercept you and see that you met a fatal end. So be it." He raised his weapon.

"Who sent you?" Taurin asked. "Surely you can tell us if we're about to die."

"Wodeners don't betray their friends. Prepare to meet your maker."

As his finger reached for the trigger, Taurin threw himself into a flying leap that landed him a kick at Brother Aron's knee. Knocked off balance, Brother Aron's shot went wild. A beam of red light sizzled through the air as he toppled backward. Taurin sprawled atop him, and the two rolled in the dust, each struggling for control. From the corner of his eye Taurin saw Sister Bertrice's skirts flying past.

"Stop her!" he shouted to Leena.

Leena charged after the woman, gasping when Sister Bertrice whirled around, clutching a knife in her hand. She pounced at Leena, grabbing her by the hair and thrusting the blade at her throat.

Taking in the situation at a glance, Taurin's face paled. "Don't harm her," he warned, his eyes glittering dangerously as his hand scrabbled in the dirt to pick up a hefty rock.

Sister Bertrice spared a glance at her downed companion. "Stay where you are or I'll kill her."

Leena held herself immobile, afraid the dirk at her throat would pierce her flesh if she moved. "Lothar, help us," she prayed silently.

Shouts from the village drew her assailant's attention, and that was when Taurin made his move. He raised his hand, and a rock hurtled through the air, striking Sister Bertrice clear between the eyes.

"Come on! Let's get out of here," he hollered to Leena.

Hesitating, she glanced at the missonaries, who lay prone on the ground. "What about them?"

Taurin gave her a glowering look. "I suspect they were with the Truthsayer movement. Let's go; we don't have time to linger."

Casting aside her regrets, Leena followed him into the

woods. They skirted the village until Taurin called for a halt beside a thicket of tall shrubs.

"Wait here. I'll see if I can recover any of our gear."

Before she could protest, he disappeared behind a stand of low-branched, leafy trees. Leena waited anxiously, biting her lip and reflecting on their close call with the missionaries—if they were, indeed, members of the clergy. It was likely they'd assumed the disguise to put themselves above suspicion.

Taurin loped into view, carrying their sacks and a couple of unfamiliar items. Cautious to avoid attention from the tribesmen, they didn't speak as they descended the hill in search of their abandoned riders.

When they did find them Taurin was dismayed that the lead vehicle had been completely dismantled by the curious natives. The one he and Leena had used was still intact. A heap of parts on the ground attracted Taurin, and he threw several items into the backseat of their rider, along with the things he'd already salvaged.

"Get in!" he yelled, jumping into the driver's seat.

Soon they were rattling downhill at a rapid pace, neither one daring to look behind to see if they were being pursued. Their only thought was to get far enough away before darkness fell.

"We've got to avoid Alber's men," Leena shouted over the engine noise and the bouncing gyrations of the vehicle.

"They won't be looking for us. Ives probably went back and told Alber we'd been conveniently lost."

Seeing the fear reflected in her face, Taurin motioned her closer. She snuggled against him, grateful for his warmth and strength. They drove for hours, each immersed in their own thoughts. Eventually she succumbed to exhaustion and fell asleep, awakening when they finally reached the valley below.

Along the banks of a stream, Taurin stopped for a break. Wild berries and trees laden with fruit provided a meal. They happily picked their fill of nature's bounty and quenched their thirst with cool, fresh water from the stream.

"Tomorrow we'll make a break for Grotus's island," Taurin said. "We need to find shelter for tonight. It's getting late, and I'd like to secure our rider in a location where we won't be noticed. Let's move on."

Leena obligingly climbed back into the rider.

He followed a paved road that twisted in and out of various settlements, whizzing through so quickly they couldn't be identified. Coming to an offshoot, he drove up a wooded hillside to a plateau, parking at the edge of a flower-strewn meadow that appealed to the gardener in him.

"These wildflowers grow in such profusion," he remarked, stretching his legs and breathing in the crisp air as dusk encroached upon the land. "I wonder why Lothar's beneficence extends here and yet plagues our land with drought. The people who live on this island don't follow the Faith. They were banished here because they're dissenters. If you ask me, I don't think Lothar is playing fair."

Leena glared at him, hands on her hips. "I thought you didn't believe in Lothar."

"Maybe you're convincing me there's something to believe in." Taurin glanced at the golden wisps of hair being blown about her face by the cool breeze. At one of their stops she'd changed behind a clump of bushes into a ruby-red gown, the velvety fabric keeping her warm against the cooler temperatures that prevailed on this side of the island.

Seeing the admiring gleam in Taurin's eye, Leena's limbs trembled. Fearing she would say or do something wrong, she turned away, walking aimlessly across the meadow. Her feet stumbled over a solid object. Stooping to get a closer look, she saw it was a piece of rock. Dear deity! This was from the same type of carved stone block she'd seen at other ruins.

"Taurin, look at this!" she cried, scrabbling in the grass until she found a similar stone. Familiar symbols were etched onto both pieces, although it was difficult to make them out after years of wind and rain had smoothed them nearly clean. Requesting that Taurin bring her the sack with her archaeological supplies, she tried to brush away the grime with her delicate tools.

"The Black Lands must be dotted with ruins," she concluded, sitting back on her haunches to gaze up at him. He stood by patiently, waiting for her to finish her examination, the breeze ruffling his hair about his head. She thought he'd never looked more magnificent than now, with the setting sun emitting a tangerine glow behind him. With his dark clothes, broad-shouldered figure, and menacing aura, one might fancy he came from the demon world—except that his expression was one of tenderness as he watched her, and it melted her heart.

"How curious that the Synod has never mentioned these finds," she murmured, ignoring the wave of warmth that seduced her senses under his scrutiny.

"It is forbidden for outsiders to come here," Taurin reminded her, his voice gruff. "These ruins must not be important enough to be studied."

"What about the crystal used by those natives in the mountains, the ones who captured us? I wish we could have examined it. The crystal may have provided a source of power for the steam heat."

"It's too late for that now. Let's make camp."

Instructing her to choose a likely spot, Taurin strode to the rider, where he obtained a large bundle of cloth he'd apparently stolen from the villagers. Spreading it on the ground among the wildflowers, he sat with Leena while they watched the sun descend in a brilliant display of colors. A perfumed scent pervaded the air as the sky darkened.

"This island is lovely," Leena commented, trying to ignore the effect his proximity was having on her. Every fiber of her being was aware of his nearness, his masculine strength. "I don't see why they call it the Black Lands."

"Perhaps it is because of the evil in the hearts of the men who are sent here." He paused. "Or is it the evil intentions of the ones who send them? I'm not sure who is in the right or wrong anymore."

Startled, she glanced at him. The thunderous expression on his face made her swallow hard. She hoped he wasn't right—that the Synod wasn't to be feared for their treachery to the people. And yet some member had stolen the horn and, in so doing, threatened their chances for survival. The horn had to be restored in order to maintain the balance of their society, not to mention stabilizing the weather situation and providing the lozenge.

Already they'd learned someone in the hierarchy had permitted the Chocola Company to harvest beans on this island. That person was profiting from the misery of the inhabitants. Raking stiff fingers through her hair, Leena wished she could contact Bendyk, but that would have to wait. On the morrow they'd make for Grotus's island, and who knew what revealing discoveries awaited them there?

In the meantime she had to spend the night here with Taurin. It was growing cold, and she was aware of his eyes on her, his silent inquiry. By all that was holy, how could she rid herself of this restless urge she had in his presence? It destroyed her peace of mind, knowing he was so near. Daring to look at him, she gasped to find his gaze locked on her mouth. Slowly her eyes raised to meet his smoldering gaze.

Chapter Nine

Taurin struggled to fight his attraction to Leena. The glow from the sky was backlit against her hair, making her seem as if she were lit with an ethereal aura. His gaze fixed on her mouth, her pink lips soft and full, and he longed to sweep her into his arms and lie with her upon the bed of flowers, making love. But the intensity of the lust raging in his veins frightened him, and he didn't want to start something he couldn't finish. One kiss wouldn't be enough, but he dared not risk hurting her with the violence of his nature. Afraid that he would lose control if he touched her, he swathed his head in the usual black cloth and settled onto his side.

"We need to get an early start in the morning," he said, his tone gruffer than he'd intended. He wanted her so badly that he couldn't keep the rough edge from his voice. "Get some sleep."

Leena couldn't help feeling disappointed. For a brief moment she'd thought he was going to kiss her, but then he'd abruptly stretched out, turning away from her. Yearning for his attention, she laid down her head on the rumpled shawl she had fashioned into a pillow and squirmed restlessly. Every inch of her was aware of Taurin lying beside her, his head shrouded. Piqued that he wouldn't remove the cloth and share his reasons for wearing it, she tried to imagine what he might be hiding but quickly gave up the conjecture as a useless exercise.

As the air cooled, the warmth from his body seemed to mingle with hers, keeping her from getting too cold. Or was it her blood, which coursed through her so hotly at his nearness, that made her feel so warm? How could she want him when he was so unlike anyone she'd ever known? Why wasn't it Malcolm's image that sprang into her mind when she closed her eyes, instead of Taurin's menacing figure? Malcolm represented security and familiarity, and she'd thought that was what she sought in life. Now she doubted that Malcolm could ever rouse her passions. She was fond of him, but as a close friend. Being bonded to someone like Taurin would be infinitely more exciting. I am wed to him, she reminded herself. Lothar save me, but I'm beginning to wish he would treat me as his wife.

As soon as the thought entered her head, she chastised herself. *Shame on you!* You're nearly pledged to Malcolm. Would you dishonor your family by taking such a man as this to bed? The marriage is in name only. It will soon be annulled. And despite the freedoms allowed in their society, she knew Malcolm would expect her to be faithful.

Yet as Taurin shifted his position, his buttocks inadvertently bumping against hers, Leena couldn't help the small gasp that escaped her lips. Every bone in her body stiffened, and she held herself rigid while he regained a position of comfort. His breathing sounded ragged, as though his rest were troubled, but she didn't dare move lest she betray her desire. He must never know how much she craved his touch and yearned to feel the pressure of his mouth on hers. After a long while she drifted into an uncomfortable sleep.

Some time during the night Taurin awakened to find her legs entwined with his, one arm thrown against his chest. As he shifted his position, she murmured unintelligibly. He agonized with each contact between them and slept very little, savoring the silken feel of her hair against his arm and the luscious warmth of her body. Overhead, a myriad of stars glittered in the night sky, and cool air swept across the meadow. Taurin wasn't cold. He desired Leena until the flames of lust consumed him, heating his blood to a raging torrent. He kept telling himself she was forbidden fruit. He couldn't have her, and it broke his heart that while she was wed to him, she was nearly promised to another. Perhaps Malcolm would reject her, and she would seek him out for solace, he thought hopefully.

But Taurin quickly discarded that notion as being absurd. Why should Leena ever come to him again? Once she was back at the Palisades she'd resume her former life, and her position did not include associating with people like him. Casting off his daydreams as being a waste of time, Taurin tucked his elbow under his head and closed his eyes. But he heard the soft sounds of her breathing and smelled the sweet, feminine fragrance that was hers alone. Sleep wouldn't come to him this night. It was his fate to live in isolation, he told himself. He'd have to isolate his emotions as well, in order to preserve his sanity.

Leena awoke to a fresh dawn, scented with the fragrance of wildflowers. With her eyes still closed she reached out to touch Taurin, seeking reassurance from his presence, but her fingers met empty air. Her eyelids snapped open and she peered at the rumpled blanket beside her. He was gone.

Frightened, she bolted upright, giving a cry of relief when she spotted him across the meadow, bending beside their rider. Standing, she stretched, shaking out her stiff joints. Then she trotted toward him. His black shirt tucked into a pair of snug matching trousers and his booted feet were a dark contrast to the brilliant flowers surrounding them.

"What are you doing?" she asked as she sauntered near. Taurin appeared to be assembling a piece of machinery.

His face brightened when he saw her, but he quickly assumed a dispassionate expression. "I am constructing our means of transportation to Grotus's island," he said, his rich voice an early morning balm for her ears.

Leena recognized a fan motor that he must have salvaged from the other rider, but it appeared as though he had a piece of sail as well.

"I got this on the ship," he confirmed, pointing to the canvas. "Here. You can help me spread it out."

He'd attached various ropes to different edges of the sail material, and she helped him spread the fabric over the dewy grass.

"What in the world have you done?" She noticed that he'd removed the seats from the rider, and the ropes were attached to the seating platform.

"You'll see. The weather is perfect. It's cool, and there's a slight breeze. According to what I've read, morning is the best time for flying these."

"According to what you've read? What on Xan are you building?"

"A hot-air balloon. It's the only means I could think of to reach Grotus's island. We can't get a boat to take us there, and the higher air currents are too turbulent for commercial flight. We should be able to make it if we remain at a low altitude."

Leena's eyes flashed at him. "But we don't even know where his island is located. There could be thousands of them in the archipelago."

"Have faith, madam. Lothar will guide us." He gave her a sardonic grin.

Leena's fists clenched in fury. "You mock me, sir."

Taurin's eyes softened as he regarded her. The fiery display of her golden hair tumbling over her shoulders and the brilliance of her blazing blue eyes made him instantly contrite that he had taunted her.

"I'm sorry. Perhaps we should say morning prayers together this morning. If there is any divine help available, we could use it.''

Leena gazed at him in astonishment. Had she heard him correctly? He had just agreed to say morning prayers with her? Taking advantage of the moment, she bowed her head and began her litany.

"Praise be to Lothar for all our blessings—for life, for work and rest, for home and love and friendship. May we continue to be worthy of your generosity, dear lord. As this new day dawns, we awake renewed and refreshed, inspired by your love for us and your graciousness. May our day be filled with beauty, goodness, and truth as we follow in the path of your righteousness. Mahala.''

"Mahala,'' Taurin murmured, then caught himself. Demon's blood! If he wasn't careful, he'd end up praying on every occasion as she did and would accomplish nothing. No, that wasn't quite true, he told himself as he resumed the task he'd set for himself. Leena was a qualified archaeologist. Her faith was part of her, but it didn't stand in the way of her goals, nor did it inhibit her personal growth. If anything, it gave her strength and the courage to carry on despite formidable odds. He admired her devotion but could never see himself in a similar position. *I wonder if she'll ever give herself as willingly to a man as she does to her god,* he thought. Malcolm might find out, but he sure wouldn't.

Taking a couple of cans from a heavy burlap sack, he rummaged around in the bag and then cursed.

"What is it?'' Leena queried, feeling the stirrings of hunger in her belly.

"These are chemical granules normally used in mixtures for fertilizer,'' Taurin explained, his brow furrowing in annoyance. "I forgot to bring something as simple as a can opener. I have tools that I found in the back of the rider, but they won't serve the purpose.''

"I brought along my archaeological equipment. There's got to be something you can use,'' she offered, hastening back to the blanket, where she'd left her gear.

A few minutes later Taurin was searching through a box containing short-handled shovels, hoes, cutting shears, a small ax, a knife, string, variously shaped trowels, tweezers, paint brushes, and assorted report forms. He chose an unfamiliar sharp-edged instrument and hacked away at the top of the can until the space was big enough for him to pour out the chemical.

"This is not the way these compounds are generally mixed," he explained as he poured them together. "Combined in this manner, they make a volatile substance that will serve our purpose well."

After they gathered their belongings and ate a quick meal of fruit and water Taurin was ready to cast off. He fired up his makeshift burners and started pumping hot air into the expanding envelope of the sailing fabric.

"What if the fabric catches fire?" Leena asked, feeling a tremor of apprehension.

"If direct heat touches it, the fabric might melt, but the melting won't spread. It can't burn," he told her.

Obeying his order, she stepped into the seating arrangement. She couldn't help hanging her arm over the side since the space was cramped. The fabric ballooned upward. Taurin joined her on the platform and tossed off the tether lines. Their makeshift balloon began to rise. The meadow below got smaller and smaller as their height increased. Leena clutched at the side of her seat as the platform swayed back and forth. She wanted to shut her eyes in terror but forced them open to observe the view.

"We'll head west," Taurin shouted over the roar of the burners. He yanked on the blast lever to send another shot of hot air up into the envelope.

Leena turned her face away from the searing heat of the blowers. Since talking was so difficult over the roaring noise, she concentrated on quelling her panic instead. Periodically Taurin used shots of the burners to lift the balloon or maintain a steady altitude as the air cooled inside the envelope. By pulling on lines connected to the vents high in the fabric, he could release air on either side of their craft. This would rotate their direction so that their voyage became a feat of juggling between heating and venting.

As they rose toward the sky, Leena glanced around in amazement, forgetting her momentary fear in the magnificence of the view. The volcanic origin of the Black Lands soon became evident. As they floated by the mountain ridge to the north, a white plume of smoke could be seen coming from a still-active vent. Taurin steered clear of the higher mountains. Lush greenery covered most of the island except for the west coast, where lava flows had reduced the land to a black, rocky void.

"So this is why it's called the Black Lands," she exclaimed in awe, leaning forward. Her motion rocked the platform and she jerked back, frightened.

"Don't move too fast," Taurin cautioned her, pulling on one of the side vents to steady their course.

Beyond the blackened shoreline was a stretch of sea that shimmered in reflection from the rising sun. Leena shaded her eyes as she peered toward the archipelago in the distance. She could barely make out the series of islands dotting the water, but they loomed larger as their craft approached. Terrified that they'd fall into the water if a gust of wind caught them the wrong way, she sat rigidly in her seat.

Taurin appeared fully in control of the vessel, however, and he took a pair of viewfinder glasses from the sack at his feet. Clamping the strap around his head, he gazed out to sea through the magnifying lenses. It wasn't until they had passed over the first of the islands that Taurin pointed excitedly.

"Over there!" he shouted.

Leena barely heard him over the roar of the blowers, but the animated expression on his face was self-explanatory. She rose in her seat to glance over the side. Taurin was jiggling a finger excitedly, yelling something at her. Sure enough, she could make out a spot of color on one of the islands below. No doubt Taurin could see more clearly through his special glasses. He was waving at her, but she didn't understand what he was saying until he yanked on one of the cords and the platform shifted. She fell back into her seat and remained there, her knuckles white as she clutched her armrests. They'd begun their descent, and her stomach lurched as Taurin vented the hot air through the top of the balloon. Their rate of descent increased rapidly. If that is Grotus's hideaway, Leena thought, Taurin is planning to put us down right smack in the middle of it. She glanced at him questioningly, but his mouth was set in a grim line, and his shoulders were hunched as though he were deep in concentration.

Scanning the island below, Leena noted that it consisted of two mountainous humps. In the valley between them sat a palatial structure with manicured lawns and formal gardens. Surrounding the estate was a natural forest with pools, springs, and streams. An approach road ran along the ravine.

They continued to lurch downward. At Taurin's suggestion, Leena had stuffed her most essential belongings into her backpack, along with whatever archaeological supplies she wished to retain. Upon his signal, she slung the pack over her shoulders. Taurin did the same with his, after removing the viewfinder glasses and replacing them in his kit.

As they veered in on their final approach, Leena's eyes widened. The exterior of the four-story mansion consisted of fitted limestone and elaborate woodwork. Winding gravel paths were bordered by lush shrubs, cultivated flower beds, and fine specimens of cutleaf maples.

Their imminent arrival had been detected, and armed guards were rushing out onto the lawns. As they briefly touched down, Taurin urged Leena to jump. She landed on a soft bed of grass and heard Taurin's thud beside her just before the balloon lifted off and drifted far into the sky.

Brushing off her clothes, she stood and watched with concern as a bevy of guards surrounded them, weapons drawn. The guards wore nondescript clothing, but the hard look about their eyes told her they knew what they were doing.

The armaments were foreign-looking devices with long barrels.

"Who are you? Why have you come here?" a flat-faced individual spat out.

"I'm Leena Worthington-Jax, representing the Synod," Leena replied, her heart palpitating with fear. "It is imperative we speak to Grotus. Our business is urgent."

The leader of the guards looked Taurin over from head to toe. "And who are you?"

"I'm her escort." His tone implied they'd be well advised to regard him with respect.

A heavy silence followed; then the man said, "Follow me."

Leena's apprehension vanished, replaced by a sense of triumph. News of the horn could be forthcoming, she thought excitedly. Muttering a prayer that their talk with Grotus would be fruitful, she strode ahead, chin uplifted with pride.

Bendyk and Swill finally found a moment to confer together in their office. They were seated at separate desks but could see each other easily from their upholstered swivel chairs.

"One of Sirvat's neighbors said she likes to travel," Bendyk told Swill, proud of the information he'd gleaned. "Sirvat always returns in a jovial mood, wearing a new piece of jewelry. Apparently, the trinkets she brings back are unlike the usual gold pieces people wear. The neighbor said they're embedded with polished gemstones that must cost a fortune. Sirvat's predilection for fancy jewelry isn't generally known because she doesn't wear the pieces while on duty, but the neighbor told me she has quite a collection."

"Is it possible she meets a male admirer?" Swill asked, twirling a strand of hair around her little finger.

"It is likely," responded Bendyk, glancing at the simple sheath dress Swill wore.

The rust color brought out the golden sparkle of her eyes, and briefly Bendyk wondered how she would look with a gold choker around her neck. She wasn't one to adorn herself with jewels, but Bendyk had a sudden urge to present her with a gift.

"You said there was a miscellaneous entry being made in the treasury records every month?"

"That's right," Swill said. "When I pressed her, Sirvat admitted that Magar was responsible for the entry. She said his department receives the incoming funds and we should ask him about it. She wasn't sure what the receipts represented."

"So basically what we have on Sirvat is that the treasury records check out except for that one entry about which we have to question Magar. Her personal finances are in order, correct?"

Swill nodded. "This matter of her traveling and coming home bedecked with jewels bothers me. That's very unlike the woman, at least according to the image she presents."

Bendyk lapsed into a thoughtful silence. "I propose we assign a couple of Caucus members to tail her. It wouldn't hurt to find out where she goes the next time she takes off on one of these trips."

"That's a good idea."

Swill smiled at him, and Bendyk's heart somersaulted with joy. He didn't understand why earning her admiration was so important to him, but somewhere along the way she'd become more than a business partner. At least he wanted to regard her in a different fashion if she'd let him. The woman fascinated him, and he found he couldn't get enough of her company.

"What about Magar?" Swill asked, gazing at him innocently.

Bendyk struggled to focus his thoughts on the task instead of on the attractive woman facing him. "I have an interview scheduled with him in the next half hour. Would you like to come?"

"Sure, if you don't think it would upset him to confront both of us. Would you like to join me for dinner afterward?"

Bendyk gaped at her, too astonished to respond. Since their last dinner together their relationship had been fairly formal, their conversations confined to the topic at hand. Although he'd been hoping for more, he hadn't really thought Swill was interested.

"I'd love to," he told her, beaming. "Thank you." Rising, he donned a gold-lined cloak over his longshirt and trousers so that he would appear more impressive when they saw the Minister of State.

Magar was waiting for him in his spacious office. His eyes widened when he saw Swill accompanying Bendyk, but he quickly recovered his composure.

"Brother Bendyk, Sister Swill. Please, be seated. What can I do for you?"

Bendyk got right to the point. "You sent my sister off with Taurin Rey Niris. How do you know the man? Where is he from?" This matter was more important to him than the inquiry involving the treasury entry. He'd get to that subject shortly; Leena's safety was his prime concern for the moment.

Magar leaned back in his chair, a sly smile twisting the corners of his mouth. "I met him during a diplomatic exchange. He wanted to relocate, so I said I'd help him."

"Why?"

Magar shrugged. "We can always use farmers here, and he said he grew edible flowers. We don't have many such growers in these parts. So I obtained permission from the Population Council for him to immigrate."

"How did he end up on a piece of your property?"

"The man didn't know anyone here. I offered to sell him a plot."

"Did he pay you in cash, or is he paying you back year by year in money or produce?"

"We made a trade." Magar's eyes skittered away, and he shifted uncomfortably in his chair.

"A trade? What sort of trade?" Bendyk was getting impatient; he sensed that Magar was evading his questions.

"Let's say we each had something the other wanted," Magar concluded.

"You told us the man was from Iman. I checked the census; there's no such person listed from Iman."

Magar's complexion grew a shade paler. "Is that so? That's just what the man told me. I didn't know any different."

"Indeed?" Bendyk raised his eyebrows, glancing at Swill. "How did you know he could protect Leena? Where did he gain his fighting skill?"

Magar's lips pinched tight. "He will take care of her," he said quietly. "You have my assurance on that."

"Why is he interested in archaeological symbols?"

"It is an interest of his."

"You said you met him at a diplomatic exchange?" Swill intervened, hunching forward. "Who were the parties present?"

Magar simply stared at her, remaining silent.

"We found a regular entry in the treasury records," she went on. "Sirvat said your department is responsible for the revenue. How do you explain the source?"

Magar reached for a pen, and Bendyk noticed that his hands were trembling. "It's a convenient category for any extra funds that overflow our receipts."

"We'll need to examine the transactions of your department for the past few years and any trade agreements that have been documented," Bendyk said.

"I don't see why that's necessary," Magar snapped. His tremors increased, and he dropped the pen. "And now I'm afraid I must call an end to this interview." He stood up, and the look in his eyes reminded Bendyk of a frightened *dier* running before a hunter. "Besides, you're wasting your time with me. You should be looking for the one who stole the horn."

"And who do you suggest we investigate?" Swill asked sweetly.

"Try Karayan. The man's too ambitious for his own good.

I'd watch out for him if I were you.''

Karayan? My father's friend is the last one I would suspect, Bendyk thought as he and Swill left Magar's office. Magar is just trying to throw suspicion off himself.

"I believe Magar is purposefully withholding information," he said to Swill as they walked back to their office.

"Why don't we enlist some of the Caucus aides to delve into his trade agreements for the past few years?" she suggested. "Perhaps we'll find the source of revenue that way. We could also obtain a record of Magar's movements."

Bendyk regarded her, his blue eyes thoughtful. "I'd like to find out how he met Rey Niris. There's something going on between those two that Magar is unwilling to discuss."

Swill twisted her arm through his. "Let's have dinner and continue this investigation in the morning, shall we?"

Bendyk was startled by her familiar gesture. "Of course. Where would you like to go?"

"I'll fix something in my apartment."

His ears perked up. Her apartment! Briefly he considered refusing; he wasn't sure he could behave with the proper decorum in such an intimate setting. Swill was a temptation he was finding increasingly difficult to resist. Wondering what she had in mind, his imagination soared with different possibilities, most of them erotic. A thrill of anticipation shot though him at the idea of spending the evening alone with her, regardless of the outcome.

Sister, he said to himself, mentally addressing Leena, I hope Rey Niris doesn't hold the same attraction for you, or you'll be in even greater danger than that posed by our enemies. Take care, he warned her in spirit.

Drawing Swill closer, he veered down the corridor that led to the private residential suites.

"Nice flowers," Taurin muttered as their captors took them between sculpted garden paths and up to the front portico of Grotus's mansion.

Leena rolled her eyes. Leave it to him to comment on the

gardens. She was too concerned that they meet their goal to care. If Grotus knew anything about the horn, they'd soon find out. Trembling with excitement, she preceded Taurin into a huge reception hall, ornately decorated with gilded ceilings and cherubs painted on silk-lined walls. Expensive objets d'art were placed in strategic locations meant to provide the maximum viewing pleasure.

Leena wondered if Grotus ever brought guests here and, if so, what method of transportation they used. A number of other structures had been visible outside. Presumably, some of them were the guards' quarters, but she had no idea what the others represented. Grotus would have to keep his own gardeners and housekeepers. Did the people live here permanently, or were they sworn to secrecy and allowed to return home for periodic visits? If the latter was the case, how did they get off the island? No visible means of transportation was evident: She hadn't noticed any aircraft or ships in the vicinity. So how did Grotus and his people come and go? For that matter, how would she and Taurin leave when it was time to do so?

While one of the guards scurried off to alert Grotus to their arrival, Leena's eyes flickered about the hall. On a center table was a recognizable set of bronzes by Anton Luye, a famous sculptor. She was familiar with his work, having seen some of his pieces in Karayan's establishment. Flanking the statuettes was a pair of candelabra made of sparkling silversheen. Woven tapestries decorated the walls, but she preferred to admire the ceiling tiles, painted with scenes from ancient legends. She narrowed her eyes at another discovery. A polished gold disk hung above a central archway. It was an artifact from the Kelleran Age, stolen, no doubt, by Grotus's ring of smugglers. Unfortunately, there were many people who were interested in collecting artifacts for themselves, and Grotus was a well-known supplier. Archaeological looting had been recorded since the time of the ancient kings, and it continued to this day. Many sites that Leena had explored had been thoroughly ravaged by looters. Illegal marketing of early artifacts recovered from unsupervised excavations made for a lucrative business, one that the Ministry of Religion had been unsuccessfully trying to stop.

Grotus was a kingpin among the unscrupulous dealers. Taking him out of action would ensure that the exploration of sites was preserved for the professionals. But Grotus always covered his tracks. No one had ever relayed a description of him, and she wondered what the man looked like. For that matter, where had he obtained his guards and the servants who maintained his property?

They didn't have long to wait to meet Grotus. They were shown into a library paneled in rich koobi nut, with a magnificent woven carpet depicting the ancient Apostles. On a mantel above a black marble fireplace stood jadestone figurines representing Vestia, goddess of water, and Demeter, goddess of the earth. Between the figures was a seventeenth-century Aurin tapestry. A globe sat in one corner behind a comfortable seating arrangement that included plush furnishings upholstered in royal blue. Bookshelves filled the walls from floor to ceiling. Placed on pedestals about the room were various statuettes carved from backen stone that Leena recognized from the Triceras Age. Loot from raided tombs, she thought, admiring the other objects in the room that Grotus had garnered from illegal excavations.

"He's quite a connoisseur of ancient artifacts," she mumbled to Taurin.

"I would expect that's his main interest." Taurin studied each object in the room as though weighing its potential as a weapon.

Remembering her status, Leena withdrew her circlet from inside a deep pocket and placed it on her head of riotous blond waves. Hopefully Grotus would respect her position, she thought nervously.

A side door opened, and in walked a tall man who might have been in his late forties. His black hair was pulled back into a severe ponytail. He had on a multicolored longshirt that was cinched at the waist by a wide leather belt with a jewel-encrusted buckle that Leena recognized as a relic from the Moradean excavation site. Baggy black pants were tucked into a pair of scuffed knee-high boots. Leena's gaze was riveted on his nose ring as Grotus approached. It appeared to be constructed of the same creamy, translucent material as the sacred horn!

"I'm told you wish to see me," Grotus said, his gravelly voice grating to her ears. "Your unorthodox arrival has drawn my interest. Otherwise I would have had you disposed of in the same manner as other trespassers. What brings you here?" His eyes widened as he noticed Leena's circlet.

"I am Leena Worthington-Jax," she said, her tone loud and clear, as though she were unaware of the guards hovering behind him, listening. "I am authorized by the Synod to speak with you. We are on a quest. Taurin Rey Niris"—she indicated her companion—"is my escort," she added for clarification.

"And her husband," Taurin put in.

Leena caught the warning glimmer in his eye but decided she could handle Grotus on her own. "We seek information," she said.

Grotus eyed her attire with a lecherous gleam. "I have some business to attend to. Join me for dinner and we can discuss this matter you deem so important. I will have my housekeeper show you to a room. I would be delighted to have you stay as my guests."

"It doesn't look like we have much of a choice," Taurin muttered in a voice low enough for only Leena to hear.

Chapter Ten

Taurin and Leena followed the stern-faced housekeeper up a curved marble staircase, Leena holding on to the wooden banister. She wondered if they'd have the freedom to move about the house. Art treasures teased her from every corner, and she longed to explore.

After showing them into a sumptuous bedchamber the housekeeper indicated a cord by which to summon assistance.

"What are we to do until dinner?" Leena queried. It was still morning; they had the whole day ahead of them. Why was Grotus making them wait? Did he really have business to attend to, or did he just want to increase their anxiety?

"Can we walk about the grounds," she asked, "and explore the house?"

"If you wish." The gray-haired housekeeper inclined her head. She wore a starched apron over a plum-colored sheath dress. "I'll have a guide escort you, say in half an hour. Will that be satisfactory? You'll be provided with midday nourishment as well."

"That will be fine. Thank you," Leena said, forcing a smile to her lips.

As soon as they were left alone, she turned to Taurin excitedly. "Grotus must have raided half the sites on Xan," she said, pointing to more stolen objects lying about the room. "None of this is authorized to pass into the private sector. It belongs to the Ministry of Religion."

"Grotus doesn't follow the rules."

"No, he doesn't."

Leena glanced at the double bed in the center of the room. "We should have told the housekeeper we need separate rooms."

Taurin's eyes darkened. "May I remind you that we are wed, madam?"

Self-conscious under his scrutiny, Leena avoided looking into his smoky eyes. He took a step closer to her, tilting up her chin to force her to meet his gaze. His eyes roamed her face as he showered mental kisses on her lips, nose, and cheekbones.

"Leena," he murmured, unable to resist her allure. Without considering the repercussions, he lowered his head and pressed his mouth to hers.

Leena was shocked not so much by his action as by the eagerness of her own response. Instead of pushing him away, she wrapped her arms around him and gave in to the incredible sensations he created within her. Her body leaned into his, pliant against his hard strength.

Sensing her willingness, he crushed her in his embrace, his kisses frantic in their intensity.

"Taurin," she whispered, wanting something more but not sure what it was. She longed to achieve a goal beyond her grasp and intuitively knew that Taurin could satisfy it. His virility outshone that of any other man she had ever known. Because he was so different he appealed to her even more.

His hand caressed her face, and he kissed her lips lightly, murmuring her name. When his hand trailed downward, over the front of her bodice, she didn't resist. They were alone, man and wife, and the wide bed beckoned to them. Taurin nudged her over, and she stretched out, sighing with pleasure as he settled his length beside her. His mouth never left hers. When he brought his hand to her chest she moaned with pleasure.

"I shouldn't let you do this."

"You're my wife."

Taurin pushed her legs apart and settled atop her, smashing his mouth to hers and his hand to her breast. Leena clutched at his back, wanting to tear his shirt off so she could feel the burning flesh beneath it. She'd never known such passion before; his kisses aroused her to a wild frenzy. She parted her mouth, inviting his tongue to enter, and when it did she met it with her own explorations. "Lothar save me, but I want you to touch me," she said in a voice so husky she barely recognized it as her own.

"If I go much farther, I won't be able to stop," Taurin said thickly, his eyes glazed with lust.

"We should be thinking of a way out of here."

"We can think later. I want you now."

Leena cried out when his hand slid inside her bodice and found her naked breast. Dear deity, what he's doing to me, she thought as he rubbed her nipple, sending spirals of delight coursing along her nerves. Please, please don't stop, she urged him silently. The muscular planes of his back rippled beneath her fingers as she held on to him as though letting go would dispel the moment.

With her eyes closed she could hear his grunts of pleasure as he rocked his hips back and forth. His bulge jabbed at her through her gown, but she wouldn't go so far as to remove her clothes. Taurin apparently had other ideas. Suddenly the front of her bodice fell away, and she realized that he'd unfastened her gown. By pushing her binding out of the way, he had full access to her breasts. Moaning as his hands kneaded her softness, she accepted his tongue into her mouth with renewed ardor. His hips moved atop her with increasing urgency and his breath came in panting gasps.

Leena felt a coil of pleasure spring up from within her femininity, and she was unable to stop its crescendo. Wrapping her legs around Taurin's, she cried out as an explosive release rocketed her to ecstasy. Taurin shuddered above her, crying her name, and then he lay still, his passion spent. Leena, stunned by what had happened, let his weight rest upon her. She had never experienced such incredible delight before, and she couldn't wait until the next time. She hated herself for being so weak, but she couldn't help it. Taurin overwhelmed her reason. He's a demon, she told herself, seducing me until I have no willpower to refuse him.

He rolled off her and lay still at her side, staring at the ceiling. What have I done? he thought to himself. I've taken advantage of her innocence. Nothing could be more despicable, especially when I know nothing can come of any relationship between us. She was the most desirable woman he'd ever known, and yet once they finished this mission— assuming they got away from Grotus's place—they'd have to go their separate ways. He was fooling himself if he thought it could lead anywhere else.

"I'm sorry," he said abruptly.

He dropped off the side of the bed and strode into the lavatory. Leena stared after him, puzzled by his gruff tone of voice. Did he regret what they'd done? Why did he speak harshly to her when words of kindness would have been appreciated? Perhaps she'd disappointed him in some fashion. Tears sprang to her eyes and for the first time she regretted her inexperience.

A rush of warmth washed over her as her mind replayed the feel of Taurin's body moving atop hers. His moods were unpredictable, and she should be wary of him, but she knew she couldn't push him away even had she wanted to. Once again they were thrust into the role of man and wife, sharing a bedchamber. It would probably be wise to pretend they were a happy, loving couple before Grotus as well. But how would that be possible when she feared Taurin's disapproval after what had just happened?

171

Indeed, he emerged from the lavatory with a scowl on his face. He seemed almost relieved when a knock sounded on their door and their guide announced herself. Blanchette was another servant, as indicated by her manner of dress, which matched that of the housekeeper. Only Blanchette was much younger—in her twenties perhaps, like Leena—with a sleek figure, shiny black hair, and a pretty face. Leena ran into the lavatory to freshen up. It took her but a moment, and when she emerged she saw that Taurin had flung the door open wide and was chatting with the guide.

Blanchette's eyes narrowed when she took in Leena's expensive gown. "Grotus tells me you're a member of the Caucus. Why are you here?"

"I'll discuss my business with Grotus at dinner," Leena retorted.

She sensed that the girl disliked her and wondered why. Perhaps it was because they were intruders. Grotus's staff would have to be very loyal to be trusted, meaning she and Taurin should be on their guard at all times. Glancing at him for reassurance, she was dismayed at the dark glare he gave her. She wanted to cry out, *What's wrong? Why are you angry with me?* But she couldn't do so in front of Blanchette. Her heart sank and a heavy weight of depression pressed down upon her. She followed Blanchette out of the room and tried to rouse some enthusiasm for the magnificent artworks displayed about the structure, but she was too aware of Taurin's silent tread beside her and the closed look on his face.

Their tour began on the second floor, one floor down from where her and Taurin's room was located. A billiard room was first on the agenda. The oak paneling was covered with sporting and theater prints, and she recognized the leather settees and chairs as being made by the well-known Morant furniture company.

"This is an interesting piece." She pointed to a bronze sculpture of a sportsman on an *enix*. She'd seen some like it from the tomb of the ruler Antiok from the third dynasty.

This was no copy, but the genuine article, as were all of the objects she'd noted thus far.

The banquet hall was next, its ceiling arches seventy feet above the huge expanse of the room. Again tapestries hung along the walls, interspersed with ornate wood carvings. The dining table itself was made of polished bennir wood, and there was seating for twenty, indicating that Grotus might often have guests. Perhaps he invited his fellow smugglers for dinner, she thought wryly, again wondering how they would be brought to the island. She'd seen no visible means of transportation.

An informal dining room provided seating for eight at an oval table set with a white tablecloth and gold-rimmed dinnerware. A music room held a stand with lyrics and a magnificent grand piano. Seats were arranged as though for a concert, and vases of flowers decorated the room.

"Does Grotus play the piano?" she asked Blanchette in astonishment.

Blanchette gave her a smile that did not extend to her eyes. "He's an accomplished musician. I'm sure he'll play for you tonight."

"He appears to be a man of exquisitely fine taste."

"Yes, except for his clothes," Taurin murmured.

Leena shot him a glance of reproach, but luckily Blanchette hadn't heard, or else she chose to ignore his remark.

"He does have a wonderful eye for art," Leena hissed on their way into a salon filled with comfortable sofas and armchairs, bright lighting, and a stenciled ceiling with linenfold paneling at the side walls.

"He's a thief, and you'd do well to remember that fact."

Leena's eyebrows lifted. He almost sounded jealous of the man, but that certainly couldn't be. He's probably wondering how we're going to get out of here, Leena thought. She was too fascinated by her surroundings to ponder the matter herself. She'd leave the logistics to Taurin, while she learned more about Grotus's operation.

"You don't see the horn anywhere, do you?" Taurin muttered on their way back up to the third floor.

They were shown a couple of unoccupied guest bedrooms, an upstairs sitting room, which Blanchette told them they were welcome to use, and a parlor filled with potted plants and wicker furniture. An air-filtering system cooled the sunny room, emitting a faint fragrance of orange blossoms. It was quite pleasant, and under other circumstances Leena could easily have spent several days exploring the place. But finding the horn was her main preoccupation, and she kept her eyes open during the tour.

"What's on the fourth floor?" she asked Blanchette.

"The servants' quarters are upstairs."

"And below?"

"Kitchens and workrooms."

"Do all the staff who work here live on the island?"

"Of course," Blanchette replied. "I believe it's time now for midday nourishment, after which I'll show you about the grounds."

"That would be delightful," Leena said, her voice expressing her approval.

Blanchette's face softened slightly, as though she hadn't expected Leena to be so congenial. "This way, please," she said, leading them back downstairs to the small dining area.

Grotus wasn't present, but a couple of ladies were seated there. They were scantily attired in silken drapes in the bright colors Grotus seemed to prefer. Leena had noticed that the curtains covering the windows in each room were rather garishly colored. It appeared that Grotus's taste in fine art did not extend to his eye for design.

Another man was present, seated at the head of the table, his unshaven face sullen as he awaited his food. A couple of servants were filling plates from a sideboard, and as Leena and Taurin took their seats opposite the two ladies, they were served their meal. It was an appetizing repast of baked cloinder fish, mixed greens, and buttered tortas. A glass of vintage wine accompanied the meal. The ladies claimed to be friends of Grotus, while the man said he was a business associate.

All three were rather closemouthed in the presence of strangers.

As soon as Leena and Taurin had partaken of the sweet pudding offered for dessert, Blanchette showed up to continue their tour. The afternoon was spent in a pleasant manner, strolling about the gardens. Taurin's face became animated as he exclaimed over the cultivated flower beds. Neither of them learned a thing about Grotus's operation, nor how he came and went from the island. Leena wondered if he already knew of their mission; he didn't seem in any hurry to find out their reason for coming to see him.

Leena's curiosity grew to learn what he knew of the missing horn, and it was with growing excitement that she readied herself for dinner some time later that afternoon. Showered and dressed, she preened before the mirror in her topaz gown. She'd only had room for three ensembles in her bag; the rest of the space was taken up by her archaeological tools, work breeches, and the tunics Taurin had bought her.

Taurin emerged from the lavatory, his jaw freshly shaven and his ebony hair damp. His black shirt was half open at the neck and tucked into a pair of tight black breeches that tapered into a pair of polished boots. Her gaze lingered on his manly physique.

"What's wrong, Taurin? Why aren't you talking to me?"

She was a vision in her yellow gown, with her golden hair streaming over her shoulders. Her eyes, wide and questioning, gazed at him in supplication. Taurin's heart twisted inside him, but he couldn't tell her how he really felt.

"Nothing is wrong," he lied, stuffing his few toilet articles back into his bag in case they had to make a hasty exit.

"You are displeased with me, aren't you?"

"Displeased with you?" He glanced up, noticing her tremulous lower lip as she tried to suppress a flood of tears. "Why do you say that?"

"I . . . I disappointed you earlier. You got up and left me, and now you seem angry."

Taurin's resolve dissipated in the face of her pain. "I'm

not angry with you, Leena. On the contrary, I'm so mad for you that I'm trying to restrain myself. If I had my way, I'd keep you as my wife. But both of us know that can never be. We cannot remain together.''

He still insisted that their marriage be annulled and said nothing about his feelings toward her. Lust must be what drove him. Leena's head hung sadly.

Taurin yearned to tell her how she brightened his life, how her inner serenity provided a balm for his troubled spirit. But their union could come to naught, or else he'd have her brother's wrath to answer to, and perhaps that of the Synod as well. Besides, he couldn't afford to allow anyone to look into his background too closely and hoped that Magar was able to fend off any questions that might be asked about him. Leena would be horrified if she learned his true nature. He didn't trust himself where she was concerned and strengthened his resolve to rein in his feelings and suppress his desire.

"I may want you," he blurted out, "but you don't need to be with someone like me your whole life. You know nothing about me."

She took a few steps toward him, as though sensing his longing. "Then why won't you tell me?" she pleaded. "I'd like to help you, Taurin."

"Help!" he spat. "I don't need your help. That's not what I require."

"Perhaps it was a poor choice of words. I mean . . . I know you're not happy."

He squared his shoulders. "I'm very happy. I have my farm and my flowers. They bring me peace and harmony. That's all I need from life."

"Is it?"

The question went unanswered because Blanchette came to lead them to dinner. They hadn't even decided what to say to Grotus, Leena realized on their way downstairs. What if he decided not to respect their authority and chose to rid himself of them like all the other unwanted visitors to his island? She wouldn't let him get away with that; on their way into the small dining room she rehearsed what she could say to convince Grotus to listen.

Grotus was seated at the head of the table. He wore a turquoise shirt encrusted with silver spangles that clinked whenever he moved. White linen pants and a white wide-brimmed hat completed his attire. His nose ring was the same, Leena noticed, but now he wore two sets of earrings in both ears and a number of flashy rings on his fingers. His shoulder-length black hair contrasted dramatically with the white hat. He was smoking a rolled mogur root, and the sickeningly pungent aroma made Leena choke. Coughing, she took her seat.

"Where are your other guests?" Taurin asked.

"I thought our conversation should be private." Grotus blew out a puff of smoke. "Would you care for an aperitif?" He rattled off a list of exotic choices. Taurin chose one, but Leena declined.

"How are you familiar with Muer's brandy?" Grotus asked Taurin, narrowing his eyes. "It's not readily available in these parts."

Taurin realized he'd fallen into a trap. Muer's brandy was made on Yllon. He knew Grotus traded with his planet; now his role was in jeopardy. "It sounded as though it would have a rich flavor."

"Ah." Grotus eyed him keenly. "What is your occupation, sir?"

"I raise edible flowers and sell them on the market."

"A farmer."

"Yes, I am."

Grotus arched an eyebrow, glancing at Leena. "You're married to this man, madam?"

Leena's cheeks colored. "Yes, he is my husband."

"Is not your father Cranby Worthington-Jax?"

He's been checking up on me, Leena thought. "That is so."

"And he gave his consent for you to marry a farmer?"

Leena felt Taurin tense beside her. "This is a personal matter that has nothing to do with our business here. We're searching for a missing artifact, one on which the Ministry of Religion places a high value. We are wondering if you have heard of its whereabouts."

Grotus signaled for the first course to be served. "What kind of artifact?" he demanded.

To Leena's relief, he stubbed out his mogur in a tray placed beside his plate for that purpose. Her throat parched, she gulped down several swallows of water from a crystal goblet provided on the table. The table settings exhibited the same discriminating taste as Grotus's art collection.

"It's a ceremonial object," Leena explained, trying not to give away too much information needlessly. "You would know what I was referring to had you seen it."

"Perhaps a more detailed explanation would aid my memory," Grotus said.

Leena felt Taurin's knee poke her under the table. "It's an unusual relic," she said. "The Synod values it more for its symbolism than for its intrinsic value. They are willing to pay a substantial sum for its return."

"I see." Grotus's eyes gleamed with avarice. "I'd be happy to do business with you, madam, but I need more information."

"If you don't have it," Taurin drawled, "maybe you know who does."

Grotus silently stared at Taurin for a full minute. "Would the same reward be offered for information leading to the return of this valued object?"

"A lesser payment, to be sure," Leena put in.

"I can't say that I'm interested in money."

Having finished his equas, steeped in a tangy cream sauce, Grotus signaled for the entree to be served. Steaming plates heaped with juicy steaks, sauteed vegetables, and fragrant cronsom rice were placed before the diners; then the servants withdrew, leaving them alone.

"Your background is in archaeology, is it not?" Grotus asked Leena.

Taurin felt as though he were being ignored, and he didn't care for this reception. Grotus was far too interested in Leena. He let his leg rub against hers under the table, but she was too engrossed in the conversation to pay attention. His resentment flared, and he found himself glaring at Grotus, wishing he could nail the man.

Leena rattled off her professional credentials, and Taurin could tell that Grotus was impressed. I'll bet he checked up on us, he thought, and wondered how extensive Grotus's intelligence network actually was. Just then a messenger hurried in with an urgent missive for Grotus. He held out a folded parchment sealed with wax.

"The source says it's urgent, sir."

Grotus's face reddened. "I said I was not to be interrupted."

"I'm sorry, sir, but I thought you'd want to see it right away. Am I to wait for a reply?"

"Not now! Get out!" Grotus thundered, and the messenger scampered from the room. He slit open the envelope, frowning as he scanned the contents. Then a chuckle erupted from his throat. "A bit late, aren't you, my little magpie?" he murmured to himself.

Leena caught sight of the seal and gasped. Why would Sirvat be sending Grotus a private message? The implications stunned her. Was Sirvat warning him of their arrival? How much had she revealed of their mission? How did she know where to contact Grotus, when she'd told Leena she wasn't sure of the island's location?

She vowed to have Bendyk look into Sirvat's relationship with the smuggler at the earliest opportunity. A sense of betrayal assailed her. Sirvat could no longer be trusted.

Finally Grotus looked up. "I may not have the information you seek, though that may come at a later point in time. For now, though, I can offer you something else in trade."

Leena finished chewing a tender piece of meat. "What's

that?'' She considered the possibility that Grotus was toying with them, that he did know who possessed the horn and was manipulating them to his own purposes.

''I know a secret guarded closely by the Synod, but it comes at a price.''

Taurin rolled his eyes. ''What do you want? The full ransom we planned to pay for the . . .'' He bit his tongue, catching himself just before he blurted out, *the sacred horn.*

''No, no,'' Grotus said. ''You have something else of value to offer me.'' His gaze swept the room. ''You see the kinds of objects I treasure.''

Taurin's eyes lit with understanding. ''Of course. I do have something in my bag upstairs. With your permission?''

Grotus appeared surprised, as though he'd had something else in mind. But he motioned for Taurin to go. A moment later, Taurin returned, holding a small book in his hand. As Leena took a closer look, she realized it wasn't an ordinary book. There was no visible means to open the thing. A circular depression marred the tooled cover, but . . . Wait a minute! Wasn't that inscription written in the same symbols she'd been studying? The same as those in Taurin's drawings?

''Where did you get that?'' she snapped.

He ignored her. ''Grotus, would this interest you in return for your so-called secret?'' He plopped the book down on the table in front of the smuggler.

Grotus's eyes popped. ''A bibliotome! I have more of these.''

He stared at Taurin meaningfully. Taurin knew where he had gotten them. ''Does this one interest you?''

''You know it does. Have you learned how to open it?''

''Not yet. Have you?''

''No, I've not had any success.''

Leena puzzled at their exchange. She had no idea what they were talking about, or where this item had come from. She'd never seen anything like it before.

"What is it you have to tell us?" Taurin said to Grotus, reminding him of his promise.

"There is a temple hidden in the jungle at Morasia. The Ministry of Religion has obliterated any record of its existence. They say Death stalks any intruders, and even my men have failed to get past the entrance. I have heard that the Temple of Light hides a great treasure."

He held out his hand, pointing to a large crystal ring on one of his fingers. "More of these," he said. "Larger and more powerful. I would give anything to find them."

Taurin leaned closer. "That gemstone looks familiar." As recognition dawned, he turned to Leena. "Isn't it a smaller version of the natives' crystal stone fixed in the pillar at the Black Lands?"

Her eyes widened. "I believe you're right! There must be a link. Strange that I've never uncovered these before on an excavation. You say this Temple of Light holds more?" she addressed Grotus.

He nodded vigorously, his nose ring jiggling. "It is said that the Temple of Light guards the secrets of the Apostles. I assume that means these crystals have a significance we have yet to fathom."

Leena's eyes glittered with zeal. "How do we get there?"

Taurin stared at her. "Are you out of your mind? We're supposed to be searching for the . . . you know."

"But to find a storehouse of these crystals! They could help to unlock the secrets of the past."

"And when you return I might have information on this valued object you seek," Grotus offered, swirling the wine in his goblet. "Come, let us retire to the library. We can have our kava and dessert in there."

Once in the library he drew a map from a locked desk and handed it to Leena. "Study this tonight. The path to the temple is delineated through the jungle."

"I'll take my bibliotome back now," Taurin said, holding out his hand.

Grotus clutched it to his chest. "You offered it to me in

trade, fair and square. I gave you the map in return.'' He glanced at Taurin consideringly. ''Perhaps you would like to engage me in a bout of ramagan,'' he said, poking Taurin on the shoulder. ''We can save dessert for later.''

''Ramagan? What's that?'' Leena asked.

''An ancient sport,'' Taurin replied, his eyes never leaving Grotus's face. ''It would be a great pleasure.''

''There's a gymnasium downstairs. Follow me.''

The two men turned, and Leena scurried after them. ''Wait a minute. What does this game involve?''

It didn't take long for her to find out, and she certainly didn't like her discovery. It was a contact sport in which opponents using long sticks tried to knock each other off-balance. Both men stripped to the waist, and she saw that Grotus kept himself in trim form, no doubt with the help of the gleaming equipment in the far corner of the room. Grotus paused in his warm-up exercises, his eyes fixed on the strange band Taurin wore around his upper arm.

''What is that?'' Leena said, coming forward for a closer look. By Lothar, it was constructed of the same creamy, translucent material as the sacred horn. She'd seen Taurin without his shirt before, but he must have kept this hidden.

''Now, that is worth a fortune,'' said Grotus, licking his lips appreciatively.

''It's not for sale or trade.'' Taurin's tone left no doubt he meant what he said.

''Where did you get it?''

''Never mind. Let's get on with the match.''

The fight lasted a good thirty minutes. The two opponents were well suited. They sweated and fought and finally called it a draw; neither one could best the other. After drying himself with a towel Taurin threw on his shirt.

''Let us retire to the salon,'' Grotus suggested. ''I'd like to show you my porcelain Apostles.''

Grotus continued to shower his attentions on Leena while Taurin stood by, seething. It rankled him that Leena was so fascinated by Grotus's personal collection of artifacts that she was ignoring him. Forcing a polite smile to his lips, he accepted a glass of honey ambrosia from the smuggler, who proudly exhibited his figurines to Leena. Grunting with disgust, Taurin finally moved away.

"I could use someone with your expertise on my staff," Grotus told Leena under his breath.

"I'm flattered." Leena cast a troubled look in Taurin's direction. He stood with his back to them, seeming to study a tapestry on the wall. She could tell by the hunch of his shoulders that he wasn't pleased.

"Where did your man get his arm bracelet?"

Grotus's casual tone didn't deceive her. She saw the blatant envy in his eyes.

"I really don't know." Discomfited, she changed the subject. "If you want us to explore the Temple of Light, we should leave soon."

Grotus gave a short, raucous laugh. "I'm afraid that's not possible just yet. We still have much to discuss." He touched her arm. "You're quite lovely, you know, and this gown makes your hair gleam like sunlight."

Leena took a step back. "I . . . I should retire if we are to get an early start in the morning." Grotus sounded as though he had no intention of letting them go anywhere; but then, he wanted them to find the Temple of Light, didn't he?

The meal had made her thirsty, so she accepted a goblet of honeyed nectar from Grotus. The drink slid down her throat, thick and sweet.

"Think about my offer," Grotus said, "while you sleep."

"Your offer?" Leena was feeling drowsy, now that he'd mentioned it. Unable to suppress a yawn, she raised a hand to cover her mouth. Grotus's face loomed larger in front of her.

"Stay here," he said, his pale blue eyes mesmerizing her. "If you work for me, I can offer you more than any farmer, and I don't just mean in wealth."

He kept his voice low so Taurin wouldn't hear. His hand darted out and rubbed her crotch in a crude manner that left no mistake of his meaning. Leena jerked back.

"How dare you! Taurin!" she called.

Glancing at her husband, she saw that he was no longer standing but had slumped into a chair. His head lolled back, and his eyes were closed.

"Taurin! What's the matter?" She started toward him, but dizziness overwhelmed her.

"Here, my dear. Allow me to help you." Grotus's voice was close to her ear.

The last thing she heard was his shrieking laughter as she fell into a deep, dreamless slumber. Her final chilling thought was that Grotus coveted her as another treasure to add to his collection, and she had the haunting feeling that wherever she went, he or his agents wouldn't be far behind.

Chapter Eleven

"Demon's blood! Where the hell are we?" Taurin demanded, sitting up and rubbing the back of his head. An unfamiliar shoreline met his groggy gaze. From the position of the sun he determined that it was morning. He and Leena had been deposited on a beach with their packs of belongings and a pile of containers he didn't recognize.

"How do you feel?" he asked Leena, who was beginning to rouse herself.

"I've felt better," she mumbled, brushing her face with her hand.

Peering inside one of the containers, he discovered a supply of food—enough, it appeared, to last them for several days. His guess was confirmed by a note, signed by Grotus, telling them they'd been dropped off at Morasia. They had five days in which to find the Temple of Light, explore the site, and return to the beach. Return transportation would be provided on the morning of the fifth day. Other than some tracks in the sand that led into the water, there was no other sign of habitation.

"We must have been drugged," Leena remarked, shading her eyes with her hand as she gazed out to sea. "I'll bet it was in that nectar drink."

In the humidity, her yellow gown stuck to her body like plaster. Taurin couldn't keep his gaze from raking her slender form. Memories from their other time on the beach flitted into his mind, and a surge of heat swelled in his loins. He suppressed his response; they didn't have time for dalliance.

"I'll bet he has a vessel that travels under the sea. That would explain why no one ever sees him going or coming from his island," Leena guessed.

Taurin narrowed his eyes. He knew submersibles existed on Yllon as war machines used to attack rival territories, but to obtain one Grotus would have had to pay dearly or make a substantial trade. He wondered if the smuggler had dealt directly with Drufus Gong, the most notorious gang leader on Yllon. His blood chilled at the notion. Drufus Gong had put a price on his own head. Should he ever learn Taurin's whereabouts, his life wouldn't be worth the price of an eulich.

Taurin swallowed hard. He'd been so preoccupied with his role as Leena's protector that he hadn't given a thought to his own safety. After seeing his bibliotome Grotus might make the connection that he was from Yllon, especially when Taurin suspected Captain Sterckle had sold him the bibliotomes he'd used to buy passage to Xan.

"Do you still have the map Grotus gave us?" he asked gruffly, casting aside his concerns.

She rummaged in her sack. "Here it is."

Unfolding the document, Taurin pinpointed their location on the beach.

"He hopes we'll find that treasure for him," Leena said, opening their canteen and gulping down a swallow of water. "It might be worth the effort, if Grotus gains information about the horn in our absence." She paused. "Sirvat told him we were coming."

Her words startled Taurin. "How do you know?"

"That message he received at dinner—I recognized the seal. It was Sirvat's personal missive. What I don't understand is why Sirvat didn't tell me she knew him."

"You can tell your brother to look into it," Taurin suggested. "Investigating the Synod falls under his jurisdiction."

Leena rose, dusting the sand from her gown. Stooping, she pulled a tan tunic from her bag.

"Where are you going?" Taurin shouted, jumping to his feet. She was walking toward the strip of tropical vegetation lining the beach.

"I need to change my clothes. I'll just be a minute."

By the time she returned Taurin had packed Grotus's containers inside his bag. "Let's move out," he urged. He added her pack, heavy with tools, to his own.

According to the map there was a trail to follow. They were able to find it easily enough, but it was mostly overgrown, and Taurin had to hack their way through with a machete, which, thoughtfully, had been provided by Grotus's staff.

Leena followed in his wake, admiring the wide set of his shoulders and the muscles rippling on his arms. The heat had made him remove his shirt so she had an enticing view of his broad back. At his urging, she took care not to walk into any of the glistening cobwebs or insect mounds blocking their path.

After a while the undergrowth thinned, and the trail began an upward climb. They passed through a stand of fragrant calyp trees and stopped beside a running stream to quench their thirst.

"Let's have something to eat," she suggested. "I'm hungry."

Leaning against a tree, Taurin ogled her legs. Although she'd slathered insecticide on her bare skin, she was aware that Taurin hadn't seen her very often without her long gowns.

187

"So am I," he murmured, and she realized food was the farthest thing from his mind.

Her face turned crimson. Realizing they couldn't afford to waste time, she stalked over to their bags and found a couple of snack packs. "Here, eat this. It'll keep us going a while longer."

The trail seemed endless as they headed up ridges and down valleys. She estimated that they would reach their target tomorrow; then they'd need another two days for the return trip. That meant they'd have one full day to explore the temple, assuming they could get inside.

Skirting around a dead root in the path, she glanced apprehensively at the sky. Clouds were gathering, and she prayed it wouldn't rain. The trail would turn into a river of mud, making their path miserable. As it was, the trek was arduous, and she had little energy to think of anything else except their journey.

Curiosity about the excavation site kept her going through the long day, the cool night, and the following morning. Taurin was solicitous of her comfort, making her yearn for his tender touch. Yet there seemed to be an unspoken agreement between them that time was of the essence; they couldn't spare a moment for personal pleasures. Nevertheless, Leena decided to take that moment when they were resting before resuming the last leg of their journey.

"I feel like we've been married for months," she announced when they'd cleared away the remnants of another snack.

Taurin glanced at her: a quick, sharp perusal. He'd kept his head swathed during the night, and she hadn't seen his eyes then, but now, in the bright morning sunlight, they gleamed like two steel disks with that curious yellow-greenish light in their depths. He'd kept them going for a while after dark the night before, and she'd wondered at his keen vision.

"I've seen you do your morning exercises every day now," she told him, sitting on a flat-topped rock and letting her fingers trail into a cool stream.

Taurin leaned against a thick tree trunk, his shirt hanging open. Leena couldn't help looking at his hairy chest and feeling the stirrings of arousal.

"I'm beginning to learn what annoys you and pleases you, but there's so much more about you that remains a mystery."

Taurin scowled. "It's best if you don't know everything about me."

"Is it?" She got up and sauntered toward him. "We're alone in the jungle, Taurin. We've slept side by side for several nights. We are man and wife. Is there not more you wish to learn about me?"

Taurin averted his gaze, but not before she saw the flare of passion in his eyes. "I dare not answer that question."

Leena knew she should stop. Her taunts would lead them down a dangerous path, but she felt compelled to continue. His mystique surrounded her, enveloped her, until she wanted nothing more than to peel away the layers and see him for what he really was. That he could follow their path in the dark she didn't doubt. He heard animal sounds before she knew the creatures were even there. And then there was that weapon strapped to his calf, a type of armament she'd never seen before until Brother Aron used one in the Black Lands. She didn't like the unknowns about him and felt challenged to unravel his secrets.

Taurin tried to slow his rapidly beating heart as she approached. Her golden hair streamed over her shoulders as her lithe figure moved toward him. He wasn't sure she knew what she was inviting when she teased him, but he wasn't going to let her find out.

"You won't like the man I really am," he warned, his voice gruff. Against his back, prickly spines bit through his shirt, but he didn't budge. The discomfort would help focus his thoughts. "My world is a far cry from yours. You wouldn't understand its violence even if I explained it. I've had to kill people."

"What? You . . . you've killed people?"

Taurin flinched inwardly when she stopped in her tracks. It saddened him that he'd had to resort to the truth, but it was necessary if they were both to avoid further pain. Despite their formal bonding ceremony, she was still considering a betrothal to Malcolm—at least she hadn't indicated otherwise to him. Upon their return her brother would annul their marriage, leaving her free to pledge herself to her former suitor. So why start something he couldn't finish?

"How can you so casually say you've killed people? I don't understand."

He leveled his steady gaze on her. "I didn't expect you would. We're from different worlds, Leena, in more ways than one. You belong with your brother and his kind."

"Yes. I suppose you're right."

As though she were too stunned to argue, Leena picked her sack off the ground and started along the trail.

He was a murderer! she thought, struck speechless with horror. Such violence was unheard of among her people. Why hadn't he been banished to the Black Lands for such a vile deed? Instead, he was living on Magar's land, with the minister's sanction. There had to have been extenuating circumstances. She knew there was goodness in his heart; he just didn't believe in it himself. Unknowingly, he ached for deliverance. Her heart was torn between wanting to show the depths of her caring and her abhorrence of what he had revealed.

Saying nothing, she continued along until they reached the beginning of the ruin. Crumbling stone walls were partially enveloped in vegetation. Tangled vines reached like spider legs to squash the stones together or force them apart. Headless sculptures lay about, covered with coarse white mold. Leena gazed upward toward the familiar, pyramidlike tower that capped all of the temples. Missing were the antlerlike decorations, the branches of life representing Lothar, that usually reached out from the superstructure.

It appeared as though the site had been partially excavated; she could see the markers laid out in a grid, the evidence of various diggings. The Ministry of Religion must have authorized an investigation, but then, for some reason, had terminated it, making her wonder why they'd erased all records of the find.

With a tremor of excitement she approached a hollow opening in one of the walls.

"This looks like an entranceway," she said to Taurin, motioning for him to come closer. Dropping her sack onto the ground, she rummaged inside it for her notebook and tools. "I'll look for the datum point."

"What's that?" Taurin's gaze skittered about, as though he sensed a threat.

Leena didn't understand what would alarm him. Exotic bird calls and the sounds of trickling water met her ears. A spicy floral scent permeated the air. It was a serene setting, as far as she could tell, marred by the crumbling ruins that were devoid of life . . . or so she hoped.

"The datum point is the spot from which all measurements originate," she explained, her eyes sparkling with enthusiasm. "During an initial survey, a permanent marker is implanted in the ground near a corner of the site, and this point is delineated on a map. It gives future investigators a place to identify where the excavation was begun, and it's often used as a starting point for laying out the grid that will cover the site."

She scribbled in her notepad and showed him a diagram. "A grid pattern is a set of squares that covers the entire site."

Gazing with dismay at the growth of jungle encroaching on the structures, she decided it would be difficult if not impossible to locate the original datum point. What was the purpose, anyway? She wasn't here to do an official survey.

Coming across a pottery shard half-buried in the ground, she dusted it off with one of her brushes, labeled it, and placed it in a small container in her bag. She was writing notes on where she'd found it, describing the surrounding physical objects, when Taurin snatched the notebook from her hand.

"Why are you wasting time picking in the dirt? Let's go inside," he growled, gathering up her tools and throwing them into her satchel.

Annoyed with herself for becoming distracted, Leena followed him toward the wide gap in the wall, in front of which vines dangled and leafy branches grew as though warning trespassers to stay away. A couple of mammoth helixcats, carved in stone, their faces partially eroded, guarded each side of the entrance.

"I'll go first," she said. "I'm familiar with these temples."

Shoving past him, she entered the gap and was pleased to see the interior passageway had walls that glowed with a strange luminescence, providing a dim illumination. Carefully, she made her way through the narrow corridor, watching her footing. The paved floor was cracked and uneven, having been worn down by age. As they got farther inside, a musty odor tickled her nostrils.

"Be careful," she warned him. "Some of these temples are booby-trapped."

"Now you tell me." His voice sounded loud in the confines of the tunnel.

"Maybe that's why the excavation was stopped," Leena mused. "Perhaps the early explorers couldn't get past the obstacles. Grotus's men wouldn't have had any more success."

Halting as she came to a wide archway, Leena glanced at the floor of the chamber in front of them. It stretched like a huge square, at the other end of which was another open archway. The floorwork consisted of an even patchwork of stones. Crouching down, she studied the pattern.

"What is it?" Taurin said, peering over her shoulder. He drew in a sharp breath. Bones littered the inside of the chamber ahead of them.

"This is the first challenge. If it's similar to ones I've seen before, there's a deadly ray that gets you if you don't step on the right stones. The trick is finding the correct combination. Give me one of my brushes,'' she told him, placing her sack on the floor within his reach.

He gave her the requested tool and perused the environs while she patiently dusted away the symbols on the floor in front of her, being careful to keep her feet firmly rooted in the passageway so her weight did not rest on any of the stones. Through the dim light she scanned the outline of the carvings on the dust-laden stones. She could barely make out the symbols, but it wasn't possible to get closer for a better look. Not yet, at any rate.

"These symbols correspond with the others I've been studying,'' she said, sitting back on her haunches to glance up at Taurin. "By the grace of Lothar!'' she cried, covering her mouth. His eyes emitted a frightening greenish-yellow glow in the darkened corner where he leaned against a wall.

He stepped forward immediately, the illumination of the passage restoring his vision to normal.

"Do not be afraid,'' he hastened to reassure her. "This is the reason why I shade my face in the dark.''

Struck speechless, Leena could only stare in wonder.

"According to local legend,'' Taurin said, "children born with eyes like mine are seen as demons. I learned at an early age to hide my vision from others during periods of darkness.''

"What demons are you talking about? What local legends?'' she queried, thrown into confusion. "I'm not familiar with any such mythology.'' She could understand why he covered his head in that cloth. To see his eyes emit that strange glow was enough to frighten anyone. It almost made him seem . . . alien. The man had said he was from Iman, hadn't he?

"Where I come from, my eyes are seen as a mark of evil, and those thus born are usually destroyed. Rather than murder me, my parents left me for a foundling.''

"Murder you! I don't understand. Who . . . what are you?''

Taurin sank onto the floor across from her, resting his back against the wall. Wearily, he rubbed a hand over his face, contemplating how much to tell her. Other than Magar, she was the first person here to learn his secret, but he dare not reveal all it meant.

Long ago on Yllon, strangers had appeared who were not kindly, like the Apostles on Xan. Instead, they promoted aggression and war. Fabled as demons, they were persecuted, and most were eventually destroyed. Intermating had occurred with the native population, and periodically their descendants showed the sign: the glowing eyes that enabled them to see in the dark. It was feared that those thus accursed could cause angry passions to surge. Fear of the demon seed was so prevalent on Yllon that even to this day their descendants were hunted down and destroyed. Since Yllon was a violent society anyway, it was difficult for Taurin to tell if he did have the power to drive men mad, as the stories claimed. Thus far he'd shown no inclination to negatively influence his neighbors on Xan, yet the possibility that this might be true was one of the reasons for his isolation.

"I seek my origins as you do," he said to Leena. "These symbols are my only clue."

He rolled up his sleeve and showed her the bracelet fixed around his upper arm. She had noticed the unique material before, when he'd bared his chest to fight Grotus, but she had not observed the symbols etched into the band. Gathering her courage, she crawled closer and traced them with her finger.

"This item was left with me as a child," Taurin went on, lowering his heavy lids so she couldn't read his expression. "It is the only remnant of the past I have left. Other than the books," he murmured.

"But your bracelet is constructed of the same material as the horn and the ring that I found on my last excavation. How is that possible?"

He shrugged. "I assume it's part of my heritage. I was hoping you could help me interpret what these symbols mean. They might explain the link relating the different objects.''

"I've never been able to decipher the symbols. Perhaps this temple holds the answers we seek.''

"How do we get in there?'' Taurin gestured toward the chamber.

Realizing she still had many questions, Leena crept over to the opening and peered at the stones covering the floor. "I've determined from my studies that there are seven symbols, presumably representing an alphabet of some kind. There's also an eighth, but it's actually a combination of two others. One particular string appears repetitively. It's the same string of symbols that is etched onto your bracelet and on the horn.''

Using her fingers, she drew the symbols in the dust at Taurin's feet. "This is the sequence. The Apostles must have left us a message, but no one has been able to decipher it. There's another design I've found on occasion.''

Drawing a diamond shape with an antlerlike branch coming out of the left corner, she frowned. "This representation doesn't appear to be associated with the other string.''

"Can you get us inside?'' Taurin asked.

Reexamining the inscriptions on the chamber floor, Leena grimaced. "Each one of the squares has a different symbol on it. Perhaps if we follow the string, we'll be all right.''

"Let's see what happens if you make an error.''

Before she could stop him Taurin withdrew a small shovel from her pack and threw it onto one of the stones. A red light shot out from the eyes of one of two huge stone statues at the far end of the room and veered toward the stone Taurin had hit, crackling through the air.

"I guess a lot of people have died trying,'' he muttered. "You'd better get it right.''

The floor was three squares wide. In the first row, Leena studied the symbols from left to right. The first one looked like a pair of mountain humps. The middle was an oval with a horizontal line dividing the center, and the one on the right looked like a backward crescent moon. Remembering that the common string she'd found on most of the digs began with the backward crescent, she decided to put her guess on that one.

"Give me another tool," she instructed him.

He handed her a small hoe and she tossed it onto the block to the right. The stone statues at the opposite end of the room remained lifeless.

"It's safe," she whispered. "I'll go first."

Before Taurin could object she gingerly stepped across the threshold and onto the first block to their right. Taurin grasped the sacks, flung them over his shoulder, and followed her. As soon as he crossed the threshold to join her, a stone slab slid from the top of the entranceway, sealing them inside the chamber. Silent walls surrounded them. Now there was no way in and no way out unless they determined the correct sequence. He waited patiently while Leena read the symbols in each row.

Fifteen squares later, they had made their way to the opposite end, where the *V* symbol with a dot in the center was the final choice. It was the correct selection, as evidenced by their safe passage through the open archway.

"You did it!" Taurin exclaimed, putting his foot forward to rush ahead.

"Wait." Leena's hand stopped him. "Each room has a way to get across. We dare not go in haste."

More bones littered the passageway into the next chamber, and he realized that the few souls who had made it across the first section hadn't survived the subsequent challenge.

Leena peered inside the next chamber. "There are carvings on the walls. I don't see anything on the floor except those odd piles of dust."

"Strange, aren't they?" He stared at the unusual mounds scattered about the room.

She walked forward before he could stop her. Again, as soon as Taurin followed her inside, a slab lowered behind them. This time there was no visible opening at the other end. The luminescent glow in the room reflected the odd light in Taurin's eyes.

"Can you interpret these inscriptions?" he asked her.

Leena leaned forward, studying the carvings on one wall. "I don't see the familiar sequence anywhere. Look, this diamond shape has the branch sticking out, but it's in the wrong place. And here's more of them."

Taurin moved beside her to peer at the strange diamond shapes with the antlerlike branch growing out of a corner. "They all look the same to me."

"Wait a minute!" she exclaimed excitedly. "See this— the branch rises from the upper right corner. There, it's on the left. And down here it's the other side. They're different!" As Leena came to this realization, a jolt rocked the room.

"What's that?" Taurin glanced around apprehensively.

Leena's hand traced the outline of a diamond shape with the antler symbolizing Lothar's branch of life on its upper left corner. As she applied pressure, the stone pushed in.

"It moves!" she cried.

His gaze darted about the chamber. Was she talking about the stone or the entire room? The walls seemed to be encroaching upon them, or was it his imagination playing tricks? "Something is moving, all right, and it's not just that stone. It's the whole place," he concluded grimly.

"What?" Leena glanced up, startled. The walls were slowly, steadily moving inward.

Taurin's eyes fell to the strange piles of dust on the floor. With sudden horror he realized what they represented.

"We've got to find a way out or we'll be crushed," he shouted.

Leena's hands splayed on the walls. "The key has to be here!"

"Perhaps there's a pneumatic door. If we step on the right spot on the floor—"

"No, I don't think that's it. Help me look for the diamond shape, the one with the branch in the upper left corner. If

197

the other stones push in with this symbol . . .''

Taurin followed her instructions, and sure enough her theory was correct. As the walls moved closer and closer, he frantically scrabbled to find all the appropriate diamond shapes and push on them. The ceiling was low enough that they didn't have to reach above their own height.

"We've found them all, but the walls haven't stopped moving," Leena cried, her voice desperate.

"No, there's got to be another." Taurin was forced into a crouch, his body pressing against hers as the walls compacted further, narrowing their space. His breathing labored as their air space decreased, and dust clogged his nostrils. "Hurry! There's not much time."

Leena stretched to examine the bottom row of stones. "I don't see another symbol with the branch in the correct position."

Taurin could clearly see the carvings with his luminous vision. "I've got it!" he exclaimed, his eyes alighting upon the only remaining diamond shape with a branch on its upper left corner. Quickly he pushed at it, and as it gave way, the floor beneath them opened.

He heard Leena's shriek of terror as they tumbled downward into blackness, their bodies slipping along some kind of slide. He squeezed his eyes shut against the enveloping void. Down, down, until it seemed as though they were falling to the depths of the underworld. Just when he despaired of reaching bottom they landed with a huge *whump* onto a soft substance.

For a moment he lay there, breathing hard. "Are you all right?" he asked Leena. She rested beside him, panting.

"Yes, I'm fine. We did it again!" she cried, sounding jubilant that they'd passed another challenge.

Taurin rolled over, sinking further into the bed of feathers that had broken their fall. His amused gray eyes met Leena's questioning glance.

"This calls for a celebration," he said, planting his mouth firmly upon hers. When she didn't resist he deepened the kiss, edging himself closer until he lay atop her.

His weight caused them to settle deeper into the fluff.

"I can't breathe!" Leena croaked beneath him.

He sidled toward the edge until his feet touched solid ground. Helping Leena to rise, he briefly brushed his lips across hers. She looked infinitely kissable with her parted mouth, dreamy-eyed look, and blond hair flying about her face in disarray.

"I'd like to continue this, but we'd better move on," he said, his voice husky.

"I'll keep you to your word," she whispered, a coy expression on her face.

"What do you mean?"

"We'll continue this later." Grinning, she straightened her clothing, stalking past him to take the lead.

Taurin gathered their belongings and cautiously followed her through a curving corridor where they couldn't see what was around the next bend. A strange, acrid odor pervaded his nostrils, and he wrinkled his nose. "What's that smell?"

Leena didn't bother to answer. Instead, she stopped abruptly, and he bumped into her, cursing.

"Uh-oh," she said, and Taurin's heart sank as he glimpsed the sight ahead. The floor dropped away to reveal a cavernous hall, the bottom of which was filled with a pool of liquid that sputtered ominously. Reaching across the room to a ledge at the opposite end was a rickety ladder that served as a suspension bridge. With its tattered ropes and broken rungs, it looked as though no one had walked on it for ages.

"Acid," Leena surmised, bobbing her head in understanding as she stared at the pool below.

To test her theory, she threw one of her tools into the pool. The liquid sizzled and boiled as the tool disappeared beneath the surface. She gazed with dismay at the dilapidated bridge. How would they get across? Their journey couldn't end so soon. She'd be vastly disappointed if they were unable to learn the secrets contained within the Temple of Light. Because of the elaborate traps, she felt this was a significant find. She'd certainly never come across anything else like it during her previous excavations. The other booby traps had been relatively simple to defeat and were probably meant to keep out trespassers in the days of the Apostles.

But this place had much more immense proportions, and the deviousness of the traps pointed to a greater importance. They hadn't come across any living quarters that might indicate this was a dwelling, nor had they seen remnants of an altar. If not a worship center or a residence for the Apostles, she wondered what purpose this temple had served. And if the Synod knew of this place, why had they suppressed all records of its existence? Had they deemed it too dangerous for anyone to explore?

She glanced at Taurin, whose expression was thoughtful. He appeared to be contemplating a way across.

"I saved a couple of ropes from *The Predator*," he told her. Stooping to reach into his bag, which he'd rested on the ground, he drew out a long cord. "I think this one will stretch across. The other we'll use to tie ourselves together in case one of us falls."

Leena gazed at him in horror. "You're not thinking of swinging across on a rope?"

"No; it'll be a safety line. We'll use the bridge as much as possible." A thought struck him, and he stared at her, aghast. "Wait a minute. If this bridge were in perfect condition, what would stop anyone from walking across? The acid pit is here for a reason."

Leena gazed back at him with understanding. "There's got to be another hazard to knock people off the bridge."

Both of them peered intently around the room. Finally Taurin shook his head.

"We'll just have to make a go for it." He tied a knot in one end of the rope. "I learned a few things on *The Predator*," he told her, a smug expression on his face. "One of the sailors taught me how to tie knots."

"That's good and welfare, but can you toss a line to the other end?"

"We'll see."

Taurin straightened, stretching back his arm. In a lightning-quick motion, he spun the rope and tossed it across the chamber. The first time he missed his target. With a grunt of dismay he yanked on the rope to retrieve the end before it dipped into the acid.

On his second try he looped it over the pointed ear of a stone gargoyle guarding the entrance into the next passageway. Tugging on it firmly, he nodded approvingly.

"This should hold," he said, tying the other end to a promontory jutting out from the wall just inside the chamber entrance. "We'll use this other cord to link the two of us together." He tied it around their waists so they'd remain attached. "Your weight is lighter," he told Leena. "You go first."

"Thanks," she said, her tone sarcastic. This was one time when she would have preferred to allow Taurin to take the lead. Her eyes fell upon the broken rungs and the rickety swinging bridge. Below, the murky pool sputtered and spit, as though awaiting its next victim.

Her limbs trembling, she grasped onto the safety line and began the trek across. The bridge swayed underfoot with each step. She was careful to test each rung before putting her weight forward. Once or twice the forward rung gave way, and she had to stretch her leg across to reach the next one over, her heart thumping wildly in her chest.

About halfway across a grating noise sounded overhead. Looking up, she saw that a panel had opened in the ceiling. Spears began pelting down upon them.

"Hurry!" Taurin yelled, giving her a light shove. He was just behind her on the bridge.

Leena shrieked, covering her head with her hands. Crouching, she advanced along the swaying ladder. When it began rocking violently back and forth she clutched at the safety line. A spear glanced off her upper arm. Pain pierced her flesh, but she didn't dare to stop.

"Move!" Taurin urged, dodging his head to the side as

201

another spear flashed past. His action rocked the bridge even more violently. He gritted his teeth, holding on to the taut cord fixed to the other end.

Leena glanced up just in time to see a spear point aimed straight at her face. Screaming, she ducked to the side. The side railing, a frayed rope, gave way against her weight, and she tumbled into empty space.

Screaming, Leena felt herself falling. Just as she thought she'd be swallowed by the acid pool, the line tying her to Taurin went taut, jerking on her back.

"Hold on," he called, his face peering over the edge of the swaying bridge.

Leena's blood ran cold and her heart hammered so fast, she could barely breathe. Beneath her, the acid swirled and bubbled.

"Pull me up," she yelled, wondering why he was taking so long.

"I've got to get my balance," he hollered back.

Gauging the angle of the spears, he was able to avoid the onslaught as he slowly tugged her back onto the safety of the bridge platform. Crawling, they finally made it to the other side. Leena collapsed onto a ledge, her body shaking violently. The ceiling panel closed, and the danger was past. But still she couldn't conquer her overwhelming fear.

"Are you all right?" Taurin kneeled beside her, his face etched with concern.

"I will be in a minute." Before she realized her intent, she'd turned into his comforting embrace. "Thank you," she whispered against his chest. His arms tightened about her, and she sighed with relief. Held in his arms, she felt warm and secure.

Feeling it wouldn't hurt to spare a few moments, she lifted her face. Taurin's eyes darkened as he lowered his mouth to hers. As he kissed her, her intuition told her what her rational mind had been contemplating. Malcolm wasn't the man for her. He'd never sweep her to the heights of desire as Taurin did just with a simple kiss.

As his tongue thrust inside her mouth, exploring her with an intimacy that bespoke of possessiveness, all sense of reason fled her mind. Pulling back slightly, she murmured, "Taurin, I don't care who you are or what you did in the past. I just want to be with you."

With a groan, he pulled her closer and plundered her mouth with renewed vigor. With one hand, he cradled the back of her head to lend support. His other hand roamed her body, inducing a rising heat within her core that made her press herself wantonly against him.

Don't stop! she pleaded silently, the dangers they had recently shared making her yearn for a passionate escape.

Reluctantly, Taurin released her, his fingers stroking her hair. In his eyes she read an unsatiated appetite, and she trembled inside, knowing his hunger was for her. Dear diety, how she wanted him! She shook with the violence of her need.

"We'd better move on," he said, his voice thick.

"Of course." Leena wanted to protest but knew he was right. They had a limited time available to explore the temple. Rising, she dusted off her clothes while he settled their bags firmly about his broad shoulders.

As Taurin prepared to resume their expedition, he considered her words. They'd been spoken in the heat of the moment. She hadn't said how she felt toward him, so he assumed her actions were provoked merely by the need for physical comfort. When they returned home she'd resume her position in the Caucus, and his role as a farmer wouldn't garner much respect. Her family considered her nearly pledged to Malcolm, and she'd probably succumb to their wishes. Shaken as he was by her declaration, he didn't give it any credit.

With a sense of regret, he pushed aside his personal longings to focus on the task at hand. Doubtless a new challenge awaited them around the next bend, and he'd need all his mental faculties if they were to survive.

Chapter Twelve

Leena took the lead, with Taurin following, down a dusty corridor, up a ramp to another level, through a maze of passages to a third level, where they came to a halt. An empty space yawned in front of them.

"Do you suppose we should descend to a lower level?" Leena asked, peering over the rim of the ledge that held them. Blackness met her gaze, except for the ever present faint, luminescent glow. "I don't see any way to get down."

Taurin frowned, bewildered by this latest puzzle. "There are more symbols carved into the walls. See if you can interpret their meaning."

While Leena studied the carvings, he squinted at his foot. The floor dipped at his toes. "Give me one of your brushes," he demanded. A moment later he'd swept the dust away, revealing a circular depression. "Haven't we seen something like this at the different entranceways?"

Leena whirled around, a spark of interest gleaming in her eyes. Hastening over, she knelt beside him to observe his latest find. Curious, she traced the circle with her fingers but couldn't fathom its significance.

"It's not a pneumatic platform trigger, is it?"

She tried stomping her foot around the circle. "I don't think so."

"Then we've come to a dead end."

His voice betrayed his dismay, and Leena felt a momentary surge of sympathy upon noting the fatigue etched on his face. But the excitement of discovery took precedence. She eyed the solid wall opposite the gap, figuring there must be a way to cross. Or perhaps the next door would open from below, as she'd first surmised.

"Do you see a doorway beneath us? We could use one of your ropes to descend."

Taurin scrounged in her bag for a torch, which he shone downward, but the beam didn't penetrate the distance, nor did his special visionary powers.

"I suppose that's one option," he muttered, though he didn't sound too happy about it.

"Let's take a break," Leena suggested, realizing they hadn't rested since they'd entered the temple. "Perhaps after a brief respite we'll think more clearly." She rummaged in her sack for their provisions.

They ate some fruit and nut bars and took long swallows of water from a canteen. Her limbs trembled from exertion, but she was eager to resume their explorations. Taurin didn't seem in any hurry to rise. He'd removed the bracelet from his arm and was twirling it on the floor, presumably as he'd done as a child. Leena was surprised at the musical tone emitted by the spinning bracelet.

"Why, that's delightful," she cried.

Taurin flashed her a wide grin. "Watch what happens when I separate the rings."

He took apart the interlocking bracelets and spun them one by one. Each emitted a distinctive melody, and all three were different than the one produced by the joined armband. "I used to do this all the time when no one was looking. It brought me comfort."

Leena saw the brooding look on his face and figured he must be thinking about his unknown heritage. A sequence of five symbols was carved onto his armband—the same sequence she'd seen elsewhere. The middle symbol was a combination of two letters, if that was what they represented. But what alphabet had only seven letters? Could it be some kind of pictorial representation? Or a metaphoric language?

One of the rings he was twirling teetered into the circular depression and spun around, emitting its haunting musical melody. Suddenly Leena felt a vibration from underneath, and she glanced at Taurin, startled.

"What's that?" He leapt up, alarmed.

"Look! We're moving closer to the opposite wall." She couldn't believe her eyes. The ledge was extending toward the opposite end, and when they reached it a hidden door slid open, revealing a passage ahead. Hastily, they gathered their belongings before the ledge retracted. Taurin snapped the links together and thrust the armband up his sleeve. After slinging their sacks over his shoulder, he headed out first into the passageway.

The trek took them up and down several other levels, using a variation of ramps, narrow staircases, and slides. They were approaching what Leena assumed must be the bowels of the temple when they heard a strange scurrying noise from up ahead.

Taurin stopped abruptly in his tracks, holding a hand up to warn Leena.

"What is it?" she whispered.

"I'm not sure. But there's something around the next bend." A creepy feeling assailed him. It was possible that they were getting closer to the treasure and that the obstacles would become even more threatening. But what could possibly be worse than what they'd already encountered?

"Wait here," he told Leena, his eyes glowing luminously in the darkened corridor.

He gave her the torch to hold and advanced slowly, flattening his back against the wall as he rounded the bend.

Leena heard him cursing and hurried forward.

"Dear Lord!" she exclaimed. Before them was a large chamber covered with the sticky entanglement of a huge web. "What kind of creature lives here?"

Taurin glared at her. "I don't know, and I don't want to find out."

"Do we have to cross through here, or is there another way?"

Taurin's keen hearing picked up an ominous rumbling coming from farther back in the corridor. "We didn't come across any intersections. There's only one way to go, and it's forward."

Leena pointed out a rounded depression on the floor. "Try spinning your bracelet in there. Maybe it'll clear us a safe passage through this room."

Taurin admired her logic and was just reaching into his sleeve to loosen his armband when a whoosh of air roared through the passage from behind, knocking him and Leena straight into the confines of the tangled web. Immediately a door shut behind them, and they were trapped, their hands and feet stuck in the gluelike strands. A strange rustling noise sounded from a darkened corner of the room, and Leena glanced at Taurin fearfully.

"What is it? What's coming at us?" She didn't need a sixth sense to know that whatever creature lived in this place was advancing on them. They were probably the tastiest meal to come along for a long time.

Her eyes widened when she saw the giant eight-legged creature with huge bulging eyes and voracious teeth. Its spindly legs manipulated the web with ease, and it seemed to have a grin on its face, as though anticipating a treat. Taurin cursed and fought, but the best he was able to do was to reach inside his pant leg and grab hold of his blaster. He hoped the creature would be susceptible to its charge.

"Fire at it!" Leena yelled, seeing the weapon in his hand.

Beads of sweat covered Taurin's brow as he struggled to move his arm into place to take aim. The sticky strands clutched at him as though they had a mind of their own, inhibiting his movement.

Leena was closer to the creature; she could see the hairs bristling on its legs. A cloudy fluid began dripping from its feet—or whatever those pads were on the ends of its legs. That might be poison, Leena thought frantically. It's going to smear that stuff on me, and I'll be paralyzed. Her heart thudding, she closed her eyes in terror.

With a growl of rage, Taurin freed his elbow and was able to take aim. He fired repeatedly while the creature howled in pain. Red laser bolts sizzled through the room, severing strands of the web that cut across their path. With a final roar of agony, the hideous creature fell back into its own entanglement, a limp, motionless form.

"Leena, it's all right. We're safe now." Alarmed, Taurin saw that Leena hung limp in the living net. Had that gooey substance touched her? Was she dead? His heart hammered as he fought to free himself. "Leena! Open your eyes!"

Had she heard him correctly? They were safe? Her eyelids fluttered open, and she was relieved to see the many-legged creature apparently lying dead.

"I'm fine," she croaked, barely able to speak.

Using his blaster, Taurin cut them both free of the web and made a path to a door on the opposite side. The door swished open at their approach, and a blast of cool air refreshed them.

"We must be getting close," Leena said weakly.

Taurin dropped his sacks and holstered his blaster. "Are you sure you're all right?"

"Yes. Let's just go on."

His eyes intense, he planted his hands on her shoulders. She had an incredible urge to sink into his embrace, to be held in the warm security of his arms. When his gaze drifted to her mouth she thought he might kiss her, but then he turned away and the moment was lost.

"Let's see what else is in store for us," he said, his voice grim.

Facing them across a short distance was a sturdy metal door without any visible latches and with no sign of a circular depression at the entryway. Two stone statues guarded the door on either side, fierce expressions on their animalistic faces.

"That's odd," Taurin said, studying the stone surface of one statue for clues. "This has a different face on each side."

"This one has variations also," Leena remarked, studying the other statue. Touching it, she was startled when the head rotated slightly under the pressure of her hand. "It moves!"

Closing her ears to the irritating grating sound the movement produced, she proceeded to push the head around by one-quarter turn. The door in front of them lifted half a foot and stopped.

"Holy waters, it's opening!" she cried.

"Not quite." Taurin shifted the head of his statue to match hers, but nothing happened. "Try rotating yours again," he suggested.

They shifted the heads around in various positions and different orders, noting which combination produced a reaction in the door. Finally, when the left statue had the feline face directed to the left and the right statue had it directed toward the rear in a certain order of moves, the door slid open. Another door immediately blocked their path.

"Now what?" Taurin said, frowning in puzzlement.

"There's a slot in the wall on this side." Sweat dribbled down the back of Leena's neck as she bent forward to get a closer look. Shining her torch inside the slit showed an empty cavity. "Wait a minute! I think there's a depression in here. Taurin, stick your bracelet inside and see what happens."

"All right."

He took off the armband and inserted it into the slot. As soon as its weight settled in the depression, the rounded area began to spin. Musical notes sounded, and the door in front of them slid open. A stale, musty odor assailed their nostrils.

Shoving Leena inside, Taurin grabbed for his bracelet and snapped it on his arm as he charged through the archway, fearing the door would shut behind them, which it did. Leena hadn't uttered a word, and now he understood why. Facing them was a cavernous hall, which contained pile upon pile of gleaming crystal rocks.

"Demon's blood!" he exclaimed. "We've found it."

Leena was stunned by the magnificence of the sight before them. "This is incredible. What can these stones signify?"

"The temple must be some kind of storehouse," Taurin muttered. "Unlike most of the other temples on Xan, the Apostles didn't want anyone to enter here. They designed this place to be impregnable."

Leena turned to him, her eyes glistening in the light reflected from the luminous walls. "Not impregnable. I'll bet anyone with one of those bracelets could enter. They act like a key."

Taurin nodded slowly. It made sense, and if his spinning rings could effect entrance into this place, what else could they do? He visualized the repository of ancient bibliotomes he'd discovered on Yllon. That the books held secrets of the past he didn't doubt. When he had immigrated to Xan, he'd traded Magar some of the texts in exchange for a plot of land, but neither one of them knew how to break the seals.

As he moved forward to examine the crystals, he remembered the circular depressions on the cover of each heavy tome. Could it be that if he spun his armband on the circle, the books would open and the contents be revealed?

"I still believe the crystals are some kind of power source," Leena said, distracting him from his thoughts.

She'd picked one up and was turning it in her hand to examine the facets, her delicate features lit with awe. Her blond hair trailed over her shoulders, and Taurin thought she'd never looked lovelier, despite the grime that covered them both. He felt a surge of desire, but her next words planted him firmly in reality.

"We saw how a crystal rock was used to heat the water in the native village in the Black Lands."

"The stone wasn't responsible by itself. The crystal caught

a ray of the sun, intensifying the beam of solar energy. And there may have been an underground heating source, such as a hot spring.''

''Well, if it is a power source, how do you activate it?''

''Maybe the crystals need the energy from the sun.''

She pursed her lips. ''Spin your bracelet and see if the musical tone does anything.''

Taurin complied and was disappointed when no effect was produced. ''There's more beyond,'' he said, catching sight of an opening into another room.

Leena pondered the possible applications of the crystals if they weren't a source of energy. Maybe they had value merely for their aesthetics, or they'd been used in a type of credit exchange. Certainly the different sizes of the stones lent credence to the latter theory. But then, why hadn't any other archaeologists uncovered these crystals at other excavations? This place held a huge stockpile of the stones. Had people fought over them so much that the ancients decided to limit their accessibility?

Too engrossed to follow Taurin, and figuring there must be more of the same in the next room since she heard no other exclamations from him, she sank into a sitting position and took a small crystal in her lap. Turning it round and round, she studied the play of the multicolored lights upon its faceted surface. The stone was a magnificent gem; Grotus undoubtedly would enjoy possessing it for its beauty alone.

''Taurin, what are we going to tell Grotus?'' she shouted.

When no response was forthcoming Leena stood and marched forward. Pocketing the crystal, she passed through the opening into the next room. Taurin was seated silently on the floor, his back toward her, surrounded by a pile of books similar to the one he'd shown Grotus. Stacked in another corner was a display of rings made out of the same creamy, translucent material as Taurin's armband, the sacred horn, and—

''Holy waters!'' she exclaimed, rushing forward to peer at the rings scattered about in different sizes. ''These look just

211

like the ring I discovered on my last expedition. Zeroun confiscated it, and I was ordered not to tell anyone of my discovery. I wonder if he knows that more exist.''

Taurin twisted around to face her. "Look at this bibliotome,'' he said, holding up the volume he'd been studying. "It's similar to the ones I own.''

"How many do you have?''

"Enough to have filled several trunks on my journey to your land. I traded some to Magar in exchange for my piece of property. I believe he hopes to learn their secrets. So far none of us, Grotus included, knows how to open them.''

"Grotus? How did he obtain them? I've never come across books like these on any of my excavations. Do you believe they were left here by the Apostles?'' she asked, excited by the notion. That would certainly account for their value.

Her eyes narrowed suspiciously. "Where did you get your collection?''

His gaze skittered away. "I, uh, came across them in a library and managed to gain possession of them.''

"A library? How odd.'' Her expression became thoughtful. "I've always wondered if the temples in use today hold storerooms down below. The regional worship center over which my father presides was built centuries ago. Only Candors or members of the Synod are permitted access to the lower levels. So even though I haven't come across these books on my digs—or any other rings, for that matter—it is possible they are stockpiled elsewhere.''

"It might pay to have a closer look at your father's place,'' Taurin mused.

"We've got to agree on a story to tell Grotus.''

"Just tell him we never made it past the first set of challenges. If we tell him that we got inside but the place was empty, he'd want to come have a look for himself. We'll bring him a few crystals for a consolation prize and tell him we found them in one of the outer chambers. Why don't you gather some now? I'd like to remain in here a while longer.''

"What for?''

"Just to look around."

Leena perused Taurin's face, wondering why she sensed he was being evasive. Suppressing the questions that sprang to her lips, she left to do what he'd suggested, intending to ask him later on.

Taurin watched her go before snatching up another bibliotome. He wanted to test his theory in the few moments to spare. Fitting his bracelet into the circular depression on the cover, he spun the entwined rings, producing the familiar musical tone. Before his amazed eyes, a top section slid open, revealing a scrolling narration. He couldn't read the words, but their meaning was somehow imprinted in his mind.

Quickly scanning several other volumes, he realized they recounted the history of the Apostles. The readings told about the scourges of disease in their time, about warfare and regional conflicts, dwindling resources and erratic weather patterns, and the people's lack of advancement. The Apostles spoke as though they were superior and told of their plan to define a new order. Taurin couldn't find any further reference to this new order, but he suspected it was the religion of Sabal, because the Apostles were the ones who had given the laws to the people. But if he'd hoped to find any truth behind the religious teachings, he was disappointed.

He figured the story continued in the bibliotomes he had brought from Yllon. He had never understood the link between their two societies, but now he had the means to unlock the mysteries of the past. The rings, in varying sizes, were the keys. He couldn't wait to get home to confirm his theory and study the books from Yllon.

The value of the crystals was still beyond his scope of understanding, but the key to that knowledge might be in the books as well. If only he had more time to study this collection.

Before he left the chamber he selected a small ring from the pile in the corner and placed it in his pocket. They couldn't risk taking more, or Grotus would question their tale.

A tender smile tugged at his mouth when he found Leena sitting on the floor in the next room, surrounded by a pile of crystals. She held one in her hands and was twisting it side to side, a look of rapt concentration on her face.

"It's time to move on," he said.

"Did you learn how to read those books?" she inquired mildly. Her eyes, large and round, regarded him with keen appraisal.

Dismayed by her perceptiveness, he fumbled for an appropriate response. He didn't think it wise to admit his knowledge. The information contained in the books might refute her people's beliefs about their religion. He couldn't reveal what he knew until he learned more.

"Not quite," he lied, regarding his statement as a half-truth. After all, he was unable to decipher the words inside the books. The contents had become known to him through some sort of mental transference that he couldn't comprehend.

"I wish we could take some of the volumes with us, but they'd be too heavy a burden," he added wistfully.

"Grotus would inquire after the source. I filled a sack with crystals to give to him."

"That should make him happy," Taurin said approvingly. While Leena dusted off her clothes, he stooped to gather their belongings. Looking around one last time, he pronounced himself ready to depart.

"It's a shame we can't take more with us. What about those rings in the next room?" Leena asked.

He shook his head. "Grotus may have us searched. Now that we know the location of this place, we can always return. I don't think we should reveal what we've discovered here to anyone at this point, Dikran and the Synod included. Agreed?"

Reluctantly, Leena nodded. "We still don't know why this excavation was closed and the records purged, but I intend to find out. In the meantime, I agree with you that we shouldn't say anything about it. Our knowledge of these items might come in handy later.''

She followed him through the temple's maze toward the exit. At each doorway Taurin placed his bracelet in the circular depression, and they passed unharmed through each challenge back to the surface. Stars twinkled in the night sky when they emerged from the temple.

''How many hours had we been in there?'' Leena asked, feeling a heavy weariness assail her.

''More than twelve,'' he replied. ''Let's make camp here for the night, and we'll head for the beach in the morning. We've got plenty of time before Grotus has us picked up.''

''I wish we could contact Bendyk. We need to tell him about the plantations in the Black Lands.''

Taurin inflated the air-filled mattress Grotus had provided. ''Let's hope he's proceeding at a faster pace with his inquiries than we are.''

Leena watched him work. In the moonlight, his eyes glowed luminously. A day's growth of beard covered his face, giving him an even shadier look than he already possessed. With his tall, well-built frame, thick black hair, and glowing eyes, he appeared as she imagined Lothar would look, had he been merely mortal.

Taurin is not of this world, she thought, and wondered where the idea had sprung from. He kept speaking of Xan as ''your world.'' Yet, if he wasn't from here, who was he? What did he represent? He spoke of demons in his past as though he feared his own heritage, but, as she regarded his magnificence, she concluded that he must have descended from the gods.

Taurin caught her staring at him and smiled. The flash of his white teeth lit his face in a devilish grin, but something very human sprang into his eyes. Suddenly Leena felt exposed in her short tunic.

''The temperature is cooler. I think I'll change into one of my warmer gowns.''

She needed a moment of privacy, a time away from him to still her rapidly beating heart. Aware that Taurin's glance followed her movements, she picked up her bag and stalked off toward a clump of trees that would hide her from view. Hearing the sound of trickling water, she made her way through the thin underbrush to a small stream. After washing the layers of dust off her exposed skin she donned her red gown. The long sleeves provided warmth for her arms, but the low-cut neckline exposed more of her cleavage than she would have liked. Aware of how attractive a figure Taurin presented, she vowed to regard him in a cool, professional manner.

She needn't have worried. When Leena returned to their encampment Taurin was already lying down on his side, facing away from her. His gentle snoring told her he'd wasted no time in falling asleep. Leena stomped her foot in frustration. The least he could have done was to stay awake and talk to her.

She was too restless to fall asleep so quickly. Taking one of the crystals from her bag, she held the small stone in her hand. Moonlight shimmered off its polished surface, reminding her of the time when she and Bendyk had played on the slippery stones in a brook near their home, laughing and splashing each other in the moonlight.

Bendyk, she said in silent supplication, are you all right? What have you accomplished? I hope we'll be able to talk to you soon.

Bendyk was enjoying another dinner in Swill's apartment. She'd invited him there several times already, and he'd returned the favor by taking her out to restaurants on other evenings. They'd fallen into the easy habit of having dinner together every night, but Bendyk hadn't wanted to press his luck by pushing Swill any further. She seemed content to keep their relationship as an easy camaraderie, and he wasn't one to argue. His dreams of her were sinfully erotic, and as penance he forced himself to maintain a safe distance between them.

"I'm getting worried about Leena," he told Swill, who sat across from him at her small dining table, staring into her glass of wine. Her short hair, glossy and black, curled about her neck with her every movement. She still refused to adorn herself with makeup, although her cheeks held a faint flush that he regarded as maidenly virtue. Her simple sheath dress, of a pale peach hue, impressed him more than any elaborate gown would have done. She wore the gold choker that he'd presented her the day before. She hadn't wanted to accept the gift, but he'd insisted, saying it was a token of his appreciation for all the help she'd given him. Having assessed the financial records of the different members of the Synod, they were moving into personal territory, which was revealing interesting results.

"Communication from your sister is overdue," Swill agreed, her amber eyes soft as she regarded him.

She knew he was worried about his sister. He'd mentioned her often the past few days, wondering why they'd received no word of her progress. Had she been able to reach Grotus, and, if so, what were the results of her visit with him?

Bendyk twirled the stem of his wine glass. "Perhaps we should send someone after her—like one of the Caucus members."

"We need them to help conduct our investigation." Swill reached her hand across the table and was thrilled when he grasped her palm in his. She didn't want to admit how much she'd grown to like his company. The man still had his pompous moments, when he spouted his religion, but he'd given up on trying to convert her, and when he acted naturally he was very appealing.

"You two have always been close, haven't you?" she said enviously, wishing she'd had a sibling in whom to confide.

Bendyk's eyes filled with anguish. "We grew closer after my mother's death. She could have blamed me, but she didn't. We needed each other then."

"Tell me about the accident," Swill said encouragingly. He hadn't spoken about it after that first time, and she hoped he'd confide in her now.

Bendyk gave a long sigh and ran his fingers through his blond hair. "It was a snowy night in winter," he said, his eyes taking on a distant look. "My father had been called away for an unexpected meeting. I'd invited some friends over and needed to go to the grocery for supplies. Mother came along to do her shopping. Being in a rush, I insisted on driving. I took Father's rider because it was the heavier one. The roads on our estate are steep and winding," he explained, his voice lowering as he continued. "Despite the bad weather, I drove faster than I should have. There's a particularly treacherous stretch near my home. The brakes failed. I . . . I couldn't . . . I lost control of the steering. We crashed through a guardrail and went down into the ravine. My mother was killed by the impact." His voice faltered, and he couldn't go on.

The silence in the room stretched taut, like a rubber band about to snap. Finally he continued, his voice ragged with pain. "I was seriously injured, pinned in place. The rider was pretty badly smashed up. I began to get cold, and I was afraid I'd freeze to death before anyone found us. Leena was visiting friends, so she didn't know we were out. No one did. I hoped that my friends, when they came to the house and found no one home, would sound the alarm. But then, they might just assume they'd arrived on the wrong night. The minutes ticked by, and then the hours. I grew numb with cold."

Bendyk shivered, as though he were reliving the horror in his memory. Swill felt a surge of sympathy for him, but she didn't dare interrupt. He was finally sharing the story with her, and she was grateful for his trust.

"My legs were broken, a few of my ribs cracked, and I had a gash on the side of my head that left me dizzy. My fingers and toes grew numb; then I could feel the coldness seeping up my limbs. I prayed to Lothar to save me. It was my fault we had crashed and my mother had died. Her body, slumped beside me, still emitted a measure of warmth, and I think that helped save me from freezing to death. My prayers kept me alert; I knew if I fell asleep, I would never awaken.''

His anguish-filled eyes bored into hers. ''Lothar heard me. He sent rescuers at dawn. I was airlifted to a trauma center, and the police had the unpleasant duty of notifying my father of what had happened.'' Bendyk lowered his head. ''That was the night I decided to devote myself to Lothar if he should hear my pleas. I've given myself to him, but I don't delude myself that this can ever assuage my grief and guilt. If I had let my mother drive, or hadn't gone down that hill so fast, we might have avoided the accident.''

Swill squeezed his hand. ''Didn't you say the brakes failed?''

Bendyk shrugged, avoiding her gaze. ''The roadway was slick. They couldn't hold the friction.''

''What happened to your rider?''

''It was taken to a garage and sold for junk metal. I really wasn't aware of what had happened for days afterward.'' Letting go of her hand, he took a large swallow of wine. ''My father was devastated. The accident happened just over five years ago. It was shortly after he'd been censured for his indiscretion.''

Swill raised an eyebrow. ''What did he do that was so terrible?''

''He misinterpreted the Apostles's teachings as written in a set of ancient scrolls. For his heresy he was sentenced by the Synod to do a year of penance. He regarded my mother's death as an additional punishment sent by Lothar.''

He rose abruptly, his face shuttered. ''Do I smell something burning?''

Swill shot to her feet. ''Cripes, I forgot about the bean fritters!'' She rushed to the oven and heaved a sigh of relief that their meal wasn't overcooked.

''You really should watch your language,'' he admonished, coming up behind her and tickling her neck with a tender gesture that belied his preachy words.

Having removed the casserole from the oven, Swill took off her mitts and turned to face him. "And just how do you intend to chastise me, Bendyk Worthington-Jax?"

"By assigning you a penance." He towered in front of her, his gaze darkening as his eyes fell to her inviting mouth. "You'll have to kiss me," he murmured, wishing he could feel every enticing curve of her luscious body. Desire welled up within him in an unwanted coil.

"Kiss you," Swill whispered, realizing she was backed up against the counter. His face hovered above hers, inches away.

"Like this," he said, brushing her lips with a brief, feathery touch.

Swill didn't want to like him; he was totally the wrong man for her. And yet she couldn't help the thrill she felt in his company. Whenever she saw him sunlight seemed to burst into the room. Could it be the religious fervor wrapped around him like a halo? Or was it merely her response as a woman to his masculinity? He wore none of his priestly robes now. His plaid flannel shirt stretched across his broad shoulders. It was tucked into a pair of navy trousers that molded to the contours of his slim hips. His shirt was modestly open at the neck, just enough for her to get a tantalizing glimpse of his blond chest hairs. She stared into his mesmerizing blue eyes as her limbs grew weak with wanting.

"No," she murmured in protest as his mouth descended once again.

Having read the longing in her eyes, Bendyk gave her another teasing kiss. He warned himself not to lose control, yet his lust grew to explosive proportions when he heard the soft sigh that escaped her lips. It took a strong effort on his part not to wrap his arms around her and crush her in an embrace, but he wanted the next move to come from her. He stepped closer, so their bodies touched, but still he kept his hands to himself.

Swill leaned forward, capturing his mouth, not wanting him to stop the kiss just yet. She swayed against him, liking the lean, hard feel of his body. Would he make love to her with the same passion as he praised his god? she thought. She'd never had a man like him want her. The other louts who'd chased after her were lowlife types who thought she'd be easy because she dressed unconventionally and came from a poor family. Bendyk was too good for her, but she could enjoy him while their relationship lasted. She might never have the opportunity to be with anyone like him again, and he'd earned her respect and admiration. She wanted to offer him comfort for the grief he'd experienced and to erase the loneliness she often felt herself.

Her fingers found their way to his shirt buttons, and she began unfastening them one by one, her mouth clinging to his so he couldn't protest. Bendyk wondered what she intended, but he decided to wait to find out. When she opened his shirt and splayed her hands across his chest he felt curious as to what she would do next. There was nothing sinful in his curiosity; it was merely an intellectual observation. But when she took his hand and, with a seductive smile, led him to her bedroom, he figured he knew what she had in mind.

"Now wait a minute," he said, hesitating.

"What's the matter? Don't you want me?"

She said it with such casualness that he wondered how many other men she'd favored with her attention. "You're a beautiful woman, and I do desire you, but this isn't right. It's improper for us to . . . to . . ."

"To what?" Swill stood with her hands on her hips, a silly grin on her face. "To have sex together? Relations are encouraged among singles."

"But . . . but we are not intending to get bonded. Nor is this the month of trial marriages. Sex is only condoned if it's part of a serious relationship."

"So what?" Swill slid up to him and glided her body languorously against his. Reaching her arms around him, she kneaded his back muscles with her dexterous fingers. "Why

221

don't you set aside your lofty aspirations for a change and experience your humanity?'' she whispered huskily, her breath hot against his cheek.

Before Bendyk had taken his vows he'd lain with women who were casual acquaintances. But since his ordination he'd strictly upheld society's mores. Now Swill thrust her leg between his thighs in a seductive motion that brought a vigorous response, and his remaining willpower evaporated.

''If we do this, it will change our relationship,'' he warned, his voice thick.

''No, it won't. We can each go our separate ways when we finish our mission. Consider this just a way to relax, to relieve the pressure of our jobs.''

''I need relief from pressure, all right,'' Bendyk gritted, nudging her toward the bed.

His body surging with need, he couldn't resist any longer. With an animalistic growl, he tore off his clothes and then waited while Swill, smiling knowingly, unclothed herself before his hungry gaze.

Chapter Thirteen

Taurin awoke the next morning noting with dismay that it was well past dawn. Leena was still sound asleep on the mattress beside him, lying on her back, arms flung wide. A heavy layer of dew glistened on the grass, and the sound of trickling water reached his ears. So did the steady drone of insects and the occasional hoot of an owl or the howl of a wild animal. Exotic bird cries filled the perfume-scented air that was heavy with humidity.

Feeling Leena would be safe if he left her for a brief moment, he followed a trail through the jungle toward the sound of rushing water. The vegetation thinned, and he came upon a clear, cascading stream. With an exclamation of pleasure he knelt by the bank and scooped cool water into his cupped hands, taking a slow, thorough drink. Reminding himself that they should refill their canteen before leaving, he proceeded to shave using the razor he'd brought along. After managing that feat without cutting himself he washed as best he could, wishing the stream were wider and deep enough for a swim.

Keeping his shirt off, he trudged back to camp. The sun

rose hot on his back, the start of what promised to be a sweltering day. They should get moving while it was still early, but he hadn't the heart to wake Leena. She appeared so peaceful in repose, and yesterday had been particularly strenuous. She needed her rest, and he wouldn't steal it from her.

After gathering their supplies and picking some fresh fruit off the trees for their breakfast he squatted on the mattress, contemplating Leena's lovely face. Her thick-lashed eyes were closed, but he could see the rapid movements that indicated dream sleep. A small smile played about her seductive mouth, and he wondered what or who she was dreaming about. Her blond hair spread out like a sheet of gold, gleaming in a shaft of sunlight. His gaze, filled with the longing that was in his heart, roamed her luscious body. The ruby gown molded to her curves, and he imagined his hands roving where his mind dared to go.

If only his situation was different, and she was not nearly pledged to Malcolm. Had Cranby, her father, already arranged the match? A hard glint shone in his eyes as he imagined the Candor's reaction should he claim Leena for himself.

It wasn't his destiny to have her. And yet as he observed her breast rising and falling, he felt a yearning so intense that it became painful.

At that moment her eyelids fluttered open, and she caught him staring at her.

Leena had been having the most marvelous dream. She and Taurin had just discovered the cache of crystals. With an exuberant cry, he'd swept her into his arms and kissed her firmly on the lips. The taste of his mouth was so delicious that she didn't want to let him go. She wrapped her arms around his neck, drawing him closer. . . .

Leena flushed under Taurin's intense scrutiny. The look in his eye almost reflected the eroticism of her dream, and a restless urge suddenly took hold of her.

Taurin saw the sexual awareness flood her liquid blue

eyes, and his loins tightened. Demon's blood, how he'd like to make slow, passionate love to her! Her parted mouth, dreamy expression, and soft, sleek body lulled him into a state of suspended reality. Here in the tropical jungle, with the spires of the ruined temple rising behind them, nothing mattered but the most primal factors of existence.

Without conscious thought, Taurin stretched out beside her, propping up his head by leaning on an elbow. With his free hand, he traced a gentle line along her cheekbone.

"Malcolm wouldn't approve of us being alone here together," he murmured.

"I don't care what Malcolm thinks." She drew in a tremulous breath that told him how much his touch affected her. "He doesn't make my pulse race the way you do, or make me restless for something I can't define. Only you do that."

Taurin sucked in a breath, unable to pull his gaze from her face. He should get up now, move away from her before he acted in a manner they'd regret later. But how could he feel remorse for bringing her the pleasure she didn't even realize she craved?

"Have you ever lain with a man before?" he asked, knowing the answer, yet needing to reassure himself that this was what she wanted.

"No." The word was a whisper on the wind. "But there's always a first time."

"Malcolm . . . your brother and father . . ."

"They've got their lives to live and I've got mine. It's time I made my own decisions." As soon as Leena said it, she realized Malcolm had always been her father's choice for her. She'd gone along with the idea because it would have been an appropriate match and she liked Malcolm. But liking him, or even feeling a deep fondness for him, wasn't love; not in the sense of a woman and a man sharing a passionate need for each other. In her heart she sensed Taurin's need for her, and it struck an answering chord within her own soul. He still held many secrets, but she sensed his innate goodness. Perhaps he didn't realize it was there, but he'd shown her concern and consideration, and that meant more to her than any of his warnings about his violent past.

All of this flitted through her mind in an instant. Taurin hovered beside her, his gaze dark with desire, his hair tousled, his jaw clenched as he waited for her to answer the question in his eyes. Her glance lowered to his bare chest, and her blood stirred as she yearned to feel flesh against flesh, body against body.

"Make love to me," she urged, stretching out her arms. "Nothing else matters right now except you and I."

Taurin's mouth split into a smile, and his eyes softened as he slowly lowered his head and kissed her. It was a gentle kiss, a mere feathery brush of his lips on hers, but now that Leena knew what she wanted patience flew out of the door. She reached up, grasped his shoulders, and pulled him closer until he lay sprawled atop her.

"Gods, Leena," he grunted, his hips moving against her belly. His movements sent a wave of heat spiraling through her core. With an animalistic cry, his mouth claimed hers in a hunger born of desperation. Slanting the angle of his mouth again and again, he kissed her senseless. When she felt his tongue thrust between her parted lips she gasped with heated pleasure. He rolled his tongue in and out in an erotic motion that inflamed her senses. She returned the favor, eager to progress, and was pleased to note how his breath quickened and the bulge prodding her thighs stiffened.

So this is what it's like to feel a woman's power, she thought, smiling inwardly.

Breaking free from his kiss, she sought to remove her gown, wishing to feel his hot skin upon her own.

"Let me help you," he murmured, his eyes feasting on her as he slowly slid her arms out of the sleeves. Moistening his lips in anticipation, he edged the garment downward, over the swell of her creamy breasts, past her trim waistline, and below the golden triangle of hair at the juncture of her thighs.

"How beautiful you are, my *angella,*" he rasped, his eyes devouring her.

Restless, she lay back and lifted her face toward him. Shyness wasn't even a consideration. It was as though this was meant to be, that Taurin was the one she'd been waiting for all her life. Now she wanted to know him as a woman knew a man; heart to heart, soul to soul, body to body.

"My wife!" he uttered, kissing her gently. The tender expression in his eyes brought moisture to her lashes.

"I . . . I'm not sure what to do to please you."

"You please me with your loveliness." After a reluctant parting kiss he sprang up and unceremoniously stripped off his pants and boots. In the next instant he was beside her again, ravishing her with his eyes. All his inhibitions and concerns about their future were gone, washed away by her allure. With his index finger he traced the outline of her lips, pleased to see the awe in her expression as she regarded the evidence of his manliness.

"You're so big. I don't know if I can—"

"Hush." Leaning over, he silenced her with a kiss. "I'll be gentle. That is, if you still want to continue." His eyes feasted on her nakedness, lingering on her breasts. They rose up like the twin humps on Grotus's island, lush and full of promise, the pink tips like mountain peaks waiting to be explored. Licking his lips, he regarded her with a solemn expression.

"Say it now if you want to stop, because if I go further, there'll be no holding back." It took a major effort to restrain the wild passion tearing through him, but he had to control himself. He cared too much to risk hurting her.

Leena's eyes glowed with affection as she tenderly stroked his jaw. "I'm not afraid. Show me what to do," she said, glancing toward his groin.

In response, he lowered his head to meld his mouth to hers.

Leena thrashed her fingers through his hair as his body covered hers. The urgency of his kiss and the feel of her breasts pressed against his chest excited her to new heights. Her nerves screamed for release from a tension she didn't understand, an ache that began between her legs and spread through her like wildfire until her nipples throbbed.

As though sensing her deep desire, Taurin's hand roamed downward even as his mouth plundered hers and his tongue claimed her for his own. Leena writhed under his searing touch as he stroked her nipple and tweaked the tip until it stood erect, sending twinges of delight along her nerve endings. He kneaded her breast gently, rubbing the nipple, until a cry of ecstasy burst from her lips.

She clutched at his back, arching beneath him, shifting her position so he lay fully atop her. His hard shaft prodded her inner thigh, and she opened her legs, wanting to accept him, all rational thought evaporating from her mind as her focus centered on the feel of their bodies pressed together. An unbearable throbbing arose from her womanly folds.

"Now, Taurin!" she pleaded.

With a heavy grunt, he plunged inside her, halting when he felt her tightness.

"Are you all right?" His eyes, smoldering with barely restrained passion, scanned her face.

She groaned. "Don't stop now!"

He watched her as he increased his thrusts, wanting to see this first experience reflected in her eyes. When her orbs widened and a violent shudder racked her body, he penetrated her fully, eliciting a small scream.

Waiting a moment for her to grow accustomed to him, he resumed his movements, an erotic rocking motion that made her soar toward the heavens. The convulsion that had begun blossomed into a cataclysmic eruption as spasm after spasm of delight shook her body. Taurin's seed spilled into her as he reached his own climax, and they clung together, lost in a whirlwind of pleasure.

Sweaty and panting for breath, he rolled off her, collapsing onto his back.

"Did I hurt you?" he asked, his voice concerned.

Leena closed her eyes, too languorous to move. "I felt a momentary pain, but then the most incredible sensations overwhelmed me.'' Leaning up on an elbow, her hair trailing over her breasts, she regarded him with womanly guile. ''Taurin, I want to do it again.''

He hadn't thought of the consequences. Now that he'd awakened her passion, she wouldn't be satiated after one experience. Yet he realized this didn't mean their lack of a future together would change. She was exploring him the same way she might one of her temples: with an innocent excitement, an eagerness for discovery. And damned if he didn't want to explore with her.

''How can I resist you, *angella?*'' he said when she let her hand wander to play with his chest hair.

He closed his eyes, enjoying the physical contact, breathing heavily when her hand dipped lower.

''Later!'' he rasped, pushing her away and leaping to his feet. ''If we don't start back for the beach soon, we may miss Grotus's rendezvous.'' After pulling on his pants and boots he began to break camp.

Leena watched him, admiring the play of muscles across his broad back and the tautness of his body. He was truly magnificent, and she ached with wanting him. He filled a need within her that she hadn't known existed, and now the desire for more consumed her.

I love him, she realized suddenly, gazing at the heavy arch of his eyebrows, the sleek line of his nose, his finely chiseled mouth, as he turned toward her. *He's the only man I'll ever want.* Malcolm was her father's choice, not hers. She'd lost interest in any liaison between them and would tell Malcolm at the first opportunity, being tactful so as to minimize any hurt feelings. In the meantime she'd try to convince Taurin that their love was meant to be. That he kept secrets from her didn't faze her; she'd learn them in good time. He was gentle with her, and that was more important.

''Your wife,'' she whispered.

''What's that?'' He gave her a sharp glance.

''Now I'm truly your wife.''

He paused in his work, gazing at her with a wistful ex-

229

pression. "Aye, you are." *For today,* he thought sadly. Who knew what the morrow would bring? She might learn the truth about him, and that would shatter her belief in him. The affection he saw in her eyes would turn to loathing. His throat constricted as he imagined the pain of parting from her, knowing he'd caused her grief. It would be better if he didn't let her get too close. Physical coupling was one thing; emotional intimacy was something else entirely. He'd been good at separating them when seeking women for pleasure; why was it such a difficult task now?

Turning away so she couldn't read his expression, he made a show of preparing breakfast.

"You go ahead and eat," he told her, his gaze averted. "I'm going to refill our canteen."

Leena watched him go, frowning. Why was he so eager to depart her company? Did he regret what they'd done? Or did he care so much that he feared losing her to Malcolm? She hadn't told Taurin she hoped to honor their marriage vows. It might help if she made up for that omission; but would he insist on an annulment for his own reasons? He hadn't admitted his feelings for her, and she wondered if his affection was skin deep or more serious. She liked to think he felt as strongly about her as she did about him.

Biting her lip with uncertainty, she dressed in a work shirt and breeches. By the time Taurin returned she'd finished her meager repast and was counting her tools to make certain all were packed.

Taurin ate in morose silence, and she was afraid to interrupt his mood. Later, when they'd trekked some distance into the jungle, he finally spoke.

Leaning against a tree trunk, he regarded her with a hooded expression. "Leena, I want you to make me a promise. We don't know what's going to happen when we return to Grotus's place. Give me your word that you'll do what I command without protest."

She sat on a flat rock beside a stream, trailing her fingers in the cool water. "I will, if your request is reasonable. Do you feel our lives will be in danger once Grotus gets what he wants from us?''

"Possibly. Danger lurks around every corner while we're on this quest. It behooves us to be prepared."

He fell silent, and Leena studied the brooding look on his face. His dark hair swept appealingly across his forehead, and the nearness of his tall, rangy form sizzled her senses. He seemed troubled, and she yearned to know what he was thinking.

At last she found the courage to ask the questions on her mind. "What's the matter, Taurin? Why won't you speak about what has happened between us? Are kind words so troublesome to your tongue, or do you not feel anything toward me now that your lust is satisfied?"

Stiffening, he glared at her. "Not feel anything! Cosmos, woman, what I feel for you can never be expressed in words! It is for your own good that I keep my distance."

She rose and faced him squarely. "And why is that?" she asked, her voice soft, encouraging.

Taurin's heart melted at the tender expression on her face. "I'm not someone you'd normally associate with," he reminded her, his tone harsh.

Comprehension dawned. "I'm no longer interested in Malcolm. Taurin, you're the man I want for my life mate."

Stricken by her words, he sucked in a breath. "You can't mean what you're saying!"

"Yes, I do. I'm in love with you."

Inwardly, his heart leapt with joy. Yet in the next instant the realization hit him that she was an impressionable young woman, likely to fall for the first man to lie with her. "It's just an infatuation. You'll get over me."

"Why do you refuse to believe I really care for you? Has your life been so grim that you regard yourself as unworthy?" She drew herself upright. "I'm offering you a part of myself I've never shared with any other man. Don't you want me?"

Feeling like a swine, Taurin pulled her into his arms and

buried his face in her hair. "Of course I do, but this isn't right. You don't belong with someone like me. You can't know—"

"All I know is that we need each other. Can you deny that is true?"

"No." His voice was muffled.

"Then let's make a deal: We'll consider this an actual trial marriage, like they have at Beltane. If, at the end of our mission, you still insist on an annulment, I'll agree with no further imposition. Is that fair?"

"Yes, it's fair." Sighing, he gazed into her glistening eyes, unable to risk hurting her further. They'd play the game her way, even though she didn't understand the stakes.

Drawing her soft body into his embrace, he kissed her thoroughly, wishing their fantasy could come true. But like many of his past desires, this one was made of the same fluff, about to be blown away by the winds of evil that were sweeping the land. If they didn't find the horn by the month of Fearn, peace and harmony would cease to exist on this world, and everyone's dreams would be shattered, not just their own pathetically fragile ones. For all their personal problems, he and Leena mustn't lose sight of their goal.

The tide had washed up on the shore during the night, leaving a deposit of wet seaweed and shells on the sandy beach.

"How much longer do we have to wait for our rendezvous?" Leena asked, using her hand to shade her face from the bright sun.

Dropping their sacks onto the beach, Taurin shrugged. "Should be soon. Remember what we're going to tell Grotus." His forehead glistened with sweat. Their trek had been long and tiresome.

"We found a few crystals near the entrance," Leena repeated dutifully, "but we were unable to get past the third challenge."

"You can embellish on the bones we saw," he added,

gazing out to sea. If he looked at her, he'd be tempted to ravish her on the soft bed of sand just as he'd had her the night before, when they'd succumbed to another bout of frenzied lovemaking.

To distract himself, he queried her about her observations at Grotus's complex. They still needed to determine an escape plan should Grotus attempt to detain them, but as soon as he saw their means of transportation, he decided that would be their route.

On the water, an immense structure slid from the watery depths to the surface, its black hull gleaming against the deep-green sea. While he and Leena watched in amazement, a small craft was launched in their direction. As the motorboat approached the beach, they could discern a lone crewman aboard.

"Come with me! Grotus is eager for news of your success," shouted the fellow.

Taurin assisted Leena into the craft and then seated himself beside her on a small bench. They veered out to sea, zipping across the waves toward the ominous black vessel, which was sleek and tapered at both ends, with a superstructure in the center. As they neared the submersible, another crew member helped them aboard.

After climbing down a hatch Taurin and Leena found themselves in a control room. Facing them was a confusing array of flashing instruments and dials.

A young crew member dressed in a tan uniform was assigned to the visitors. "My name is Stoker," he told them. "Can I help you with your bags?"

"We'll manage, thank you," Taurin responded. They were shown to their quarters, a narrow stateroom with twin bunks, a built-in set of drawers, and a small desk. Compared to their cabin on *The Predator,* this one was spacious.

"The toilet's at the end of the corridor," Stoker said, backing toward the door as though intending to leave them alone. A shuddering vibration indicated they were underway.

"Any chance of our getting a tour?" Taurin inquired, raising his eyebrows. "This is a fascinating vessel." In an aside to Leena, he whispered, "We should learn all we can. We may have need of this knowledge later."

The crew member, gullible in his youth, responded in the affirmative. Taurin took advantage by asking numerous questions, pretending he was merely curious but sharply observing the details. He coaxed Stoker into explaining the operating systems, communications network, and navigational computer. Taurin was familiar with computer technology from Yllon. The Synod had repressed any development of advanced electronics on Xan, presumably because they wished to keep the people at a level amenable to easy control. Grotus's clout must be far reaching for him to be able to smuggle in an item as huge as this submersible, Taurin thought. Or maybe he had friends in high places.

"How many crew members are aboard?" Leena asked as they were given a tour of the machine shop.

"There're four of us. We don't need many for a sub this size. Some of the fleet's larger vessels hold a crew of twenty."

"What fleet?"

Stoker gave her an appreciative glance. "Grotus has a worldwide fleet," he said proudly. "I can't show you the cargo hold, but our main assignments are for short runs. The other vessels are larger and capable of traveling a longer range."

"Where does Grotus get the ships?"

Stoker shrugged. "Who knows? He pays well and gives generous benefits. That's all that matters to me."

"When do you estimate we'll reach Grotus's island?"

"The trip will take about twelve hours." He led them back to their quarters. "If you're hungry, help yourself to chow in the galley. We don't have a regular cook."

Left alone, Leena stared at Taurin, who restlessly paced the small cabin. "Grotus keeps a whole fleet of these vessels around the globe," she said. "This must be how he smuggles his contraband out of the different territories."

"It makes sense," Taurin agreed, hoping to learn more from Grotus himself when they reached his lair.

It was late by the time the submersible pulled into its berth at an underwater complex. Now at least they knew how Grotus's visitors came and went from the island, Leena thought as they were guided through a series of brightly lit chambers to a lift that took them to the surface. Through a window she saw that it was night, and the lateness of the hour was confirmed when they were directed to the guest quarters and told Grotus would see them at noon the next day.

They lazed in bed in the morning, enjoying a bout of leisurely lovemaking.

"I could get used to this," Taurin murmured, flicking his tongue at Leena's earlobe. He held her naked body in his embrace, luxuriating in the soft, warm feel of her.

"Me, too." She writhed against him, loving the security his hard, lean body provided. His hot breath in her ear drove her wild with desire. "Kiss me!" she demanded, wishing this interlude would never end. Their time together truly was like a dream. She was afraid it would dissolve once they returned to the Palisades.

Taurin's mouth crushed down on hers and their bodies entwined in a twisting, desperate tangle. He entered her in a smooth thrust, his passage eased by her slickness. Instantly, she brought her legs up to wrap around him, clutching at his back, riding him like a frenzied *enix*. She'd never wanted anything in life as much as she wanted to be with Taurin, and being joined with him was the ultimate joy.

Taurin thought his heart would burst from pleasure and something else he felt deep inside and couldn't yet acknowledge. As his thrusts deepened, a low growl rolled from his throat, and all rational thought flew from his mind. He and Leena were one, united in the ageless rhythm of the universe, and that was all that mattered.

Was it? he asked himself later, when they were resting side by side. Analyzing his emotions, he realized he had nothing to fear from the violence coiled within his soul.

Treating Leena with the gentleness she deserved came naturally to him. His response only confirmed his notion that the supposed demonic influence was nothing more than a myth.

"What are you thinking?"

Leena's voice cut into his thoughts. He glanced at her, smiling at the lovely portrait she made with her hair trailing across her bosom, her eyes still languid from their spent passion.

"I'm thinking how important you've become to me," he said truthfully.

She touched his arm, letting her hand linger on his skin. "I hope our marriage works," she whispered.

"What are you going to tell people when we return to the Palisades?"

Her expression clouded. "I'd like to tell Malcolm and my father about us first. Would you mind if we delayed our announcement?"

He was more concerned for her safety. There were still things about him she didn't know, other reasons why he kept himself hidden away in Lexington Page. "Not at all," he replied. "Let's wait until the horn is recovered. That would be a more appropriate time for a celebration." They still had a lot of work to do, secrets to learn. She might despise him after certain factors came to light. If Grotus had news of the horn, it would speed their path.

Breakfast was served in their room and the morning passed quickly. Later, they were ushered into the private dining room to greet their host.

"I was quite impressed with the mode of transportation that brought us here," Leena remarked, chewing on a bite of egg bread spread with fruit jam.

Grotus stuffed a leafy stalk of saltreed into his mouth. He'd changed his nose ring to one holding a topaz-colored gem that flashed with each movement of his jaw. His sleek ebony hair was tied into a ponytail at the base of his neck. As before, he wore a multicolored longshirt over a pair of baggy trousers. His jewel-encrusted belt, Leena noticed, was a relic of the Brotzoa Age.

"No one has ever been able to determine what method of transport my agents use," Grotus said. His gaze raked Leena from the top of her loose, wavy hair down to the bodice of her ruby-colored gown. "Even if you inform the Synod, they'll not be able to track our movements. You haven't the equipment or the knowledge."

"Your operation is well organized." Her compliment drew a pleased look to the smuggler's face, and Leena surmised that flattery could work to her advantage. "Do you keep the most valuable finds for yourself, or do you sell them to select buyers?"

Grotus didn't pass up the opportunity to impress her. "Many of my collectors don't care how the merchandise is obtained. They pay me well for the right goods." He beamed at her. "Some of the better treasures I keep for myself. I'm sure a woman of your talents would appreciate them."

Leena lowered her eyes demurely. "Your taste in art is exquisite," she murmured.

"No more exquisite than your beauty."

Seated on the opposite side of Grotus, Taurin coughed loudly. "Have you any news regarding our quest?" he asked, raising an inquisitive eyebrow.

Grotus didn't bestow on him the courtesy of a glance. He kept his gaze fixed on Leena while they consumed their meal—a curious mix of delicacies that Leena was only partly familiar with. She fed herself automatically, more interested in the conversation than the food. Grotus chewed thoughtfully on a piece of ambermeat.

"We did agree to a trade, did we not? Were you able to get into the Temple of Light?" His gaze swung to Taurin's, and there was no friendliness in his cold black eyes.

"The temple was booby-trapped. We couldn't get too far," Taurin announced. "But we did manage to bring you back a sack of these, which were near the entrance."

He withdrew one of the crystals from his pocket, handing

it over to Grotus for examination. Leena thought his expression looked skeptical and figured he needed further convincing that their tale was true.

"I was familiar with some of the traps from other temples I've been in," she said, "so we were able to get farther probably than your men or any previous explorers. The third challenge was impassable, however. We barely escaped with our lives."

Grotus turned over the crystal in his hand, licking his lips avariciously. "How many of these did you say you got?"

"A whole bagful," Taurin replied. "I'm sure they're quite valuable. Now what of the horn?"

Leena's mouth dropped open. They hadn't told Grotus before what had been missing, just that it was an important artifact. Grotus didn't seem in the least bit surprised by the news. He must have already known the horn was the object of their quest, Leena concluded, remembering the message sent by Sirvat.

"Unfortunately, my agents were unable to pick up any hints of its whereabouts," Grotus said, placing the crystal on the table. "The sacred artifact has not been presented to me for sale, so I have as little knowledge as you do about who has stolen it. Rumors are spreading among the people about the disasters that have befallen them. Apparently they don't accept the story of a substitute trumpet being blown at the Renewal ceremony. They're aware of greater tragedies ahead if the horn isn't recovered."

He spread his hands, a wide smile on his face. "I am just as eager as anyone to see the horn reinstated. My little empire is quite prosperous. Should disaster occur because the horn isn't blown in time to reset the cycles, I would be most unhappy. My agents will continue to make inquiries, and if I learn anything, I'll let you know."

"Taurin and I will need transportation back to the Palisades," Leena said, acutely disappointed at their failure.

Grotus's expression turned sly. "Don't be in such a rush, madam. I have much to show you."

Taurin gave him a suspicious glare, but Grotus ignored him, signaling for one of his attendants to clear their plates. Dessert followed, while they discussed the varying weather patterns.

"Go to the garden," Grotus told Leena when they had finished. "Blanchette is waiting for you. She'll take you to an overview of a nearby lake that's quite pleasant. Your husband can join you shortly."

Taurin remained, sitting rigidly in his seat, wondering what Grotus wanted with him. He didn't have long to wait. As soon as Leena left the room, all traces of pleasantry were erased from Grotus's face, replaced by a snarl.

"When you find the horn," Grotus told Taurin, "I want it."

Taurin stared at him. "Why would I give it to you? You just said you want this world restored to order as much as we do."

"That relic is worth a lot of money. Dikran will pay highly for it. You will give it to me first, and I will ransom it back to the Synod."

"Go to the devil."

Taurin half rose as though to leave, but Grotus stayed him with a gesture. "Who are you to speak of demons, Taurin Rey Niris? I know where you come from, and there they call you demon seed. Do you wish me to tell your enemies where to find you?"

Taurin sank slowly into his chair, too stunned to speak.

Grotus picked idly at his teeth with a lacquered fingernail. "After seeing your bibliotome I had my suspicions. Captain Sterckle had sold me some bibliotomes that came from Yllon, or so he said. I made inquiries about you and learned you had booked passage on his ship. Then there is your bracelet, constructed of the same material as the elusive horn. Are you still wearing it?"

Taurin nodded.

"I'll pay you a good price if you sell it to me."

239

"No deal, Grotus. And you're not getting the horn if we find it first."

Grotus leaned forward, hunching his shoulders menacingly. "If you don't cooperate, I'll tell your friends where to find you. You're under a death sentence on Yllon. You won't last long if they come for you here."

A spearhead of panic shot through Taurin's veins, more out of fear for Leena's safety than his own. She was in danger merely by associating with him. His mind raced frantically as he sought a method of appeasement. "We brought you the crystals. Didn't we fulfill our part of the deal?"

Grotus chuckled, a nasty, evil sound. "Whoever said I was an honest man? My agents will be watching you. Should they learn that you have recovered the horn and not handed it over to me, I will immediately contact your prior associates."

"How can I get in touch with you?"

Grotus's smile broadened. "Sirvat knows how to reach me."

Taurin's eyebrows rose. "So Leena was correct about the two of you. What is your relationship?"

"The Minister of the Treasury would do anything to please me." Grotus's eyes held a mocking light as he spoke of the female Synod member. "She has long coveted my attention and provided me with certain tidbits of information in exchange for my . . . uh . . . favors." He examined his fingernails. "If you tell Sirvat that you need to contact me, she'll be most happy to oblige. Now, if you'll excuse me," Grotus said, rising, "I wish to make your wife an offer." The way he emphasized the word *wife* showed that he didn't think much of their bonding.

Taurin shot out of his seat, his fists clenched by his sides. "What do you mean by that remark?"

"It doesn't concern you." Grotus snapped his fingers, and a couple of guards arrived—armed guards, Taurin noticed. "You will escort our brother to his chamber," Grotus ordered.

Seeing it would be useless to argue, Taurin went willingly, his troubled mind imagining all sorts of threats Grotus might make to Leena. *They couldn't be as bad as the one he made me! If my identity is exposed . . .* Taurin shuddered, blocking the violent images from his mind.

Chapter Fourteen

"Where is Taurin?" Leena asked, having been shown into the music room by Blanchette and left alone with Grotus. She'd had a pleasant stroll to the lake with her guide, but now she yearned for Taurin's company and wondered why he wasn't there to greet her.

"I wished to have a moment alone with you, my dear," Grotus said, his dark eyes gleaming maliciously. "Come, please be seated. If you're thirsty, help yourself to a beverage from that carafe on the table."

Leena remembered the last time she and Taurin had taken a drink from Grotus and refused his offer. Curious as to what he wanted from her, she sat herself in an upholstered armchair and waited. Grotus lowered himself onto a bench behind the magnificent keyboard instrument in the center of the room. In moments his fingers were flying over the keys, producing a beautiful melody that lifted her spirits and relaxed her mind.

"You play wonderfully," she remarked in astonishment.

"I've practiced for many years." As he played, his eyes

roved over her, his expression leaving no doubt in her mind what he wanted.

Compressing her mouth, Leena glared at him meaningfully. "My husband would enjoy hearing you play. We should summon him."

"He complained of fatigue and is resting upstairs. Come, sit here on the bench with me, and I'll show you the music."

"I can hear quite well from this spot, thank you."

Grotus lit a candle of incense. "This is my favorite scent," he told her. "I think you'll enjoy it. Come closer," he commanded, and this time she felt compelled to obey.

The spicy fragrance tingled up her nostrils as she sat beside Grotus, modestly spreading her skirt about her legs.

"Have you ever played an instrument?" he asked her.

"No." Leena gave a small smile. "My brother Bendyk used to play the hironrod, but I was never musically inclined."

"Your artistic talents simply run in other directions." Grotus showed her how he placed his fingers on the keys. "There are seven basic notes to play, plus three tabs and notches. Once you learn the basic sets the rest is easy."

Leena shook her head. "It could never be easy for me."

Grotus played a fast, catchy tune that caught her fancy, and she swayed in place, dreamily breathing in the tantalizing scent of the incense and enjoying the crescendo of the music that thundered her senses.

"That was marvelous," she said breathlessly when he had finished with a flourish. His nose ring seemed unusually large as she gazed at him. He didn't seem quite as unappealing as he had before, and that strange gleam in his eyes held her transfixed.

"If you like my music, perhaps there's some other things I can share with you," he said, taking her hand and guiding her away from the bench and toward a doorway. In the library, Grotus rotated a book high on a third shelf. A section of wall swung aside, revealing a passage beyond. "Go ahead," he urged. "I'll follow you."

Her mind in a state of numbed tranquility, Leena strode ahead. Facing her was a short corridor with a door ahead. Behind her Grotus laughed as he swung the hidden panel back into place. Recessed lights provided illumination as he sauntered next to her and pushed a touchpad beside the far door. It swung open, and Leena gasped at the brightness within.

"This is where you keep your precious objects," she exclaimed, rushing forward to finger the meticulously restored artifacts and other works of art he'd gathered here.

"I knew a woman of your fine taste would appreciate these. But they're nothing compared to my newest treasure," he told her. "Follow me."

"What is it?" she asked, licking her lips eagerly. Again the smell of incense drifted into her nostrils, lulling her into a calm serenity.

The next room appeared to be a bedchamber, with a large, round bed on a central dais. Black and gold drapes decorated the space, gleaming reflectively from mirrors covering the walls and ceiling. She was too intent on observing her surroundings to notice the sound of a door latching. The smell of incense was particularly thick here, clogging her nostrils until it was almost difficult to breathe.

"I don't feel very well," Leena said. "I think I should find Taurin."

"You can rest here," Grotus said in a soothing voice, motioning to the bed. "Lie down, and I'll see that you're well attended."

Feeling dizzy, Leena did as she was told, but instead of leaving to seek her husband, Grotus sat beside her.

"I've never met a woman of your unique beauty who also has such excellent taste in art. It's an irresistible combination," he told her, trailing his fingers down her arm.

Leena felt too weak to protest, or even to wonder why she felt so strange. The soft bedding felt comfortable, and she couldn't have moved her limbs had she tried because they felt so heavy. Grotus leaned over her, his face growing larger as her vision blurred.

"I'd like you to stay with me, Leena. Your man can find the horn. I need someone of your intelligence to appraise my acquisitions."

"Stay here? No! No, I can't." Leena began to rise, but Grotus pushed her down.

He studied her face, an expression of concern on his visage. "You look pale, my dear. I think perhaps your gown is too tight, I will help you unfasten it."

Before she could murmur a protest he rolled her to the side and unstripped the fastening in the back. His fingers lightly caressed her flesh, and a shudder coursed through her veins, disgusting her.

"Don't . . . don't do that," she protested weakly.

He pushed her onto her back and gazed into her eyes, smiling evilly. "I will show you the pleasures that will be yours should you decide to remain. You don't need to go away with that farmer. You'll stay here and reap the glories of my empire. Rey Niris will find the horn, and he'll bring it to me," Grotus snickered. "He has no choice."

"I'll not be your hostage," Leena murmured, misinterpreting his remark.

Grotus's hand groped inside her bodice, finding her breast. As he stroked her, his knee nudged her legs apart. "No, not a hostage. You will be the supreme addition to my collection. A treasure beyond comparison," he gloated.

Leena couldn't understand why the incense didn't bother Grotus. Choking from the cloud that pervaded the room, she closed her eyes, barely aware of Grotus's hands roaming her body. Her mind wandered and replayed the tune he'd performed in the music room.

C-D-E-F. Leena rattled off the keyboard notes that Grotus had taught her, only there were some missing. Try again, she told herself, focusing her mind on her one rational thought. *C-D-E-F-A-B.* Was that right? She counted them all together. *C-D-E-F-G-A-B.* That's it! There were seven notes, plus the other notches he'd pointed out to her that made for the different combinations. Seven. Why did that number ring a bell? Leena flinched as she felt Grotus's probing touch between her thighs.

"That's it, my dear." Grotus chuckled. "I knew you would enjoy this. The perfumed incense is very hypnotic, is it not?" A grin spread across his supercilious face. "I am immune to its power, but you, my dear, are quite susceptible."

Seven notes, Leena thought. Just like the seven letters that she couldn't decipher in the ancient symbols. If they were letters, that is. Her mind replayed the tone of Taurin's spinning bracelet. Wait a minute! What if the symbols represented notes? That would explain why there were only seven! Stunned by the revelation, she sat upright and stared at Grotus.

"Get away. I must speak to Taurin."

"You're not going anywhere."

"Oh, yes I am." The fog dispelled from her mind by a sudden clarity of thought, she leapt off the bed and started for the door.

Grotus reached her in two quick strides and grasped her by the arm. Leena whirled about, her eyes flashing angrily while she adjusted her gown.

"What would you do? Keep me hostage here while sending Taurin off to locate the horn on his own? Is this how you hope to obtain it for your collection?"

Enraged by her defiance, Grotus glowered at her. "Rey Niris will bring me the horn, but you are not the bait. I want you here for my own reasons."

"May I remind you that without me Taurin has no way to verify the authenticity of the horn?"

"You will authenticate it here."

"The Synod would not stand for you to hold me captive. My brother Bendyk is a partner in this investigation. He would see to it that you were hunted down."

Grotus snickered, his fingers digging into her arm. "No one can reach this island."

"We did." Leena thrust out her jaw stubbornly. "I'll not work for you, no matter what you do to me. Release me at once."

Grotus, staring into her lovely eyes glittering with anger, considered his options. He wasn't certain she and Rey Niris were telling the truth about their sojourn into the Temple of Light. It was possible they'd penetrated farther than they'd indicated, but he had no way of knowing for sure without forcing the truth from them. This he couldn't do, because retrieving the horn was more important. He enjoyed his way of life, and to see Xan descend into chaos should the horn not be found and blown would mean the destruction of the empire he'd so carefully built. He wanted to see the horn restored as much as anyone, and it was true that Leena and Taurin together had the best chance of finding it. His spies could tell him when they located the sacred object, and then he'd capture the duo and bring them here. He would force Leena to submit to his wishes by threatening to harm Taurin if she didn't cooperate.

Abruptly, Grotus released her. "Very well. I will make arrangements for your return to the Palisades." Besides, he told himself, Rey Niris will return to me of his own free will. He has to bring me the horn or I'll expose his identity, and that would make his life here worthless. Either way, the odds are in my favor.

After escorting Leena to the main hallway and summoning an attendant to take her to her chamber, he hastened into the library, closed the door, and put through a private call to a certain influential lady's private residential suite in the Palisades.

"Sirvat," he said when he heard her voice on the line, "I am sending our two little birds back home. They have failed in their quest thus far, but I would appreciate it if you'd keep me informed of their progress." His voice lowered seductively. "I should be most grateful."

"Of course, Grotus." He could almost hear her purring on the line. "I miss you. When am I going to see you again? It's been a long time since our last meeting." Her voice was edged with the desperation of a woman who knew that her man was not nearly as attracted to her as she was to him.

"Soon, my dear. Have you any news to report?"

"Karayan and Zeroun have expressed doubts about Magar. They're unsure of his relationship with Rey Niris."

Grotus knew very well what their relationship was, but he didn't share this information with Sirvat. "Be cautious. Leena and Taurin are aware of our liaison. Call me if anything else develops."

He terminated communications, realizing that he had no more clues to the horn's location than did Leena or Taurin. He'd have to impress upon his agents the urgency of the matter, and see that any information they gained was passed on anonymously to the duo. A rage of helplessness shook him. Not only did the Synod have to rely upon the pair to find the horn, but so did he, and Grotus didn't like having to depend upon anyone.

Leena and Taurin were summoned to a conference with Dikran almost immediately upon their arrival at the Palisades. The Arch Nome greeted them in his private reception chamber. Sitting in a large, thronelike chair, his figure seemed dwarfed by the furnishings about him. His gaunt face and slumped shoulders indicated a weariness that went beyond his years. But his keenness of mind hadn't faded, Leena was relieved to note; his sharp gaze was riveted on her and Taurin as they were escorted into the room by a Caucus member. The aide left, and the three of them faced each other alone.

"Well," Dikran asked in a tremulous voice, "have you brought me the sacred horn?"

Leena hid her failure by lifting her head proudly. "No, your grace. We have not recovered the holy relic, but we've made other significant discoveries."

A look of anguish passed across Dikran's face. "You've not found the horn! Then what are we to do?" he cried. "The people are growing restless. No one believes that tale about the trumpet substituting for the horn. The Truthsayers are making loud noises about rebellion, and Zeroun's enforcers are hard-pressed to quell the people's fears."

After a moment of heavy silence, Dikran addressed Taurin. "Where do you come from?"

Taurin was taken aback by the directness of the question. "I own a farm, sir, in Lexington Page."

Dikran nodded. "Karayan told me your property abuts Magar's estate. How do you two know each other?"

Taurin shuffled his feet. They hadn't been invited to sit, and he envied Leena's composure as she stood beside him, an elegant figure in an emerald green velvet gown. The crispness of autumn had finally arrived in the area, and she'd wisely chosen to wear a heavier fabric.

"Magar and I met during a trade exchange between our two lands," he explained. "I expressed interest in immigrating, and he agreed to help me. I raise edible flowers, which is not too common in your territory."

Dikran folded his gnarled hands in his lap, his gold robe reaching to his feet. He'd forsaken his headdress, and without it he appeared merely as he was—an old man who kept his dignity but had lost his strength. His powers of observation had not been lessened, though, and Taurin felt the intensity of the Arch Nome's gaze boring into him.

"The trade records have been examined. There is no report of a meeting between you."

Taurin shrugged. "Magar probably deemed it insignificant. My background is not the issue here. We didn't find the horn, but we did come across several clues."

Her voice pitched high with excitement, Leena told the Arch Nome about their excursion to the Black Lands, including the attempts on their lives and the illegal transactions of the Chocola Company on the exiles' island. Dikran's brow furrowed, and he promised to look into the matter. Then he urged them to continue their story. Briefly, Leena described their encounter with Grotus, omitting any mention of the Temple of Light. Their knowledge of the treasures therein might prove useful later on.

"If Grotus could tell you nothing," Dikran commented, "what are we to do next?"

"I have an idea," Taurin said, shifting his weight. "Brother Aron, the missionary who tried to murder us, mentioned that Wodeners don't betray their friends. I gather he was from the Woden district. Leena and I could travel there incognito to see what we can learn about the Truthsayers."

Dikran raised an eyebrow. "It is possible Grotus may still hear news of the horn, but we cannot rely on him. I will make arrangements for your journey to Woden."

"Just give us a rider," Taurin said, making an impatient gesture. "We'll do this our way."

Leena glanced at him in surprise. His tone of voice denoted no disrespect, but it sounded as though he were ordering Dikran, not the other way around.

Dikran pursed his lips, studying the younger man. "Less than two months remain before Lothar is due to reset the cycles. If the horn is not blown at the Grand Altar by then, disaster will ensue. The people may not wait that long before they revolt. The Truthsayers are using the situation as a weapon against the Synod. They must be stopped!"

He leaned forward in his chair, hunching his shoulders. "You and Bendyk are our only hope. You have to locate the horn."

Leena bowed her head, too choked with emotion to speak. It was a heavy burden, and she didn't feel worthy of it, especially after their lack of progress thus far. After promising to report as soon as they had news, she followed Taurin out.

"Your brother said he would wait for us in his office," Taurin reminded Leena, putting his hand lightly on her shoulder. Her body drooped, and she looked as though she needed support. He hoped her brother had achieved greater success than he and Leena had.

"Leena!" Bendyk's handsome face burst into a grin when she and Taurin appeared in the doorway of his office.

"Bendyk! Oh, I'm so glad to see you!" Leena rushed forward into her brother's arms, crushing him to her. How good it felt to be held in his warm embrace.

"I must bless your return," Bendyk said, giving Taurin a solemn nod of greeting.

Behind him, Swill rose from behind her desk, giving Leena a friendly smile. All four of them fell silent as Bendyk raised his hands and intoned, "We give thanks to you, O Lothar, for delivering these two children back unto us in safety. You are our lord, the source of life and its blessings. The harmony and grandeur of nature are representative of you. We owe you our eternal gratitude for your sanctifying our life and granting us peace and tranquility. Mahala."

"Mahala," Leena murmured, and both she and Bendyk were surprised to hear Swill and Taurin mutter in unison after them.

Bendyk's gold medallion flashed against his white shirt as he motioned for Taurin to close the door so they could talk in privacy. They moved their chairs into a circle so each could see the other.

"Swill, how are you?" Leena asked the tall, slender girl.

"I'm fine, thank you."

Swill cast a fond glance in Bendyk's direction, and Leena raised her eyebrow. She would have expected a snappy retort and wondered what had occurred between Swill and her brother in her absence.

"Did you find the horn?" Bendyk asked without preamble.

"No," Leena said, and proceeded to relate to him everything they had already told Dikran.

"Yes, I think that's your wisest course," Bendyk said of their plan to go to Woden.

"I'd like to go home first and visit Father," Leena said, casting Taurin a sly look from beneath her long lashes.

"Why? You'll waste valuable time," Bendyk retorted.

"I wish to show Taurin our estate and Father's temple," she said, emphasizing the last word.

Taurin caught the gleam in her eye. "Of course. I would be most honored."

"Father doesn't know about your vows," Bendyk said, looking from one to the other. "I could annul the marriage now if you wish. It has served its purpose."

Leena cleared her throat nervously, glancing at Taurin. "We've decided to consider this a trial marriage, such as the ones performed at Beltane. Taurin and I have reached an understanding, and we'd like to stay together." She was gratified to see the admiration in Taurin's eyes as he returned her gaze.

"But . . . but . . . what about you and Malcolm?" Bendyk stuttered, clearly taken aback by her announcement.

Leena was amused to see Swill's wide smile as she witnessed the intimate family scene. "I'm no longer interested in Malcolm. I'll tell him so when I have the opportunity, but I'm eager to introduce Taurin to Father."

Bendyk was about to say that their father would be disappointed, but he held his tongue, wondering, perhaps, if Leena had made the better choice. Rey Niris was a man of character, whereas Malcolm was accustomed to the easy life. He enjoyed the accoutrements of wealth through his inheritance and lacked the ambition to further his intellect. Leena was an archaeologist. She'd been educated and pursued her career with alacrity. Taurin had come to this land with nothing to his name and had developed his farm into a thriving business. They undoubtedly shared the same type of enthusiasm for their work. His sister probably would be better suited to a man who met challenges head on and could protect her in times of adversity.

He was still concerned about Taurin's irreverent attitude toward Lothar, but since meeting Swill he had come to realize that everyone had the right to his or her own point of view. It no longer seemed so important to convert those who were weak minded enough to doubt their faith. His calling should be more in the line of helping people, as Swill tried to do.

Pleased with his conclusions, he decided to bless his sister's marriage and pray that Lothar would grace her union with beneficence.

"Congratulations, Brother," Bendyk said, extending both his hands to Taurin. "I offer my blessings to you both and my counsel should you require it for any reason."

Taurin accepted his handshake, a pleased look on his face. "I will look after your sister," he promised.

"We'll pretend to be new settlers when we go to Woden," Leena told her brother. "Dikran is arranging for the proper documentation. Now tell me, what progress have you and Swill made?"

"We've made some interesting observations," Swill said, pulling at the long sleeves of her burgundy blouse, which was tucked into a black skirt that hugged her slender hips. "Magar makes regular unexplained entries in his receipts, which Sirvat deposits into the Treasury. Magar refuses to elaborate on the source. Sirvat's financial records are impeccable, but the odd thing about her is these trips she takes every so often, returning with a new piece of jewelry each time. She's usually not one to adorn herself, but the items are apparently created with rare gemstones."

"I'll bet I know where she gets them." Taurin related what they knew about the liaison between Grotus and Sirvat.

"I don't believe it!" Bendyk shouted. "She seems so straitlaced."

Leena gave a small smile. "Perhaps she hides a passionate nature. She certainly has a peculiar bent to fall for a man like Grotus." She grimaced in disgust at the memory of the smuggler. "You know, some of those items I saw in Grotus's mansion are similar to ones in Karayan's place." She stared at her brother. "Karayan has quite an extensive art collection."

"Are you implying that he buys his artworks from Grotus?" Bendyk asked, horrified.

Leena wasn't implying anything of the sort. "Not really. They just seem to share the same kind of taste. Although Karayan is a much better dresser."

Beside her, Taurin snorted. "We're not here to discuss anyone's preference in art or in clothes. Did you investigate Zeroun? As Minister of Religion, his department is responsible for administering the Black Lands. Someone there has granted the Chocola Company illegal rights."

"We'll check into it," Swill assured him. "We've cleared most of the other Synod members but weren't sure about Sirvat's trips and Magar's secretive dealings in his trade commissions. I still feel he's withholding information from us."

"You're wasting your time with Magar," Taurin snapped. "I suggest you check out Zeroun. The Minister of Religion would also be responsible for . . ." He held his tongue; he'd nearly said, ". . . *for excising any records of the Temple of Light.*" ". . . for the Black Lands," he finished lamely.

"Karayan wants to see you," Bendyk told Leena, "to make certain you have arrived back safely. He's been stopping in often, asking after you."

"Of course," Leena said, pleased that her father's friend would take such an interest in her well-being. "I'll stop in and say hello before we leave. Why don't the two of you come home with us?"

"Swill and I made plans to go to the Festival of Hathalat tomorrow. All the offices will be closed."

Leena's eyes widened. "But the Festival of Hathalat is where young maidens are . . ."

She stopped when she saw the laughing expression in Bendyk's eyes. How was it that he and Swill were socializing together? Could it be that their relationship had progressed beyond a professional one? They certainly seemed to share an easy camaraderie. Swill showed little of the rebelliousness she'd first demonstrated, and Bendyk wasn't at all his usual pompous, preachy self. What an unlikely couple!

Rising, she turned to Taurin and linked her arm with his

when he stood. "Let's keep in touch, Brother. Dikran said the people are getting restless. We must conclude this business soon."

Karayan was not in his office, so Leena and Taurin proceeded outside to the sleek blue rider that had been lent to them. Taurin started the engine, then glanced at Leena. "Why did you not tell Bendyk and Swill of your discovery regarding the symbols?"

"What? That the symbols represent seven musical notes and that the common string stands for Cadega, the constellation? We have no idea what it means," she told him.

"It means the Apostles might have come from there," Taurin said, careful to keep his hands on the wheel and his eyes on the road ahead.

"Are you saying they might have come from another planet?"

"Why not? Didn't you tell me yourself that the horn is constructed of a material unlike any other found on Xan?"

"With the exception of your bracelet and the rings we found."

"Doesn't that mean the material could have come from another world? It would explain why the Apostles were so much more advanced than the native population."

His words fired her imagination, confirming a theory she'd held but hadn't dared to acknowledge. "Wherever the Apostles came from, they brought us Lothar's teachings."

Taurin shook his head. "I think they established the worship of Lothar because they knew it would appeal to the primitive intellect of the inhabitants. The Apostles wrote the laws as guidelines for an orderly society. There was no supernatural entity involved." He'd always felt that the Apostles, who were regarded with such awe on Xan, had also come to his world, where they'd been condemned as demons. What had happened to make the difference he had yet to discover, but he hoped to find out while on Xan, feeling it related to his destiny. He was a direct descendant of those ancients, and learning more about them would help him understand himself and his purpose in life.

"Are you saying there is no Lothar?" Leena demanded.

Taurin shrugged, as though unwilling to commit himself to a direct response. She fell silent, lost in her own musings about Lothar, the Apostles, and the history of her world.

At the Palisades Bendyk was having second thoughts about taking Swill to the festival. Ever since that first night, when they'd made love in her apartment, Bendyk had been visiting her several times a week. Neither one of them said any words of commitment. Swill had made it quite clear that physical satisfaction was her main motivation, and Bendyk wasn't going to admit to any stronger emotions as far as she was concerned. The purpose of the festival, which was to induce young maidens to succumb to their suitors' charms, gave him a moment of guilt. He was using Swill as she was using him, and such selfishness was unworthy of Lothar's blessing. A bonding ceremony was still the ideal goal for most young people, and his continuing to enjoy Swill without any plans in that direction began to weigh on his conscience.

The same night that Leena and Taurin left, he went to Swill's apartment. Aware that she was not expecting him, he was nonetheless surprised when she opened her door wearing nothing but an overshirt with a scooped neckline. His gaze swept from her damp hair to her bare legs and feet, and he surmised she'd just come from the shower.

"Please come in," she said, her face coloring to a becoming shade of crimson. She led him into her living area.

"I don't think we should go to the festival tomorrow," he said bluntly. "Let's go visit Father instead. I'd like to show you around our estate."

Swill's mouth dropped open. "You want to take me home?"

Bendyk saw the doubt on her face and interpreted her hesitation as being due to her desire to continue their work at the Palisades. Accordingly, he paced the room, hands folded behind his back, and addressed a topic he wouldn't have spoken of otherwise.

"Before the accident that killed my mother Father had spoken out against the teachings of the Synod. Studying ancient scrolls had always been his avocation, and the ones he'd been examining were a recent find from the caves of Halea. His interpretation was grossly misguided. Charged with heresy, he was threatened with banishment to the Black Lands unless he rescinded his words."

He paused, fingering a pottery vase displayed on Swill's bookshelf. "Zeroun was responsible for assigning him penance. Father was allowed to keep his position, but the censure destroyed his faith in himself."

He fell silent, and when he said nothing more she asked, "Why are you telling me this?"

His steady blue eyes locked on hers. "I told you the brakes failed on our rider the night of the accident. I didn't see the mechanic's report, but my father told me it showed nothing irregular. Now that we are investigating the Synod, I am wondering . . ."

He let his voice trail off, confusion and doubt assailing him. He'd had his suspicions, but they'd been suppressed in the aftermath of the tragedy, and until now he'd had no reason to bring up the matter again. He wasn't sure he even wanted to dig any deeper at this point in time; but then, he didn't have to be the one to pursue the subject. Swill could do it.

"Of course," she said when he explained what was to be done.

Leaving Swill so she could prepare for their excursion, Bendyk contemplated the possible consequences of this angle of their investigation. What if his suspicion was true, and the brake failure hadn't been an accident? Did he dare mention the matter to his father? It would only throw the government into a further state of chaos if someone at a high level was implicated. Hunching his shoulders as he strode down the corridor on the way to his own suite, he decided there was no other choice: Father might know what really happened that night. He resolved to discuss the matter with him to clarify the issue once and for all.

Satisfied with his reasoning, he never once considered why he needed an excuse to bring Swill home to meet his father.

Taurin was impressed by the richness of Leena's familial estate as she conducted him on a tour. He'd met Cranby earlier, enduring an interrogation worthy of a Gang Inquisitor from Yllon. Cranby must have been satisfied with Taurin's responses because he'd offered his congratulations and dismissed them both, shuffling off to his library to pursue his studies. Leena had excused herself to make a private call to Malcolm.

"This is too easy," Taurin muttered to himself, inordinately gratified that Cranby had accepted him so readily. Apparently the older man was happy to see his daughter wed, as long as her mate was honorable and offered the proper respect.

"How'd it go?" he asked when Leena strode into the foyer where he awaited her.

"I'd hoped to see him in person, but Malcolm has a business appointment later. I told him the news over the messager. He was . . . outraged and deeply hurt." Her eyes reflected her pain. "Once he thinks it over I'm sure he'll realize this way is best for our mutual happiness. I just hope he doesn't complicate matters by speaking against us. His comments were not very complimentary."

"His pride is wounded, but he's a good catch. Someone else will snare him before long. If he's a gentleman, and you've given me the understanding that he is, I doubt he would malign you to others."

Advancing toward him, she kissed him soundly on the mouth. "You make me feel so much better. I'm glad you're mine."

He embraced her, sensing her need for comfort. After planting a light kiss on her forehead he stepped away. "How about completing our tour?" he said encouragingly.

They were just finishing when Bendyk and Swill arrived.

Save BIG!
4% Off!

"What are you doing here?" Leena said, greeting her brother with a big hug as he strode in.

Swill, trailing behind him, gazed with awe at the gilded entranceway.

"We decided not to go to the festival today," Bendyk said. "I'd rather show Swill around, especially since you're here. We're just in time for midday nourishment, are we not?"

"Of course," Leena said, and she and her brother showed their guests into the family dining room. Her father retained several servants, and providing for the extra pair of visitors was an easy task. They sat around a table laden with gold-rimmed dishes and gleaming silver flatware.

"Is Father not joining us?" Bendyk asked, his brow furrowing with concern.

"He's engrossed in the library," Leena said, her lip curling downward. "You know that he doesn't like to be disturbed."

Bendyk rolled his eyes before helping himself to a biscuit and butter. Leena engaged him in conversation while Taurin ate in brooding silence. Swill wasn't one for idle chatter either, and she ate quietly, casting nervous glances at Bendyk each time a new course was served.

"What are you two planning to do this afternoon?" Bendyk asked, finishing his meal with a slice of juicy porcheberry pie.

"I was going to show Taurin around Father's temple." Leena glanced at Swill, who'd barely said a word throughout the entire meal. "What about you?"

"Swill is going into town to make some inquiries." Bendyk put a hand on Swill's shoulder.

"What sort of inquiries?" Taurin asked, sounding mildly interested.

"I want her to check into the report of brake failure on the night of the accident."

"What!" Leena hunched forward. "What brought that subject up?"

Bendyk looked uncomfortable. "I was never fully satisfied with Father's explanation of the mechanic's report."

"You mean you don't believe the brakes failed? How would you account for the accident otherwise? Unless you blame it on your reckless driving."

"Don't open old wounds," Bendyk spat, his eyes expressing his pain. "I'm just looking for a better explanation of what happened."

"But why now? Why not five years ago, when it happened?" she cried.

"I knew Father believed that the accident was an extra punishment sent by Lothar for his blasphemy. The way things have been going around here lately, I'm not so sure we should let the matter go so readily."

"What did your father do?" Taurin asked quietly.

Leena twisted her head to gaze into his eyes and found reassurance there. "He interpreted an ancient scroll to read that Lothar exists in men's minds and was created in the spirit of love. He made an erroneous judgment. We should serve Lothar with love, and he will bring peace to our land. If we don't maintain harmony, Lothar will become angry, and you've seen what's happened with the weather disasters."

Taurin raised an eyebrow. "You mean your father actually said that Lothar exists merely in men's minds, implying that he is not a supernatural entity, as the rest of you believe?"

"Father admitted he was wrong," Leena gritted. "He apologized for his misinterpretation and has paid the penance." She glanced at her brother. "One of the reasons why I joined the Caucus was to find a way to clear his name. It hurts me to see him behave so differently around the Synod members, and even his peers. His scholarly efforts have always proven valid. I can't help wondering if there is any truth to his finding, although it goes against everything we've been taught."

Bendyk compressed his lips, as though he didn't give credence to the idea. "I intend to have a talk with Father. I'd like to hear his opinion about the cause of the accident.''

The four of them rose, and an awkward silence descended.

''Swill, do you know the way into town?'' Leena asked, feeling sorry for the girl, who'd mostly been left out of the conversation.

Swill lifted her chin. ''I'll find the way.''

''Let me walk outside with you.'' Once they were alone she turned to Swill. ''How do you feel about my brother?''

''He's the most unusual man I've ever met,'' the young woman admitted, casting her gaze upon the circular brick driveway.

''He cares for you.''

''We're working together. It's a business relationship.''

''No, it's more than that. He's never brought a girl home before.''

''I'm not his girlfriend,'' Swill protested. ''And even if I wanted to be, I'd never fit into a place like this.''

Understanding lit Leena's features. ''Do you mean to tell me you don't think you're good enough for Bendyk?'' She laughed aloud, astonished by the realization. ''By all that is holy, Swill, he needs someone like you!''

Swill shuffled her feet. ''I don't come from a background anything like yours.''

Leena's face sobered. ''Listen to me: Bendyk didn't plan to be a missionary. He took on the calling after the accident. Before that he was spoiled and aimless. Religion has given him a purpose in life, but it's not enough for him, Swill. He yearns for something more. I think your liaison has been good for him. He's looking happier than he has in a long time.''

''What of you?'' Swill asked softly. ''You're married to a farmer.''

''I love Taurin. He may be a flower grower, but there's much more inside him than that, just as there is in you, Swill. You have to believe in yourself. Give yourself the respect you want others to feel for you, and the rest will follow.''

Swill's expression clouded, but not before Leena saw the

longing in her face. "I have to be going. Bendyk asked me to interview the mechanic who inspected the wrecked rider after the accident."

Leena grasped her shoulder. "Tell me what you find out, will you? And Swill, I . . . I do appreciate the help you're giving Bendyk."

"He's lucky to have a sister like you."

On an impulse, Leena embraced her. "Be careful."

Hours later, Leena and Taurin were exploring her father's temple. The regional worship center consisted of a complex of buildings located in the center of town. The characteristic antlers—the branches of life representing Lothar—could be spotted from miles away, sticking up as they did from the various spires and the central pyramid point of the temple itself. Having explored the outbuildings, Leena was now showing Taurin the main temple. He'd seen the cathedral, side chapels, and offices, but when they entered the Candor's private robing chamber Leena hesitated.

"I suspect the entrance to the lower chambers is in here, although Father has never admitted it. What's down there is a secret known only to the Candors, given to them by the Synod when they take office."

"Is this where your father does his private worship?" Taurin asked, standing before an altar at the far end.

"No," Leena replied. "You see that receptacle?" Beneath the statue of a naked male cherub was a wide dish fashioned entirely of gold. "Lothar's lozenge pops out of the . . . er . . . loins of the statue each month of Mistic."

"You mean the lozenge comes out of the . . ." Taurin pointed to the very masculine appendage on the cherub.

"Not just one tablet, but hundreds of them. They overflow the basin. Yet Lothar always seems to know how many people to provide for. The count is nearly accurate, with only a small variation."

"Your father keeps a census tabulation, does he not? He can tell Lothar how many lozenges to provide." Taurin's mouth twisted wryly. He had no concept of how the lozenge was created or how Lothar could gauge the quantity required around the globe. This prevention of sickness was one of the wonders of Xan, and it made him almost want to believe in the god himself. Snorting derisively, he cast his gaze around the rest of the room.

"Where do you suppose the hidden entrance is located?"

Leena shrugged. "I've not been in here that often. Your guess is as good as mine."

"Another puzzle," Taurin murmured, his black-garbed figure moving briskly about the room as he poked and prodded at various objects, hoping to push a secret lever. "Did you check your father's desk? Perhaps a clue can be found in there, or maybe there's a key." He frowned thoughtfully.

Leena hesitated, feeling guilty. "I don't know if I should."

"Demon's blood, woman! We're already trespassing."

Leena was rummaging in her father's desk when voices sounded outside the room. Her eyes widened in panic, meeting Taurin's gaze.

"Go see who it is," he hissed in a loud whisper. "Let me know if your father is coming."

"He said he had a meeting with the town council this afternoon." Shutting the desk drawer, she hastened to the doorway.

"Close the door behind you," Taurin ordered. He continued to search the office until she returned a few minutes later.

"It was just some villeins seeking solace in the chapel."

"Perhaps it would be best if you stood guard outside."

Leena appeared to weigh his words. "All right," she agreed finally. "Call me if you find anything significant." After vowing to return to check on him after a half hour's time she left, closing the door silently behind herself.

Taurin paused before the cherub at the altar, studying the exaggerated features, including the enormous organ that brought forth Lothar's lozenge. The figure certainly didn't impress one with its heavenly origins, despite the halo. His eyes fixed on the curly ring floating atop the cherub's head. Wait a minute! Wasn't that the same creamy, translucent substance as his bracelet? Grasping hold of the halo, Taurin was surprised when it snapped off in his hand. Held thus, it appeared as a ring similar to the ones they'd found in the Temple of Light.

Unsure of what response his action would produce, Taurin spun the ring in the gold basin beneath the cherub. A light, musical tone reverberated throughout the room, followed by a low, grating noise coming from behind. Taurin whipped around in time to see a partition opening as a large painting swung aside. A dark hole gaped from the wall.

"That's it!" Taurin exclaimed and, without considering the consequences, he dashed over and plunged into the darkness.

Chapter Fifteen

Taurin groped about the narrow passageway for a light switch. Finding none, he had to rely on his own vision, which showed him that the path led to a stairwell just up ahead. He descended carefully, perplexed when he faced four blank walls at the bottom.

''Demon's blood! I hope this place isn't full of traps like the Temple of Light,'' he muttered to himself.

Feeling around, he smirked in the dark when his fingers found a familiar depression in the floor. Removing his bracelet, he hoped that the ring from the cherub wasn't required and that his own armband would serve in its place. He needn't have worried. The musical tone produced the desired effect, and a wall swung open, revealing a series of chambers opening one into the other.

As he entered, each room was illuminated automatically, but the first few he passed through quickly. Old records were stored there, and he didn't have time to search through them. What interested him more was found in the fourth chamber. The immense hall must have taken up an entire square block beneath the temple, and it was brightly lit. He strode about, staring at the matrix of glowing crystals.

I'll be damned, Taurin thought. The crystals are some kind of power source, after all. But how do they work? Some of the crystals appeared dark and lifeless, and he wondered why they didn't glow as the others did. But he pushed his questions aside to enter the next chamber, where glowing wires ascended into the roof, and a crystal display on a wall showed their attachment to the antlerlike decorations on the temple's edifice.

"Those things aren't just decorations," Taurin remarked aloud. "By the Gods, they're an antenna system." He stared with awe at the display, his computer knowledge enabling him to interpret the data. Those radar devices were sending signals back and forth to the weather satellites orbiting the planet. There must be thousands of them centered on temples around the globe.

So this is how Lothar controls the weather system, Taurin thought, aware that there still had to be a central monitoring station, which was likely located at the Palisades. Did the Synod know how to manipulate the controls, or was it totally out of their grasp, the reason why the system was failing? Computers had never developed on Xan, but they were commonplace on Yllon. Was this a legacy that the ancients had left behind?

Everyone who extolled the Faith, except for the Synod and the Candors, believed that Lothar controlled the weather, including Leena. How could he disillusion her by telling her their climate was monitored by a series of radar stations and weather satellites?

Stroking his jaw, he contemplated the function of the sacred horn. Was its blowing merely ceremonial, or did it somehow serve to reset the central computer? Supposedly it had to be blown at the Grand Altar in the Palisades, meaning there had to be a link between the sound of the horn's frequency, or the tune played, and the main weather system equipment. Since the Synod was so frantic to find the relic, he assumed it was actually needed to reset "Lothar."

Curious to see what he'd discover next, he strode ahead. The immense hall beyond contained a power grid large enough to supply the entire town and the surrounding region with electricity. Taurin followed a line of cables back to the room with the glowing crystals and realized this was the power source for everything. He'd known about the solar collectors on the roof, but apparently they weren't adequate to supply the demand for power.

How were the crystals activated? When he and Leena had seen them in the Temple of Light they were as lifeless and dark as some of those trapped in the matrix here. Did they die out with age, or was there a way to get them to work that was beyond the comprehension of the Synod? Or was the mechanism for delivering their power faulty, and the Synod technologically incapable of repairs? It seemed likely that the dying crystals were the cause of the weather disasters.

A disastrous thought struck him, and he sucked in a sharp breath. Upon entering Xan airspace in Captain Sterckle's cargo transport, they'd waited for a window to be opened in Xan's protective energy screen. How was that defensive shield maintained, and who operated it? Could the shield be powered by these same crystals, some of which were failing?

Another possibility entered his mind. What if the horn had to be blown to reenergize the crystal lattices each year? If that were so, then the horn had to be blown to fortify the defense shield. Now it seemed even more imperative that he and Leena recover the holy artifact.

Frowning, he debated what to tell Leena as he ascended the stairs back to the Candor's private robing salon. A partial truth would be better than the whole, he decided, not wishing to be the one to tell her that a machine was responsible for the weather cycles on Xan, rather than her god. In any event, he hadn't confirmed it yet himself. The pieces of the puzzle were just beginning to come together. He feared the people's horror should they learn the whole of it for themselves.

When Leena rushed into the Candor's private robing salon she found Taurin lounging in a chair behind her father's desk.

"Did you find an entranceway below?"

Taurin shrugged, averting his gaze so she wouldn't see how it pained him to evade the truth. "I was unsuccessful. Let us return to your father's house. We need to prepare for our trip to Woden."

Leena agreed, but her eyes narrowed as he continued to avoid her gaze. "Are you sure you didn't find anything?"

Taurin rose and hastened to her side to allay her suspicions. "Wouldn't I tell you if I had?" he said, brushing his finger across her lips.

Her large blue eyes stared into his with a look of accusation.

"Don't you trust me?" he murmured, stooping his head to lightly kiss her mouth. He hated himself for deceiving her, yet she'd despise him even more for revealing the truth. Like the bearers of bad news to kings in days of old, he didn't want to face her wrath, or be the one responsible for destroying the illusions of her faith.

Cupping the back of her head with one hand, he let the other roam her body, intending to seduce her to distraction. But when she swayed against him, encouraging his caress, he moaned her name aloud. As she kissed him back, he nearly lost his reason. It took a strong effort to exert his self-control and step away.

"Not now; not here," he said tersely.

"We'll finish this later." A smile of promise played enticingly on her lips as she gazed up at him, a coy look on her face.

Despite her outward show of enthusiasm, Leena felt ashamed of her behavior. How easily he bedeviled her senses. Imagine succumbing to his caress in her father's holy quarters! She should exert more control over her responses unless they were together in private.

Gathering her skirts, she spun around, ready to depart. As

before, in the Temple of Light, she had the distinct impression that Taurin was withholding valuable information, but she'd question him later, when they were home.

"Bendyk!" she cried, spotting her brother, who was stalking toward them from the cathedral. "What are you doing here?" Her face flushed guiltily, as though they'd been caught red-handed doing some vile deed.

"I thought I'd stop in to say hello before meeting Swill." He glanced at Taurin, a scowl on his face. "What are you doing in Father's private robing chamber?"

"Greetings, Brother," Taurin drawled. "We're searching for the entrance to the lower chambers. When you're at the Palisades next try to locate the secret entry."

"What are you talking about?"

Leena touched her brother's arm. "Each major worship center has a lower level. Father never lets anyone into the one here, and we haven't been successful in finding the entrance. It would be useful if you could find the access point at the Palisades."

"But why?" Bendyk shook his blond head in obvious confusion. "Only the Candors and the Synod are privy to the secrets of the temples. Why were you looking here, in Father's place of worship?"

"We'll explain another time," Taurin inserted hastily. For a brief moment of insanity he considered telling them what he'd learned and showing them the wonders below, but would they believe him that a machine was responsible for the weather cycles? It would still seem logical to Leena and Bendyk that their god provided for the people. After all, who had programmed the main computer?

"I don't see any reason to delay our journey until morning," he announced to Leena. "We can get in a few hours of driving before dark. Woden is four days away."

Leena looked crestfallen. "But I'd hoped to visit with Bendyk and Swill later."

"You should go," Bendyk agreed. "There's no sense in waiting. Just be careful. It is said Woden is a den of Truthsayers. If they learn you are a member of the Caucus, Sister, your life will be worthless.''

"We'll be traveling incognito," Taurin said, "and we'll only stay long enough to learn whether they have the horn."

Bendyk muttered a brief prayer of blessing, and Taurin followed Leena's example by bowing his head. How can I destroy their faith when it occupies such a significant part of their lives? he thought. And yet, if I don't, someone else might. Already the people were clamoring for explanations about the missing horn. If it wasn't returned soon, the Synod would lose credibility, and anarchy would result.

Escorting Leena down the hall, Taurin vowed to himself that he'd never let that happen. This world was his now, and peace had to be maintained. If his identity was exposed as a result, perhaps Lothar's will was at work after all.

Woden was one of the larger towns in the province of Prefectus. Being unfamiliar with the environs, Leena suggested that they stop at the worship center and introduce themselves to the local priest. He could offer suggestions as to where they might find housing.

"What about a realtor's office?" Taurin countered, eyes straight ahead as he drove down a tree-lined thoroughfare in a business sector. Banners were strung out along storefronts welcoming members of the International Merchants Association.

"The priest would know more about the people. If this place is the center of Truthsayer activity, as we suspect, he should be aware of the dissension."

"But if we're seen in his company, it'll link us with the Sabal order." Taurin shook his head, his mouth set in a determined line. "I think we should steer clear of any connection with the priesthood." Glancing at Leena, he gazed approvingly at her attire. Gone were the elegant gowns and the revealing circlet. She wore a simple day dress with a fitted bodice and a flounced skirt in a pastel floral print. He'd chosen to forego his usual black attire in order to appear less noticeable. So it was he wore a blue longshirt belted at the waist, navy pants, and nondescript black work shoes. They should both blend in well with the inhabitants, he thought, noticing how the businesspeople scurrying about their afternoon rush were similarly attired.

In the end Taurin won out, and they entered a real estate office. Admiring female eyes turned in his direction as he sought a free agent to serve their needs.

"We're looking to rent a place," he said, draping a possessive arm around Leena's shoulders.

An attractive brunette approached them and smiled. "Good and welfare, citizens. Please have a seat." She gestured at two chairs facing her desk. "How can I help you?"

Taurin chose his words carefully. "We want to be among other young people with progressive ideals. We've just been married"—he beamed at Leena, making her heart flutter wildly, even though she knew his action was only a pretense—"and have received permission to relocate." He drew the appropriate document from his pocket and handed it over. "We heard Woden was a good town because people here are . . . dynamic. You know, not stuck in the old ways."

The woman's green eyes glittered at him. "I see. You might like Brantome. It's a restored area in the eastern part of town by the river. Very pleasant, and the locals have a sense of community."

"Sounds good to me. How about you, *angella?*" He didn't know where the endearment had sprung from, but it brought an instant image to his mind of the first time he'd seen Leena framed in the doorway of the tavern, her golden hair backlit like a halo about her lovely face. She'd brightened the depths of his soul and showed him how faith could give courage and hope. Despite his wish to deny the impact she had made on his life, he was unable to do so effectively.

Leena turned to him, and what she saw on his face took her breath away. "Darling, that would be perfect," she whispered, both the look in her eyes and the way she spoke making him want to sweep her into his arms.

271

Anxious to be alone with her, Taurin completed the rental agreement.

"It's a good thing you're not looking for a hotel," said the realtor, eyeing Leena enviously. "There's a convention in town and all the rooms are booked."

"The International Merchants Association?" Taurin guessed.

"The organization has its roots in Woden, you know. Stephan Tom is the president. I believe he has a home in Brantome. You might even run into him. Talk about a dynamic character!" The brunette pursed her lips. "Some of his views are downright heretical. But I shouldn't be telling you this, should I?"

"Heretical? What do you mean?" Leena asked, leaning forward, a look of keen interest on her face.

The realtor glanced at her co-workers before lowering her voice. "If you're interested in progressive viewpoints, check out the White Enix Pub. You'll find it easily enough. It's in a reconstructed mill by the water."

Concluding their business, Taurin thanked her and left, the keys to their new home in hand.

" 'Prefectus, a lushly forested district cut by deep rivers, is noted as much for its flower-strewn meadows and rolling hillsides as it is for its classic cuisine and wild-growing *rushtees,* a type of fungus valued as an edible delicacy,' " Leena quoted from a guidebook handed to them along with the rental papers. " 'Woden began as an early settlement by the Organdy River. Originally the town consisted of a cluster of stone houses, a school, a small worship center, and a mill. As the town expanded, this part became known as Brantome, named after one of the founders.' "

She glanced at Taurin, thrilled at the prospect of exploration. "The former religious house has been turned into a museum. Maybe we can stop in there one day if we have time."

Taurin nodded, having been only half tuned in to her recital. He was eager to view the White Enix Pub. Following a road that led toward the river, he drove slowly past the old stone building, where a waterwheel churned in the swiftly moving current. Weeping willows and red-leafed syca trees lined the riverbanks. Through the open windows of the rider, the sounds of rushing water played music in his ears.

Turning away from the seductively peaceful scene, he entered a residential sector and drove along narrow streets graced by buildings with arched doorways and fluted chimneys spouting pungent woodsmoke. Blooming flowerpots kept company on windowsills with collections of colored glass bottles.

"What a charming neighborhood!" Leena exclaimed, delighted. Peering out her side window, she sniffed the cool, brisk air. Which one of these tidy little homes was theirs?

They found the designated address and emerged from their parked rider to stare at the stone facade of a modest two-story structure. Its red-tiled roof was marred only by the antenna of a modern messager system. Taurin grunted as he withdrew their luggage from the trunk. They'd bought new suitcases and filled them with wardrobes suitable to their current mission. Leena hoped they looked like a normal young couple as they proceeded into the house, using the key the realtor had given them.

"Oh, I love it!" she exclaimed, rushing from the living area into the kitchen and small dining alcove, then upstairs to view the bedrooms. A spacious master bedroom faced the street, while two smaller rooms took up the rear upstairs floor.

Taurin trudged up after her, setting both suitcases heavily onto the carpeted floor. Straightening his spine, he gave her a lazy grin.

"We're home, *angella*." His arms stretched out for her, and she ran into his embrace, lifting her chin so he could kiss her.

As their mouths melded together, Leena wished this was their home and that they were starting a new life together.

Drawing back excitedly, she said, "We'll have to buy food and cleaning supplies."

"Hold on," Taurin said, touching a finger to her lips. "Remember, we're only here temporarily."

"We still have to eat." She had the most incredible urge to keep house now that Taurin was her husband. *Husband.* The word thrilled through her as she gazed at him with deep affection.

"I'll go downstairs and see what's in the kitchen while you unpack," he agreed, his tender smile making her heart soar with joy. "Or should we even bother with the suitcases? I was hoping we wouldn't be here that long."

His words reminded her of the urgency of their mission. Chastising herself for becoming sidetracked by personal desires, she gave him a rueful grin. "I'm forgetting why we're here because I want so badly to be alone with you. Please forgive me."

"There's nothing to forgive." His eyes darkened until they were like two chunks of coals pierced by a faint luminescent tinge. "Remember, we'll have that four-day drive back to the Palisades when we're finished in Woden."

The sensual curve of his mouth told her how much he'd enjoyed their nights together in the various hostelries along the route, safe houses where their security had been assured by the Synod.

Before she could respond, a loud knock sounded from below. They exchanged surprised glances, and then both rushed downstairs.

"Who's there?" Leena called out.

"My name is Lilot," a singsong female voice replied. "I'm your neighbor from across the street."

Curious, Leena flung the door wide, aware of Taurin's protective stance behind her. She smiled at the young woman standing on the doorstep.

"Good and welfare, neighbors." The woman's reddish-blond hair reached her shoulders, where it curled under in a soft style. She wore several layers of pink- and rose-colored clothing: a tunic top, an apron, covered by an over-blouse, beneath which peeped out a pair of tight dusky rose leggings tucked into high-topped, sturdy black shoes. Her single item of ornamentation was a pendant necklace depicting vegetables.

"I saw you pull in and was just taking my criche out of the oven," she said, offering Leena an aromatic casserole dish. "I thought you might like this, since you won't have much time to make preparations. I grow all my own vegetables, so you don't have to worry about contaminants." She beamed happily. "After the festival I'll bake you a loaf of my bundan bread."

"Thank you," Leena said, accepting the dish. "My name is Leena, and this is Taurin." As she introduced him, Taurin settled his hulking presence at her side, nodding a greeting at their neighbor.

"I hope we'll get to know each other better," Lilot continued, "but I must hurry to complete my own arrangements."

"Arrangements for what?"

"Why, tonight begins the festival of Tu Imbol."

Leena's jaw dropped. Engrossed in their pretend homecoming, she'd forgotten all about the holiday! Her gaze swung to Taurin. "All of the restaurants will be closed tonight, and that includes the White Enix Pub. We won't be able to dine out."

Lilot gave them a quizzical glance. "You'd best get to market if you want to do any shopping. It'll be closing by four today."

"We're new here," Taurin said, stating the obvious. "Where do we go?"

Lilot gave them directions. Waving as she turned away, she shouted, "Let me know if you need anything! I've got to take my qiana fritters out of the oven."

She trotted away, and Leena slowly shut the door in her wake.

"We're going to have to wait until the day after tomorrow

to visit the White Enix Pub," she exclaimed in dismay.

Taurin glowered at her. "We'd better do what Lilot said and get to the market before it closes." Taking the keys to the rider from his pants pocket, he asked, "Are you ready?"

He didn't seem at all pleased by this turn of events, but it couldn't be helped. Grabbing her carryall, Leena nodded.

"I'd like to attend services tonight," she said. "Tu Imbol is an important holiday. The grove festival—"

"No!" Taurin spun to face her, steely eyes blazing. "We don't go near the worship center."

Riled by his tone of voice, she was about to make a waspish retort when she realized he was right. "Yes, of course," she said, averting her gaze. "We cannot afford to be identified with the religious order. I'm sorry, Taurin."

If they couldn't attend the sacred celebration, she'd just have to follow her own worship service at home. And even though she understood Taurin's rationale, she was upset he didn't share her disappointment. His tone of voice made it clear what he thought of religious services, and she wondered how their differences would ever be reconciled. While on this mission, they were working things out together, but what would happen when she moved in with Taurin permanently?

Slinging her bag over her shoulder, she stepped outside into the bright afternoon sunshine. This region should have been colder by now, with the beginnings of frost. Instead it was like early autumn, with a fresh pine scent in the air. She took the abnormal climate as another sign of disruption in the weather cycles and mentioned her observation to Taurin.

"Perhaps we'll gain some useful information at the town market," she said optimistically.

"Let's hope so." Touching her elbow, Taurin guided her toward their parked rider. "Otherwise we can write off today as a loss."

Luckily, the market turned out to be the heart and soul of the town. Its colorful sights and tantalizing smells converged to give it a sense of community that Leena found highly appealing. She counted more than fifty local farmers who tempted consumers with an array of fruits, vegetables, natural fiber clothing, and homemade products such as honey, cheese, wine, baked goods, and jams.

A flower seller attracted Taurin's attention, while Leena was fascinated by the varieties of mushrooms for sale. From the guidebook, she'd learned that this area was renowned for its edible fungi, but she'd never seen so many different kinds.

"Who's cooking tonight?" Taurin asked after he'd rejoined her.

Leena gave him a quizzical glance. "I assumed it would be me."

Taurin flashed her a wide grin. "Wild mushroom tart is one of my specialties. I can't resist when they're so plentiful here. And then there's my chocolate salad." He'd procured a wicker basket and began negotiating with various vendors as she trailed after him, her mouth open in astonishment.

"I didn't know you could cook," she exclaimed.

His dazzling smile took her breath away. "I've got to do something during those long lonely hours I spend by myself."

"I thought you studied archaeological texts and worked on your drawings."

"They don't put food in a man's stomach," he said, chuckling, and Leena was amazed to glimpse this other side of him.

They walked past stalls offering garlic, leeks, carrots, and an assortment of leafy vegetables unfamiliar to her. Clothes merchants, fishmongers, butchers, and cheese sellers hawked their wares. Live chickens, geese, and ducks strutted about fenced cubicles, their squawking adding to the general cacophony. Bundles of produce spilled into the aisles, which were crowded with buyers. Citrus fragrance spiced the air, along with the aroma of ripened fruit warming in the sun.

Taurin stopped before a baker to order the flour and other supplies he would need to make his mushroom tart.

"I'm lucky I got me bakery," said the baker, a stout fellow wearing a flat-topped cap on his balding head. "Those produce farmers, they's real worried about the weather. If it don't get cool, their crops'll be ruined for next season.''

A young man with an unshaven face and baggy pants overheard the remark. He gave up inspecting the stall offering squash and sauntered over. ''It's a ruse by the Synod to get us to tighten our belts. If you ask me, they're causing these weather disasters. They know that when things are righted again we'll be so grateful that we won't mind an extra tribute to Lothar.'' With a disgusted grunt, he spat on the ground.

The vendor's eyes darted about nervously, as though he were afraid someone in authority would overhear their conversation. Taurin took up the slack. It wasn't too difficult to force an interested expression to his face.

''I'm in full agreement with you, Brother,'' he said, handing a bag of flour to the baker so it could be weighed. ''Things have gotten out of hand. It's beyond me what can be done about it, though.''

The stranger narrowed his gaze. ''You're new to these parts, aren't you? Are you here for the merchant convention?''

''No, sir.'' He put an arm around Leena's waist and smiled down at her. ''We just got married and have permission to settle here. I have some experience in growing crops and was hoping to land a job on one of the local farms.''

''The farms won't have any jobs if the soil dries up.'' The man lowered his voice to a conspiratorial whisper. ''We're fixing to do something about that real soon.''

''What do you mean?'' Taurin asked, his mild tone belying the keen interest that sprang into his eyes.

''You'll find out if you stick around long enough,'' said the stranger, winking before he sauntered off down the lane.

They completed their shopping, sensing an undercurrent of tension permeating the marketplace. Obviously something was in the works, but despite their determination, they failed to learn what was going on.

When the vendors began putting away their goods Leena

and Taurin gave up trying to coax information out of the reluctant merchants and headed for home. True to his word, Taurin cooked a savory mushroom tart, which he put aside so they could consume it along with their neighbor's vegetarian casserole. As he was making dessert—his renowned chocolate salad—Leena peered over his shoulder to observe his technique.

"When we're ready," he told her, his hands moving deftly, "I'll combine these berries with the chocolate and orange sorbets we bought. Normally I'd include some of my edible flowers, such as pansies and violets, but there weren't any for sale at the market. I'll have to talk to my distributor about supplying this region," he concluded, putting the bowl of rinsed berries into the cooler unit.

Dusk was descending rapidly, and he was starving, but when he glanced at Leena, all thoughts of food fled from his mind. She appeared so delightfully domestic, wearing an apron she had purchased, with her hair pulled back into a low ponytail.

As though following his train of thought, her face broke into a wide grin. "Let's save that for dessert. The sun is setting. We must commence our prayers."

For once Taurin didn't argue. He knew this was an important holiday, although he wasn't familiar with the ritual. In deference to her sensitivities, he helped her set the table for their repast.

"You can uncork the wine," she instructed. "We'll need both bottles opened, but pour the white first."

When they were seated Leena raised her glass of wine, speaking to Taurin from across the table. "Our first cup of wine is entirely white, reminding us of winter, when nature sleeps and the land is often covered with snow. Let us give thanks that we are together to join in this celebration."

After she had uttered a prayer she and Taurin sipped from their glasses. "Observe the fruits on the table," she said, pointing. "Each type of fruit represents a season. Let us first partake of varieties with a peel or shell that cannot be eaten."

She selected for herself a thick-rinded citrus, a furry kemeris, and a nut with a hard shell. Taurin reached for a large, round plung and began peeling off the thick red skin.

"If I'm going to have to endure your rituals, the least I can do is make them more fun," Taurin said, tearing off a section of fruit and offering it to Leena.

At first she was shocked by his sacrilege, but when she thought about it she agreed that there was no harm in making the traditions more enjoyable. With a smile, she leaned forward, taking a bite of the juicy piece of fruit. The tangy flavor was tart on her tongue, but she licked her lips, eager for more of a taste—more of Taurin than the fruit.

"Pour a bit of the red wine into your glass of white," she ordered. "This symbolizes springtime, when the sun's rays thaw the frozen land. The earth changes its color as the snow melts, and as the pink blooms of cyclamens appear in the mountains. Before we drink we hold up our glasses and recite the prayer."

This time Taurin humored her by repeating the prayer in unison with her.

"You may choose fruits with pits or seeds that cannot be eaten." Their eyes locked, and Leena watched as Taurin popped a few cherries into his mouth and spit out the inedible innards. She took a cherry for herself and bit daintily around the pit, but when Taurin reached for a date, her hand stilled his.

"Allow me." With her knife, she cut out the pit for him. Then she held the date toward his mouth and fed him. He plucked a plum from the dish and returned the favor. Leena didn't even notice the flavor. She was too engrossed in looking into his mesmerizing eyes.

"Don't forget the blessing over the fruit." Taurin's lip curled in a half smile.

She uttered the prayer, the words appearing automatically on her lips. "We need to refill the wine cups," she said, already feeling the effects from the first glass. She felt as if she were floating on air—or was that because Taurin's attention was centered on her?

"Which color?" he asked, pointing to both bottles.

"Fill the cups with red wine and just a dash of white. This mixture symbolizes summer, when flowers bloom and the ground softens."

"The time of plowing and sowing," Taurin said, nodding. "I assume we eat from the third category of fruits, those that are edible both inside and out." He didn't need any prompting to say the blessing over the fruit; the words were out of his mouth before Leena even thought about them. Then they were feeding each other juicy red grapes and plump, moist figs.

"I don't know if I can drink another cup," she murmured.

"We have to complete the ceremony." Taurin filled their glasses with red wine. "Summer ends, and the crops grow tall as autumn approaches. The harvest season. This is why you bought these packages of seeds, isn't it?" he asked.

"Tomorrow we are supposed to plant them, but we don't have a garden."

"We'll find a spot. Drink your wine," he urged, uttering the prayer for her. After she'd complied he rose to get his wild mushroom tart from the oven. "I don't know about you, but the fruit just teased my appetite. I'm ready for the main course." He would have preferred to accompany Leena upstairs for a more tempting dessert, but the tart was best eaten freshly baked.

A flavorful aroma reached her nostrils as Taurin placed the dish on the table, along with their neighbor's casserole. Despite her inebriated state, Leena's stomach growled in anticipation of a solid meal.

Jabbing her fork into a soft slice of the mushroom pie, she raised it to her mouth and took a tentative bite. The distinctive taste pleased her palate.

"This is delicious," she said, delving into her second piece. "What are your other culinary specialties?"

"I prefer to cook mostly vegetarian dishes. Don't worry;

I have no intention of usurping your role in the kitchen.''

She glanced up and noticed that his eyes were dancing with mirth. Nevertheless, this was a topic that had to be addressed. ''We should talk about the household chores. My term in the Caucus lasts for two years. During that time I'll be able to commute from Lexington Page and will be off on weekends. After that I'll probably return to my job at the museum.'' She'd already told him about her position as Director of Archaeological Studies for the Javis Museum of Natural History. It would be a half hour drive from where he lived.

''I thought you were undecided about your plans.'' His expression had turned serious, as though he knew this was a subject that concerned her.

''After exploring the Temple of Light I realized that archaeology is my passion . . . aside from you,'' she teased. ''If I succeed in my goals, I won't seek a higher office or further training within the religious order. I only joined the Caucus to learn the secrets of the Synod.''

Taurin shielded his reaction. She wouldn't want to know all the secrets being slowly revealed to him. He feared such knowledge would destroy the basic tenets of her beliefs.

''Isn't there a museum at the Palisades?'' he asked.

''Yes. They've offered me a position as curator, but I refused because it would mean I'd have to give up the field work that I love.''

Taurin rolled his eyes. ''So that means half the time you'll be off on some archaeological dig, and the rest you'll be commuting to the museum every day. So much for our idyllic family life.''

''Marriage is an adventure in itself, and I'm greatly looking forward to exploring it with you. Now, shall we clear the table and retire for a brief interval?'' Untying her apron, she fluttered her eyelashes at him. ''I'll offer you my brand of dessert before we taste yours.''

Upstairs, Taurin was more than happy to loosen her gown. ''I've never dared dream about having a wife or family,'' he murmured as the garment slid to the floor.

Leena smiled at the somber expression on his face. "That's another thing we'll need to talk about."

"Huh?"

"Starting a family."

Taurin glanced at her, startled. "I am up-to-date on my birth inhibitors," he announced stiffly.

She laughed. "It really doesn't matter."

His eyes gentled as he regarded the lovely picture she made with her golden hair floating about her bare shoulders. Standing naked before him, her breasts were exposed, firmly uplifted as though waiting for his caress. His eyes languorously explored every curve of her body.

"It's a little too early to be talking about children," he said, thinking of how many obstacles still lay before them.

"Is it? Why do I get the impression that you believe something is going to come between us?"

His jaw clenched. "Because I love you too much, and I'm afraid of losing you."

Her mouth gaped. "What did you just say?"

"I love you, Leena." He grasped her by the shoulders and pulled her close, burying his face in her hair, clutching her in his embrace as though he'd never let her go.

She sensed his desperation and wondered what made him feel so insecure. Obviously he didn't have much faith in her love for him. What could possibly happen to destroy their feelings for each other? Did he know something she didn't that made him afraid she'd leave him?

If anything, she should be annoyed that he didn't trust her. She knew he'd read the bibliotomes in the Temple of Light. Had he withheld his knowledge because he was afraid of her reaction should she learn the truth about the Apostles? And how would these truths, if that were the case, affect their relationship with each other?

"I just want to be with you," she murmured, tightening her arms around him. Her breasts pressed flat against his massive chest, and she leaned her head on his shoulder.

283

They'd resolve their differences later. Right now all that mattered was that they were together.

Lifting her face for his kiss, she felt a swell of joy when his mouth covered hers. Her body ignited as he moved his hips against her naked belly, and rational thought fled from her mind as she gave herself up to her passion.

"You're so beautiful. I want to enjoy every part of you," he said in a husky tone deep with desire. After trailing a line of kisses across her throat and down along her breast he took a nipple into his mouth and gently suckled it.

Leena closed her eyes and cried out with pleasure. "My love, you're killing me with ecstasy."

"Then I will die with you." He moved to her other breast, his tongue rhythmically stroking her nipple until she moaned in heated frustration. Crouching, he aimed his tender ministrations at the juncture of her thighs.

"Taurin, dear heaven!" Opening her legs so he could have better access, she let her head loll back, concentrating on the building tension within her core. "I've got to lie down!" she rasped, her knees failing her.

Taurin stripped off his clothes and joined her on the bed. Eager to please her, he sought her port of entry with his fingertips. Her slickness made him groan with restrained passion. With a mighty thrust, he entered her, smiling at the cry of pleasure his action elicited. "You are mine, *angella*," he said, his lips finding hers.

They melded together, flesh against flesh, a primal need consuming them both as they spiraled toward the pinnacle of desire. Taurin's explosive release stimulated her own climax, and shuddering spasms shook her body until she lay spent beneath the weight of his taut, muscled form.

"Maybe we should stay here and never go home," he muttered, rolling onto his back.

Too content to move, Leena slid him a sideways glance. "Why are you so afraid things are going to change?" When he didn't respond she feared he was taking his role as protector too seriously. He withheld knowledge that he assumed would be distressing to her, and she resented his patronizing attitude.

"I'm not afraid to learn the truth," she told him quietly. "If you would share what you read in those bibliotomes—"

"Let's go have dessert," he said abruptly, rising.

"Taurin, I don't like the way you're treating me. Trust has to be the foundation of a marriage." Dismayed, she watched as he threw on his clothes without a single glance in her direction.

Fully dressed, he stood before her, his expression softening. "I'll share what I know when I learn the whole story. There's no need for you to be upset at this point, when we have to concentrate on finding the horn."

She sat up, pulling the sheet to her waist. "I can make my own decisions about what I need to know. You're not my keeper."

"Oh, yes, I am." And his closed face told her he'd accept no further arguments.

Chapter Sixteen

The next morning, Taurin received a rude shock. He peered outside the living room window after opening the drapes and noticed a fellow hovering beside a strange blue rider. His blood pressure rocketed when he realized it was the same fellow who'd conversed with him in the market about the adverse weather conditions. Was this a coincidence, or had the man been posted here to keep an eye on them? In which case, for whom did he work? The Truthsayers? Or was he perhaps one of Grotus's agents, sent to keep tabs on their movements?

He didn't mention his concerns to Leena when he suggested over breakfast that they pack a picnic for the day. "We'll find a spot of dirt to plant our seeds. It'll give us a good excuse to explore the environs. And bring that wicker basket," he suggested. "We can always say we're hunting for wild mushrooms while we're in the woods."

"Are you going to cook again tonight?" she teased.

"Tonight we're going to the White Enix Pub, remember?"

"Of course," she said, puzzled by the brooding look on

his face. He hadn't said much after they'd returned to their room last night following dessert. His chocolate salad had been fantastic, and she'd raved over it, hoping to earn back the look of warm regard in his eyes. But he'd remained aloof after their discussion, and even as she tossed restlessly in their bed, he'd fallen asleep instantly, dashing any hopes she might have had for further intimacy.

Adding a shawl to her ensemble, she pronounced herself ready to go out. "Shall we start by the river?" she said when they emerged into the brisk morning sunshine. Glad she'd put on a long-sleeved wool day dress, she wondered how warm it would get in the afternoon.

"That's as good a place as any to begin exploring." Taurin stood on the front stoop, picnic carrier in hand, glancing around, as though expecting to see someone he knew.

"What's wrong?" she asked, shifting the empty wicker basket to her other hand.

"Nothing." Shrugging, he started down the steps.

She had the distinct feeling that he was lying. The street was quiet at this early hour, theirs being the only rider parked by the curb. So what was the cause of the frown on his face?

They began their expedition by a cluster of old stone houses along the riverbanks, enjoying the gracefully overhanging trica branches, whose fallen crimson leaves floated on the surface of the water. Ducks swam past, searching for their morning meal. Next to a cluster of palmelo reeds, a bridge led across the water to the ruins of an old abbey, which had been converted into a museum. Since it was a holiday the museum was closed, much to Leena's disappointment.

They passed the ancient mill that had been turned into the White Enix Pub, then followed a medieval road circling up a wooded hillside. The dirt was packed firm, indicating that the trail was well used. She enjoyed the smell of clean air and fresh autumn leaves. They hiked for some distance before coming to a meadow near an overlook where they could view the entire town and the twisting river.

"This is the perfect spot for a picnic!" she exclaimed, hoping he'd agree. Their trek had left her thirsty and eager for refreshment.

Taurin had brought along a cloth to spread over the grass. They'd just settled onto it when a rumble shook the earth at their feet.

"What's that?" Leena cried, spotting a cloud of dust where the woods joined the opposite side of the meadow.

"Let's go see," Taurin said, jumping up as though he were primed for action.

Disappointed that their idyllic interlude had been interrupted, she stood, shaking out her shawl, which had become covered with fallen leaves. "Should we fold the blanket and bring our things with us?"

"That might be wise." With impatience written across his features, he helped her repack the items, then shouldered the burden himself.

"These are truck marks," he said when they came to the site of the dust cloud.

Leena's brow furrowed. "What would a truck be doing in these parts? And why today? No one works on a holiday."

"Let's follow the tracks and see where they go."

The tire marks led into the woods and ended at a clearing beyond what appeared to be a construction site. Since no one was about, Leena rushed forward, anxious to see what they'd discovered. Maybe it was an excavation—a ruin that had been unearthed! Her feet flew over the grass as she raced ahead.

"Leena, wait!" She heard Taurin's voice call out behind her, and then her body crashed into an invisible barrier with stunning force. Pain exploded in her forehead, and she teetered backward.

Taurin steadied her with a hand around her waist. "What happened? Are you hurt?"

"S-Something stopped me," she stuttered, pointing.

Taurin noticed the construction site straight ahead. Where had that truck gone? A trail of dust indicated that it must have been driven into the forest beyond. "I don't see anything in our path," he said, a puzzled frown on his face.

"There's some sort of barrier. Look for yourself!"

Releasing his hold on her, Taurin stretched out an arm. "You're right." Splaying his hands against the obstacle, he followed its outline for a short distance. His stunned mind processed the new information with chilling clarity. The barrier was an energy shield, meant to keep out unwanted trespassers. Xan did not possess this technology. It could only have come from one place: his homeworld, Yllon, a world fraught with violence.

Demon's blood! Now their doom was surely at hand. He couldn't conceive of how his fellow Ylloners were involved here, but he was determined to find the answer. Rather than attempting to breach the barrier, he suggested they return to the village.

"Tonight, in the White Enix Pub, we'll learn what's going on. I suspect the Truthsayers are mixed up in this, but they must be getting help from somewhere else."

"I agree," Leena said, biting her lip. "This wall is unlike anything I've experienced. Let's go. I can't wait to check out that pub!"

The White Enix Pub was bustling with activity when they entered after dark. The rustic interior of the old mill was rife with the smells of sawdust and ripening barrels of red wine. A cacophony of noise hit Taurin's sensitive ears, and he grimaced as he scanned the bar area that took up the entire first floor. He'd been told there was a restaurant upstairs and had called ahead to make reservations. Giving his name to a host, he allowed Leena to precede him up the stairs.

The dining room was intimate, with charming yellow and white checked tablecloths, votive candles, and rural paintings decorating the walls. Wooden beams and hanging plants contributed to the coziness of the decor. The tables were set far enough apart, and he was gratified that they might talk without danger of being overheard.

Leena ordered an appetizer of mushrooms sauteed with herbs and wine, tender fillets of kalmagn fish, crisp corn fritters, and a frozen chocolate souffle with salisberry sauce. Taurin chose a simple salad of mixed greens, a pollentine with fig preserves, and nougat ice cream made from a local wildflower honey.

Despite his penchant for practicing the culinary arts, his everyday tastes were simple. On his home planet, scrabbling for a day's food was a major occupation, and the cause of many conflicts. He'd learned to eat frugally and accept whatever fare was available. Spare plots of land, which were few in the urbanized centers on Yllon, were often converted to gardens. Heavily fenced in, they provided fresh produce for the lucky owners. Taurin's gang leader had let him tend a small piece of land, which gave him his first taste of farming. It wasn't surprising that he'd chosen to pursue agriculture as an occupation when he'd moved to Xan. Blessed as it was with rich earth and plentiful rains, Xan offered vast expanses of fertile soil to its fortunate inhabitants. Toiling in his fields, feeling the sun on his back and the sweat dripping from his brow, Taurin had tried to erase the days of hunger from his memory and the fear that there wouldn't be enough food. He'd spent hours raking his fingers through the dirt, reveling in its richness and his blessing at being able to reap the fruits of his labor. Growing edible flowers paid off the debt he felt he owed to Baker Mylock.

A warm log of satisfaction settled into his stomach, lulling him into a tranquil state. Studying Leena, who was seated across from him, he decided she looked especially lovely in the glow from the candlelight. The periwinkle blue of her gown highlighted her eyes, making them seem deeper and larger.

"Tell me about your youth," he said encouragingly. His large hand snaked across the table to grasp her smaller one, and as she recounted tales of her childhood, he traced small circles in her palm.

"Stop that!" she said, blushing.

His gaze fell upon her lips, slightly parted. Her mouth, a rich, full pink, tempted him with its sensual outlines. She reminded him of the tulipett blossoms he grew in his fields. Feeling the way a honeybee must when it was drawn to a brightly colored flower, he craved a taste of her nectar.

"I like to feel your soft skin," he crooned, widening the pattern of his circles.

Leena withdrew her hand. "You're making me lose my appetite . . . at least for my meal." Her knowing gaze met his amused gray eyes. "We'll forget our purpose here if you keep this up."

"You're right. We must focus on our mission."

As soon as they finished their repast they headed downstairs to check out the bar scene. The din assaulted Taurin's sensitive ears as he descended the stairs. An argument about mushroom hunting prevailed among the patrons.

"You've got to leave enough stem for the fungi to grow again," one red-faced fellow proclaimed. "And don't use plastic bags. A wicker basket allows the spores to drop through and regenerate, which they'll do in four or five days, given the right conditions."

"I pulled in fifteen hundred chekels yesterday," bragged a bearded fellow in a work shirt and cap.

"You've gotta keep a steady pace," the first speaker agreed. "We're lucky we had the rains in this district, or it would have been a bad season. Still, if it doesn't turn colder soon, we'll be headin' for trouble."

Someone else chimed in, "Other territories have it worse. There's no reliability to the weather anymore. But at least Lothar hasn't totally forsaken us yet!"

Snickers of laughter greeted that announcement. One man stood up from the bar, whirling around. His eyes blazing, he addressed the crowd. "You know Lothar has nothing to do with our climate changes. The Synod is responsible. They're trying to force us to bend our knee to their laws. I say we've had enough of their oppression. It's time we stood up for ourselves and exposed them for what they are: a group of power-hungry old men who rule the populace with fear.''

Leena stared at him in shock. How dare he utter such blasphemy? Yet no one else seemed surprised by his rhetoric. People were nodding in agreement around the room.

''Our numbers are growing,'' the man went on, his tone quiet. A hush fell over the crowd as everyone listened. All eyes turned in his direction. The man was tall and lean, and intelligence sparkled behind his eyes. His business suit indicated that he was a person of some position, more educated perhaps than the majority in the lounge.

''Who is that?'' Taurin whispered to a well-dressed woman behind him.

''Why, he's Stephan Tom, our president.''

''President?''

''Of the International Merchants Association. Aren't you a member?'' The woman looked at him with disdain, as though anyone who was not a member of her organization was unworthy of respect.

''Er . . . uh . . . I'm new to the group,'' Taurin muttered.

''Stephan, what will happen if the horn is found?'' someone called out.

''It'll never be recovered,'' the leader retorted. ''And everyone will see the power of the Synod is an illusion created to subdue the populace. If Lothar were our true god, he wouldn't be making people suffer. Religion should be no part of our government. It's time we established an order where the people come first. We need elected officials, not an elite religious hierarchy, to govern our land.''

''Hear, hear!'' someone cried, and a cheer went up.

''We must spread the word through our organization,'' proclaimed Stephan Tom, his eyes fired with zeal. ''Our businesses cannot flourish unless we have the ability to expand. It's not right that we have to ask permission of an impersonal board to develop branches in other towns. Population growth cannot proceed naturally at this pace. I say the time for change has come. We're lucky we have friends in our struggle for freedom.''

The man standing next to Stephan Tom, facing the bar with his back toward the crowd, turned around. Beside her, Leena heard Taurin suck in a sharp breath.

"Demon's blood! What is *he* doing here?" Taurin muttered. Grabbing Leena's elbow, he steered her toward a dark corner. "Come on; let's get out of this light."

"What's the matter?" she cried, jostling into people as he threaded their way through the throng.

Stephan Tom continued his rhetoric, inciting the crowd.

Taurin wanted to get a better view of the fellow beside Stephan Tom without being seen. From his pocket he withdrew a familiar piece of cloth and swathed it about his head so his face would be shaded.

"That person standing next to Tom—I know him," he said to Leena, his voice low so they wouldn't be overheard.

"Who is he?" Leena asked.

Taurin shook his head. He couldn't tell her the man was one of his gang members from Yllon. What was the fellow doing here? Terror struck his heart as he heard Stephan Tom tell how, with their friends' support—and he distinctly used the plural there—their organization would march forward.

"Which organization is he referring to?" Leena whispered. "The International Merchants Association, or the Truthsayers?"

"I believe the two organizations are one and the same," Taurin said, leaning against a wall where he could watch the crowd without being noticed. "It makes perfect sense. That's how the Truthsayers are able to spread their heresy—through the Merchants Association. The business sector would have the most to gain from a laxity of the rules, and it appears they have outside help."

His thoughts swirled in panic. Leena was in danger merely by associating with him. If that Ylloner, whose name was Testi, spotted Taurin, he was in deep trouble. Taurin had left Yllon with a death sentence on his head. Exposure now would mean an end to his security. He had to know what the Ylloner was doing here, and how he'd received permission to travel. Normally, no one from Yllon was allowed free run of the planet. The two worlds had a restricted trade agreement, but Yllon's existence was known only to the Synod and a few trusted individuals on Xan. Aliens were not permitted outside of the spaceport.

So who had let Testi in, and why was he here? Was Stephan Tom aware that his friend was an alien? Someone in a knowledgeable position had to be involved in this, and Taurin wondered if it was the same traitor who'd stolen the horn. Weighing his choices, he decided his best course of action would be to follow Testi. That the Ylloner was involved in an attempt to overthrow the government along with the Truthsayers was obvious, but there was more here than met the eye.

"I want to hang around a while," he told Leena. "If you're tired, I'll find someone to escort you home."

"I'm not leaving just when this is getting interesting," she retorted. "Besides, you haven't told me who that man is." She indicated the fellow standing next to Stephan Tom.

"His involvement concerns me because it means outside interests are involved. I can't let him see me, or he'll recognize who I am."

"So what?" Confusion shone in her clear blue eyes.

Taurin's mouth tightened stubbornly, and Leena narrowed her gaze as she stared at him in the dim light.

"It's time you told me what you know, Taurin Rey Niris . . . if that's your real name."

Their eyes locked and held, hers demanding answers, his evasive and wary. "He's leaving," Taurin said suddenly. Testi was heading out the door, with Stephan Tom and several others among the crowd.

Outside the air was cool, and the scent of evergreens refreshed the night. Leena drew her shawl about her shoulders, shivering in part from the fear of what they would discover. They followed the crowd, blending in with a couple of stragglers and pretending to be part of the group. Gravel crunched underfoot, and overhead a myriad of stars shone in the darkened sky. The rush of water filled her ears as they passed the huge waterwheel churning in the river, a last remnant of the old mill that had been converted into the pub.

"Time to go to work on putting up the new village, eh, pal?" slurred a drunken fellow next to Taurin, winking a bleary eye.

They followed a familiar trail into the woods, climbed a hill, and crossed the same meadow where they'd attempted to picnic earlier. Ahead of them, brightly illuminated by hidden spotlights, was the building site they'd observed. The energy field had apparently been deactivated because noises of construction rang heavily in the night air and villeins in all manners of dress were working at the site. Testi strode over to one of the men calling out orders and consulted with him.

"Get to work!" Stephan Tom exhorted his followers. "Once this place is completed our friends will bring in the weapons we need to empower our liberation from the Synod."

Leena gasped. *Weapons.* They were planning an armed revolt. "They're building an armory," she whispered to Taurin. "We've got to warn Dikran."

Careful to avoid detection, Taurin moved about the foundations, inspecting the layout. This was no armory. That huge slab of dormite was reminiscent of a launch pad, and the other structures had the marks of hangars and maintenance sheds. These people weren't building an armory; they were building a landing site.

Demon's blood! He stopped in his tracks, his eyes widening in shock. That could mean only one thing: Yllon was planning an invasion, and now he understood with perfect clarity why the horn had been stolen. It wasn't for money; that's why it hadn't passed through Grotus's hands. If his theory held credence that the annual blowing of the horn served to reenergize the crystal lattice structures, and the crystals powered the defensive perimeter around the planet, then the horn had to be blown by the month of Fearn in order to strengthen the defense shield. Otherwise the perimeter might crumble, and Yllon's ships would be clear to enter the atmosphere.

Whoever had stolen the horn had to be in league with Yllon in planning an invasion. Taurin thought his former associate, gang leader Drufus Gong, was involved. But which Synod member was a traitor, and why? What did he or she hope to gain?

"What is it?" Leena asked, her eyes bright with concern as she touched his arm.

"We have to get away from here," he said, suddenly conscious that Testi was patrolling the site, talking to each of the workers. At any moment the Ylloner might spot him! Taking her hand in his own, he hastened her away, avoiding explanations until they were safely home.

Or were they safe? Rushing into the living room, he pulled aside a drape and looked outside. A strange rider had just pulled up to the curb. Someone was still keeping tabs on them, but who was it? Someone working for the traitor in the Synod, the Truthsayers, or Grotus's men? He didn't think the Truthsayers suspected their identity, considering the lack of interest in them in the pub. That left the other two possibilities, neither of which pleased him.

"Pack your things," he told Leena abruptly. "We're leaving."

She'd been hovering behind him, questions on her lips. She could tell by the hunch of his shoulders that something awful had happened tonight, something that related to the fellow they'd seen in the pub.

"Taurin, I'm not going anywhere unless you tell me what's happening. It's time you trusted me enough to tell me the truth."

Taurin spun around, a scowl on his handsome face. "You don't want to know the truth. It will hurt you, and you'll blame me for whatever myths I destroy."

She flinched at the pain that flashed across his countenance. "Why don't you let me be the judge of what I can or cannot accept?'' Striding forward, she brushed a lock of dark hair off his forehead. ''Trust me, Taurin. I love you. Nothing will ever change the way I feel about you.''

With a desperate cry, he swept her into his arms and kissed her. She was his haven, his safety among the swarm of hornets that threatened to sting him. She had no concept of the danger that threatened them now. It was far worse than he could have imagined. Stepping away, he pondered the implications of Drufus Gong's involvement, his blood icy with foreboding.

Leena remained silent, as still as one of the stone statues in the Temple of Light. At a loss for words, he swept his hand across his forehead in a gesture of helplessness. How was he to tell her she was married to an alien? That there was, indeed, life on other planets, and his homeworld was preparing a hostile invasion? Would she laugh at him for creating wild fantasies, scream in rage, or recoil in terror?

He'd feared this moment ever since he'd begun to care for her, which was almost at their first meeting. But now, when he needed her desperately, it was worse. He didn't think he could bear to see revulsion in her eyes.

Standing with his back to her, he faced a painting, depicting a lakeside scene, that hung above the fireplace mantel. The artist had frozen a duck in still life, its black feathers ruffled and its white neck erect, its orange beak jutting in the air as the creature glided on the water. Alone, it pursued its hunt for food, heedless of its loneliness on the vast body of the lake. He'd felt like this: adrift on a sea in the fabric of the universe, alone until Leena had entered his life and brightened the dark gray depths to a sunny blue hue. How could he tell her who he was?

''Do you believe that life exists on other planets?'' he began, unable to look her in the eye.

Leena wished he would face her squarely. ''I'm open to the possibilities,'' she replied, her tone cautious. She didn't see where the question was leading.

''The rings and the horn . . . the Apostles themselves . . .

may have come from another planet. A system in the Cadega constellation, perhaps.''

''So? We've had this discussion before.''

''What if I told you that Xan isn't the only world in our star system that supports life? Seven planets rotate about our sun, and two of them have human populations—Xan and Yllon.''

''You mean the Apostles came from this other world?''

''No, the Apostles visited Yllon just as they did Xan, and it's likely they seeded both our civilizations.''

Leena frowned. ''I don't understand. What does this have to do with you?''

''How do you think I know so much about Yllon?'' He whipped around, his eyes glowing luminously as a shadow crossed his face. His skin appeared darker, the angles of his jaw more clearly delineated; his glowering countenance intensified the menacing aura that normally radiated from his being. ''I'm from Yllon, Leena. I traveled here in a spaceship.''

Leena gasped, inadvertantly taking a step backward. ''What?''

He repeated his confession, hating what this would do to her, to *them.*

''I don't believe it! You said you're from Iman. What kind of joke is this, Taurin?''

He shook his head, wondering how he could convince her of the truth. ''It is no joke. You wanted an explanation; now accept it. I had to say I was from Iman in order to protect my true identity. Iman is a remote region; I thought no one would question me about my relocation.''

''B-but you can't be from another planet! You look just like us.'' She stared at him, horrified. Could there be any validity to his words? No, it couldn't be true!

He scowled at her. ''Look closely at me. Does anyone else you know have eyes like this? Can anyone on Xan fight with the fury I feel when rage runs through my veins? Go on,'' he said, his gaze narrowing, ''say you want to be rid of me.''

Stunned by his admission and yet stricken by the look of pain deep in his eyes, she didn't know what to say.

"I knew you'd be repulsed," he muttered.

"I . . . I just don't know what to believe anymore." She dashed a shaky hand through her hair. By the Grace of Lothar, was he for real? Did he truly come from another world, and not just from a faraway region of Xan? Her mouth went dry at the possibilities. "Perhaps if you explain how you came to be here, or more about your world . . ." It was as though he'd become a stranger, and the feeling saddened her. Yet logic told her he was being truthful, and his admission coincided with her unspoken theories about the Apostles. She'd dared to believe they might be visitors from another planet, and now Taurin's story was telling her this was a logical assumption.

Overwhelmed by the implications, she sank onto an armchair and waited expectantly for more details.

Taurin took a seat opposite her, his expression wary. "Yllon is a violent world rife with gang warfare," he began, staring at his lap. "Rauch's gang is probably the biggest group, led by Drufus Gong. Drufus Gong is the one who found me when I was abandoned by my parents. He took me under his wing and raised me as he would any other young child of a gang member."

Leena frowned in puzzlement. "Who were your parents? Why did they desert you?"

"I had the sign of the curse." He lifted his head, and she gazed straight into the dancing, luminous lights in his eyes. "I told you about our legends. Many eons ago demons came to Yllon, causing men to go mad and instigating killing sprees that destroyed our civilized society. Pogroms wiped out most of these demons, but their bad seeds had already been sown. Every few generations the genes come together in the right combination, and a child shows the demon's sign. The fear from ages past has not dissipated, and a child thus afflicted usually meets with a quiet, unexplained death. Apparently my parents decided to give me a chance.

"Drufus Gong had ambitions of his own. He saw my special gift and decided to take advantage of it. I could see in the dark, an ability he used to conquer his enemies. Together we hid my special visionary power from others. It was feared that one would go mad in the presence of a demonic offspring, but I could never tell if this were true because everyone on Yllon was hostile. Killings, beatings, and rampages are the norm."

"How horrible," she remarked, shuddering at the images such a violent society evoked.

"This armband is the only clue to my heritage," he said, raising his sleeve so she could see it. "I told you how I used to separate the bracelets and spin them. I'd always thought it was a child's toy until I noticed the symbols carved on the side when the rings were banded together. But it was some time later before I observed those symbols elsewhere."

Leena interrupted him. "Isn't it your theory that the Apostles visited both our worlds? In that case, why didn't they establish the reign of Lothar on Yllon?"

Taurin shrugged. "That's one of the answers I'd hoped to find here. Their visit to your world prompted an orderly society, whereas on mine it engendered violence and warfare."

"Could it be some quality in the environment that makes the difference?"

"I don't know." Taurin crossed his legs and then uncrossed them again. Other than Magar, she was the first person on Xan to learn his history, and he was glad to be sharing it with someone else. His eyes roamed her lush golden hair, lovely features, and lithe, graceful body. Gods, how badly he wanted her to stay with him.

"I was sixteen," he continued, "when my gang went on a rampage and destroyed a bakery thought to belong to a rival group. I was walking out of the demolished interior when I heard the sounds of someone sobbing. I whirled around and was surprised to see the baker stooped over, his hands covering his face. We all believed the rival gang would restore the baker's business, but it was a way of sabotaging their efforts, so to speak. When I saw the baker hunched over it struck a chord within me, something I hadn't felt since I was a young child, alone and lost.

"After everyone else had gone, I went back and asked the proprietor why he was so upset when his gang would fix up his establishment. Baker Mylock shook his head sorrowfully, saying he was just paying them protection money. Now his livelihood was destroyed and he had a family to support. I couldn't leave him when he appeared so forlorn, so I offered to help him rebuild the shop. I returned in secret and helped him restore order to his business. He introduced me to his wife and children, and soon they became the family I had never had. Drufus Gong was never a father figure to me. He remained a distant leader, demanding and ruthless. Baker Mylock treated me kindly and taught me how to read. I discovered a side to myself I hadn't known existed."

He paused, getting up to pace the room restlessly. Leena watched him silently, grateful he was at last confiding in her. A marriage couldn't succeed if there were secrets between the partners, and she hoped he would tell her everything he knew . . . no matter how traumatic the revelations.

"A year afterward," Taurin said, stopping in front of her, "my gang attacked what we believed to be a weapons storehouse for another group. I was the scout man. When I broke inside I discovered not weapons but a treasury of books. I tricked my mates into giving me responsibility for blowing up the place. That night, with the help of some local hired hands, I secretly transferred the books to an abandoned warehouse. Looking them over, I discovered a collection of bibliotomes, ancient texts with symbols written on the covers that seemed to match the ones on my bracelet. I had to know what they meant. Eager to learn more, I risked contacting the rival gang leader, hoping he could tell me how to open the sealed books. I offered to return them to him if I could have use of the library."

Leena saw a veil of pain descend over his face. "I was betrayed. Drufus Gong realized I had lied to him. The price for treachery on my world is death. The rival gang leader put a mark on me for stealing their property. Pursued by both gangs, I was forced to flee my world. I had met Captain Sterckle, who traded with Xan, and I offered him some of the bibliotomes in exchange for passage on his ship. My only recourse was to seek asylum on Xan. Captain Sterckle introduced me to Magar, who is in charge of off-world relations.''

"Magar!" Leena cried, straightening her spine. "He's in charge of affairs of state!"

He gave her a wry grin. "That includes relations with other worlds, namely Yllon. Magar directs the trade relations between our two worlds. Yllon provides technology, and Xan sells us her food surplus. Population overcrowding and constant warfare have depleted our resources. Food is a valuable commodity. Normally no one from Yllon is allowed to leave the spaceport, and the workers there are sworn to secrecy. I believe the Synod and the spaceport crew are the only ones who know of Yllon's existence.''

"So Magar offered you a piece of land on his property?"

"That's right. He probably figured he could keep an eye on me if I was close at hand.''

Leena was unable to fully comprehend all he was telling her. It was too much information to assimilate at once, and she still couldn't believe he was an alien. Dear deity, how could she conceive of such a thing?

Excitement welled within her as she considered the ramifications. Space travel was an actuality, at least within their star system. The Apostles might have come from a world located in the Cadega constellation. Taurin was beginning to fill in the blanks in the information she sought, yet there were still many questions left unanswered.

"Why did you decide to run a flower farm?" she asked.

Taurin flashed her a boyish grin, and her heart warmed toward him. Perhaps he wasn't such a stranger after all. "Baker Mylock always used expensive candied flowers on his sweet breads. I decided to pay him back for his kindness by growing edible blooms and sending them to him once a month. Magar makes sure the shipments reach him.''

''Why has Magar been so good to you? He never knew you before Captain Sterckle introduced the two of you. Why would he let you, and no one else, settle on Xan?''

Taurin's gaze narrowed. ''I offered him my bibliotomes in exchange for permission to immigrate and a piece of land. He recognized their worth and accepted the deal immediately. Although none of us knew how to open them, that they were valuable was obvious. I had to swear I would never reveal my identity to anyone, and I chose to keep apart from others in case the curse was true—that I could drive men mad by my presence.''

''Surely you don't still believe that to be so?''

''I guess not.'' Taurin's eyes glowed happily at her. ''You showed me I have nothing to fear from my violent nature— at least not when I'm with you. I keep it leashed, like a wild animal, yet it's there should I need it.''

His face darkened. ''Unfortunately, I may be needing my skills rather soon. That man we followed from the pub? His name is Testi. He's one of Drufus Gong's best lieutenants. It alarms me that he's here on Xan, undercover. I don't believe the Truthsayers know who he is.''

''Testi may be the source of weapons Stephan Tom referred to,'' Leena remarked. ''But how would Yllon benefit if the Truthsayers gained power?''

Taurin shook his head. ''The Truthsayers may have been led to believe they are constructing an armory, but I recognized the structures. It's a landing site.''

Her eyes widened. ''Meaning?''

''I think Drufus Gong is planning an invasion.''

Leena leapt up, her heart thumping in alarm. ''First you tell me you're an alien; now you're saying we can expect a hostile invasion from outer space?''

Taurin sent her a grim nod of acknowledgment. ''This planet has a protective energy shield, and when the trade ships come through, a window is opened to allow their passage. Just how the system works is unknown to me, but I suspect Lothar is involved.''

''Lothar? What does the Holy One have to do with this?''

''Lothar provides the main source of energy for your planet. He regulates the climatic cycles, supplies the lozenge against sickness—and I believe he is also responsible for the protective barrier. That means that if the horn is not blown by the month of Fearn to awaken Lothar the shield will fail. Your world will be open to invasion.''

Leena covered her mouth with her hand. ''Holy waters! Do you think that's why the horn was stolen?''

He nodded. ''It wasn't taken for money, or it would have passed through Grotus's hands by now. The Truthsayers didn't take it to discredit the Synod. You heard them say in the pub that they hope it's never found. That means they don't have it. Whichever member of the Synod stole it still possesses the horn, and if he or she took it to lower the energy shield, that person is in league with Drufus Gong.''

''But how could anyone have been in contact with Drufus Gong when relations between the two worlds are so highly restricted?''

''Magar is in contact with them.''

''Karayan and Zeroun suspect Magar because of his relationship with you.''

Taurin grimaced. ''They may be right. It's time we had a talk with Magar ourselves.''

Leena noticed his expression and wondered if he was feeling betrayed by Magar, whom he must have regarded as a friend. ''Shouldn't we get proof to show the Synod? Photos of the landing site or something equally impressive? Otherwise it will be your word against Magar's.''

Taurin frowned. ''I don't know that proof is necessary. Our other option is to stay here and follow Testi.''

''We could also talk to Stephan Tom,'' Leena suggested.

''To what end?''

''The Truthsayers think they're building armories and will receive weapons. Testi didn't just show up on the site. He must have been introduced to them by someone else. Someone who is secretly supporting the Truthsayers.''

''You mean taking advantage of the Truthsayers for their own purposes. They're pawns being used in this game of interstellar politics. I don't think we should talk to the Truthsayers just yet. Let us seek out Magar first. If he's guilty, he'll confess to using them for his own aims.''

''What if Magar doesn't confess to anything? How will we prove our case against him?'' Leena's eyes lit up. ''The construction equipment at the landing site! We could trace the supplier. Maybe there's a link.''

''I didn't notice any markings on the crates, did you?''

She shook her head, crestfallen.

''We'll have to make another trip to the site,'' Taurin determined. Changing the subject, he said, ''Grotus knows who I am. He tried to blackmail me into giving him the horn when we found it, in exchange for keeping quiet about my identity. He's aware there is a death sentence on my head.''

''And so is that fellow Testi. You can't run the risk of having him discover your presence. It would be too dangerous for you. I'll go to the construction site by myself,'' she said.

''No way. You're in danger just by associating with me. You should return to the Palisades now, while you have the chance, to get safely away from here.''

''I'm not leaving you.''

They stared into each other's eyes, each one determined not to yield.

''Very well,'' Taurin said tersely. ''We'll wait for morning. Hunting for mushrooms is a major occupation here. We can pretend we're stalking the woods for valuable fungi. As soon as we get the necessary information, we'll head straight for the Palisades. Hopefully the crates or other equipment will have notations that are traceable.''

''What if the barrier is in place?''

''Let's worry about that later. We'd better get some sleep.''

His voice shook with weariness, and Leena realized his confession had been an ordeal for him. She was overwhelmed by all they'd discussed and readily agreed to his suggestion. It didn't take her long to prepare for bed. As she snuggled beneath the covers, Taurin's lean, hard body beside her, she felt a deepening sense of dread that chilled her bones.

"Come here," Taurin said, spreading his arms.

She folded herself into his embrace, grateful for the warm security he provided. She hoped he realized she would never desert him, no matter who or what he was. But . . . an alien? His body was nothing foreign, she told herself. He was quite human, with manly urges and the delightful ability to gratify her desires. And he had human feelings, as well. He'd been afraid she would reject him once she learned the truth.

Feeling a compelling urge to offer him reassurance, she said, "Taurin, you're still my husband. Just because you're from . . . somewhere else . . . doesn't mean we can't stay together. I still love you."

Tightening his arms around her, Taurin buried his face in her loose waves of hair. "What did I ever do to deserve you? You belong with Malcolm and his kind, not the likes of me."

"That's not true. You're the perfect mate for me." She knew him as a gentle, caring man, and that was all that mattered now. Murmuring his name, she let her hot breath caress his ear. She flicked out her tongue, tickling his earlobe, until he moaned with rising passion.

Flipping her onto her back, he gazed into her eyes, which she knew were already glazed with desire. With a whoop of exultation, he brought his mouth down on hers, his tongue thrusting forth as though thirsty for intimacy. She met his movements with eager ones of her own. She wanted him, here and now, regardless of any dangers encroaching on them from the outside world. *Their* world was all that counted.

Her mouth still pressed to his, she reached for him, letting him know what she had in mind. A gratifying gasp came from his lips as she found her mark. He expanded under her bold touch, showing her how much she aroused him. A swell of pure feminine power filled her with exaltation as she craned her neck so he could kiss her throat.

Pushing her hand away, he let his own hands wander over her body. Holding her breasts as though he were starving and they were a source of sustenance, he nudged her night-shirt aside with his powerful thighs. When he massaged her naked flesh a gasp of pure pleasure escaped her lips.

It took him but a moment to shed his clothes, and then he was atop her once more, plunging inside, letting loose an animalistic howl that threw her into a frenzy. Panting, sweating, she rocked her hips to match his rhythm, clutching at his back. Liquid heat rose from the well of her being, sapping her will, rendering her helpless against the onslaught to her senses.

''Taurin!'' she screamed when her body exploded into a cataclysm of delight. He moved against her, and she felt his spasms as he joined her at the pinnacle of pleasure.

Eventually, he rolled off her, his strength spent. Listening to his steady breathing beside her, she relaxed her mind and drifted toward sleep. Her final thought was that he hadn't told her what he'd read in the bibliotomes.

Chapter Seventeen

Before they left the house the next morning Taurin revealed the presence of the watchdog on the front street by briefly pulling back the drape in the living room.

"The Truthsayers would have exposed our presence here by now," Leena exclaimed, cautiously peering out. "That fellow has to be Grotus's man. It's not only the horn he's after. Grotus hopes to add me to his collection."

"What do you mean?"

Leena related what had transpired during their last visit to the smuggler's haven.

"Curse the man! I'll kill him for that!"

"No, you won't," she said soothingly, putting her hand on his arm as he allowed the drape to fall back into place. "We've too many other important things to do. By the way, you forgot to mention what you read in those bibliotomes in the Temple of Light."

He gave her a quick, assessing glance. "We don't have time to talk now. Let's go before that hound realizes we've moved our rider to the rear of the house." Lifting their bags, he stalked into the kitchen and opened the rear door, glancing outside. Seeing their path was clear, he signaled to Leena to follow him.

A crisp, cool morning breeze ruffled the hairs on her skin as she watched him load their bags into the trunk of their vehicle. He made a dashing figure, his black garb snugly outlining the muscled contours of his body. She moistened her lips, wishing their interlude here had lasted longer but eager to move on.

A winding rural road took them in the direction of the construction site. Along the way, Taurin explained how they would proceed. He found a secluded spot behind a clump of bushes in the surrounding woods and parked the rider.

After trudging a short distance across the meadow he halted abruptly. Leena stopped directly behind him, waiting while he tested the space ahead. Sniffing the pine-scented air, Leena enjoyed the sensation of sunshine warming her back. The material of her day dress was fairly thin, and standing in the shade by the rider had made her cold.

"Demon's blood! That damn barrier is in place again," Taurin said. He hesitated, considering a course of action. "I'll use my blaster," he decided. "The villeins don't expect anyone to have weapons of this caliber. I can probably short-circuit the thing, but the discharge might set off an alarm in town. At the very least, I would expect Testi to be alerted that something is amiss. We'll have to act fast."

"Just do it," Leena said, standing back as he pulled his weapon.

Zing. Red laser fire cut through the air, impacting with the energy shield in an eruption of sizzling sparks. For an instant they could see the entire defensive perimeter in highlight, like a neon sign flashing erratically. In the next moment it went dead.

"Let's go," Taurin yelled, hölstering his weapon.

They dashed toward a truck that stood empty by the road-side. Searching for a vehicle tag, they were disappointed to find none.

"You check out the construction equipment. I'm going to look at those crates over there," Taurin told her.

A few minutes later they regrouped.

"Got it," Leena said. She showed him the name she had written in her notebook.

Taurin nodded. "Westner Alliance Corporation. We'll enlist those members of the Caucus who are not busy helping your brother. They can trace this to find the owners."

"Right." Leena nodded, eager to be off. "Too bad we don't have a camera."

"Someone's coming!" Taurin pointed to an approaching cloud of dust ascending from the road to the village. "Let's move!"

But as they turned to go, the protective shield flickered into life, and they were trapped inside. Taurin pulled his blaster and fired, but the level of the shield must have been strengthened because this time he didn't make a dent. With a growl of rage, he drew Leena to his side as a four-wheel vehicle thundered into view.

"Who are you and why were you snooping around?" a thin-voiced fellow with a sallow complexion asked Taurin.

They'd been taken prisoner and were now being held in a cellar beneath the White Enix Pub. Taurin gathered that the pub served as the headquarters for the Truthsayers, of which, they'd learned, Stephan Tom was definitely the leader. He spread his gospel through the International Merchants Association. Most of the small businesspeople wanted the rules relaxed so they could expand as per their own wishes and didn't like the restrictions placed upon them by the Synod. Taurin had a lot of questions to ask himself, but right now he was the one being interrogated.

He glared at the fellow's pale yellow eyes and smiled amiably. "I told you, we were hunting mushrooms."

"Aye," the man sneered. "But your wicker basket was empty, and you were found within our defensive perimeter.

Where did you obtain this weapon?'' He held up Taurin's blaster.

Taurin cringed. "It was given to me. We're simple farmer folk.'' He spread his hands. "We were simply looking for some premier cepes. I thought I'd spotted a ring of *pieds de moutons*.'' He nodded toward Leena. "She was after a bed of golden chanterelles. You know they're hard to find.''

Their captor regarded them with obvious disbelief. "Are you spies for the Synod? Is that why you were sent here?''

They'd been left alone with this man, the heavy wooden door shut behind them and guards posted outside. He and Leena stood side by side, holding hands. He felt her tense at the man's question.

"Of course not. We're newlyweds who have just settled in the region. Actually, we'd heard about your group and were interested in joining.''

The man lifted the blaster and pointed it at Taurin's chest. "I think you're lying.'' The man's rough manner of dress indicated that he wasn't one of the businessmen involved in governing the Truthsayers. He might be more prone to violence than his counterparts.

Taurin compressed his mouth, unwilling to say anything further that might incriminate them. The cellar was a wine storage vault, and the fruity aroma of wine-soaked oak assailed his nostrils. A musty odor tickled his nose, making him want to sneeze. He suppressed the urge, holding tightly on to Leena's hand. The two men locked gazes; after a moment their captor's faltered.

"I have orders not to hurt you,'' he said. "You'll be tried at a hearing. That's not the way I would do it, but I'm not the one in charge.''

"A hearing?'' Leena said, her voice squeaky. "Under whose authority?''

"Ours, madam,'' the man snarled.

Sticking Taurin's blaster into his belt, he pivoted and strode toward the door. A loud knock on the door brought a response from the guard on the other side. He stalked out, and the door slammed shut after him, the heavy lock clicking into place.

Leena's rueful gaze lifted to meet Taurin's. "Got any bright ideas?"

He shook his head. "Not at the moment. Let's look around and see if there's anything we can use to defend ourselves."

"You don't think they would hurt us, do you?" Alarm shot through her.

The look he gave her was solemn and sent chills up her spine. "That depends on who's giving the orders. If it's Testi, I'd say we're in big trouble."

"Maybe they already know who we are," she mused. "If we were betrayed by someone on the Synod—"

"I don't think that's the case. We got caught because we tripped an alarm." He strode down an aisle bordered by huge oak barrels on one side and filled wine racks on the other. "At least there's plenty to drink in here."

"This is no time for jokes." Leena's voice was shrill. "How are we going to get out of here?"

"We could try reasoning with Stephan Tom."

"By telling him the truth?"

He stopped and glared at her. "That's one alternative. Can you think of another?"

"We could insist we're just an innocent couple caught hunting mushrooms, that we were in the wrong place at the wrong time."

Taurin's mouth twisted into a wry grin. "Sure. And every simple farmer goes around with a blaster strapped to his leg."

Leena grimaced. "I forgot about that."

"If Testi sees it, I'm a dead man."

Terror struck Leena's heart, and she stared wide-eyed at Taurin. "Don't say that! I couldn't bear it if . . . if anything happened to you."

"Oh, my sweet *angella*." Walking over, he swept her into his arms and brushed his lips across her hair. "I'm supposed to be protecting you from harm. I haven't done very well."

"We've made it this far," she said encouragingly, tilting her face upward so he could kiss her.

Time passed swiftly as they consoled each other physically. Several hours later, a guard entered with a tray of food.

"I must talk to your leader," Taurin said to the man, a swarthy individual wearing a longshirt, dark pants, and muddy boots. A wicked-looking knife stuck out of his belt.

"You'll get your chance this evenin'," the guard said, handing him the provisions. "They's all at their meeting now."

"What meeting? The Merchants Association convention?"

The fellow nodded. "Aye. The boss man's giving his orders."

"Stephan Tom will be here to see us later?" Taurin persisted, hoping that Testi wouldn't be the one sent to question them.

A sly look came over the man's face. "You'll see for yerself," he snickered before leaving them alone once again.

It was getting cold, and Leena was shivering in her day dress, despite its long sleeves and ankle-length skirt. Taurin tried to warm her by putting his arms around her, but she shivered in his embrace, partly from fear and partly from the cooler temperature. There was no window in the cellar, but her timekeeper told her it was past the dinner hour. Surely someone would come for them soon.

Taurin cursed inwardly at his ineptitude. He didn't know what odds they would be facing, so he couldn't make any bets about their chances for escape. Taking out the guards was always an option, but he was reserving that one because he would rather talk to Stephan Tom while they had the chance.

Unfortunately, they weren't going to be allowed a private conversation. Just when they were giving up hope that anyone would come for them that night, the latch clicked and the door was shoved open. Four armed guards strode into the room, and two of them bound Taurin's and Leena's hands behind their backs.

"Outside," ordered one of the guards.

"Where are we going?" Taurin asked as they were marched along a hallway, up a flight of stairs, and out into the cool night air.

"Back to the place where youse was caught. The boss said we can't spare no time from our work."

Taurin's heart sank as he saw who awaited them at the building site. Testi was in a heated argument with Stephan Tom, but they halted their conversation when the group approached.

"This is the couple we caught snooping around," said one of the guards, shoving them both forward with a light push on their shoulders.

Testi's face blanched as he caught sight of Taurin. "You!" he exclaimed. "What are you doing here?"

"Do you know this man?" Stephan Tom asked. Tall and broad-shouldered, he wore a charcoal business suit. A thatch of muddy brown hair settled carelessly on his head, crowning a narrow forehead that was creased into a suspicious frown. Making a quick assessment, Taurin decided the man's passion for his ideals outweighed the importance of his manner of dress, and his respect for Stephan Tom rose a notch.

Testi was a different sort of character, reminding Taurin of a predatory insect. Small, beady eyes rose over a long, hooked nose and a thin mouth. His rounded posture was not improved by the rust-colored tunic that covered his torso, or by the loose trousers tucked into a pair of scruffy boots.

"A pleasure to see you again," Taurin said sarcastically, nodding his head at Testi.

"This is someone I knew in the old country," Testi said in an aside to Stephan Tom, who stood studying Taurin and Leena with keen, penetrating eyes. "He was a criminal, wanted for theft and willful destruction of property. He was convicted, but he escaped before his sentence could be carried out. You see that he has the light of madness in his eyes.''

With his hands secured behind him, Taurin had been unable to swathe his head in the protective cloth, and Stephan Tom recoiled at the sight of his glowing vision.

''You don't have to bother yourself with him,'' Testi continued. ''I'll be happy to handle this matter.''

''What were you doing here?'' Stephan Tom demanded, asserting his authority.

''My wife and I were hunting for mushrooms.''

''Don't take me for a fool,'' Stephan Tom snapped, his eyes blazing. ''You're spies. Who do you work for?''

When Taurin and Leena remained silent Testi turned to the Truthsayer leader. ''Let me take them aside and question them. I know ways to get a man to talk.''

''Will you tell me who you are and why you're here, or do I let this man have his way?''

''If you leave us with him, he'll kill me,'' Taurin announced. ''Just how much do you know about *his* origins? Where did he say he was from, and why is he helping you?''

Leena had been considering their dilemma. From the look on Testi's face it was clear he was barely restraining himself from carrying out Taurin's death sentence on the spot, but that would incur the Truthsayer leader's shock and fury. Somehow he'd get Taurin into his custody and then either hand him over to his fellow agents or kill him himself and collect the reward. She had to do something to intervene!

''Why don't we just kill them both?'' suggested Testi with an evil snarl. ''I'll be happy to do the job. We don't want them alive to tell tales.'' His hand reached for a strange-looking rod clipped to his belt.

Stephan Tom compressed his lips. ''Obviously neither one of them is going to talk without persuasion of a more violent nature, but you know I'm opposed to anything—''

''Nonsense,'' Testi cut in. ''What do you think we intend against the government? This is just the beginning. If you want to be liberated, you have to fight for your beliefs.

Throughout history spies have been executed. Let me take care of them now.''

He drew forth the rod, pointing it at Taurin, whose face had suddenly gone pale.

''Wait!'' Leena cried, her heart thudding in her chest. ''I'll tell you what you want to know.''

Testi's attention had been so focused on Taurin that he'd barely noticed her. Now he swung his beady eyes in her direction. ''Don't listen to her. She'll tell you lies. He's probably mesmerized her with his evil stare. Look at how his eyes glow.''

Taurin tensed his muscles, wishing he could avoid a physical confrontation, though it appeared it would become inevitable. ''Leena, don't say anything,'' he warned.

''Why not?'' she countered, her face bravely uplifted, trails of golden hair blowing about her face in the wind. ''You said you wanted to talk to Stephan Tom. Now's our chance. Let's tell him what's going on here. Let him learn the truth and see how he and his followers have been duped.''

''I would hear this,'' said Stephan Tom, directing a meaningful glance at the Yllon agent. He walked up to Leena, lifting her chin and examining her face in the glare of an overhead spotlight.

''You said you would tell us the truth, Sister. Speak now, or I will see to it that your tongues are cut out so you may speak of this to no one and your fingers mutilated so that you cannot write. I will not have you killed, but you will wish you were dead.''

Leena stared at him, struck speechless by his threats. Would he dare do such a thing? How could anyone conceive of such cruelty?

''You speak as if you're from his world,'' she cried, tilting her head in Testi's direction. ''Has he so poisoned your mind that you're willing to commit acts of violence so readily? If you must know why we're here, it's because we are searching for the missing horn, the one that was stolen from the sacred closet in the Palisades. We thought your people might have it. But we've gathered that you have no idea where it is.

"We stumbled onto this site accidentally. You've been deluded into believing it's an armory you're building, but actually it's a landing site for spacecraft. A neighboring planet called Yllon is planning an invasion. Ask Testi to confirm my words. He's one of their agents."

"She speaks the truth," Taurin said, continuing, despite Stephan Tom's skeptical glance, "I come from Yllon, where vision like mine is regarded as a curse. Forced to flee my homeland for my own safety, I settled here. Gangs dominate Yllon, and warfare is prevalent. The uncontrolled population rate and the build-up of technology have depleted her resources. Xan must be trading food surpluses to Yllon in exchange for technology like farm machinery. But if Yllon had the chance to conquer this world, it would jump at it. Someone is handing them that opportunity by stealing the horn."

"In other words," Leena added, "you're being used, Stephan Tom. You think you're leading a revolt against the government, but you're actually paving the way for an invasion."

"Ha! You expect me to believe these lies?" the Truthsayer leader cried. "That's the most absurd tale I've ever heard in my life." He turned to Testi. "See if you can force the truth from them before you cut out their tongues. But remember my sentence. They are not to be killed; I will not have their deaths on my hands."

As he turned to walk away, Taurin shouted desperately, "Listen to me! This is a landing site for spacecraft. Can't you see that slab is a launch pad?"

Stephan Tom turned back, his laughter a harsh echo in the night. "That's the foundation for our weapons storehouse, and Testi is a friend. I don't think he likes having aspersions cast on his character."

"But where do you think the weapons are coming from?

Who is supposed to supply them?'' Taurin's words drifted away in the air, and he received no answer. Clenching his jaw, he realized a fight was inevitable. Testi was motioning for a troop of locals to surround them. He shuddered to think what would happen to them if they were left to Testi's mercy. He remembered Testi's reputation for sadistic cruelty.

Leena caught her breath in alarm as one of the guards took her by the elbow and shoved her forward. What was going to happen to them? Testi knew they were telling the truth; he didn't need to question them further. Would he kill them outright or torture them first? Or would he do as Stephan Tom had ordered—cut out their tongues and do other unspeakable horrors to them? Dizziness assailed her as she swallowed her fear and stumbled forward.

A low growl erupted from Taurin's throat as he burst into action. At nearly the same moment an explosion on the opposite side of the field drew everyone's attention. Taurin used the moment to his advantage, shoving aside the nearest guard with his shoulder and flipping another one over his hip. Leena screamed a warning as she saw Testi raise his rod. Suddenly their escort was overwhelmed by people who came out of the woods camouflaged with leaves. Leena couldn't even tell if they were male or female because their faces were blackened, and they wore dark, shapeless clothes. One of them moved toward her, and she shrieked in fright.

"Hush, Sister, we're setting you free," he hissed, slicing through her bonds with a knife.

In an instant Taurin was freed. He would have thrown himself into the fray, but he was yanked aside by their savior.

"Come with me. You have to get out of here."

Taurin didn't need any further persuasion. Grabbing Leena's hand, he charged after the fellow, through the woods. "Who are you? Why are you helping us?"

The man stopped, and Taurin got a good look at him. By heaven, it was the man who'd been their watchdog these days past, taking up a post outside their house.

"I work for Grotus," the man said. "My name is Jette.

318

You haven't found the horn yet, and Grotus's orders are to keep you safe until you do. I've moved your rider. You can leave this place, but we'll be keeping a watch on you. Here is your weapon.'' He handed Taurin his blaster and showed him where he'd moved their vehicle. ''Remember, my employer expects compensation. As soon as the horn is in your possession, you must contact him.''

''Like hell I will,'' Taurin gritted, easing himself into the driver's seat while Leena quietly slid in beside him.

Jette bared his teeth in a feral grin. ''No one lives who plays games with Grotus.''

Taurin nodded in the direction of the construction site. ''My presence is known here now, so Grotus's threats bear no weight with me.''

Jette's face darkened. ''Heed my words, Rey Niris: Grotus will exact vengeance upon you and your loved ones.'' His nasty glance flickered in Leena's direction.

Taurin started the engine and backed away in a squeal of tires, drowning out any further warnings.

''At least we know that Grotus still hasn't any news of the horn,'' Leena remarked once they were safely on their way out of town.

Taurin took a circuitous route to make sure they weren't being followed. ''That doesn't help us much,'' he commented. ''We still have no clues as to who does possess the horn.''

Leena fell into a thoughtful silence until they'd reached a reasonable distance from Woden. ''Let's head straight for the Palisades. We can take turns driving through the night.''

''Aren't you too tired?'' He glanced at her, concern for her welfare showing in his eyes.

Her heart warmed toward him. He must be exhausted as well, yet his first thought was for her. ''I'll be fine. When it's daylight I'd like to call ahead and alert the Caucus members to check out the name of that equipment company. Hopefully by the time we arrive they'll have some answers.''

Taurin grimaced. "I wish we'd had the chance to learn more from Stephan Tom."

"You may have planted seeds of doubt in his mind, and that could be more important." Frowning, she shifted her position. "This is getting so complicated. Whoever stole the horn must still have it, don't you agree?"

Taurin kept his eyes on the winding country road. "I'd like to think the horn remains at the Palisades. I wonder if your brother has had any success in his investigation."

With a tired sigh, Leena leaned her head against the headrest. "Wait until he hears that a member of the Synod stole the horn in order to lower the defense perimeter around Xan, and that an alien invasion is planned!" A smile quirked the corners of her mouth. "I can imagine his reaction. What I don't understand is why a member of the Synod would want to be involved in such a plot. It doesn't make sense to me."

"The guilty party must crave either money or power."

"But the Synod wields full authority."

"Dikran remains at the head of the government. He might stand in the way of whoever wants to be in charge."

"Dikran is an old man. Why not simply wait until he dies?"

Taurin shrugged. "There may be factors involved of which we're unaware." He gave her a somber glance. "You should call Bendyk in the morning to warn him of this new threat from Yllon's agents. Somehow I doubt Testi is the only operative. Others might have infiltrated the Palisades."

"I don't see how that is possible. Whoever works in the holy center undergoes the most stringent scrutiny."

"Nevertheless, we must be extra cautious upon our return." Testi would alert any other agents on Xan to hunt him down. Stephan Tom's organization was international, and that meant there could be many different cells around the globe—a notion that chilled Taurin. How many other landing sites were already completed? And how much of the defensive perimeter had failed simply because some of the crystals providing the energy source had lost power?

In his mind's eye he saw the crystal lattice structure that had been beneath the temple presided over by Leena's father. It was likely a similar grid existed at the Palisades, and that crystalline network probably provided power for the defense shield. It was imperative that he find the entrance to the lower levels in the Holy Temple. A central control station had to be located there, and he needed to adequately assess the damage.

"Grotus will know we're heading home to report to Dikran," Leena said, cutting into his thoughts. "I wish we could find a way to stop him. We've been trying to catch him for years but never had anything concrete to pin on him. If only we could devise a way to put the man out of action! Otherwise, we'll always have to watch our backs."

"Hasn't anyone ever tried to set up a sting?"

"Of course, but he's too smart. It's never worked."

"Maybe the right bait wasn't used."

Leena gave him a suspicious look. "Your tone of voice tells me you have something in mind. You're not thinking of using *me* as bait, are you?"

That remark elicited a low chuckle from him. "I wouldn't think of putting you at such risk, *angella*. Grotus wants the horn more than he wants you. It would bring him a fortune were he to ransom it back to the Synod. I know that's what he intends to do, because Grotus told me he needs to have the horn blown as much as the rest of us. If the weather cycles continue to be disrupted, it would interfere with his smuggling operations."

Leena's forehead creased as she considered the possibilities. "I'll bet Grotus doesn't know anything about this plot from Yllon. He has his connections at the spaceport, but he must be in the dark as far as what's really going on. I don't think he'd condone a takeover. He's too content with the way things are run now. If I were in charge of regulations, I'd make them more stringent to disallow him access to the ruins."

"Are you saying someone is purposefully being lax?"

"It is a possibility. Before all this started, I never would have thought a member of the Synod was open to a bribe, but now I'd believe anything." Her voice rang with the bitterness of disillusionment.

"Sirvat could be involved."

"Yes, that's an avenue worth exploring, although I believe the excavations come under the auspices of the Ministry of Religion. Bendyk was investigating Zeroun. Perhaps he's uncovered something important."

Taurin tightened his grip on the steering wheel. A series of sharp curves was up ahead. Luckily the road was well-lit by bright overhead lighting. He could almost feel the lines of fatigue etching his face, just as he could feel the lead weight in his stomach. They were still no closer to finding the horn than they had been when they started out on this quest. Grotus's smuggling operations were minor compared to what faced them now, although he wondered what Grotus would do were he told of the threat from Yllon.

"I have an idea," he stated, "but we'll talk about it after we see Dikran. We may need to enlist Grotus's aid."

Leena glanced at him curiously. "Bendyk's discoveries might set us in a new direction. I'll call him as soon as it's daylight."

She settled back into her seat, thinking of Bendyk and the night he'd driven along a winding road like this—the night of the accident that had killed their mother. What had Swill learned from the mechanic in town? Had Bendyk discovered anything new from his discussion with their father? She couldn't wait to compare notes with him and Swill.

Snuggling against the soft upholstery, she let her eyes drift closed. Too many confusing thoughts assailed her mind; she blanked them out until the blissful peace of slumber overwhelmed her.

Bendyk wasn't in his office when Leena called in the morning from a public messager at a recharging station along the road, but she did manage to connect with Dikran via a private, confidential line he'd given her. Quickly she related what they'd learned and asked him to set the Caucus on the trail of the equipment supplier.

The Arch Nome was stunned by her words. "It has to be Magar," he said. "He's in charge of off-world relations. He's the only one who has regular dealings with the representatives from Yllon."

"Wait until we get there," Leena pleaded. "Taurin will know what to say to him. What of Bendyk? Has he reported any news? I tried to reach him but couldn't locate him. He's not in his office or his apartments."

"You'd best speak to him yourself," Dikran said, his voice gruff. "Nothing is as it seems anymore. I don't know what will become of us," he muttered.

"Your Grace?"

"Never mind. Just get back here as soon as you can, child. And see to your own safety."

Back in the rider, Leena related her conversation to Taurin while she took a turn at the wheel.

"We'll find out what Bendyk learned soon enough," Taurin commented, closing his eyes.

Noting the weary look on his face, she fell silent, biting her lip with anxiety. They had too much to worry about during the long drive to the Palisades. Why not think of something pleasant instead? This interlude provided time for them to be alone together. Soon enough, they would be forced to face the treachery of the various Synod members. And if they succeeded in recovering the horn, what then?

Her stomach churned. She was unable to shake off a nagging sense of anxiety. Instead of appreciating Taurin's company, she wondered what would happen to their relationship once the horn was blown and stability was restored. He'd brought up some valid points to be considered, such as their differences in religious beliefs. These past few days had been woefully inadequate as an example of married life. All she knew was that she wanted to be with him.

Glancing at his profile, which was charmingly vulnerable

in repose, she let a small, affectionate smile play on her lips. In many ways Taurin still seemed like a stranger to her, yet she knew, deep down inside, that they were compatible and needed each other. Her faith complemented his skepticism; his strength of presence erased her fears. Together they would face whatever obstacles lay ahead of them. And wasn't that what marriage was all about—meeting life's challenges together?

Her grip on the steering wheel relaxed as her mind emptied of its worries. They'd get through this and settle into a routine that suited them both. Lothar would guide them. Praise be the Holy One whose beneficence provided for her people.

Taurin awoke to hear her mutter a prayer aloud, and a vise tightened around his heart. Whatever discoveries awaited them at the Palisades might set her against him. She'd blame him for withholding his knowledge about Lothar, but it was the Synod's fault for deceiving the populace. It wasn't his place to reveal the truth, and doing so would break the oath he'd made to Magar not to interfere in their world's affairs.

Magar. Was the man a traitor? Did he support the Truthsayers, urging them to armed rebellion while secretly plotting an invasion with the Ylloners?

Forcing those troublesome thoughts aside, he returned his attention to Leena. How much he needed her to go home with him when this was over! Maybe they could work things out satisfactorily, but there were still many problems to overcome. Shifting in his seat, he wondered if there would ever be an end to them. Darkness seemed to loom ahead of their steps, no matter the direction they chose. If only he shared Leena's faith, it would make his outlook so much brighter. But was it faith in Lothar or his faith in her that was lacking? Walls were tumbling down around him, Magar's potential treachery being the most painful. Leena's love was the guiding light that uplifted him, drew him out of the darkness of despair. She was his savior, his *angella*. And he prayed—

for almost the first time in his life—that he'd be able to keep her by his side.

Magar was not in his office when they returned to the Palisades two days later. A cold front had finally passed through, and the air in the complex was chilly despite the efforts of the central heating system. Leena wore a topaz brocade gown and a gold-sashed blue robe, signifying her status. Her golden hair floated about her head like a mist sprayed by a waterfall, gleaming in the shafts of sunlight that penetrated through the beveled glass windows.

Taurin wore one of his usual black outfits. They stood in the corridor outside the Minister of State's suite of offices, discussing their next course of action. Upon their arrival he'd presented her with a wedding gift: the ring he'd slipped into his pocket at the Temple of Light. It was small enough to fit her slender finger.

"This signifies our bonding," he'd said to her, his tone solemn, as they'd prepared themselves in her apartment for their audience with Dikran. "I want everyone to know you are my wife."

She'd raised herself on tiptoe to kiss him. "I shall be proud to make the announcement."

But Dikran wasn't there when they went to see him.

"We waited too long!" Leena said, a look of frustration on her face. They'd arrived by four in the afternoon but had decided to freshen up before making an appearance.

"Try locating Bendyk, but use a public messenger in the lobby. The communication system in your apartment might be bugged."

She acquiesced to his command, but neither Bendyk nor Swill were available. "Where is everyone?" she cried; then comprehension dawned when she realized how quiet the corridors had been. "Of course! Today's the Festival of Lanterns."

"What does that mean?" Taurin growled, wondering how

anyone could get their work done when there were so many religious holidays.

"They've gone home to light lanterns and say a prayer for the dead. As though in mourning, one is to pursue no forms of entertainment, including answering the messager system. It would be a sacrilege to disturb anyone during this solemn time. We'll go back to my apartment. I have some lanterns there we can light."

"No. We'll go to my place."

She shot him a quizzical glance. "You won't be needing your apartment here any longer."

"I meant we should go home to Lexington Page, to my farm."

"Oh." Leena stared at him, aghast. Surely after such a long journey from Woden he didn't intend to spend another hour and a half on the road? But when she saw the firm set to his jaw she realized he meant just that. "But why?" she asked.

"We can still be here early in the morning to speak with Dikran. In the meantime I have chores to do at home."

Leena acquiesced quietly, understanding that it had been quite some time since he'd set foot in his house, and that he probably wanted to reassure himself that all was well there. The recent frost might have killed his crops, without him there to tend to them. She'd have to remember to ask Dikran to compensate him for their loss.

But checking on his crops seemed to be the farthest thing from Taurin's mind when they arrived at his home two hours later. They'd found a food market nearby that was still open and stocked up on a few supplies, and Leena bought lanterns as well. As she set about preparing their meal and lighting the lanterns in the appointed places in different rooms of the house, Taurin closeted himself in his bedroom.

"Won't you join me in prayer?" she called out, standing outside his closed door.

"I'll be out in a minute."

She turned away, hurt that he would exclude her. What

was he doing in there that required privacy? Disturbed by his behavior, she finished her meal preparations. The aroma of spiced vegetable soup wafted in the air. Warmed by the hot stove and the efficient heating system, she'd removed her cloak and donned an apron. In another pot, thick noodles simmered in an orange-spiked tomato sauce, peppered with bits of dried rasenbret.

"Something smells good."

Leena whirled around, smiling at the sight of Taurin in the archway. His tall figure and fiercely handsome features raised her temperature another notch. He sauntered into the kitchen, a seductive grin on his face, but behind his eyes were traces of anxiety.

"The food is just about ready," she told him. "Let us say our prayers while we're waiting."

The smile on his face vanished. "Must you follow all of the traditions so diligently?"

"Does it bother you if I do?"

"No, so long as you don't expect me to be so compliant."

Leena sighed, wiping her hands on a dry towel. "I wish you believed in Lothar. It would make all of this meaningful to you. I get the feeling that you're humoring me by participating in the rituals."

His expression softened. "I just want to please you, *angella*." Advancing closer, he lowered his head and brushed his lips across hers. "Let's get on with these prayers, shall we?"

Their prayers finished, they ate their hearty repast while engaging in light conversation. Scrubbing the dishes afterward, Leena wondered how they would ever reconcile their differences. She didn't care for the notion that Taurin's prayers were hollow, that he pretended tolerance just to pacify her. Ideally a marriage should be based on a common value system. That he thought so little of Lothar distressed her and boded ill for their future together. Or perhaps she was the one being intolerant. She'd been raised from birth to believe that everyone worshipped Lothar. Why shouldn't someone be entitled to believe differently?

Taurin placed a hand on her shoulder, startling her.

"Why don't you leave that for later?" he whispered, nuzzling against her neck.

She sighed with pleasure. This part of married life she was definitely going to enjoy. She turned off the water and dried her hands before moving into his arms. Immediately his mouth came down on hers as she folded her body into his embrace.

"My bed is large enough for two," Taurin drawled. "It's about time I had a wife to warm it for me."

His arm around her, he led her to the bedroom, muttering a curse when she noticed the bibliotomes scattered on the coverlet. Hastily he scooped them up and piled them on a table in a corner of the room.

Leena's eyes narrowed suspiciously. Had he been reading them? His next action diverted her attention. He stripped off his clothes and stood before her naked.

"You're next, my love. I want to see you in all your glory."

Needing no further prompting, Leena slid out of her gown and undergarments, watching as her husband studied her from head to toe.

"Beautiful," he murmured, circling around her to examine every pore of her being.

"You're embarrassing me."

"Nonsense. Looking at you brings me pleasure. See what it does?" He pointed to his erect appendage.

Leena's blood sizzled as a responding heat arose within her. The bed looked inviting with the covers thrown back, the white sheets crisp and clean. She felt the barest breeze against her exposed skin, a drift of warmth from the heating system that hummed in the background.

Taurin flipped off the light switch, leaving the room in the soft glow of the lantern light. Every room in the house was lit with lanterns, remembrances for those long past.

We are here to celebrate life, she told herself, opening her arms as Taurin approached. And celebrate life they did, joining together as one, murmuring words of passion in each other's ears, melding together in a frenzied declaration of their love.

"I need you so much," Taurin whispered, still locked in her arms after they'd satiated each other's driving lust.

She kissed him on the mouth. "I need you, too. You make my life complete." Her hands splayed across his broad back, kneading his taut muscles. The manliness of him drove her wild, and she never wanted to let him go. Entwining her legs around his, she reveled in the feel of his rock solid body against her softness. She'd never felt so feminine as when she was with him, and it was a joy to experience such a wonderful part of life.

"My wife," he uttered in a hoarse cry, and in it was an echo of the desperate longing in his heart. If only he could come home to her every night, he would be a happy man for the rest of his life. She was his haven, the peace he'd been seeking, not the farm on this tiny bit of land.

He realized now that this was what he'd always wanted—a family of his own. He'd admired the bonds between Baker Mylock and his brood but hadn't realized it was something he sought for himself. He wouldn't let Leena leave him, no matter what happened.

The way he held on to her convinced Leena that he was troubled. "What bothers you, my darling?" she asked, staring into his glowing eyes.

He gazed back at her with such love and affection, she thought she would melt. "I'm afraid," he murmured, searching her face.

"Afraid of what?"

"That you'll leave me; that you won't want me anymore after . . . after we finish this."

She realized he was talking about finding the missing horn. "Time is running out. We have to recover the horn and blow it so that Lothar may awaken."

"*Lothar*. Always *Lothar*." Taurin withdrew, flopping onto

his back. Would that her god had never come between them. The horn wasn't the issue here; it was really all about Lothar. The Truthsayers might have been right when they accused the Synod of securing power for themselves to the disadvantage of the people.

He'd learned many revealing facts in his examination of his bibliotomes, but there was still much missing information. Grotus had some of the books, obtained from Captain Sterckle, and Magar had others. The things he had learned were piecemeal, like segments of a puzzle that had yet to be fit together. The books in the Temple of Light were a valuable resource, but he believed there must be another repository located in the Palisades. He'd asked Bendyk to search for the location of the hidden lower level and wondered if he'd been successful.

Other than the bibliotomes, the symbols carved into the walls of the ancient temples were the only valuable clues they had relating to the Apostles. Leena could interpret them, but he wouldn't ask for her help unless it became absolutely necessary. He was able to read the bibliotomes only because the knowledge contained therein was transmitted via some sort of telepathic imprint. He didn't quite understand how the method worked, but at least he was not required to read the symbols. He hoped a new source of bibliotomes would reveal the knowledge required to repair the crystals.

The secrets of Lothar had to be contained within the Palisades. Tomorrow, Taurin vowed, he would force Dikran to disclose everything.

Chapter Eighteen

The next day they met briefly with Dikran. "I directed the Caucus to check into the name of the equipment company you mentioned," the Arch Nome told them, appearing even more frail than when they'd seen him last. A vein in his forehead throbbed conspicuously as he regarded them with a defeated expression. He sat, dwarfed by his thronelike chair, while they stood in front of him like sergeants being summoned before an officer.

"The trace led to a larger corporation called Amiaus. The Caucus is checking into the details now."

"What of the defense shield around the planet?" Taurin asked. "Is it weakening?"

Dikran nodded. "Ever since Lothar began malfunctioning. I should have seen this coming, but I was convinced someone stole the horn for the money."

"Lothar's malfunction!" Leena piped in. "What are you talking about? The weather disasters?"

Dikran cast her a startled look. "Eh? Oh, yes, child. Lothar is displeased because of the Truthsayer movement. You say Stephan Tom, the president of the International Merchants Association, is the leader behind this group?" Dikran frowned. "That means it reaches a wider audience than we have imagined. It's a strong organization that began as a grass-roots movement that sprang up promoting greater freedom of choice. It's grown in popularity over the years. Those people chafe against any restrictions imposed upon them."

"Why doesn't the Synod open talks with the Truthsayers?" Leena suggested.

She really hadn't considered the Truthsayers' viewpoint before, but in some respects they were right. Why couldn't people migrate where they pleased? Why did one have to obtain permission to change settlements? If society was to grow, change was inevitable. And if that meant progressing from towns to cities, with all their problems, perhaps that was the way of destiny. Progress was the goal of mankind. Perhaps it was time for the Synod to make some allowances to meet needs more suitable to the modern age.

"You forget," Dikran told her, shaking a crooked finger in her direction, "Lothar set the rules. We follow his laws, madam."

"And who wrote the laws?" Taurin asked quietly.

"The Apostles wrote the laws that were handed to them by Lothar," Dikran cried.

"Really?" Taurin raised an eyebrow. His eyes met Dikran's, and for a moment he saw a flicker of uncertainty in the Arch Nome's expression.

Dikran scrutinized his face, then turned to Leena. "Leave us for a moment, child. I wish to speak to this man in private."

"Now wait a minute," Leena said, highly insulted that they would have a discussion without her.

"Go find your brother," Taurin said, a kindly, indulgent look on his face. "I'll join you in a few moments."

"Very well," Leena snapped before turning and storming out of the room.

Slowly Taurin turned back to face Dikran. "I know about

the power grids. They relay information to the weather satellites orbiting the planet. The central control station has to be here.''

Dikran compressed his lips, saying nothing, so Taurin continued. ''Lothar isn't displeased with the people. Your power source is failing. I've seen the crystals.'' He noted with gratification the look of surprise in Dikran's eyes. ''Not all of the crystals are functioning properly, are they? They're deteriorating, and that's what's wreaking havoc with the weather. What's happening, Dikran? Are the crystals wearing out? Were they a legacy from the Apostles that no one understands?''

Dikran's posture slumped. ''You know too much, son. Does *she* know?''

''Leena? No, she hasn't a clue. She believes faithfully in Lothar. We are married, your eminence, and I love her dearly.'' He gave a wry smile at the Arch Nome's astonished look. ''I cannot be the one who disillusions her with the truth.''

''So I see.''

''May I suggest that you and I make a deal? I'll tell you what I know if you lay all your cards on the table. I give you my solemn vow that what you reveal will not go beyond this room.''

''Why should I trust you?'' Dikran said, his probing dark eyes inspecting Taurin.

''Because I'm from Yllon.''

''What!''

Taurin explained his background. ''I know what kind of terror my countrymen are capable of bringing to your people. The defense shield has to be strengthened if you want to repel the coming invasion. Maybe I can fix the malfunction if I know what is causing it.''

Dikran spread his hands helplessly. ''But the horn has to be blown to reawaken Lothar.''

''Lothar be damned! You know there's no god as well as I do. I figure the horn has to be blown to reset the weather cycles, but what role does it play regarding the crystals?''

"Blowing the horn has no effect on them. We don't know what is causing them to fade. Sounding the horn serves to reset the climatic patterns, as you surmised, but it also provides a temporary energy boost that can fortify the defensive perimeter, at least for a short time. It won't solve the problem in the long run. If the crystals continue to deteriorate, eventually all power will be drained.''

With a swish of his robe, Dikran rose, his movements majestic despite his dejection. "Follow me," he said, heading for a doorway at the rear of the chamber.

"Are you taking me to the lower level?"

"The entrance is in my private robing salon, behind the Grand Altar in the Holy Temple."

"Of course." Taurin followed him through the suite of offices and out into the maze of corridors that wound through the Palisades complex. They strode past administrative wings, small chapels, and open courtyards before reaching the Arch Nome's private entrance to the Holy Temple. Along the way, Taurin filled Dikran in on the details he and Leena had omitted before: their discoveries in the Temple of Light, Taurin's relationship with Magar, and his encounter with Testi. The only thing he didn't reveal was the use of his armband. It might come in handy as a playing piece later on, and he didn't want to give away the game at this early stage.

"We closed the Temple of Light for excavations because it was deemed too dangerous to explore," Dikran admitted after Taurin questioned him. "We had no idea what might be found therein except that it must be highly valuable. I'll have to discuss this with the Synod. They may want to reopen the site now that you know how to bypass the traps."

"Be sure to include Leena in any professional excavation," Taurin advised. She'd be deeply upset if they excluded her after her skills had gained entrance.

In the robing salon, Dikran shuffled up to a statue of a cherub, similar to the one in Cranby's office.

"How is Lothar's lozenge created?" Taurin asked, frowning.

Grasping the halo and spinning it in the golden disk, Dikran shook his head. "A gift from Lothar. It just appears during the month of Mistic, and the count is almost always accurate. We have been unable to conceive how they are produced."

Taurin's admiration of the Apostles grew. Certainly they were an advanced civilization, but why had they left and where had they gone? And what relation were they to him? Some of the answers he'd gleaned from reading his bibliotomes, but the rest might be here, through the secret passageway that had just opened in the far wall.

A flight of steps led downward to a level filled with huge chambers, featuring vaulted stone ceilings, recessed lighting, and an air-filtering system that kept the temperatures on an even keel.

The first room held an array of equipment that surprised Taurin in its complexity. Row after row of computer banks flashed with different buttons and dials. Peering closely, he noticed monitors linking the houses of worship run by the Candors. A liquid crystal map grid made up an entire wall, displaying the global weather system. The sophisticated setup impressed him. This level of technology was beyond anything he'd seen before.

"Amazing," he murmured, staring around the room with awe. "You and the Synod are the only ones aware of this place?"

Dikran nodded, his expression sad. "We know so little." He gestured toward the control consoles. "None of us understands this, nor did our predecessors. Magar said he would consult with his contacts in Yllon about repairs."

Taurin pointed to a pulsating brightness ahead. "That's a crystal lattice structure, isn't it?"

Dikran stopped in front of a receptacle before the entrance to the next room and withdrew two pairs of dark glasses. "Here, put these on. It's too bright otherwise."

Taurin donned the glasses and proceeded into the adjacent chamber. Most of the crystals in the honeycomb structure glowed brilliantly, but a few flickered, and others appeared to be dead.

"Why haven't there been any power failures? Don't these grids supply electricity, as well as power the satellite system?"

"They do in part," Dikran acknowledged, "but we have solar generators as backups. They've been able to function adequately. If more of the crystals fail, however, I don't see how the generators can be maintained either."

Taurin stalked into the next room. Inside was a repository of inactive crystals, heaped in piles like so many inanimate rocks. Again he wondered how to activate them, and puzzled over what was causing their demise. Perhaps the next chamber held some answers.

The next room held an immense library of bibliotomes. Stacks and stacks of books rose toward the ceiling. In the center of the room, on a raised pedestal, under a glass cover, was the largest bibliotome he'd ever seen. Walking over to peer closely at it, Taurin noted the familiar sequence of symbols on the creamy, translucent cover.

"What is this?" he called out.

Dikran's voice was a hushed whisper behind him. "The sacred Book of Laws. It is the bible for our society. The Apostles—"

Taurin pivoted, his eyes flashing angrily. "The Apostles came to this world, possibly from a star system in the Cadega constellation. They set up their own laws and established the rule of Lothar to suit their needs."

"They brought order and peace to our society," Dikran countered, his eyes gleaming. "They stabilized our weather, provided rain for our crops, gave us the lozenge to fight sickness. Is there not the hand of a god in all this?" Dikran swept his arm to encompass the room. "Perhaps the Apostles did create all of this. But who gave them the gifts? Who were their progenitors?"

He stepped closer, his gaze piercing Taurin's. "I truly believe there is a higher order of intelligence, a superior being who is responsible for the patterns of life. This entity's name may not be Lothar, but he . . . or it . . . is the holy one I worship."

"Why don't you reveal the truth to the people? Are you afraid they will revolt against the authority of the Synod?"

"Of course I am afraid. But I see that progress is inevitable, even though it may not be for the best. The winds of change are blowing, and there is nothing I can do to stop them."

"Not unless you get the horn back and figure out what's wrong with the crystals."

"Can you assist us?" Dikran asked, his tone pleading. "The other Ylloners claimed that this technology was beyond their scope of knowledge."

"What other Ylloners?" Taurin demanded.

"Why, the ones Magar consulted, of course. No, wait a minute. I think it was Karayan who suggested we bring in technicians from Yllon to fix the malfunction."

"You actually had people from Yllon down here? How do you know they didn't sabotage the system?"

"It was already failing!" Dikran shouted, throwing his arms into the air. "The technicians said they had to examine the regional worship centers in the outlying districts. They felt the fault might be there."

"So you actually gave approval for agents from Yllon to scour the countryside? That's how they were brought in," Taurin said, a thoughtful gleam in his eyes. "And you say it was Karayan who suggested consulting with these technicians?"

The old man's face crinkled with thought. "I believe so," he said, his gnarled fingers plucking at his golden robe.

Taurin's mouth compressed. "I'd like some time down here alone to figure this out. Do you think you could notify Leena that I'll be late? I'll meet her back in our apartment."

Dikran gazed at him consideringly. "Why is it you did

not make your marriage public?''

Taurin shrugged. ''We thought it best not to do so during our mission. Leena's life is governed by her religious traditions. I can't tell her about any of this.''

''There is no need to disillusion her,'' Dikran agreed. ''We'll tell her only what is necessary. See what her brother has learned and what you can piece together here. Then we'll meet again to determine a course of action.''

''I tried to tell Stephan Tom the truth, but he wouldn't listen.''

Dikran nodded. ''He's blinded by his own ambition. We'll put the Truthsayers in their place once the horn is recovered.''

''Whoever stole it planned on the defense shield failing by Fearn. Yllon's agents are now planted around the globe. This plot must have been in the works for some time.''

''Magar and Karayan are the most likely candidates,'' said Dikran, his voice grim. A wisp of white hair fell into his face, and he tossed it back with the air of a man determined to fight his foes despite his advancing age. ''We need evidence in order to bring a charge against one of them, or perhaps both, if they're in this together. I'll look into the matter while you're occupied here. Contact me when you are ready for another meeting.''

''It may not be safe to talk in your office,'' Taurin cautioned him. ''The traitor, with the aid of his Yllon friends, may have placed listening devices about the Palisades. We know that Sirvat leaks information to Grotus, who could have spies here as well. I have an idea as to how we can use Grotus to aid us, but we'll talk more about that later.'' Taurin felt the smuggler would remain a threat to both himself and Leena unless the matter of the horn was resolved.

As Dikran's footsteps faded into the distance, Taurin slid off his armband and disengaged the bracelets. The three large rings created a musical harmony when he spun them in unison, having selected a bibliotome to research. The soothing tone brought memories of his childhood, when he'd simply stared at the spinning rings, enjoying their music. The rings were the keys to this library. He only hoped the books didn't contain a complete account of the Apostles' culture, because then it would take weeks or months for him to find the answers he needed. They didn't have that kind of time with Fearn less than two weeks away. This was his last hope to learn how the crystals functioned and how the horn served to reset Lothar.

Leena paced agitatedly in Bendyk's office while her brother and Swill awaited her reaction in silence.

"You're telling me the brake line was cut the night of the accident?" she cried, glaring at Swill.

The young woman bobbed her head of short black hair. "The mechanic had been paid to say it was an accident."

"Paid by whom?" Distressed, she brushed a hand through her golden hair. How could Bendyk have suspected this before and never confided in her?

"A representative from the Ministry of Religion was responsible," Bendyk answered. He sat at his desk, his manner composed. His medallion gleamed brilliantly against his royal blue longshirt. "Father had a meeting that night and would have taken his rider but arranged instead to be picked up by a friend. Mother and I got in the rider intended for Father."

"But he apologized for his transgression. You're saying that someone still considered him a threat?"

"Apparently so." The corners of Bendyk's mouth turned down. "The mechanic will testify, and the representative from the Ministry of Religion has agreed to act as a witness. He received his orders directly from Zeroun."

Leena gasped. "But that means Zeroun ordered our father to be murdered."

Bendyk nodded grimly. "Others who have defied the faith have vanished mysteriously. If you remember, Karayan came to Father's defense, citing his exemplary record as a factor to be considered in his sentencing. Zeroun must have realized that if his verdict was too harsh, he would be censured, and so he took matters into his own hands. He's zealous about his faith, quick to punish anyone who deviates from the norm.''

''You mean anyone who threatens his power structure,'' Swill put in, her tone sarcastic. ''He wouldn't have taken the horn. It's too important to him to maintain Lothar's stability.''

''But he's a murderer!'' Leena cried.

Bendyk held up a hand to pacify her. ''That is a matter that must be dealt with separately.''

''How can you sit there so calmly? He was responsible for the accident that killed Mother and injured you. We must tell Dikran immediately.'' And then she remembered that Taurin was with Dikran, in a secret meeting that didn't include her.

''I wonder what he's telling Taurin,'' she said, a moue of disgust on her face.

''We learned something else,'' Swill said gently, her eyes gazing at Leena with sympathy. ''Those plantations in the Black Lands—the ones that grow beans for the Chocola Company—the land rights were granted to the Amiaus Company, of which Karayan is a large shareholder. We've received reports from some of the aides in the Caucus that Karayan has made some bad investments in the past few years. He would be in dire financial straits if it weren't for this additional income. Illicit income, I might add.''

Leena stared at Bendyk, horrified. ''Is there no end to the corruption?'' Her father's closest friend was guilty of illegal business transactions, Zeroun was responsible for murder, and they already knew Sirvat was prey to Grotus's whims. But which one of them had taken the horn? They'd eliminated nearly everyone else.

''Wait a minute. What about Magar? Magar is responsible for contact with the off-worlders,'' she reminded her brother. She'd told him about their sojourn in Woden and their discoveries. "He could be in league with Drufus Gong from Yllon."

Bendyk hunched his shoulders thoughtfully. "All of our probes have come up negative on him. He appears to be clean."

"I'll bet Taurin knows more about Magar."

"Then we'll just have to wait and see what he says, won't we?" Bendyk said.

The messenger rang. It was Dikran's aide, telling them that Taurin would be delayed and would meet Leena back in their apartment later.

"Drat!" Leena cursed, knowing he was up to something.

She looked so disconsolate that Bendyk gave her a sharp gaze. "How are you getting along, Sister?"

"We're managing fine except that he . . . he doesn't trust me." She broke down and told him about their discoveries in the Temple of Light. "I believe he's figured out how to read those books, but it's something he won't share with me."

"Interesting," Bendyk mused. Leena could tell by the bounce in the word that he was excited by the prospect. "I'd like to have a talk with him myself. There are too many questions that need answering at this point, and if he's got some of them figured out . . ." His voice trailed off. "We're working as a team," he said. "Taurin will tell us what he knows, or else." '

"Or else what?" Leena couldn't imagine her brother physically defying Taurin. Taurin's strength and skill would outweigh him by far, though her brother was no slouch.

"I still have the power to annul your marriage," Bendyk said, standing and squaring his shoulders. "If I must invoke my authority, I shall do so."

"But I don't want an annulment."

"If he loves you, he won't risk losing you. He'll tell us what we want to know."

Leena was disturbed by the prospect of forcing Taurin to reveal his knowledge. He should trust her enough to confide in her himself. Her hurt went deep, and she carried it with her to her apartment. It began as a sinking feeling in her gut and rose as a throbbing ache in her heart when he didn't return. Too weary to wait up for him, Leena went to bed, depressed as she crawled under the sheets, cold and empty without her mate.

He must have a reason for his behavior, she rationalized. Maybe he felt he was protecting her, but protecting her against what? The truth? What truths would she fear to hear? She considered her question and the various options it presented but was unable to reach any conclusions. Fatigued, she let herself drift into sleep.

Bendyk sank down onto the sofa in Swill's living area, having been to her apartment in the Palisades enough times to feel at home. After their visit to his family estate he'd noticed a reticence in her behavior toward him and wanted to address it, especially after hearing Leena's doubts about Taurin. Lack of communication was plaguing both of them, and he thought it was about time he and Swill had a frank discussion about where their relationship was headed.

He'd proposed discussing the new developments as an excuse to accompany her home, although both of them knew that wasn't what was on his mind. Swill had gone into her bedroom to change into something more comfortable—presumably, one of the seductive nightgowns he'd purchased for her. Heat warmed his face as he recalled his embarrassment in the clothing shop, but he'd wanted to give her a gift of finery, and what better choice than a couple of silk shifts to wear against her soft skin?

The heat spread through his veins, spinning him into a sensual coil as the image of her naked body came to mind. *Stop it!* he chastised himself. He hadn't come here for that purpose.

"Bendyk, you look uncomfortable in that longshirt," Swill's low voice crooned as she sashayed into the room.

The burgundy lingerie revealed a tantalizing glimpse of her cleavage and bare legs.

Bendyk gave her an appreciative glance. "Let's talk first," he suggested, making room for her on the couch. As soon as she sat, nudging her hip against his, a wave of desire rocketed through him. He suppressed his reaction. "I was troubled to hear of Leena's difficulty with Taurin," he began. "For a married couple to get along, they have to share their secrets. Mutual trust must be at the foundation of a relationship."

Swill observed him warily. "I agree."

He cleared his throat. "I get the feeling you are not being entirely honest with me. Ever since we visited my father you seem more reserved. What is bothering you?"

Something flickered briefly behind her eyes. "Why does it matter?"

He'd asked himself the same question. "It just does, that's all. I . . . I care about what you think."

Swill lifted an arched eyebrow. "I felt uncomfortable in your home, as if I didn't fit in. You saw how I was raised. I'd never belong—" She bit her lip, cutting off her words.

His arm snaked out, and he began tickling the soft skin on the underside of her wrist. "When order is restored to our land I'd hate to see you waste your talents on the tithing counts. You have a keen mind and an admirable grasp of finances. Have you thought about applying for a higher position?"

A look of disappointment crossed her face, as though she'd expected him to say something different.

"Not really."

"I should like to be able to see you, and if you were to live nearby—" He shook his head. "No, that's not what I want to say." Rotating his body, he gazed directly into her wide amber eyes. "You've made me see that there's more to life than preaching the words of Lothar. Thanks to your insights, I no longer feel I have to assuage my guilt over my mother's death. You've given me a new lease on life, Swill, and I need you with me. Say you'll be my bonded mate.''

Swill stared at him, her mouth gaping. ''You . . . you really want me?'' she asked in a small voice. ''I hadn't dared hope . . . I mean, I dreamed about this, but I never . . . Bendyk, do you love me?'' she asked in her endearingly blunt manner.

He planted a teasing kiss on her forehead, a promise of more to come if she accepted his proposal. ''I love you, and I'll cherish you as my mate. Being with you is all that matters.''

She threw her arms around his neck. ''You've just made my dreams come true. I promise I'll make you a good wife, even if I have to bring you down from your pedestal from time to time.''

Bendyk laughed, feeling more lighthearted than he had in a decade. ''I'll look forward to that, my sweet.''

As he led her into the bedroom, he felt gratified to think that on this night rest would be a long time in coming.

At some point in the night, a low, clicking noise startled Leena into wakefulness. Her groggy mind wondered if it was Taurin returning. As her hand stretched out, it encountered a warm, lifelike presence. He was here, lying by her side. Glancing in his direction, she noticed that his eyes were open, glowing luminously. He appeared to be listening. When he realized she was awake he put a hand on her arm, indicating she should be quiet.

''Someone is attempting to break in,'' he hissed, pulling his blaster from under the pillow, grateful that Grotus's agent had retrieved it for him in the ruckus of their rescue. ''Perhaps we should allow our intruder to kill his mark.''

''What do you mean?''

Her heart thumping wildly in her chest, she paid careful attention while Taurin described his plan.

Concealed behind the tall wooden wardrobe, she waited with a racing pulse and sweaty palms while footsteps sounded on the padded carpeting, coming from the living area. Taurin was secreted behind the door, blaster ready. Pillows were propped up on the bed to look like bodies—an old trick, but they hoped it would work. And if it didn't, no one would hear her screams for help in this unpopulated wing of the residential complex.

She held her breath as the intruder approached the door to the bedroom. A floorboard creaked, and the invader stopped, hesitating for a moment before advancing. Leena saw his tall, lean shape framed in the doorway as he pointed a rod-shaped object at the bed. Before he could discharge his weapon, Taurin smashed the door into his shadowy figure. The impact slammed him backward against the wall, where he accidentally hit the light switch. It flicked on to a dim setting.

"You!" Taurin exclaimed, aiming his blaster at Testi.

"Demon!" growled the agent from Yllon, clutching his back. Having dropped his weapon, he glared at Taurin. "What they say about you is true."

Taurin's glowing gaze never wavered. "Stand up straight. I want some answers out of you."

"Fat chance." Testi drew a hidden blaster and fired at Taurin.

Taurin's weapon crashed to the floor as he stumbled back with a surprised cry. Testi raised his blaster to fire again, but Taurin dodged the sizzling gust, throwing himself into a somersault that landed him at Testi's feet. He yanked his opponent off balance, and the two grappled on the floor. Rage boiled through Taurin's veins as his hands reached for Testi's throat.

"Tell me who the traitor is on this world. Is it Magar, Karayan, or both of them? Talk!"

Testi's face was growing red. Hovering behind them, Leena feared he would choke before uttering a word.

"Taurin, let him speak," she urged.

Taurin's jaw worked as he fought to gain control of his temper.

"You're under a death sentence," the agent croaked. "It is my duty to carry it out."

"You're the one who's going to die," Taurin shouted, tightening his hands.

"No, Taurin! Stop!" Leena screamed, trying to push him aside.

As though he were swatting a fly, Taurin shoved her out of the way. "Keep out of this!"

But his motion cost him the advantage. Testi thrust his fingers at Taurin's eyes. Howling with pain and momentarily blinded, Taurin fell back.

"Drufus Gong will reward me for carrying out his sentence," Testi said.

He pounced on Taurin, fastening his wrists and ankles before he could make a move in self-defense. When Taurin was sufficiently trussed up by some cords Testi had apparently brought along, the agent sat back on his haunches, satisfied by his work. Taurin glared up at him.

"Why bother tying me up? You might as well kill me and be done with it."

"Not yet, Taurin," Testi sneered, approaching Leena. "I think I'll have a little fun with your woman first."

Leena shrieked and tried to run past him, but he grabbed her by the hair, yanking her back with brutal force. Forcing her head back, he brought his mouth down on hers, his foul breath making her want to vomit.

"Now you can show me what he sees in you, lady," Testi said, leering at her. He shoved her onto the bed, face first. "Your nightshirt barely covers your knees. Let's see what's underneath."

Leena scrambled to crawl off the bed, but he seized her arm, forcing her onto her back. Her wide, frightened gaze met the sadistic gleam of his dark, beady eyes. "Get off me!" she screeched, rage at her helplessness giving her courage.

A glow came from the darkened corner of the room where Taurin struggled against his bonds, watching them in fury. "Curse you," he cried. "I'll kill you if you hurt her."

"This is nothing compared to what I'm going to do."

Moving his hands to her shoulders, Testi found her nerve centers and pinched hard. An agony of pain shot through her, and she squeezed her eyes shut, biting her lip to keep from screaming. He was tormenting Taurin by hurting her, she told herself, trying to steel her body against the pain. But Testi's onslaught was relentless, and she couldn't help the cry of anguish that escaped her lips. Weakened by the pain shooting down her arms, she didn't resist when he kneaded her breast, chuckling evilly.

Taurin could see them from where he sat, and he cringed when he saw Testi place his hands on Leena's intimate parts. I'll murder him, he thought, enraged. Straining at his bonds, he fought to free himself, a sense of fury and hopelessness washing over him. I won't let this happen, he cried silently. I won't let him maul the woman I love. I'll kill him first. As his wrists strained against the cords binding him, he pictured Testi's throat in his hands. How he'd like to squeeze his fingers taut, tightening them against the man's neck, blocking his airway until he was dead.

Leena's eyes were closed against the assault, but suddenly Testi jerked back, and she glanced at him in astonishment. In the dim light she saw him clutching his temples, his face a mottled shade of red.

"Stop it! The pain! It's killing me!" he croaked. He began to drool, continuing to mutter incoherently, and then his eyes rolled up in his head and he toppled over, dead.

Leena sat up and stared at Taurin, who'd suddenly gone still. Tightly bound, he sat on the floor, glaring back at her. In another instant she was by his side, untying the cord that held him a prisoner.

"I've killed him," Taurin said, his voice filled with revulsion as he got up to examine Testi's body.

"*You?*" Leena said, sinking onto the bed in exhaustion. She trembled with fear and relief and would have sought comfort in his arms, but the look she saw on his face forbade her to act. "He seemed to suffer a stroke."

"I thought of strangling him, and so he died." He gazed

at her, his eyes horror-stricken. "It's true, the curse. I have the power to—"

"To what? Drive men mad? He was already insane with the killing instinct. You didn't cause him to feel that way."

"No, I just killed him." Taurin retrieved his blaster from the floor and changed the setting. "This has four levels," he explained in an impassive tone. "Levels one and two are light and heavy stun; they affect the nervous system. Level three is the kill mode. And level four . . . well, see for yourself." He aimed and fired. As Leena gaped in horror, Testi's body vaporized into the air.

"Good riddance," Taurin mumbled. Pulling on a robe, he stumbled from the room.

Leena stared after him, too stunned to move. But after a moment she decided his need for support was greater than her shock at his casual disposal of their attacker. Rushing into the living area, she found him seated on a couch, his head held in his hands. A surge of tender emotion overwhelmed her, and she sank down beside him.

"Don't be so harsh on yourself," she said in a soothing tone, putting her arm about his shoulders. "You've shown me nothing but kindness. Perhaps this . . . this curse, if it actually exists, pertains only to people who are already aggressive in nature."

Taurin glanced at her, and she cringed at the look of anguish on his face. "The entire populace on my world was affected. When the Apostles came they inspired madness. It is their genes that I carry."

"But I don't understand. How could they have done so much good on my world and then traveled to yours and committed evil?"

Taurin compressed his lips, apparently unwilling to say more. "Perhaps we should ask Bendyk to perform an annulment in the morning. It would be best for you if you were rid of me as soon as we recover the horn."

She stroked his cheek lightly. "I don't want to hear you talk that way. We belong together."

Taurin said nothing, but she didn't like the brooding look on his face and hoped he wouldn't take any action on his own that they'd both regret. Realizing it was useless to comfort him, she returned to her bed, shivering despite the warmth of the blankets. The memory of Testi's disgusting breath on her skin made her flesh crawl, but wishing for Taurin to soothe away her unpleasant remembrances was a waste of time. Instead, she turned on her side, pondering how best to get Taurin to share his secrets.

Chapter Nineteen

"Did Taurin tell you anything last night?" Bendyk whispered to Leena as they awaited an audience with Dikran. Having met earlier in his office, he and Swill had revealed their news to Leena and Taurin. His sister and her mate had wished them a hearty congratulations, but he'd sensed an undercurrent of sadness in Leena, and it disturbed him.

She shook her head. "He's still hiding something."

Bendyk's face darkened with anger. "It doesn't bode well for a marriage if a man withholds confidences from his wife. I shall speak to him."

Before Leena could warn him that Taurin wasn't a man to be coerced the doors to the reception chamber opened, and they were ushered in to a private audience with Dikran. The old man sat in regal glory on his throne, dwarfed by his voluminous golden robes. A resplendent headdress crowned his thin white hair. It gave him height and dignity, affirming the intelligence in his eyes, commanding respect.

"Report," Dikran ordered, his voice unwavering.

Bendyk revealed what he'd learned about Zeroun's responsibility in his mother's death and Karayan's financial status. "As for the plantations in the Black Lands," he went on, "we found out that the property rights were granted to a corporation called the Amiaus Company."

"The Amiaus Company!" exclaimed Taurin. "Isn't that the same one that's supplying the construction equipment to the Wodeners?"

Dikran nodded solemnly, meeting his gaze with a penetrating one of his own. "Aye, so it is."

"Karayan is a major shareholder in the company," Bendyk added. "This is the link we've needed. It means he might be the one involved with the Ylloners."

"What about Magar?" Leena queried. "I thought he was in charge of off-world relations." She still found it hard to believe her father's friend could be involved in such a devious plot. Karayan had always been so supportive.

"I've been unable to speak to Magar," Taurin cut in. "He's away at a district meeting, but he should be back later. It doesn't matter; I have a plan to coax the thief into the open so we can recover the horn."

"A trap!" Swill shouted. Her face held an exultant look, as though she were enjoying herself immensely.

No doubt it was pleasing to her to get the goods on the Synod, Bendyk thought, his amusement mixed with a tinge of sadness. It was possible the Synod did wield too much power. For the first time he seriously considered the Truthsayers' rhetoric. Perhaps it wasn't so much rabble-rousing as much as a push for true human rights.

"Call a meeting of the Synod for tonight," Taurin directed Dikran. "I'll let it be known that Leena and I have found the horn. We'll say we paid ransom money to get it back from an antiquities collector to whom Grotus directed us. Because of her desire to please Grotus, Sirvat stole it some months ago. She gave it to Grotus in exchange for a fake reproduction. Grotus sold it to the collector, who in turn ransomed it back to us. Leena has verified that it is authentic. As Renewal approached, Sirvat got nervous and stole the fake horn in order to avoid detection. The thief will believe he has a reproduction. He'll want to exchange it for the real thing.''

Leena snorted. ''But Sirvat will be right there. She'll refute your story.''

Taurin gave her a cold stare. ''She won't be able to deny her liaison with Grotus. Leaking information at such a high level of government is a punishable offense.'' He directed a quizzical gaze at the others. ''How do you get rid of unworthy Synod members? Zeroun has overstepped the bounds by committing murder and Karayan is engaged in illegal financial transactions. They need to be removed from office.''

''I appointed the Synod,'' Dikran pronounced. ''I have the power to dismiss them from their posts.''

''How are you going to support your claim that we have the sacred horn?'' Leena asked.

''We'll announce a new Renewal ceremony to be held four days hence,'' Taurin said. ''I'll say I'm going to blow the horn to reset Lothar. As far as I understand, there is no training required; normally the honor is bestowed on the horn blower as a form of special recognition. The ceremony must occur at the Grand Altar for Lothar to respond. I would expect the guilty party will show up on our doorstep before the appointed time. Now, about the security arrangements: Can anyone give me a layout of the Palisades?''

''I can.'' Dikran withdrew a document from a pocket in his robe. ''I thought you might be needing this.''

Taurin spread the map across the surface of an ornamental table, and the others hovered around, including Dikran.

''This is the Holy Temple,'' Taurin indicated, pointing to the pyramid-shaped structure that dominated the complex. ''And that's the residential wing. But what are these other buildings?''

''This entire structure encompasses over one thousand rooms,'' Leena told him. ''Most are connected via internal corridors, or walkways through landscaped gardens. This sector here belongs to the Arch Nome. These other areas contain the residential wing, reception halls, dining commons, chapels, and museums.''

''Museums?'' He lifted an eyebrow.

''The Palisades Museum contains a priceless collection of statuary, valuable antiquities, and modern religious art. The Archives, which you see over here,'' she said, pointing, ''hold religious and historical documents. And the Library has one of the world's largest collections of early manuscripts.''

''Any bibliotomes?''

''No,'' Dikran responded. ''Those are stored in repositories found elsewhere.''

''How do you prevent thieves from stealing the valuable works of art?''

''We have our own internal security force, the Elite Guard. They're unarmed, of course, but are well trained in surveillance techniques and self-defense maneuvers. We've been fortunate not to have had too many incidents.''

Taurin's face darkened with a heavy scowl. ''If the traitor in our midst makes his move alone, we'll have little trouble. But if he calls for backup assistance from his Yllon friends, we'll need people who can fight. There's only one avenue we can turn down for aid, as I see it.''

''The Caucus?'' Bendyk interceded, a puzzled frown on his face.

Taurin laughed, but his eyes lacked mirth. ''One force on this planet is adequately trained to come to our defense against an armed attack.''

''The Truthsayers!'' Leena exclaimed. The group was planning their own insurgence, but if Stephan Tom could be made to realize the truth, he might exhort his followers to join an alliance to fight off the Ylloners.

Taurin rolled his eyes. ''Stephan Tom's people are playing at being soldiers. I mean Grotus's ring of smugglers.''

''Grotus!'' She dropped her jaw, astounded.

''He can get here quickly using his submersible fleet, and his men are armed.''

"But why would Grotus agree to help us? He wants the horn for himself."

"Grotus may want to get possession of the horn, but I'm aware that he actually intends to ransom it back to the Synod. He wants the weather restored to normal conditions, like everyone else. Otherwise his smuggling operation is in jeopardy. The same goes for an invasion from Yllon. Grotus favors the current power structure; his transgressions are being overlooked. If someone else takes over the government, that may not be the case. I'm willing to take a gamble on him."

"Fearn is rapidly approaching," Leena warned, brushing a golden strand of hair from her face. "If the horn is not blown by then, you say the defense shield around Xan will crumble, allowing Yllon's forces to invade. But we need to allow Grotus time enough to get here."

"How will you get in touch with him?" Dikran queried.

"We'll tell Sirvat what's going on!" Leena said excitedly. "Perhaps her sentence can be made lighter if she cooperates."

"Agreed," the Arch Nome said, "but we'll wait until after we announce the new Renewal ceremony to the Synod. Her response to our accusations will be more credible if she believes herself to be wrongly accused of stealing the horn."

"What excuse do we use in the meantime for the delay?" Leena queried. "Why not just blow the horn at the meeting? Wait, I know—I'll need to restore the horn to its pristine condition. We can say it was slightly damaged during its sojourn."

"Good idea," Taurin said approvingly, his warm smile heating her blood. Distracted by the lights of desire she saw dancing in his eyes, she forced her attention back to their tactical discussion.

"The traitor should allow me to complete the job of restoration if he wants the weather cycles stabilized once he's in power," she said. "Does that mean I'll be relatively safe until my job is completed?"

Taurin shook his head. "He could make a move at any

time. For that reason you'll never be left alone. Either I or Bendyk will be with you at all times. We'll post the Elite Guards around the grounds, but I fear they won't be an adequate force if the Ylloners attack before Grotus arrives. There's got to be something else we can do to beef up security.''

A thoughtful gleam entered Leena's eyes. "Your Grace," she addressed Dikran, "the Holy Temple—are there any booby traps such as the ones I found on my other excavations?''

Dikran gave her a startled look. "No, child. This temple has been in continuous use since the days of the Apostles.''

"Not the entire temple," Leena countered. "Just the central, older portion, right?'' At Dikran's nod, she pondered the possibilities. "It's likely traps were built in here just as at the other temples, but they were never activated. I would like to take a look around. Now that I know how to read the carvings, perhaps they'll provide a clue.''

Taurin touched her elbow, trailing a flood of warmth up her arm. "We'll set you up in one of the workrooms in the museum,'' he said, his eyes shining with the thrill of the hunt. "That's where you'll do your supposed restoration, but during the quieter hours you can study the carvings in the Holy Temple.''

She smiled as a warm glow of satisfaction filled her. At last Taurin was showing respect for her contributions. Maybe now he'd be more willing to include her in his secret talks with Dikran.

"I can talk to Sirvat," Swill offered, "while you become established in the museum.''

"You need to emphasize the gravity of our situation to her," Taurin instructed.

"What if Grotus demands a reward in return for his services?'' the young woman asked.

"Tell him we found more crystals. That should be enough of an enticement.''

Late that evening, when all the Synod members had returned to the Palisades, they set their plan into action. A special meeting was convened, at which time Taurin revealed that he and Leena had recovered the horn and would be blowing it at a Renewal ceremony four days later.

"Praise be to Lothar!" Zeroun shouted, throwing his arms into the air. "We are saved!"

"Where is the horn?" Magar piped in, his blue eyes regarding them with admiration. The silver-haired gentleman wore his priestly robes with dignified grace despite his portly figure.

"After its sojourn the horn truly does need a cleaning," Leena said. "I'm going to work on it over at the museum."

"Where did you find it?" Zeroun asked.

Taurin set his play into motion. When the accusation about Sirvat's role in the theft was made the woman turned pale with outrage.

"I didn't steal it!" the red-haired Minister of the Treasury cried. "I had nothing to do with the theft."

"You don't deny your liaison with Grotus, do you?" Leena snapped. "When you speak with him next express our gratitude that he aided us in recovering the horn."

"I'll do no such thing! That lying bastard! He told me he knew nothing about the horn's whereabouts."

Leena smiled grimly. Sirvat had just proven herself guilty of leaking information to the smuggler. She'd have to cooperate with their plan now.

Swill stayed behind to talk with Sirvat, while Taurin and Leena set off for the museum. Bendyk assumed the direction of the Elite Guard and went off on his own.

Leena selected an appropriate workroom, which Taurin approved after inspecting the premises. Their preliminary job done, they headed back toward the residential wing. They were passing through the Holy Temple when Taurin stopped.

"I need to consult with Dikran about something," he said, his eyes averted. "You go on ahead. I'll catch up to you later."

"Oh, no, you don't!" Leena snapped, hands on her hips. "I'm coming with you."

Taurin's gaze met hers, his expression unreadable. "You need to concentrate on deciphering those carvings," he said, his sweeping gesture encompassing the ornate interior of the nave. "If there are booby traps around here, we need to activate them. Your role is important."

Leena wavered, considering what she should do. Logic told her to start looking for an alternate means of bolstering their security arrangements.

"I'll meet you at our apartment," Taurin said, stalking off in the opposite direction.

Muttering a quick prayer for tolerance, Leena decided to follow him at a discreet distance. She ran into Bendyk and Swill, who were just rounding a corner ahead of her.

"Where are you going, Sister?" Bendyk asked, giving her an indulgent smile. His arm was draped around Swill's shoulder. Gazing at them, Leena considered how her brother had mellowed under Swill's influence. His change of attitude was commendable; it would make him more approachable to his flock.

She smiled at Swill and was pleased by the knowing grin the woman returned. "Taurin is going off by himself again, supposedly to confer with Dikran," she replied. "I was following him. I won't let him exclude me anymore."

"We'll join you," Bendyk said.

The trail led to the Arch Nome's private robing salon. Entering through the partially open doorway, they were surprised to see no one inside. An empty gap yawned at a far wall across the room, from which they heard muffled voices.

"I don't understand why you refuse to tell her," Dikran was saying as they approached.

Leena peered down a long staircase. The voices seemed to come from just beyond the landing; she hovered in the passageway, straining her ears to listen.

"Her religious traditions are very important to her," Taurin's voice responded. "It will destroy all she's ever believed in if she learns the truth. Those rituals give her life meaning. What will she have left if she learns that Lothar is nothing more than a mere machine, a computer?"

"Lothar is more than a computer that controls the weather cycles and provides our lozenge against sickness. Believing in Lothar is a sign of faith, my son. Maybe Lothar doesn't exist as the image people hold in their minds, but don't you think there is a higher intelligence somewhere out there?"

Leena could almost picture Dikran gesturing toward the heavens. Lothar, a machine? What were they talking about? She glanced at Bendyk and Swill, both of whom were listening in rapt attention.

"I've read our history in these bibliotomes," Taurin went on. "The Apostles came here from another world because their sun was dying. They hoped to live in peaceful coexistence with the indigenous population on Xan, but they discovered that their presence caused problems. Used to communicating telepathically with each other, they hadn't realized their intense mental energy would adversely affect the human population. The minds of primitive men could not accept the powerful neural stimulation. Analysis showed that exposure to the telepathic waves caused a disruption in the cross-communication of brain hemispheres, producing headaches and mental aberrations in the native inhabitants."

"So they devised Lothar's lozenge to prevent illness," Dikran said. "But they brought order and civilization to our world."

"Yes, they made the laws. They didn't give us an interpretation of Lothar's laws. They created the rules, and that's what's in that bible in the next room. When they saw that their influence, although beneficial, was still physically painful to the humans, they decided to leave. Some of them who did not wish to travel to the stars once again journeyed to the next habitable planet, Yllon, where they set up a society with a noninterference rule. They thought perhaps if they did not influence human affairs, as they had done on Xan, the Ylloners would not be similarly afflicted with headaches. But for some reason the effect of their presence on Yllon was worse. Already possessing a high degree of aggressiveness in their nature, the Ylloners went berserk. Eventually the newcomers were killed off, but not before they had seeded the population so as to ensure the continuation of their species. They didn't know if their mother ship would make it to the star system it was heading for.''

Leena glanced at her brother, aghast at what she was hearing. If Taurin was correct, then Lothar was no god; he was simply an invention of the Apostles, an entity created to appeal to the primitive native inhabitants. Mechanical devices were responsible for the weather cycles and lozenges. She'd begun to suspect something wasn't right when the climatic disasters started, and now her suspicions had been confirmed. But why was the horn still needed to awaken Lothar? Couldn't the computer be reset in another manner? What was causing the disruption in weather? Dammit, why hadn't Taurin confided in her?

She marched down the stairs, her fists clenched at her sides. Her brother's heavy breathing behind her told her he was as outraged as she. Swill murmured something, no doubt attempting to soothe him. Down below, an array of strange flashing equipment met her gaze. She'd never seen anything like it, not in all her experience.

"So it is true," she accused Dikran, catching him and Taurin off-guard. "The Synod does control everything. You've been perpetuating the myth about Lothar in order to retain power."

Dikran shuffled forward. "I tried to convince your man that you would accept the truth, child."

Her angry gaze slammed into Taurin. "You have no faith in me, do you?"

"I didn't want to disillusion you." He spoke soothingly, as though she were a young girl rather than a grown woman whose intelligence deserved respect.

"What does all this mean?" she demanded, glancing about the room. Bendyk and Swill moved to either side of her, as though to lend their support.

"It means the Truthsayers are right," Bendyk said. "Lothar only exists in men's minds. Isn't that right?" He directed his question at Dikran.

The old man's expression crumbled. "The concept of Lothar was created to give hope to the people. Believing in a higher intelligence gives them strength to carry on. They need something to believe in."

"But you're not letting us progress," Swill cried. "Don't you see what this falsehood has done? You've restricted our intellectual growth. Do you believe this was the Apostles' intent?"

"The Apostles gave our people their laws and helped our civilization to blossom. They tamed the weather, gave us the lozenge to prevent sickness. People should be content to live under Lothar's beneficence."

"It must have been their goal that their seed would enrich the developing species of mankind and accelerate the time frame when their descendants would begin to reach for the stars," Taurin added. "It is likely we are all the descendants of some progenitor race that seeded all of us. In that respect we may all be part of a oneness, a unity that's greater than all of us combined. A higher form of life, if you will. Besides, Lothar is more than a machine. Come with me and I'll show you what I mean."

He led them into the room of crystals, and Leena gasped. Even wearing her protective eyeglasses she could detect the brilliance of the pulsating matrix.

"I was able to read the bibliotomes," Taurin said. "I didn't need to be able to decipher the symbols; the contents are revealed through some sort of scrolling telepathic imprint once the bibliotomes are opened. Lothar, if you wish to give all this a name, is a biomechanical construct that functions from the feedback of positive telepathic signals. The Apostles must have been able to activate the crystals with merely a thought. Rising discontent with the ruling Synod is what has most likely caused some of the crystals to fail. They feed off positive vibrations or feelings.''

''Then my father was right!'' Leena cried. ''His interpretation was that we must serve Lothar with harmony and love, and now you're saying that Lothar—or this machine—can't function unless there is peaceful coexistence.''

Taurin nodded. ''Stephan Tom's inclusion in our plans is essential, since the Truthsayers' dissension is the main cause of the malfunction.''

''Assuming the horn blowing is still needed to reset Lothar . . . er, I mean, the computer,'' Leena said, confused by her reasoning. ''What if our plan fails and we don't recover the real horn by Renewal?''

Taurin's mouth curved in a sly grin. ''Let me handle that problem. Regardless of how we accomplish the Renewal ceremony, the Synod will have to make concessions. Dikran accepts the need for change, but others will have to be convinced. First, we have to repel the threat from Yllon. If Stephan Tom and the Synod can air their differences, perhaps a cooperative spirit will be produced, which will please Lothar. The malfunctioning crystals might reactivate under those circumstances. I believe that is necessary for the integrity of the defense shield to be maintained, and to stabilize the weather cycles.''

Dikran adjusted his robe, which hung loosely over his thin frame. ''I fear these matters are going beyond the ken of an old man. Perhaps the time has come for me to pass the torch.''

''Please don't say that, Your Grace!'' Leena cried, distressed. ''Your knowledge and wisdom are needed now more than ever.''

''After we get rid of the vipers in our midst a new government will be formed,'' Dikran mused. He glanced at each one of them in turn. ''I have in mind certain replacements. It's time for some fresh, young blood in the upper echelons. If I do retain my position, I'll need trustworthy advisers. Your father will be one of them,'' he promised Leena.

''Father will be glad to have your redemption,'' she told

him in a humble tone, feeling intensely gratified that all of her goals in joining the Caucus were finally being met. It made her continuation in the aide corps almost an afterthought. She supposed she'd have to serve her time, something she'd totally forgotten about in her involvement with the missing horn. Her museum job was waiting for her; she'd regarded her appointment to the Caucus merely as a sabbatical. She realized now for certain that her true calling was in archaeology. And since she could decipher the carvings, there was much work to be done.

As the others conversed, her thoughts drifted to their earlier discussion. It seemed inconceivable that the god she'd believed in all her life was nothing more than a collection of . . . what? Her people had no knowledge of such technology. Apparently it was even beyond the advanced Ylloners' capabilities. If the Apostles had left them a legacy through the bibliotomes, they had much to learn now that Taurin knew how to open them.

"How did you unseal the holy books?" she asked him.

He gave her a wry grin. "I spun my rings in the depression on each cover."

"Those rings have a lot of uses," she murmured, a thoughtful expression on her face.

Dikran addressed Bendyk. "You'd better prepare your evidence against the guilty members of the Synod."

"You mean Zeroun and Sirvat."

"And don't forget Karayan," he said sadly. "He's involved in illegal business transactions. We still don't know Magar's part in all this."

"Magar claimed at the meeting that he knew nothing about a plot with Drufus Gong. We should wait and see who shows up at Leena's workroom," Taurin interjected.

They stayed to discuss the security arrangements and then split up in different directions.

The trap was laid. Now they only had to bide their time until someone fell into it.

*   *   *

Back at their apartment, Leena was preparing for bed. As she brushed out her long waves of blond hair in front of the mirror at her dressing table, she searched her soul for her true feelings regarding Taurin. Even though she'd finally learned his secrets, she felt betrayed by his lack of trust in her. She couldn't find it in her heart to forgive him easily for his deficiency of faith. Maybe Lothar wasn't a supernatural being, but the traditions of her people still had meaning. They were based upon an agricultural society, and celebrations of the harvest and such were still worthwhile. As for her prayers, she felt a higher intelligence must exist. Perhaps Lothar was merely a tool produced by the Apostles, but the natural beauty of her world could only have been created by a superior entity. Now that she knew there was life beyond the stars, a greater joy enveloped her, and her heart swelled with gratitude to the creator. Taurin was wrong to dismiss her allegiance as belonging solely to Lothar.

Her philosophical musings carried her through the rest of her nightly preparations. She was applying a lotion to her hands when Taurin's footfalls sounded from behind her.

"I can do that for you," he said, his tone soft.

Seated at her dressing table, Leena glanced back at him, unable to contain her joy at his presence. She tried to calm her rapidly beating heart, telling herself she should be angry with him, but it was difficult when he took the tube of cream and began smoothing a palmful across her bared neck. She closed her eyes, enjoying his gentle ministrations, until a rising coil of desire made her spring from her seat.

Turning, she wrapped her arms around his neck, drawing his head down for a kiss. "I love you, Taurin." Despite his lack of faith in her, she couldn't help feeling a surge of affection for him. She knew he regarded himself as her protector, but did that mean protecting her from life's disappointments as well as its physical foes? He didn't give her enough credit, although at the moment she felt the total satisfaction of a woman being cherished by her man.

Letting her hands roam the broad planes of his bare back,

363

she gave herself to the deep yearnings she felt for intimacy and security. Evil forces were stalking her world, and only this man could protect her and her people. He was the keeper of the rings, the keys to the storehouses of knowledge contained within the bibliotomes.

But none of that mattered now. The outside world disappeared as she yielded to his tender touch. Everywhere his fingertips met her flesh, her skin was seared with heat. As his mouth claimed hers again and again, she writhed against him, wanting to join with him, to be united as husband and wife.

"You're mine," he murmured huskily, showering her face with kisses. Guiding her to the bed, he slowly removed her flimsy nightdress, devouring her with his eyes. With a cry of impatience, he tugged off his briefs and they lay naked, side by side. He caressed her skin, searching for her secret places until she clutched at him, moaning for him to complete her satisfaction.

Moving over her, his passion surged. With a mighty thrust he slid inside her, filling her so completely that she cried out with pleasure. If only they could stay like this, attached to each other, with all the cares of the world gone from their minds. Rational thought escaped her as Taurin urged her to match his rhythmic movements. When his hands found her breasts she whispered his name. A sheen of sweat covered her body as she surged under him, tension springing through her body. Soaring to the heights of ecstasy in a cataclysmic release, she shuddered against him. His own explosive response spilled inside her. Stars danced before her eyes as waves of pleasure coursed through her. Life could never be more complete than this!

Their scenes of passion were repeated in the nights that followed. To Leena it seemed like an idyllic interlude before all hell broke loose. As time wore on and the day of Renewal approached, Taurin became more fearful that his plan wouldn't work.

On the last day a knock sounded at the door to the work-room. It was one of the Elite Guards, announcing a visitor.

"Minister Magar is here to see you, sir."

Taurin felt the color drain from his face. He'd dared to hope that Magar was not the culprit, but his visit was a good indicator that he was the thief who had stolen the horn. No doubt he'd come to get a look at the supposedly authentic one that Leena was restoring. He threw open the door, and Magar shuffled inside.

Taurin stood aside so the silver-haired Minister of State could enter. He felt a deep sense of disappointment that the man who had sponsored his immigration might be a traitor.

When Magar's ready, warm smile descended upon Taurin it was like a knife twisting in his gut. Like Baker Mylock, Magar was a figure whom Taurin had admired and respected. Now all that remained was the bitter taste of betrayal.

"I regret not having had the time to visit with you more often," Magar said, his voice tremulous as he glanced about the compact work space. His hands plucked nervously at his robe.

"I suppose you have come to see the horn," Taurin remarked, leaning against a counter.

Magar appeared surprised by the suggestion. "Why, the idea had not crossed my mind. I admit I was looking forward to hearing it blown at Renewal, but I understand Leena is restoring it to its prior condition." He glanced at her, bending diligently over a tracing of the carving she'd done earlier.

"If you're not here for the horn, why did you come?" Taurin persisted. A glimmer of hope rose within him that he'd been wrong about Magar, but he couldn't let his emotion enter his voice.

"I could tell from the way you looked at me during the meeting that you knew." Magar clasped and unclasped his hands. "Did you inform Dikran?"

Taurin stared at him. "What are you talking about?"

"My . . . my problem." Magar's blue eyes were troubled as he regarded his protégé.

"I have no idea what you mean, sir." What problem? Upon further examination, Taurin noted Magar's strange pallor and fine tremors. The man didn't look well. What was disturbing him so greatly that it afflicted him thus?

"I have the Agus," Magar mumbled, so low that Taurin had to strain his ears to hear.

At Magar's pronouncement, his eyes widened in shock. "The Agus!" This was a genetic disease for which Lothar's lozenge was ineffective. In one's later years it produced tremors and progressive debilitation and, eventually, death. "Have you been to a clinic for a solid diagnosis?"

Compressing his mouth, Magar nodded mutely, and for the first time Taurin read fear in his eyes. Striding forward, he grasped Magar by the arm.

"I will help you. Whatever I can do."

Magar shook his head. "There is nothing. I thought you already knew, but now I see that I was mistaken." He stared at the floor. "You know what this will mean when word gets out, don't you?"

"There are medications that can help. It doesn't have to mean you must leave the Synod." Especially not now, Taurin thought to himself. Not when there are so few we can trust. Shame swept over him like a tidal wave. To think he'd suspected Magar of complicity in the theft of the horn! How could he have been so faithless?

"We could use your advice," Leena said, rising from her seat. She'd kept silent during their conversation, but now there were things she had to discuss, worries she needed to bring into the open. "Drufus Gong probably knows Taurin is here by now. He could be in danger from Yllon's agents. There's a death sentence on his head."

She recapped their adventures for Magar's benefit. During her recital the Minister of State gazed at her with a shocked expression.

"I will help you in any way I can to catch those felons," Magar stated in a firm tone. His eyes gleamed with renewed strength as he squared his shoulders like the proud man

Taurin remembered. Despite his illness, he still bore his heavy weight well. "Your security arrangements are sound, but I'll keep my ears open. Count on my warning if I see any Ylloners around."

"It's best if you pretend ignorance," Taurin cautioned him. "We don't want to tip our hands that we know who is responsible for stealing the horn. He hasn't come forward yet."

"Karayan may be too smart to fall for our ruse," Leena said worriedly. She still couldn't believe he was so deceitful, and yet it all fit in—his extensive art collection; the upkeep of his mansion, which, according to Swill and Bendyk, was above his means; his ambitious nature. Dikran himself had said that it was Karayan's idea to bring in agents from Yllon to consult about Lothar's malfunctions.

"He's waiting for the right opportunity to make his move," Taurin predicted. "It has to be after you finish your supposed restoration. We should make an announcement that your work is completed."

"He may also be waiting for reinforcements from among his Yllon friends. You're in danger by being so exposed," she told him, her anxiety reflected in her tone.

"I'm more concerned about your safety," he retorted.

Planting her hands on her hips, Leena glared at him. "First you wouldn't tell me anything because you didn't trust me, and now you think I can't protect myself. When are you going to learn that I'm not one of your flowers that's going to wilt at the slightest pressure?"

"Leena, you're not accustomed to this sort of thing," Taurin said, his voice carrying a dangerous edge. "You have no conception of the violence these people can perpetrate."

"Yes, I do! That's why I'm so worried about you." Had he forgotten she was the recipient of Testi's unwanted attentions? "If you'd stop treating me as though I have a brain the size of a tupa, you'd realize I've dealt pretty well with our situation so far. I really resent your patronizing attitude."

Confounded, Taurin could only stare at her in response.

What the devil was she talking about? "My job is to keep you from harm, or did you forget why you came to see me at Magar's suggestion?"

At the mention of his name, the Minister of State gave an embarrassed cough. "Children, this isn't the time—"

Ignoring his presence, Leena continued her tirade. Now that she'd gotten started, it felt good to ventilate her ire. "You've tried to protect me from everything, afraid that I couldn't handle even the slightest test of my beliefs. Let me tell you that your findings have confirmed my faith in Lothar, only now I know he's more than a god who maintains our planet. His is not a physical manifestation. So a machine is responsible for controlling the weather cycles and producing the lozenge, but somewhere out there"—she raised her hands toward the heavens—"he, or rather it, still exists."

Taurin wasn't in the mood for another philosophical discussion. "What you believe in doesn't matter here," he cried, exasperated. But deep down inside he knew she was right. He had doubted the steadfastness of her faith, only it wasn't Lothar she believed in so much as the concept of a higher intelligence. He couldn't discredit that idea himself. He'd regarded her as his own personal angel, feeling her purity to be far above his, but in reality she was merely a woman. A strong woman, who followed her ideals and took courage from them. She wanted to be admired, but not worshiped. He'd made the mistake of putting her on a pedestal. Perhaps it was time for him to respect her as an equal. But first a show of trust was called for in order to win back her affection.

"I want to check on Bendyk's progress with the Elite Guards. Come on, Magar; I'll escort you back to the administrative wing. Will you be able to manage by yourself?" he asked her, fully intending to be within calling distance once he'd finished talking privately with his mentor.

"Of course." Her smile was triumphant. Naturally she could look after herself, and it was about time he gave her the credit she was due!

After spending another hour studying the pile of bibliotomes she'd brought into the room, she decided to focus her attention on the carvings in the Holy Temple. She'd located a couple of booby traps, but there had to be more.

She was getting ready to leave when a commotion sounded outside the door. Thinking it must be Taurin returning, she didn't pay any attention until the door crashed open.

Glancing up, Leena gasped.

Karayan's tall figure was framed in the doorway. And there was no sign of the Elite Guardsman or anyone else outside the room.

Chapter Twenty

The Minister of Justice was groomed impeccably, as usual, from his carefully styled brown hair to his tailored navy blue frock coat and matching trousers. He strode into the room with a friendly smile on his face.

"Leena, how's it going?"

"Uh . . . very well," she stuttered, her gaze flickering apprehensively toward the corridor. Where was the guard?

Karayan sauntered closer, his smile widening. "May I see the horn? Have you restored it to its previous condition?"

"Well . . . yes." She noticed for the first time the briefcase in his hand. It bulged strangely, as though there were an object inside with an irregular shape. "What have you in there?" she asked, keeping her tone on an even keel.

Karayan stopped in front of her. "I'll show you after I see the horn. Where is it?" His eyes fell upon the bare work counter and on the bibliotomes, on a small table. "What are those?"

"Those are some books recovered from an excavation," she lied. "I've been reading them. They reveal much about the Apostles."

"I don't see the horn."

Leena felt a sheen of sweat cover her face. If he had the real horn in that briefcase, she had to get it from him.

"I finished restoring it," she said.

"Where is it?" His tone had lost any hint of friendliness. His cold gray eyes assessed her.

"You brought the counterfeit horn, didn't you?"

Nodding, Karayan withdrew a cloth-covered object from his case. Whipping away the material, he showed her the sacred horn. At last! Leena's heart leapt with joy, but she erased all emotion from her face.

"Why did you do it, Karayan?"

He put the horn back in the sack, tightened the loop, fastened it, and slung it over his shoulder. "This world is run by a bunch of old men and women. People are getting out of hand with their uprisings. We need a strong hand, a leader who rules with iron."

"And that's you," Leena scoffed.

His eyes turned as dark as a thundercloud. "With the Ylloners backing me, no one will deny my power. They can offer us technology beyond our dreams. We have the agricultural resources that they so desperately need. An open exchange of trade between our two worlds has been too long in coming. I merely intend to speed the process and lead this world into a new age of enlightenment."

"So you stole the horn, knowing that the defense shield around Xan would fail by Fearn if the horn wasn't blown."

"Once the takeover is complete and I am recognized as the new Arch Nome, I will blow the horn myself and restore Lothar to his former status. I need the weather cycles restabilized and the integrity of the defense shield maintained. That can take place only after I am in power."

"But you're already a member of the Synod."

"That's not enough! I intend to put this land on the right track. Dissenters must be punished ruthlessly. Technology has to advance. The Synod is too smug. I am the catalyst for change!"

"You mention dissenters, and yet you're using the Truth-sayers. Do you intend to squash them once you've achieved your aims, or do they share the same ideals as you?"

"They're a bunch of fools who will follow anyone with charisma. Once my order is established they'll obey my dictates or perish."

"You've profited from the status quo," she pointed out. "You get money from the Chocola Company for land rights to the plantations in the Black Lands."

He gave her a sardonic grin. "Once I'm in power I won't have to worry about income any longer."

Leena bit her lip. She couldn't keep him talking forever. Wasn't anyone going to show up to help her? Why didn't Taurin stop by to see how she was doing, or her brother?

Karayan read the expression on her face and smiled. "You've stalled long enough, Leena. Where are you hiding the horn?"

She compressed her lips, remaining silent.

Karayan withdrew a wicked-looking blade from an inner pocket of his frock coat. "Don't force me to use this," he said, approaching her. "Your face is too pretty to ruin. Just tell me what I want to know."

"It's not here," she cried, backing away until she came up against the counter and could move no farther. Karayan had an odd light in his eyes that made her swallow hard. "I'll take you to it," she offered, hoping to elude him along the way. The only problem was getting hold of the horn in that sack.

"If you're lying to me, I will kill you," Karayan threatened. He gestured toward the doorway. "Move!"

Outside the small workroom, she searched for the guard, but he was nowhere in sight. What had Karayan done to the man? Praying desperately that she'd meet someone along the way to whom she could appeal for aid, she led him through the maze of museum corridors and outside to a cloister with vaulted archways and graceful columns.

Crossing a courtyard, they passed through the western entrance to the Holy Temple. They crossed the chantry adorned with fifteenth-century sculptures, climbed a flight of steps over the south ambulatory, and walked between other chapels ornate with carvings. A number of vaults followed. The eerie silence brought Leena's nerves to the breaking point.

What if Karayan's allies from Yllon were already here? They might have taken out the guards one by one throughout the Palisades complex. That would explain the absence of any familiar security forces. She had to warn the others, but how?

Karayan caught hold of her arm. "Don't make a sound." She felt the point of the blade pinch her back as he emphasized his warning.

The Holy Temple was devoid of worshipers, and she realized he'd chosen a good time of day to make his move. It was evenlight, when most people were home preparing their supper and making plans for the day ahead. The populace had cleared out by now, and all the administrative offices were closed. She was alone, with only her own wits to save her.

Staying in the shadows, Taurin glided silently after Leena and Karayan. He'd purposely kept away from her workroom, intending to give the thief who had stolen the horn a golden opportunity to confront her. It had worked, but now the problem was how to get her safely away from him.

She appeared to be winding in circles in the Holy Temple, and it wouldn't take long for Karayan to figure out her ruse. Then he'd have no choice; he'd have to make his move without any backup. Karayan wouldn't be any problem, but Taurin was puzzled over what had happened to the guards. He feared that Karayan's forces had arrived before Grotus's. Dikran was unavailable, being closeted with Stephan Tom, who'd arrived earlier that day. If the Truthsayer leader was willing to listen to reason, maybe they could yet convince him that this plot was real. Unfortunately, he couldn't count on Stephan Tom's people for assistance in the immediate future.

The silence of the Holy Temple unnerved him. This felt like the calm before a storm. Stealthily, he followed his quarry, biding his time until it was safe to act. Leena appeared to know what she was doing. He'd let her play her hand unless Karayan became too threatening.

A surge of rage filled his veins as he watched her being marched along at knifepoint. Her crimson gown was a splash of color against the gold-painted cherubs and religious ornaments adorning the temple. Her hair, hanging free down her back, cascaded like a thick curtain of silk. The thought of Karayan harming her made his throat constrict, and he could almost feel his mind reaching out to touch the thieving bastard. . . .

No! With a jolt, Taurin realized what he was doing. After what had happened to Testi, and from what he had read in the bibliotomes, he realized that some of the Apostles' telepathic powers must remain in him. That was the demon's curse if he attempted to use it, not any innate power to drive men mad. And if he directed his newfound ability for an evil purpose, wouldn't he be as drenched in sin as his compatriots from Yllon? Wouldn't the ease of it tempt him into using his power again and again, until he couldn't distinguish right from wrong? He should not be allowed to abuse his heritage in this manner. The Apostles had inadvertantly caused pain through their use of telepathy. For him to purposely do so would be a grievous wrong. He must avoid temptation and forbid himself to ever use his telepathic powers again.

Squelching any thoughts of mentally assaulting Karayan, he focused his attention on Leena. What plan did she have in mind?

In the Inner Sanctum, Leena approached the Grand Altar with trepidation. The awesome splendor of the hall challenged her to defile its sanctity. A shadowy movement down a side aisle caught her attention, but she saw no one. The light was dim in the late afternoon, little brightness coming through the stained-glass windows. The interior lanterns had not yet been lit. Slowly she climbed to the dais, where the initiates had been honored when they entered into the Caucus.

The Caucus! Where were all of the aides? They were supposed to be helping to catch the thief, yet she hadn't seen a sight of any of them. Her skin crawled as she realized the place was dead of all activity. But her path had been determined, and she stuck with it. Facing the colorful frieze above the altar, representing scenes from the lives of the Apostles, she paused. Beneath her feet was an engraved pavement of porphyry and marble. Candleholders with long tapers stood on either side of the altar. Statues of the Apostles marched across the rear wall, divided by the holy closet itself.

"I put the horn back in there," she said, pointing to the closed carved wooden doors.

"Open it!" Karayan ordered her. Impatience shone in his eyes. He clutched the sack that held the horn.

Leena approached the sacred doors, feeling as though she were committing a sacrilege just by stepping on the carpet leading to the holy closet. To open the hallowed doors without it being the appointed time of year was a horrendous sin. The Apostles had known this, and one of the traps was located here.

When she'd been making her rounds, inspecting the carvings, she had dared to come to this holy place and peruse the carvings on the wooden doors. Noting a depression in a tiny recess in the wall to the side of the doors, she'd spun in it the ring Taurin had given her. According to her interpretation of the carvings, that had activated the booby trap. Now the trick was to get Karayan to open the doors.

"I will not commit such a sinful act. You will have to open the doors," she told him, raising her chin defiantly.

"Hold this."

Karayan thrust the sack at her, apparently unconcerned that she might take off with the fake horn inside. As far as he knew, the authentic relic was inside the holy closet. His eyes gleaming with the lust for power, he approached the carved wooden doors. Leena carefully backed away. She had no idea of the nature of the trap; she had just been able to discern its existence.

Just as Karayan reached out to open the doors, he hesitated. Narrowing his eyes, he glared at her suspiciously. "Come here. I'd rather you open the doors, madam."

"No, I won't!"

Karayan took a menacing step in her direction.

"Run, Leena!" Taurin's voice sounded from behind. "I'll take care of him."

"Wait!" she called, whirling around. "You don't understand."

But it was too late. Karayan tossed his blade through the air in Taurin's direction. Taurin easily dodged the missile, but as he stumbled, off balance, Karayan lunged after Leena.

"Bitch! You tricked me!"

"Stop!" she screamed as Karayan caught hold of her arm, jerking her backward. The sack she held in her hand tumbled to the floor. Both she and Karayan flung themselves after it.

"Now!" Karayan screamed. "Get them now!"

From hidden recesses emerged a troop of men, armed to the teeth with blasters and odd-shaped objects similar to the one Testi had been carrying. They all wore black, as though that were the uniform of Yllon. Taurin spun about, clenching his fists as he realized they were surrounded. Slowly, Leena rose from a crouching position, and Karayan, chuckling, grabbed the sack containing the horn.

"Damn you, Taurin," Leena hissed. "I nearly had him. The holy closet has a trap."

He cast her a startled look but didn't respond because Karayan, who had been issuing orders to his men, turned his attention on them. Triumphantly, he held up the sack. "Your ruse failed. I understand this is the authentic horn. Good try, Leena." He addressed them both. "You'll be confined with the others."

"What others?" Leena croaked.

"Dikran and your brother. The Caucus and Synod members. They're all being held in the crypt. You'll join them."

"What do you intend to do?" Taurin asked.

"The invasion will come in a few days' time. The take-over should be swift, once Yllon's ships arrive. After I'm proclaimed Arch Nome I'll decide your fate. Perhaps I will banish you all to the Black Lands." He threw back his head and laughed, the sound of a madman.

Leena stared at him, wondering how she had ever regarded him as a friend. The man was truly power crazed.

"It won't work," Taurin muttered to her as they were led away. "If he blows the horn after the takeover, the crystals will continue to fail. He won't be able to restore the weather patterns to normalcy."

"So what?" Leena retorted as they were marched past the choir stalls. "Once Yllon invades everything is lost."

At the north transept they were forced down a narrow spiral staircase toward the crypt below. Leena and Taurin were dismayed to find there the other members of the Synod, the Caucus, and most of the Elite Guardsmen.

"Bendyk!" Leena said, rushing into her brother's embrace. "Where's Swill?"

"With Sirvat. They went to meet Grotus."

"Karayan has the horn," she said bitterly as Dikran and Stephan Tom approached.

The Truthsayer looked her in the eye. "I'm sorry I didn't listen to you earlier, madam. Your story was true. This fine man is your sibling, is he not?" He put an arm around Bendyk's shoulder in a brotherly fashion. "He and I have been having an interesting discussion."

"Yes," Bendyk said, his smile broadening into a grin. "It appears as though we have a lot to learn from each other."

She glanced from one to the other, then to Dikran, hovering in the background. The Arch Nome didn't appear to be very distressed by recent events.

"Aren't any of you worried about what's going to happen

to us?'' she asked, puzzled by their calm demeanor. They couldn't rely on Grotus. Karayan's men might intercept him.

Bendyk said, ''We're not really trapped down here, Sister. There's an exit into the lower levels.''

''Where is it?'' Taurin asked, his voice amazingly nonchalant by Leena's standards.

Bendyk's gaze darted about. ''Let's keep this among ourselves. If Sirvat and Swill are meeting Grotus, we've got to warn him that Karayan's allies have taken over the Palisades. Dikran made an announcement that the Palisades would be closed to the public until the Renewal ceremony, which has been unavoidably delayed. We don't have to worry about innocent citizens being hurt until things are straightened out. Now let's hurry. There's still the chance Karayan might decide to do away with us all.''

Leena grasped Taurin's hand, holding him back from the others. ''What about you?'' she whispered. ''Testi may have spread the word about your presence here. Even if the rest of us are spared, you're under a death sentence from Yllon.''

His jaw tightened. ''I'm aware of that. Let's go.''

''Where are you young people heading?'' a familiar voice called out behind them.

Taurin spun around to regard Magar, hastening in their direction. The silver-haired Minister of State held out both his hands in the customary greeting. Taurin grasped his hands firmly, an affectionate look on his face. He blamed himself for ever doubting Magar's intentions.

''There's a way out of here,'' he confided. ''We're going to get help. You stay with the others and try to keep their attention diverted.''

''I'll do my best, son.'' Magar held his hands a moment longer. ''May Lothar guide you,'' he added, his voice quivering.

Turning away, Taurin put a protective arm around Leena's shoulders as they hurried forward and out of sight. Passing through the interconnected chambers of the lower levels, Leena was dismayed to note how many more of the crystals appeared to be lifeless. At this rate they'd all blink out by Fearn if harmony wasn't restored to her world. When this was over, assuming Karayan was defeated and the horn was returned to its proper place, should the people's faith in Lothar be reaffirmed? That path would certainly cause less disruption than telling the truth, as proposed by Stephan Tom. It was a weighty decision, but it was Dikran's choice to make it.

If it had been hers, what would she do? Was it better for everyone to believe that Lothar's beneficence provided for them? Or should they understand that their fate was subject to a network of circuitry and their own ingenuity? In order for peace and harmony to prevail, concessions for reform had to be made. That was the only way the crystals would function at their full capacity. The truth had to be told.

A heavy weight of sadness settled over her as she recalled the traditions that had made her life so meaningful. Who would everyone worship when they realized Lothar was a mere machine?

The answer sprang into her mind. The carvings she'd been studying . . . they didn't apply to Lothar, a false creation of the Apostles. Initially, the Apostles believed they would be remaining on Xan. The inscriptions spoke of their own faith, a belief in a higher intelligence, an ideology she shared.

Understanding brightened her mind in a brilliant flash. "Dear deity," she whispered. The answers had been in front of her all the time. She just never understood them. She glanced at Taurin, who was deep in conversation with her brother. Somehow she knew he'd share this new faith. Searching for his destiny, he hadn't recognized it was in the stars, as well as in his heart. Overlapping the vast reaches of space and the inner depths of the human soul, a thread of life encompassed all living beings. The changes about to occur could be part of their evolution as a race. They might even be part of a divine plan.

But if not, she couldn't let Karayan get the upper hand!

As they approached the exit into Dikran's robing salon,

the Arch Nome announced his intention to remain behind and guard the entrance to the lower levels.

"Where is Swill?" she asked Bendyk, her voice a hoarse whisper.

"By the east gate of the Palisades," he replied.

Dusk had fallen, and the evening air was cold. Luckily, Leena's heavy velvet gown kept her warm as they moved stealthily through the cloisters and open corridors.

"We're going the wrong way," she hissed when she noted the direction in which they were heading. Having spent several weeks in training for the Caucus, she was more familiar with the grounds than her brother or Taurin. "Follow me," she ordered, turning left down a garden path crossing in front of the north entrance to the archives. A pungent smell of woodsmoke permeated the air, a comforting aroma.

She approached the east gate, a massive wrought-iron structure set into a wall that surrounded this part of the Palisades. She heard voices and saw movement up ahead. Bendyk also noticed the commotion and charged ahead, yelling for Swill.

"Quiet!" The young woman stepped out of the shadows.

"Swill." Bendyk swept her into his arms and pressed his mouth to hers in a frantic kiss.

"Save that for later!" Leena said, relieved that Swill was safe. "Has Grotus arrived with his people?"

"I'm right here, madam." His loud voice made her jump.

Pivoting, she stared into the glittering gaze of the renowned smuggler. He'd toned down his style of dress; instead of his usual flamboyant longshirt, he wore a military-style belted jacket and pants with enough armaments hanging off his belt to take out a squadron of opponents. Taurin strode up to him, holding out both his hands in greeting. After a moment's hesitation Grotus returned the gesture.

"Thank you for coming," Taurin said stiffly.

Grotus inclined his head in acknowledgment. "In this case, your fight is my fight." He turned to his men, who were regrouping behind him. "Prepare for assault. Who is the traitor?" he asked Taurin.

"It's Karayan. He's sequestered the members of the Synod and other personnel in a crypt beneath the complex. Karayan has the horn, and he also has the following of Yllon's agents."

Grotus noticed his assessing glance. "The rest of my troops are taking positions at the other gates. At my signal we will rush the complex, but I need to know where Karayan is stationed."

Leena spoke up. "If I may venture a guess, I'd say he's trying to move up his timetable." Her intelligent gaze met Taurin's look of warm regard. "The window that is opened in the defensive perimeter each time a spacecraft approaches—where is the control panel located?"

Taurin's glowing eyes bulged. "The spaceport is outside the town limits, but Magar once mentioned the control station is here at the Palisades. Demon's blood! Magar knows how to open the window. Karayan will force him to lower the defense shield."

He turned and ran off into the night before anyone could stop him. Terror pounded in Leena's heart. She gestured for Grotus to follow. "Hurry! If we lose the protective energy screen, we're doomed."

Grotus mobilized his men, and they all charged down the floodlit path after Taurin, Leena in the lead. She didn't know if Bendyk or Swill followed; she was merely concerned with catching up to Taurin, assuring herself that he would come to no harm.

Grotus's men engaged the Yllon agents almost immediately. The Ylloners were guarding the various entrances to the Palisades' structures. Taurin had veered toward the east ambulatory, presumably because that route would take him into the Chapel of the Benedines, from whence he could easily access the Arch Nome's robing salon and the lower levels.

But if Karayan had gone after Magar, he would have

headed through the crypt. Hoping to cut him off, Leena entered the Holy Temple through a different entrance. As she passed a stone effigy of Avus, the third Arch Nome, she heard loud voices coming from the Inner Sanctum. Crossing the nave, she passed the choir stalls and halted by the screen that shielded access to the organ loft.

"You'll lower the defense perimeter *now!*" Karayan shouted.

A loud slap resounded, the sound of a hand hitting flesh.

"I will do nothing," Magar's tremulous voice cried. "Kill me. I refuse to leave our world defenseless."

"Foolish old man. I know it has something to do with playing this organ. What is the correct sequence of notes?"

Collapsing against a wall, Leena gasped. Seven notes, seven symbols. Could the secret Karayan sought be the same repetitive string she'd encountered elsewhere?

"Why don't you try blowing the horn?" Magar's voice sneered. "See if that opens the defense shield for you."

"Do you take me for an idiot? The horn must be blown at the Grand Altar or it doesn't work. Besides, blowing the horn would strengthen the shield. You're just trying to trick me."

Leena heard Magar give a low chuckle. "Maybe you don't really have the horn in your possession."

"Of course, I do," Karayan gloated. She heard a rustling noise and imagined he was pulling the horn out of its sack. "See? Here it is."

"Give it to me."

Sounds of a scuffle ensued, followed by thuds and grunts. Holy waters—the two men were fighting. Magar was no match for Karayan. Rushing up the stairs, Leena spotted the horn lying on the ground. She made a dive for it, slithering along the cold marble floor until her outstretched hand grasped the sacred object.

Her cry of triumph drew Karayan's attention, and he leapt up from where he'd been bending over Magar's limp form. "You!" he cried, vaulting after her.

Shrieking, she tripped over a protuberance on the floor. As she flailed her arms to regain her balance, the horn slid from her grasp. For a moment Karayan hesitated, a look of indecision on his face, as though he didn't know whether to attack her or retrieve the horn. With an angry snarl, he pounced at her, grabbing her by the sleeve and hauling her to within a hairsbreadth of his fierce face.

"Show me!" Karayan screamed at her. "You know how to lower the defense shield, don't you?"

"No!"

"You understand the symbols." He shook her violently until her teeth rattled, then shoved her at the organ keys. "Make it work!"

"She doesn't know how to play music as well as I do," crooned a deep male voice from the entranceway.

Leena glanced up in surprise as Grotus sauntered into the room, stooping to pick up the dropped horn.

"At last!" the smuggler exclaimed.

"Give me that. It's mine," Karayan hissed, taking a threatening step in his direction.

Grotus's face purpled with rage. "You've done enough damage. It's time you reaped the consequences. Leena, get out of the way."

Leena rushed over to Magar. Stooping, she felt for a pulse. The beat was rapid and thready, reassuring her that the older man would live. Straightening, she noted with dismay that her escape route had been cut off. What could she do to help Grotus? The smuggler clutched the horn, unwilling to let it go even in the midst of a deadly struggle against his opponent. The smell of sweat filled the air as the two men battled each other for supremacy.

"Leena!" She heard Taurin's voice call from far away.

"I'm here!" she screamed. "In the organ loft."

Her eyes centered on the huge musical instrument. What would happen if she played the sequence of seven notes? Would it reset Lothar, or might the action open another window in the defense shield? If only she knew, she'd be able to influence the course of events in their favor. Hesitating, she watched the frenzied fight.

As physical opponents, Grotus and Karayan were evenly matched. Karayan was older, but he was seized with madness. Grotus's propensity for fine foods slowed him, even though his muscles bulged. Perspiration trickled from the edge of his slicked-back raven hair to his wide forehead. His nose ring quivered as he fought off Karayan's assault.

"Leena, take the horn." He threw it in Leena's direction.

Jumping forward, she caught the sacred artifact before it hit the floor. Sinking to the ground, she cradled the horn in her lap, inspecting it for signs of damage. Karayan had taken good care of it. The creamy, translucent surface was unmarred.

"Aargh!"

She looked up to see Grotus's face turn an ugly shade of purple, a dirk sticking out of his chest. Her face blanched as the smuggler slid to the floor, a death mask on his face.

"No!" she cried as Karayan slowly turned in her direction, an evil smile on his face.

"Hand over the horn," Karayan demanded.

"No, I won't." She rose, choosing to defy him.

"Give it to me!" He pulled a blaster from the holster inside his frock coat and aimed it at her. "I will not hesitate to kill you, Leena, but I'll spare you if you obey. Do as I say!"

"Catch it." She threw the horn into the air.

Startled, Karayan's finger twitched on the trigger. His shot sizzled through the air in a bolt of red laser fire. One instant the horn was in midair; the next, it had vaporized, caught in the stream of fire.

"Dear deity," she whispered as she ducked, missing the edge of the shot. Her large, rounded eyes reflected her horror. "The horn. It . . . it's gone."

Karayan turned on her with a murderous look. This time his blaster was aimed directly at her chest. "You made me lose it!" he shrieked. "You won't interfere with me again!"

Behind them, footsteps thundered up the stairs. Taurin flew into the organ loft, snatching at Karayan's legs and jerking them out from beneath him, making his shot go wild.

Knocked down, Karayan rolled to his side and then jumped to his feet. Having regained his balance, he aimed a vicious kick at Taurin's stomach, doubling him over. As though realizing Taurin was an adversary who demanded respect, Karayan muttered an expletive, threw Leena a regretful glance, then charged down the stairs toward the north transept.

Taurin recovered sufficiently to dash after him.

"Wait!" Leena cried.

They had more important things to do. The horn had been destroyed. How would they reset Lothar in time for Fearn? Even if Karayan had been exposed, the Ylloners would commence their attack. Drufus Gong would be more than happy to take over the leadership position.

Taurin had already vanished in Karayan's wake, so she turned back to assist Magar, who was regaining consciousness. She tried to shut out the sounds of battle as she assisted Taurin's mentor into a sitting position. It was a sacrilege to have fighting going on in the Holy Temple. Then again, who would care? Lothar didn't exist. This place was holy to no one except the Apostles who had erected it.

Their purpose in doing so came to mind, and their faith filled her with renewed hope. Her own faith wasn't lost, it had just been misguided, and so it would be with her people.

Her eye fell upon a familiar symbol carved into a column beside her. The diamond shape, with the antler rising out of its upper left corner. Of course—why had she never realized it before? Now she finally understood what it represented!

A ruckus from below caught her attention. Someone stumbled up the stairs, and she leapt up with joy when she saw it was Taurin, disheveled and battle weary. Uttering an exclamation of relief, she rushed into his arms. He held her tightly, as though she were his haven of peace.

"He got away," Taurin mumbled against her hair. "Karayan escaped, along with the agents from Yllon. We couldn't close the window in time. I suppose he'll seek refuge on their world.''

''It doesn't matter,'' she said soothingly. ''He won't be a threat to us here any longer.''

''I'm not so sure of that.''

Leena learned what he meant when Dikran convened an emergency council meeting two days later, after the remaining men in Grotus's party finished the clean-up. They'd left by now, and Dikran addressed an assembly gathered in the Inner Sanctum. All of the Candors were present, along with the Caucus and certain members of the Synod. They sat facing the Grand Altar.

Leena was explaining her theory. ''The diamond sign represents the Cadega constellation,'' she said, smoothing down her sky blue gown as she stood facing the others. She wore her hair loose, aware that the darker blue of her veil contrasted sharply with her golden hair. The circlet crowning her was a source of pride. Her marriage had been formally announced, and she'd happily accepted her friends' congratulations. Now she only needed to fulfill certain obligations before she and Taurin could be alone. She smiled at him, lounging casually in the front row.

''Look at how this constellation is shaped.'' In the air she drew the points of a diamond. ''The branch in the upper left-hand corner represents a particular star system, and I believe this offshoot indicates the second habitable planet orbiting its sun. According to the inscriptions left to us by the Apostles, this is where they headed when they departed from Xan.'' Her voice shook with fervor. ''If we ever achieve the means to travel beyond our own system, we could visit their descendants!''

Dikran gave a tired shrug. ''What good does that knowledge do us now, child? The horn has been destroyed. We have no way of resetting Lothar.''

He'd already revealed the truth to the Candors, and they'd

all agreed to call the computer device Lothar. It would be more understandable to the people. Besides, there was a higher faith now to worship, since Leena had shown them the way. Having decided it was time for them to take control of their destiny on a more concrete level, Stephan Tom was included on the Council, and various positions were being discussed for replacement.

Silence fell heavily upon them. No one wanted to acknowledge their defeat, but Fearn was nearly upon them and there was no horn to blow.

"Have a little faith," Taurin said, smiling as he rose and strode toward Leena. "I should let you do the honors, *angella*. It was your faith in me that got me through all this." He slipped his armband off his muscled limb.

Leena stared into the amused light in his eyes. "What are you talking about?"

"That receptacle in the recess beside the holy closet—that didn't set any trap. You must have misinterpreted your symbols. I suspect the horn, when it was blown, contained inside it a set of rings similar to these, but smaller."

He took apart his bracelet, showing the viewers what he meant. "The air sent the rings spinning inside the horn, where they rubbed against protruding nubs. This produced a musical tone. Watch!"

He climbed onto the dais and headed for the depression in the wall beside the holy closet. Into the depression he set his rings, where he spun them one by one.

"Your little ring didn't have much effect," he told Leena, "but observe this!"

With the specialized acoustics, the musical tone from his spinning bracelets reverberated throughout the great hall. The lights, which had been dim, suddenly brightened.

"Behold the Renewal ceremony!" Taurin shouted triumphantly.

Dikran, who'd been sitting during Leena's explanation, shot to his feet. "You have reset the computers?"

Taurin nodded. "Consider it a done deal. The rings are

the keys. They can unlock the secrets of Lothar and the Apostles. The horn is no longer required. Spinning the rings will serve the same purpose at Renewal, but it must be done in this receptacle.'' He snapped his bracelets together and shoved the armband back in place. ''Dikran, I expect you to keep your promise,'' he added, tilting his head at the dignified leader.

Dikran clasped his gnarled hands together, his golden robe swishing at his feet. ''We have several vacancies to fill among the Synod. First, I have created a new Ministry of Internal Affairs, of which Stephan Tom will be minister.''

Applause sounded, and the Truthsayer leader beamed happily. He seemed pleased by the concessions made in his favor as Dikran elaborated on his duties.

''Sirvat has resigned as Treasurer,'' the Arch Nome continued. ''Swill, I hereby appoint you as Minister of the Treasury. You have proven your worth. Even though you are not of the religious faith, I think it is time we had representatives from the laity on our council. We need to broaden our viewpoint. Bendyk, you will replace Zeroun as Minister of Religion. I believe your directives will be more sympathetic to the people.''

Bendyk jumped up, enthusiasm lighting his face. ''I have learned my lesson well, Your Grace. We exist to serve the people's needs, not to impose religious doctrine upon them. Hopefully they will come to seek our counsel and respect us for our wisdom, rather than fearing reprisals for misconduct.''

''Hear, hear,'' the other council members agreed.

''Father,'' Bendyk said, turning to Cranby, who was among the Candors present, ''I seek your permission to wed Swill. Thanks to her, my eyes have been opened.'' The blond young man beamed at his intended bride, who sat in the second row, beside her father.

''You have my blessing, son,'' said Cranby.

Dikran turned his attention to the Candor. ''You were censured for your honesty, sir. Your study of ancient religious texts has been forthright and accurate, and it is known that your work as a judge is widely respected. I hereby appoint you as Minister of Justice in Karayan's stead.''

"What of Karayan?" someone shouted. "Has he been found yet?"

Taurin descended from the dais, glowering at the assemblage. "He escaped with the Ylloners. We tried to close the window but failed to do so in time. The agents escaped, and Karayan went with them. We shall have to bolster our defenses against the Ylloners, in case they find a way to pierce the shield in the future."

Dikran's penetrating gaze focused on Taurin. "I would ask you, sir, if you will head a new Defense Ministry. You shall be known as Keeper of the Rings, since you understand their function. Will you accept this office?"

Taurin stood before Dikran, his head bowed. "I should be honored, Your Grace. At last I have found my destiny, and it is among your people. I shall ensure that no further threat from Yllon remains."

"Fine. Then that leaves you, Leena," the Arch Nome said, smiling broadly at her.

Leena glanced at him, startled. She had supposed she would go back to work at the museum once her term in the Caucus was over.

"It has come to my attention," said Dikran, "that the regulations concerning archaeological sites need to be updated. I propose creating an Office of Antiquities, with you as Director, with full responsibility for coordinating the work at excavations. It will no longer come under the auspices of the Religion Ministry."

Leena's expression brightened. "*I* get to set the rules?" Her mind reeled with the possibilities. She wouldn't have to give up her fieldwork. On the contrary, her new role would necessitate frequent on-site inspections, and she'd ensure that professional archaeologists did the excavation work. Grotus's smuggling ring had been put out of operation by the death of their leader, but there were other unscrupulous individuals eager to gain possession of valuable artifacts, either for their own collections or to offer them for sale. She'd like nothing better than to put them out of action.

"If you wish, I'll release you from your pledge to the Caucus so you can assume this position immediately," the Arch Nome offered, his eyes twinkling.

"I accept," she announced proudly.

After the shouts of congratulation had died down the party split up. Leena said good-bye to her brother, Swill, and Cranby. She and Taurin were returning to his farmhouse for a much needed rest before assuming their new duties.

"I can't believe you reset those computers with your bracelets," she told Taurin later, when they were home alone, relaxing in the living area. She'd lit candles about the room, and the flames flickered, casting shadows in the far corners.

"Do you mean to say your faith in me lapsed?" he teased.

She turned toward him and lifted her face. "I always believed in you, Taurin, and I always will, now and forever."

"And I'll believe with you, my *angella*. Wherever your faith takes you, I will go with you. Your loves sustains me and carries me beyond this sphere to the heights beyond."

She stared into his glowing eyes. "You are the one I'm going to worship from now on."

"No." He put a finger to her lips. "We'll pray to Lothar or whatever you wish to call the god of the Apostles and give thanks for being brought together. For I truly believe it was divine will that sent you to me."

He lowered his head and gently brushed his mouth across hers. "I love you, my darling."

As she melted into his embrace, they joined together in the rapture of the heavens while the gods spun them a song of love.

LEGACY OF LOVE

From the Middle Ages to the present day, these stories follow the men and women whose lives are forever changed by a special book—a cherished volume that teaches the love of learning and the learning of love!

JOIN US—
AND CELEBRATE THE LEARNING OF LOVE AND THE LOVE OF LEARNING!

ALL PROFITS WILL BE DONATED TO THE LITERACY PARTNERSHIP!

COMING IN JANUARY 1996!

MADELINE BAKER
"To Love Again"

Madeline Baker is the author of eighteen romances for Leisure. Her novels have consistently appeared on the Walden and B. Dalton bestseller lists, and she is the winner of the *Romantic Times* Reviewers' Choice Award. Her newest historical romance is *Apache Runaway* (Leisure; March 1995).

MARY BALOGH
"The Betrothal Ball"

With more than forty romances to her credit, Mary Balogh is the winner of two *Romantic Times* Career Achievement Awards. She has been praised by *Publishers Weekly* for writing an "epic love story...absorbing reading right up until the end!" Her latest historical romance is *Longing* (NAL Topaz; December 1994).

ELAINE BARBIERI
"Loving Charity"

The author of twenty romances for Jove, Zebra, Harlequin, and Leisure, Elaine Barbieri has been called "an absolute master of her craft" by *Romantic Times*. She is the winner of several *Romantic Times* Reviewers' Choice Awards, including those for Storyteller Of The Year and Lifetime Achievement; and her historical romance *Wings Of The Dove* was a Doubleday Book Club selection. Her most recent title is *Dance Of The Flame* (Leisure; June 1995).

LORI COPELAND
"Kindred Hearts"

Lori Copeland is the author of more than forty romances for Harlequin, Bantam, Dell, Fawcett, and Love Spell. Her novels have consistently appeared on the Walden, B. Dalton, and *USA Today* bestseller lists. Her newest historical romance is *Someone To Love* (Fawcett; May 1995).

CASSIE EDWARDS
"Savage Fantasy"

The author of fifty romances for Jove, Zebra, Harlequin, NAL Topaz, and Leisure, Cassie Edwards has been called "a shining talent" by *Romantic Times*. She is the winner of the *Romantic Times* Lifetime Achievement Award for Best Indian Romance Series. Her most recent title is *Wild Bliss* (Topaz; June 1995).

HEATHER GRAHAM
"Fairy Tale"

The author of more than seventy novels for Dell, Harlequin, Silhouette, Avon, and Pinnacle, Heather Graham also publishes under the pseudonyms Heather Graham Pozzessere and Shannon Drake. She has been celebrated as "an incredible storyteller" by the *Los Angeles Times*. Her romances have been featured by the Doubleday Book Club and the Literary Guild; she has also had several titles on the *New York Times* bestseller list. Writing as Shannon Drake, she recently published *Branded Hearts* (Avon; February 1995).

CATHERINE HART
"Golden Treasures"

Catherine Hart is the author of fourteen historical romances for Leisure and Avon. Her novels have consistently appeared on the Walden and B. Dalton bestseller lists. Her newest historical romance is *Dazzled* (Avon; September 1994).

VIRGINIA HENLEY
"Letter Of Love"

The author of eleven titles for Avon and Dell, Virginia Henley has been awarded the *Affaire de Coeur* Silver Pen Award. Two of her historical romances—*Seduced* and *Desired*—have appeared on the *USA Today*, *Publishers Weekly*, and *New York Times* bestseller lists. Her latest historical romance is *Desired* (Dell Island; February 1995).

PENELOPE NERI
"Hidden Treasures"

Penelope Neri is the author of eighteen historical romances for Zebra. She is the winner of the *Romantic Times* Storyteller Of The Year Award and *Affaire de Coeur's* Golden Certificate Award. Her most recent title is *This Stolen Moment* (Zebra; October 1994).

DIANA PALMER
"Annabelle's Legacy"

With more than eighty novels to her credit, Diana Palmer has published with Fawcett, Warner, Silhouette, and Dell. Among her numerous writing awards are seven Walden Romance Bestseller Awards and four B. Dalton Bestseller Awards. Her latest romance is *That Burke Man* (Silhouette Desire; March 1995).

JANELLE TAYLOR
"Winds Of Change"

The author of thirty-four books, Janelle Taylor has had seven titles on the *New York Times* bestseller list, and eight of her novels have sold over a million copies each. Ms. Taylor has received much acclaim for her writing, including being inducted into the *Romantic Times* Writers Hall Of Fame. Her newest historical romance is *Destiny Mine* (Kensington; February 1995).

WHO WROTE THE BOOK OF LOVE?
ELEVEN OF THE TOP-SELLING ROMANCE AUTHORS OF ALL TIME— THAT'S WHO!

DON'T MISS

Love's Legacy

MADELINE BAKER
MARY BALOGH
ELAINE BARBIERI
LORI COPELAND
CASSIE EDWARDS
HEATHER GRAHAM
CATHERINE HART
VIRGINIA HENLEY
PENELOPE NERI
DIANA PALMER
JANELLE TAYLOR

ALL PROFITS WILL BE DONATED
TO THE LITERACY PARTNERSHIP!

___4000-X $6.99 US/$8.99 CAN